PANTHEON OF LIFE

JADE ANDREWS

Printed in Australia

Cover and internal design by Shawline Publishing Group Pty Ltd

First printing: March 2024

Shawline Publishing Group Pty Ltd

www.shawlinepublishing.com.au

Paperback ISBN 978-1-9231-0137-1

eBook ISBN 978-1-9231-0138-8

Hardback ISBN 978-1-9231-0181-4

Distributed by Shawline Distribution and Lightning Source Global

Shawline Publishing Group acknowledges the traditional owners of the land and pays respects to the Elders, past, present and future.

A catalogue record for this work is available from the National Library of Australia

PANTHEON OF LIFE

JADE ANDREWS

THANK YOU

My sister – I cannot put into words all you did for this book and the role you played in bringing it to life. You are the one other person who has loved Azraelle as if she were your own. I am eternally grateful.

My love – for the brainstorming sessions that helped me see this book through and all the ways you endlessly support and love me.

My found family – I would not have been able to write this without your help growing into the person I am today and all the love as I grew.

Brad and Jodie – for bringing me into the fold and allowing me to live a life surrounded by stories.

Jess Chaplin @jesschaplincreative – for a cover that is more gorgeous than I could have imagined.

Katrina Burge – for the edits and the final words of positivity that allowed my bravery to surface one more time, just long enough to put this into the world.

To all whose mind serves as its own cage.

For just a brief moment of freedom.

Sensitivity/Trigger Warnings

This book contains:

- explicit sexual content

- swearing

- depictions of torture

- death

- scenes of battle and gore.

While fantasy is a place we all love to use to explore themes and ideas that may be at times difficult to confront in real life, I am intent on the creation of a safe reading experience for all intended audiences.

PROLOGUE

AZRAELLE

The mortals had thousands of sayings over the millennia, all of which Azraelle had heard some variation of once or twice. She couldn't remember the origins, or even the times when the sayings held their popularity, but one in particular had been on repeat in her mind from that fateful moment: *The dice of Zeus always fall luckily.* She'd thought it untrue, thought that all the warnings her mater had broken into her would never come to pass. Not that they couldn't, just that they wouldn't. Azraelle would not let them, would not be so stupid as to get caught.

It's a child, Edda had said, kneeling on the sun-soaked pavement of the central courtyard of Eviria. Edda would not stand until Azraelle gave her the command, a command Azraelle offered quickly enough. Edda would never shirk away from her duty, would never have outright asked Azraelle to take the duty and assign it to someone else. But Azraelle knew – without the conversation ever occurring – that Edda was still recovering from the last child. Azraelle also knew that Edda was so new, so untried. It was better not to push her too fast so early on in the immortal task as Death's deliverer.

I haven't ferried a soul for a while. I'd like to see this one through, Azraelle had deemed. Edda's eyes showed nothing but relief as she dipped her eyeline down, dropping her head as a sign of respect and acceptance of Azraelle's offer.

As you wish, Primus, Edda responded.

Azraelle should have known, should have investigated it further. Yet from the briefing it looked as any of their jobs had previously looked: a dead mortal, in need of passage between the mortal realm and their next life. It was no different to anything she or any of the other Ravens had been doing for thousands of years and Az had not looked any closer. Perhaps, since it *was* Azraelle's fuckup, she deserved the consequences of her stupidity.

1

Travelling from Eviria to the mortal realm was a trip Azraelle had made countless times before. With Hades' permission branded on the back of her left hand as it was every one of the Ravens, there was no issue exiting through the Gate of the Underworld and into the wilds of the mortal realm, following the thread of the soul that beckoned to her. Once she had locked in on that golden thread of her target, there was nothing that would keep her from finding them; like a hound with a scent, she could follow it across the realms. Following that child's soul was no different.

Finding the boy had not been the difficult part; it was making sense of his tangled threads enough to understand why Azraelle was there in the first place. There was no reason to indicate that it was the child's time – the thread of his destiny still weaved through the world bright and clear. It was too early. Yet, here was this boy, not even ten years old, who lay dead in front of her. Azraelle had every right to ferry him to his next life, to lay her hands on him and beckon his soul gently to follow. But Azraelle honoured Destiny, obeyed its command as much as she obeyed Death's, and Destiny was not done with this boy.

Azraelle did what she'd only had to do a handful of times before. It wasn't often that Destiny malfunctioned and took one before it was their time, but she still knew how to place her hands gently across the boy's chest to find the tethers of his life. Once she found them, it took mere moments to bring him back from the sleep of death, the boy's mouth at once gasping for air. With her hands still pressed on the boy, she'd felt the burning of his lungs as he gulped desperately, had felt the panic as he shot upright and his eyes darted around the empty alleyway.

It had been too easy; she knew that now that she'd had time to reflect on it. The boy wasn't supposed to have died but he was a pawn in a game much bigger than him. Much more significant than even Azraelle.

Azraelle had barely begun her journey back to the Gates of the Underworld when she felt herself unable to move, her wings unable to carry her further. An electric current coursed through her, locking her muscles into jolting paralysis. Pain lanced from her thigh and, straining to peer down, Azraelle noted what was trapping her – a single arrow straight through the thickest part of her upper thigh. Not a regular arrow, of course, but one of Artemis', imbued with her paralysing power. Azraelle was trapped and nothing could be done, not as she lost consciousness, blackness swarming her senses.

How long she was kept imprisoned in Zeus' infamous cells, Azraelle had no idea. Time as a concept lost its significance when you existed for eons. In mortal time, she was sure years had passed, decades maybe even. Az never saw the marbled walls and floors of Olympus from the first moment she was thrown into the cell, but it felt as if all the Olympians had their turn inflicting pain. Through the glimpses Azraelle could get from her door creaking open and shut, she saw the guards standing watch outside, their uniform glistening in their whiteness compared to the bloodied walls and floor of her cell.

Zeus was always going to make it painful for her, a fact Az had prepared herself for the moment she'd seen Artemis' arrow sticking from her thigh. He held such a disdain for her mater that Azraelle had made it a point to stay far away from Zeus' reach out of fear of how he would take that out on her. She'd suffer the pain for her mater, the woman who'd created her, raised her and trained her to do so, and as the time passed Azraelle tried her best to reconcile with the fact that her mater would not pull her from her misery – that she *could* not pull Az from it.

Olympian's faces were her only company during her imprisonment. Zeus of course came to see her daily, but oh, those faces, and their cruel hands, and the tools they wielded against her, she saw those often enough as well. There were recurring visitors, some who took more pleasure than others, but a day was not let to pass without a visitor of some kind coming to her own personal cell.

It didn't shock Azraelle what people subjected her to. Even people who'd known her previously, who had visited her at a time in the Underworld or had once considered themselves close with any one of her numerous siblings. They were at war, and Azraelle was merely a casualty. Loyalty and friendship meant nothing when she was the enemy.

The lower Olympians, those who had once been mortal but now fought in the army of Olympus, were savage and power-crazed in their attempts to torture her, but Azraelle understood them better than they could have ever imagined. As they became more comfortable knowing the bindings that held Azraelle's wings framed behind her would keep her limbs and magic contained no matter what, the Olympians gave in to their depraved thoughts and torturous musings. They were fuelled by the sight of her bound form before them. For many of the Olympians who took their time with her, it was a fulfilment of their desire for power, specifically power over something they never should have been given the chance to touch. She was Death's deliverer, her magic could have crushed them from the inside out, but the toxins dripping down those barbed bindings, bleeding into her sliced wings and muscles, kept her magic weak and useless.

Barbed chains reached from the back two corners of the room, twisting around and through parts of Azraelle's black wings. The memory of Zeus himself jamming the spikes through the most sensitive of parts played through her mind every day she saw his face, keeping the memory fresh of having the barbs wrapped around and around until her wings were drawn to their fullest length behind her, arcing up to the top corners of the room. The way he'd smiled at her, his dark lips pulling back to reveal glistening, white teeth as he smiled and the laughter lines splashed across the perfectly composed face, betraying a man who spent much of his time smiling. The contrast so at odds with the bloodied cell around them.

Nothing could alleviate the pain. The acid that dripped down the chains at all points of the day kept her wings from sealing around the chains, kept the wounds fresh and Azraelle's agony unbearable. So intense was the pain of the acid on her wings that by the time it reached the open lashes across Azraelle's back it almost felt like a relief, before acid was dripped anew.

Through all the manners that they poked and prodded, still Azraelle did nothing – could do nothing. The physical lashings and tortures were painful but not insurmountable. As the time passed, she found it easier and easier to leave the constraints of feeling her physical body. She had prepared for this, trained to endure torture for thousands of years, and the limited creativity of the once mortal men would not be the thing that broke her. Whatever they thought to do with her body, to her skin, she would withstand it.

It was the gods that Azraelle had to really focus for, those who had been trained in breaking through the mental shields she had trained extensively to put in place. Azraelle supposed she also had her mater's upbringing to thank for how well her mental defences held up beneath those assaults.

Time passed this way until Zeus finally deigned to bring her from that cell. Apollo granted her what was basically a sack to conceal her body as they walked the halls, an act of privacy that had not been granted to her since she'd been thrown in the cell. The only item they had not been able to strip from her that first day was her pendant necklace, the Ravens symbol, its chain a simple silver that burned all who would attempt to touch it besides Azraelle herself. They knew enough to not even attempt its removal.

Az did not grant them the satisfaction of a reaction as they pulled the barbs from her wings, though internally she was so broken by the pain she wanted nothing more than to drop to her knees and sob. She would never have given in to the torture, would never have told Zeus anything he desired to know, but if Azraelle had only been able to move her arms she would have already ended it all, magic or no, whether she had to claw her own throat out to do so.

Finally outside the thick barred door, Az was escorted through the brightly lit halls of the top levels of Mount Olympus. Apollo himself stood to her right; his beautiful face twisted into a contorted grin. Artemis stood on Az's other side, on her face merely a blank expression. The twins were so similar in appearance – black hair each as long as the others, golden accessories glimmering over their dark skin, and lithe limbs designed for their respective fighting styles. The major difference came only on their expressions; Apollo had an arrogant smirk constantly affixed on his lips, while Azraelle had rarely seen any emotion cross Artemis' face.

This is not exactly how I imagined being pinned between the two of you, Azraelle had taunted as Artemis and Apollo led her through the marbled halls. Artemis didn't react and Az wasn't surprised, but Apollo gave a crooked grin, his fingers brushing beneath Azraelle's breast against her ribs. She did her best not to retch at his touch.

If only there was more time. Apollo's lips were so close to her ear as he whispered that Az felt them brushing against her. She knew then, it was to be the end. Finally.

When they reached their destination, the gathered crowd was significant but small. The room around them one of the grandest Azraelle had ever set foot in. Columns lined the outer ring of the room, every surface visible made from white marble. The dais at the head of the room was raised a full metre from the ground with marble steps leading up. An empty throne sat atop the dais with two occupied chaises either side. Despite the eons Azraelle's life had spanned for, she had never seen the inside of Mount Olympus, let alone the decorated hall she had been led into. She'd begged extensively over the years to her mater to be allowed to visit but had been endlessly denied. Every time it had been a different reason why not.

Artemis closed the giant marble doors behind their entrance, the sound echoing across every surface in the room. The endless white marble provided such a contrast to the dark halls of the House of Hades, and the mountains of Eviria.

Zeus stood in front of the empty throne dressed in his full battle regalia – a sign of the formality of the occasion. To his left, his first wife Demeter, mother to Artemis and Apollo, lounged on one of the chaises atop the platform. Her cruel beauty was unmatched by no one else in the room save for Apollo himself. And yet, that beautiful, sharply angled face of hers was also twisted into a wicked grin, her eyes shining with joy at Azraelle's dishevelled and scarred appearance.

Hera, Zeus' second wife, sat on the chaise to Zeus' right, never lifting her gaze to acknowledge Azraelle's presence in the room. Her hands remained clasped in front of her, her eyes downcast through the entire procession. As well as Artemis and Apollo, a few more of Zeus' sons were scattered through the room, but Azraelle barely noticed them when her gaze landed on one of the last people that she ever thought she'd see again. The breath caught in Az's throat at the sight of the Moirai. What were the Fates of Destiny – Az's very own sister – doing in Zeus' throne room?

Her sister's spirit was complex to comprehend, even for others who had lived for eons as Azraelle had. She was one person, but many forms. After all, the task of weaving Destiny required more than one set of hands. At times, the Moirai appeared in a single form; other times, when more was needed, they took the form of the three Fates. Today, there was simply the one. Her sister's raven black hair was pinned ornately around her face, filled with lavish gems and golds that Azraelle had never known her sister to like. Even the dress that covered the Moirai's body was decadent and full, so opposed to anything Az had ever seen her wear before.

Azraelle flashed back to the one question they had asked her every day someone entered her cell. Had the Moirai simply given them the answer? Was that why Azraelle's torment had ended? Had Zeus found out that Erebus was gone, and that Az's mater was vulnerable?

Azraelle, daughter of Night and Darkness, came Zeus' echoing voice, *you have been charged with the crime of altering the course of Destiny by bringing a mortal boy back to life. Your own sister stands witness against you. What say you?*

Of all the charges Zeus may have lain against her, she never expected that one. That boy's destiny had not been designed to end at that time and the Moirai should have known it. The Moirai stood in front of the dais that Zeus and his wives occupied, straight ahead of where Azraelle stood firmly in Apollo and Artemis' grasp. No emotion crossed the Moirai's face, no hint that she believed Azraelle was innocent.

Innocent, Azraelle said anyway, her voice more confident than she felt on the inside. *I would never dare to take Destiny into my own hands.*

And yet you have, the Moirai said, beginning her move forward to where Azraelle stood. *And I will see your confession.*

Azraelle braced herself as the Moirai finally came to a stop in front of her and placed her hands on either side of Azraelle's temple. She braced for the pain that came when one of the Moirai peered into a psyche to glean the untold truths of one's mind. There were few entities in the realms who had the power to step straight past mental defences, and the Moirai was one of them – kept only in line by her own promise to Destiny to not abuse the power. No pain came. Instead, Az heard her sister's voice, not harsh as it was when she had spoken a moment ago but loving and tender. Was that sorrow Az detected?

Please sister, came the Moirai's voice. *It needs to be this way. Forgive me.*

Why are you doing this? Azraelle was unable to prevent the burn in the back of her throat as she pushed back tears.

When the choice was to let you be destroyed or to kill you myself, I knew I would not be the one to have the strength to do it, the Moirai replied.

The Moirai's hands left Azraelle's face, and she turned to walk back to her position in front of Zeus. Azraelle frowned at the lack of clarity given with the Moirai's answer.

Guilty, the Moirai said. *Guilty as I said.*

Zeus smiled. Azraelle was firmly where he wanted her.

She was damned either way, and she had never been the kind to let anyone see her defeated. A smirk pulled at the corner of her lips and, despite the aches she felt over her entire body from the past years of torture, in the first movement she'd been able to make on her own, she threw her arms wide and unfurled her own wings, pain lancing through her as she did so.

Yes, I'm as guilty as they come, she cried. Zeus' face flickered with rage, his long silver hair crackling slightly with energy.

Azraelle always feared what it would feel like to have her wings ripped from her, but nothing could have possibly prepared her. It was as if a fire whip was cracking over her back again and again. Like the tendons that ran through them were being flayed from between each vein one by one. The agony flared as the fibres that knotted into her back were untied bit by bit. It was excruciating. Her vision blurred then blackened, and throughout the fading in and out of consciousness, the pain never ceased.

The last thing she could remember was the feeling of falling, hurtling through space at a speed faster than anyone could possibly survive. A small smile crossed her face at the final thought that flitted through her mind.

At least I will give this mortal realm one more shooting star to admire.

ONE

XADRION

It had been a fucking long two weeks. Ilyon had insisted on a hunting trip for his birthday, which his brother would only deem worthwhile if he'd felt doted on enough for the duration. It had been long, tiring, and Ilyon had made sure that every day was treated with the same magnitude as his actual birthday always was every year.

'Come on, Xadrion. Tell me you at least had fun,' Ilyon teased. They'd made camp for the night and were finally going to head into their final day of travel before they got back to the city and all the luxuries of their regular lifestyle.

'I enjoy time away from the castle as much as any man does. I'm just tired,' Xadrion answered.

Ilyon smirked, as if he could see straight through the half-truths. Yet, he didn't really care if Ilyon was satisfied with his answer or not. He had been away for two weeks, accompanied only by his brother Ilyon and the guards who worshipped the very ground Ilyon walked on. He'd missed weeks of his scheduled meetings and duties for this trip. He'd also missed the comfort of a woman beneath him or over him, with not even the privacy at night-time to take care of himself.

Xadrion loved his brother, there was no doubting that, but there was also no end to Ilyon's love for himself. And sometimes, just sometimes, especially when forced to spend two solid weeks with him, that really became totally and completely intolerable.

But Xadrion *had* been excited to come on the trip. As much as he preferred the comforts of the castle and his schedule, tension had been building inside Xadrion for months now and he hadn't been able to shake it. He found himself getting frustrated at the smallest of inconveniences, found that he was having to bite his tongue ever harder to keep himself from snapping remarks at those trying to help him. He was angry all the time and he was so tired of feeling that way. The opportunity to escape the walls and spend a few weeks in the forest had seemed like a great idea. The first day had felt different and the hope that Xadrion had of feeling calm once more was rekindled but instead, as the trip continued, he simply began finding other things to be irritated at. By that second to last day he was ready to suffocate half the guards who had accompanied them for breathing too loudly.

The camp for the night had finished winding down with most of the others tucked warmly away in their bedrolls. Xadrion himself would have been fast asleep if it weren't for Ilyon's incessant chatting. As it was, Xadrion was laying on his own bedroll, warmed by the nearby campfire, hearing his brother pondering endlessly aloud, wishing for the peaceful silence of sleep, when he saw the night sky above him change. A sphere of light appeared, staying steady for a moment, before imploding in on itself. The light contracted inwards, then suddenly and magnificently expanded. A flat circle of white light shot outwards from the central point before finally settling into the shape of a shooting star. Awe washed through him as it shot towards the ground, far off in the distance from where they were camped.

'Tell me that was worth being outside the castle walls for,' Ilyon remarked, as transfixed with the star as Xadrion had been. Xadrion merely grunted, rolled over in his own bedroll, and set to falling asleep. Yes, it was a magnificent sight, but it still didn't compare to a body in the bed beside him.

The next day brought about a quick pack up and resaddling of the horses. Finally, they had entered the last day of travel before they would reach the castle once more. The cart being pulled behind them was filled with the spoils of their hunt, the only main success being a large boar they'd shot on the final day.

This close to the castle now, there would be no dangerous paths and bandits would be almost guaranteeing their deaths if they chose to attack a travelling party so close to the walls of Fennhall. The paths were defined and the forest surrounding the city was sparser than the woods their party had been travelling through for the last two weeks. Xadrion stayed in a restful guard state as they rode, but he wasn't worried. He had traversed this road so many times throughout his life that he felt sure of every rock, tree and branch in the area. He felt that way right up until they broke through what was supposed to be a narrow pathway and instead found themselves in a sizable clearing entirely unfamiliar to Xadrion.

The guards pulled to a stop on his command and naturally fell into their observation formation while he scanned the perimeter for any sign of danger. Silence fell over the clearing, not even a horse hoof making noise on the dirt, until he felt sure there were no surprises waiting for them outside the clearing. Finally, he looked to the centre.

Destruction met his gaze as the ground in the clearing was coated with ash and char. Trees smouldered on the boundary of the levelled area and there was a notable crater leading to the centre of the clearing. There, in the centre of the crater, Xadrion's eyes caught.

Curled in on themselves was a single naked figure. A woman. Her back was facing their party, her knees tucked in against her chest, her arms curled around her knees. Xadrion slowly dismounted, approaching cautiously. There was no change from the trees around them as he moved closer. As he approached, most out of alignment with what he was seeing, a silver necklace with an emerald pendant nestled around the woman's neck. It glimmered against her otherwise naked skin.

The woman's hair was long, so incredibly long, and thick; it spread through the dirt surrounding as if a blanket had been lain beneath her. Xadrion had never seen hair so starkly white in shade, the colour of it only marred by the dirt and blood that coated the ground, the blood coming from two gashes running the length of her spine. The wounds ran from the tip of her shoulder blades down to her waist and were so deep he could see the bands of muscle beneath as if they had been cut through.

The gashes on her back weren't the only injuries the woman had sustained. Her skin was pale but covered in mottled bruising over most of the surface, with deep cuts criss-crossing everywhere he looked.

'What the fuck?' Xadrion whispered beneath his breath, the sight in front of him incomprehensible.

He pulled his coat from his own body, giving in to the panic slightly as he rushed to where she lay, now certain there was no surprise attack coming from the trees around them. He placed the coat around her back, anchored his arms beneath her, and lifted so she curled back towards him to rest against his chest. The woman's eyes stayed closed, remaining unconscious, thankfully, given how badly he was sure it would have hurt to have his hands touching the open wounds on her back.

'Is she alive?' Ilyon called from behind, all the guards still mounted. They were on the defensive now, covering Xadrion as he made himself vulnerable to collect the woman.

Turning to them and hurrying back to the horses, he could hear her breathing, faint as it was. It sounded like fluid was rattling in her chest.

'She is, but we need to hurry,' Xadrion responded. Two of the guards dismounted their horses to help as he rushed to the cart. They hauled the boar off and to the ground, clearing a space large enough to lay her down. Xadrion jumped in after he had placed her down. Someone had to stay next to her, monitor her, after all.

'Let's clear out,' Ilyon commanded the moment Xadrion had settled in the cart. The party instantly started moving once more, this time with an increased pace. The woman's status didn't seem to be changing, but before long, Xadrion's coat was bled through. He removed it from her, tore it into shreds and did his best to bind it around her torso, hoping to slow the bleeding. The amount of blood that still came from the wounds left Xadrion wondering how such a small frame could have lost so much and still be living. He would have given anything for Emera, their healer, to be with them. Xadrion demanded a coat from the guard who rode closest to them and covered her naked body with it.

Whatever had happened to this woman, he was sure she didn't also want her body on display to the host of men they travelled with, especially when they had to travel through the city to reach the castle. The castle towers came into view first, towering over the trees that surrounded their party. The castle walls made the surrounding city look small in comparison, despite the city being expansive in its size.

Their surrounds changed from trees to farms and eventually to more densely packed stone streets. The people of Fennhall made their final leg slower, as much as they tried to clear the streets to allow the royal party through. It became slow going, and Xadrion kept switching his gaze between the pale, bloodied woman in the back of the cart and the curious eyes of the people in the streets.

Despite feeling like slow process, they eventually arrived at the base of the castle wall, the large, grated gate open and welcoming. Guards lined the ramparts above and stood either side of the gate.

'One of you ride ahead, get Emera ready for us,' Ilyon commanded, and one of the leading guards peeled from their group, increasing their speed so that before long, they were out of sight.

When the rest of the party made it through the gates, Emera was standing in the welcoming courtyard next to the guard who had retrieved her. Emera took one look at Xadrion in the back, half crouching over the pale form beneath him, and turned on her heel.

'Bring her quickly,' Emera commanded. Xadrion jumped to the ground, pulled the too-light frame into his grasp, and hurried after her.

It wasn't a long walk to Emera's rooms, and the girl barely felt like a weight in his arms. Xadrion worried if this was just her or if this was some indication to how close to death she was. It wasn't until he had lain her down onto one of the cots Emera had for that exact purpose, when Emera had removed the coat covering her body and undone the makeshift bandages binding her back, that Xadrion was able to fully see the state of the woman he had been carrying. Her abdomen, her chest, across her thighs, hips and shoulders. Everywhere was marked by bone-deep cuts and scars comparable to many Xadrion had seen on battle-worn soldiers. He had seen the aftermath of torture once before, a sight that still haunted his sleeps, but the woman's body surpassed anything he had seen before.

'Move, Xadrion,' Emera snapped, pushing him away from the cot and into the corner of the room. In front of him, Emera set to moving at a pace he had never been able to follow, her hands flurrying in action over the unconscious woman.

It took another glare from Emera to finally send him from the room, leaving the events inside to unfold without his gawking. Adrenalin still pumped through him, but he wasn't useful in this part, so he decided to do his best to settle his thoughts.

Outside Emera's room, blood had dripped onto the carpeted runner and when Xadrion looked down to himself, he saw blood had seeped through the torn coat he'd wrapped the woman in and covered his clothes.

He detoured by his own chambers to change and freshen up, moving around Darlene, one of the keepers for the royal chambers, as she unpacked his belongings from the hunting trip. Finally, he headed to his father's study. A debrief was needed, if Ilyon had even bothered to tell their father that they had returned. He gave a short knock on the doors, to which his father's voice called out for him to come in. When he entered, his father was sitting behind his giant desk, dressed in the most casual clothes he probably owned as the king.

His father, Rhoas, didn't enjoy the customs of being king. He was even-headed and calm, but, unless there was reason, Xadrion didn't often see Rhoas in full court attire. Even that day Rhoas' crown sat to the left on his desk, covered in papers and notes – at hand if he needed it for appearances but disregarded in private.

'Ah, Xadrion. Good to see you're back. How did the hunting trip go? Was Ilyon satisfied for his birthday?'

King Rhoas was a point of pride for Xadrion. He was a fair king, loved by the people and nobility alike. While there were some downsides to having a king as a father, he felt proud when he was displayed the respect from their people due to their love for Rhoas.

Rhoas was older now – his hair and beard had greyed, and his sun-kissed skin creased at multiple points on his face – but he still maintained an athletic build, and Xadrion was sure there would be many more years before he would have to think about taking up the role as heir to the throne. Xadrion and Ilyon didn't hold many of Rhoas' features – from the memories Xadrion had of his mother, they'd gotten their darker skin and long black hair from her. Ilyon shared more features with Rhoas, evident through their deep brown eyes, but mostly Xadrion and his brother were closer to each other's appearance than their father's.

'Ilyon is satisfied. We had some success with the hunt, but we encountered a curious problem on the way back,' Xadrion answered. He detailed the length of their journey and took time explaining the events of that morning, including the current status of the woman in Emera's rooms. Rhoas showed only vague interest in the recounts of the woman and dismissed him finally with the comment that they would investigate more if she managed to survive.

And so, despite the eventful start to the day, Xadrion found himself falling back into his regular schedule. They had a few visitors to court that he made it a point to visit, he checked in on the training grounds to watch the progress of the guards in training and went to the dining hall to take his dinner, which he quickly realised was his first meal of the day. As Xadrion settled back into his own schedule, the ever-looming irritation began to prickle beneath his skin once more, despite its absence for a majority of the day's events.

The light began to dim outside, the candles in the castle hallways began their daily routine of being lit by the staff, and the castle was overall going through the regular events, as if there wasn't a woman somewhere there fighting for her life. Xadrion eventually headed back to his rooms, debating if he wanted to call someone for company – especially given that Emera was preoccupied – when there was a rap on his door.

A moment passed before the door creaked open and Emera walked in, changed into fresh clothes from the last time he'd seen her. She looked exhausted, her eyes rimmed by dark circles and her deep red hair tussled from its normally collected state.

'Are you okay?' Xadrion asked, walking to her and grabbing her hands. He tugged her gently back to his bed, folding her into his arms as they lay.

Their relationship was not one that usually held many words. It had been agreed early on that what they needed from each other was purely physical and Xadrion had other women who frequented his bed. He knew Emera did too, women and men. It didn't bother him and he knew Emera didn't care to know his other habits.

'This one took a lot out of me. Her wounds were grievous.' Even though she had been working on the one person for most of the day, Xadrion knew it was not that which had tired her. Emera's position in the castle relied on her healing abilities – her magical healing abilities. Magic was uncommon in their kingdom, Thesadel, as it was uncommon nearly everywhere else, but not impossible to locate. Despite it being more accepted in Thesadel, Emera did not have much help with the workload.

Rhoas had created Fennhall and most of the surrounding towns to be accepting of magic among many other things, but the same couldn't be said for the other kingdoms of their land. Sodarin, Luzia and Vaeba all had legislation still enabling discrimination against many groups of people, magic users primarily, but Thesadel didn't have the power on its own to influence change amongst them. The neighbouring kingdoms, Ceotor and Gaeweth, had a more open mind, and so were diplomatic allies in the conversations between kingdoms, but their lands were still largely disrupted in their social values. When the king of Thesadel had two sons with skin darker than was accepted in most of the other kingdoms, it made for slow change and hard-earned respect.

Most of those who had some magical ability had come to Thesadel to train over recent decades and dedicated themselves to healing professions, as Emera had. Still, their numbers were small. Xadrion had seen the physical impact it took on Emera before, when he'd witnessed her healing others in the past. It always took a lot of her energy, leaving her needing to recover for at least a few days if it were particularly bad.

'Will she survive?' Xadrion asked.

'I believe so. I've healed most of her wounds, at least at a surface level. She will need her own time, so I have induced a healing rest to allow her body the time to do so. She won't wake for some time – days, perhaps weeks even.' Emera pulled out of Xadrion's arms and moved to her knees beside him. She was rattled, Xadrion could see that, but she didn't want to talk about it. Instead, Emera cocked a half-smile at him, her hands moving to his chest as she straddled him.

Xadrion's body reacted instantly to Emera's touch; the two weeks spent alone created a desperation within him that he hadn't felt so intensely before. Feeling Emera straddling him with her hands on his chest, feeling the heat emanating from Emera legs, caused Xadrion to harden and the strain against the waistband of his pants became unbearable.

'You've been gone a long time,' Emera teased. 'I would have thought to find someone already in your bed tonight.'

Xadrion laughed, moving his hands so that they were gripping the sides of her hips. He squeezed his fingers as he pulled her down harder against him, his fingers digging into her soft, round hips.

'Maybe I was hoping you would find your way here.'

No more words were spoken between them that night except the hushed demands and affectionate names. There was something about physical touch that helped Emera with her magic's recovery. She had tried to explain it once to him before, how a certain level of intimate relations with another person could help rejuvenate her powers and give her energy, but at the time he had been too aroused to comprehend her explanation.

As aroused as he had been then, it was nothing compared to what she made him feel that night. He had been gone for weeks, not a single woman in sight, and since the adrenalin of the day had finally worn down, Xadrion found himself needing more from Emera than he'd ever asked of her before. Emera didn't seem to mind, as if she needed the same, as if she needed that amount of time with Xadrion to help her recover from the day's events as well.

When their night eventually ended, Xadrion said nothing as Emera slipped from the covers, dressed and left his rooms. Not long after that, he slipped into a deep and relatively peaceful sleep.

***

From the next morning, things went seemingly back to normal. Xadrion began taking his regular meetings, both with the townspeople and the nobles throughout the castle. He reported to his father, held his training sessions and signed his name on all the relevant paperwork. The only notable exception to his schedule came when he stopped by Emera's rooms each morning to check on both her and the woman. Emera had set her up in a more private cot, the room not displaying any of the gore that had been present.

Her back had been properly bandaged and a white dressing gown had been located to dress the unconscious woman in. Still, on her bare arms and the glimpses of her legs he saw when Emera was fussing with the blankets, scars covered the pale skin. Most were thick and he knew they would have been particularly deep, but even in between the larger ones Xadrion could see smaller, fainter scars as if they were many years old.

Cleaned up and sleeping, the woman looked so different to that first day. Someone had washed and braided her hair, revealing her face clearer than Xadrion had previously been able to see. She was beautiful, her hair so white now that it was clean that it gave her an otherworldly appearance. The chain to the woman's silver necklace still remained around her neck, the emerald pendant hidden beneath the dressing gown. For every morning that passed, nothing changed. She stayed sleeping, a peaceful expression on her face.

Emera and Xadrion spent the first nights together, as Emera had to use her magic every day to keep the resting sleep upon the woman. After the first week or so, they pulled back to their usual amount of a couple of times a week. Xadrion began entertaining a few of the other ladies in the castle once more, and life seemed to be back on its normal path.

Two weeks passed from their hunting trip and as the calmness of the castle life returned, Xadrion's anger simmered beneath the surface of his skin once more. His visit to Emera's rooms was uneventful and he had no other commitments for the day except for a ceremony for the graduating guards where his only responsibility was to stand to his father's right as Rhoas said a few official words for each guard. Ilyon needed to be present also, his position to his father's left. It was a familiar ceremony; one they'd performed several times a year for each of the advancing guards.

Each guard would be spoken to by Rhoas and receive the embroidered green and black patch that marked them a member of Thesadel's army, then everyone would relocate to the event dining hall for the night's feast.

Two

AZRAELLE

Azraelle was alive.

Reliving the pain of her wings shredding from her back as she fell, she could barely believe it was true. Yet, as she slowly gained feeling through her body, she realised she was very much alive. Azraelle could feel a bed beneath her, a pillow softly cushioning her head. She was on her back, arms by her side and, at the feel of the sheets against her back, a sob tore through her lips. Her bare back. There was nothing beneath her, no feathers that brushed against her arms or rigid bone-like structure in the centre of her spine marking where the wings attached.

Her wings were gone. And where they used to be, her back was on fire.

Azraelle searched around as best she could with her eyes closed, trying to detect if there was anyone nearby. Now was not the time for emotion. Right now, she needed to establish her surroundings, determine any danger and establish a route home if she was not already nearby. Survival first, emotions second.

Az pulled at her power, desperate to feel the comforting nudge of her shadows between her fingers or around her body, but nothing responded. Her magic wasn't answering – not surprising given the damage her body must have just gone through but devastating all the same. Unless... her magic hadn't answered in the cell from Zeus' binding of it. She'd fallen, she knew that for sure, but had Zeus found her once more and locked her up again?

When Azraelle didn't pick up any presence, she opened her eyes. She was on a bed, in a small, plain room. A bowl of water sat on the table beside the bed with a washcloth folded neatly next to it and the door from the room stood ajar. In the next room over, there was no movement. She wasn't on

Mount Olympus anymore; the lack of glowing white marble being what told her that. Instead, the colours around her were wooden, stone, reds.

As slowly as she could, Azraelle pushed herself onto her elbows, wincing at the movement. Other pain registered from other wounds, but nothing compared to the pain in her back, the feeling that strands of her insides had been pulled from their deep connections, setting all of her nerves on fire. Az hoisted herself to a sitting position, swinging her legs over to the floor, wincing at every moment. She'd been dressed in a white dressing gown of sorts, but her feet were bare, her hair was braided behind her, clear of her face, and her pendant still hung loosely around her neck, thankfully. Azraelle wondered if someone had tried to remove it and their reaction to finding themselves unable.

Someone had been taking care of her – healing her. Azraelle had no idea how long had passed since her fall, but her body didn't feel as awful as it should have. While fire rippled through her muscles, it wasn't the pain of open wounds that hit her now. Zeus had healed her daily on Olympus, if only to allow the same torture to repeat, but the injuries she'd sustained on the final day before her trial would have been enough to leave her on Death's door. Add into the mix the fire that had burned her wings from her as she fell, Azraelle should have been dead.

Was she somewhere on the mortal realm? Reason dictated that she had to be, unless someone had found her and taken her after her fall. She could be back in the Underworld, but… no, it didn't feel like she was. The sights around her were too unfamiliar.

Slowly, Azraelle began to move. First, she trialled standing by taking a few hesitant steps in the room. Once confident that she could walk without stumbling, she determined it was time to leave. Beyond the rooms Az had woken in, it looked like she was within a castle. Stone hallways extended away in several directions and wooden doors lined the length of all of them. Still, no one came into sight. It was definitely mortal architecture that surrounded her but there was nothing Az could piece together to confirm exactly where she had wound up.

The castle halls were empty, no noise drifting from any of the hallways except one. Az followed, eagerly anticipating any information as to where she was. It was a fair walk before the noise started getting louder, though it wasn't consistent – sounding as if there were long parts of silence followed by loud bursts of cheers and clapping.

Feeling exposed, Azraelle attempted to blend. If she could just get her magic to respond, she could blend into the shadows and move as only wisps of air. It had once been as easy as breathing to her, yet when she reached down into her well of magic, she felt gutted. It was all gone.

Another cry nearly broke free as she realised the hollowness inside her, leaving her feeling empty and vulnerable. She stumbled and reached her hand out to steady herself against the stone wall, her chest feeling as if it were cracking in half. The tidal wave of emotion nearly knocked her down, nearly convinced her to give up and wait for something to find her curled up on the stone of that hallway, to let whatever fate was coming her way come.

A moment passed and when she felt like she could move again, she continued walking. All the training she had ever done was the only thing that kept her silent and contained, but the pain washed over her in waves, leaving no time between torrents for her to catch her breath. It was, unfortunately, at this moment that someone came into view. She'd continued walking, turning a corner to see giant wooden oak doors looming ahead of her, the noise she'd been following coming from behind them. In front of the doors, there were two stationed men.

It wasn't Azraelle's usual reaction to behave rash and without thinking things through carefully. Maybe it was the torture at Zeus' hand, maybe it was having no idea where she was, most likely it was because of the weakness she felt in that very moment. But when they called out to her, Azraelle registered a threat, where the small sliver of logic in her mind told her that there probably wasn't one. When Azraelle felt threatened, the last thing she ever did was run.

The men were slow to react and she had reached them and got one to the ground before the second even had the time to react. They were mortal, and even without her powers she could handle mortals. She was trained as a Raven, and Ravens were more than just guides for the dead – they were warriors, trialled and trained to be the army for Destiny.

Her body was in pain, a remnant of the worst pain she'd experienced, but none of that registered as she choked the first one into unconsciousness and turned to face the second. The man's eyes betrayed his fear and inexperience; the poor man had probably never seen a real fight.

Before she could get to the second guard, he tripped backwards, grasping one of the doors behind him and falling through it, revealing the room beyond. He kept stumbling back, Azraelle stalking after him. Around her, panicked noises start to rise. A brief glance showed her a packed room, most of its inhabitants kitted with weapons. At the far end of the room there was one kneeling figure in front of a crowned man, with two younger men standing on either side.

Azraelle may have stopped in that moment, determined to discover answers from these people rather than keep fighting, but her entrance was not received peacefully. It wasn't surprising; in fact, she could only imagine the sight that she presented to these people. One body, unconscious and visible through the doors, another guard panicked and retreating. And Azraelle – well… she could only imagine her appearance to them. The haze of battle descended over Az's vision and her mind cleared of any thoughts except to defend, to fight, to win.

Several of the armed guards closest to her had advanced, pulling their weapons from their sheaths. Ceremonial blades, every single one of them, but still blades they were. With her powers, Azraelle wouldn't have been worried. She wouldn't have even batted an eye as she levelled the room. Without her powers, well, it might just be an even fight.

There was something about the haze of a battle, something Azraelle had never been able to control. Once she was fighting, it became nearly impossible to think past what moves she needed to make and what she needed to do to walk out of the fight alive. Battle also brought with it a funny sense of belonging, as if she were exactly where she was supposed to be. A smirk crept across her face as she leapt into action.

Where one sword came down on her location, she was no longer. The mortals were slow, and even in her weakened state, it was of little effort to step out of range of their slowly arcing weapons. If someone advanced too close, they received a swift kick to the gut, or neck, sending them flying backwards. Azraelle had no weapons of her own and no idea what her end goal was. Would she stop only when the room was floored?

What felt like a short minute was all that was allowed for her to make her way through the guards before an echoing order bellowed across the room.

'Lower. Your. Weapons.'

Within an instant, everyone around her had stopped their advancing, bringing their swords back to their resting grip. Almost simultaneously, Azraelle felt a sort of heaviness settle over her body. Her movement became so hard it nearly felt impossible, and she had to dedicate all her remaining energy to not dropping to her knees from the pressure. Panic rose in Azraelle's throat, the feeling of paralysis all too familiar. The memory of Artemis' arrow buried in her thigh overwhelmed her and a guttural cry escaped Az's lips at the anger that followed.

She glanced up, eyeing where the command came from, to see the crowned man at the head of the room begin his descent to where Azraelle stood. The men who had rushed her began to pull back, opening a pathway from him to her. Beside the crowned man a girl followed, her hand resting on the crook of the man's elbow as they walked, her hair fire red.

Azraelle pushed back against the pressure, sending her own signals down its line to see where it was originating from. She watched as the air quivered in front of the girl keeping to the man's side. Azraelle sent another signal, gauging the strength of the pressure, but in her weakened state she could feel she was no match for this magic – the mortal girl's magic.

'I'm going to need you to stand down,' the crowned man said, coming to a stop a few steps ahead of her.

Azraelle whipped her eyes back to look at him. The girl next to him looked afraid of her, and Azraelle again wondered at the sight she must be. The crowned man, however, only looked at her with compassion, and was that… understanding?

Azraelle couldn't talk, couldn't do anything with the pressure from the girl's magic pressing down on her.

'As you can see, I've pulled my men back to show you we mean you no harm. But I need you to stop also. If I get Emera to lower her barrier, can you promise me you will not harm another of my guards, and let us talk about this as rationally as we can?' The crowned man didn't look at Az as if she were a threat, even though every single person in the room still looked at her warily. They all kept their distance, respecting the command of this man, their king. As the panic of being frozen retreated and Azraelle knew it was not the gods that had descended upon her once more but a mortal woman, her fear begin to dissipate.

Azraelle pushed through the pressure enough to give a slight nod of her head, and she instantly felt the pressure begin to fade. Those who had been fighting her shuffled cautiously, seeing her movement slowly begin to return. Azraelle flicked her gaze around the room, taking stock of every detail she could, feeling as utterly trapped as she ever had. The king in front of her watched her, observing as if she were an experiment.

After a moment more of watching her, the king turned and smiled, throwing his arms wide in an attempt to relax the mood of the dozens of people in the room.

'Everyone, please continue to the dining hall where a feast awaits. The remainder of our ceremony will be rescheduled once we have sorted out this minor matter of ours,' he commanded, his tone light and joking. Wary expressions remained but the audience for the ceremony were shepherded from the room, giving Az as wide a berth as could be achieved.

'Father, I'm not sure sending the guards away is such a good idea,' came a new voice. One of the boys from the top of the room approached, cautiously eyeing her. He was the older of the two who had been stationed to the king's side. When Azraelle let herself fully look at the king's oldest son as he walked towards her, she couldn't bring herself to look away.

He was beautiful.

Something deep inside Azraelle stirred when she looked at him, a feeling as unfamiliar to her as the weakness she felt with the absence of her wings. While the feeling was unfamiliar, Az could not rip her gaze from him. There was something about him… something that felt eerily familiar. Inside her mind, the desire to fear him and the desire to be near him were battling at once. He was danger. And yet, he wasn't. The burden of trying to work through the emotions caused a sharp, lancing ache to spear through her temple and Azraelle forced her gaze away. She did not have the strength to push deeper, had never had the strength to push beyond that spear of pain that encircled *something* in the depths of her mind. What did this mortal prince have to do with whatever it was buried so far within Azraelle's own mind she had never been able to discover?

'Nonsense, Xadrion. Gabe will stay, as well as you and Ilyon, and Emera can keep her contained. I don't see why there's any need for concern,' the king answered. Emera's pressure was not completely gone, only light enough that Azraelle could speak, if she wanted to, and move within limited means.

When the room had cleared out, one single guard moved to close the doors and stationed himself in front of them, facing into the room. Gabe, Azraelle assumed. Ilyon must have been the other boy at the head of the room when she first entered. One glance told her that Ilyon and Xadrion were brothers, both sharing long black hair, dark complexions and thick lips. Their eyes were the main difference Azraelle noted, Xadrion's resembling the colour of silver ore, while Ilyon shared the king's eyes – deep and brown. Ilyon's hair was uncontained, wavy and below his shoulders. Xadrion on the other hand had his bound behind him, two thin braids remaining free to frame his face, the ends of the two braids reaching to his shoulders.

'Now,' the king resumed, turning his attention back to Azraelle. 'Would you come sit, and we can figure out what is going on together? It looks like you've torn some of your stitches. Emera can take care of those if you'd let her.' The king reached his hand forward, offering it to Azraelle. He didn't cross too close to her, clearly allowing her the choice to close the final distance.

One look down to her own hands showed her blood dripping to the stone floor, trickling from her back, down her arms and finally to her fingertips. It wasn't often that Azraelle was surprised by someone's behaviours, but this king left her feeling unsure. He was offering to let her *touch* him. She who had just barged into this room and been fighting her way through his guards – successfully at that.

Azraelle looked back to the king, wary and unsure, but nothing in her screamed against him. Without letting herself think too hard about it, she closed the distance between them and laid her own hand in his. The king didn't flinch at the blood that transferred from her fingers to his.

The older son, Xadrion, kept his hand firmly on his sword at his hip, ready to draw at a moment's notice. The king ushered Az to one of the benches the audience had just vacated and sat her down. Emera moved behind her, examining her back.

'I'm going to open the back of your dressing gown now. Is that alright?' Emera asked.

Azraelle nodded, not trusting her words. She felt the fabric rip to expose her back, followed by the feeling of two hands pressing against her bare shoulders. Healing magic began to flow through the point of connection. Mortal and young as she was, Emera's magic was strong and it instantly made Azraelle feel calm.

Ilyon and Xadrion remained standing, both on guard and cautiously watching her. The king, however, sat backwards on the bench in front of hers, leaning towards her and never letting go of her hand.

'There, now we can talk,' he said gently. 'My name is Rhoas Mescal and behind you is my physician Emera. These are my sons, Xadrion and Ilyon, and that is my commander general, Gabe.' He pointed to each of the people as he spoke their names. 'Who are you?'

Azraelle opened her mouth but a hoarse croak was the only sound that occurred. She frowned, closed her mouth, cleared her throat and tried again.

'Azraelle,' she managed to say, the croak gone but the hoarseness still present. She watched Rhoas as she spoke, determined not to look once more at the son who had stirred that unfamiliar feeling inside of her.

'Okay, Azraelle. Now, you are currently in the castle at Fennhall. My sons' – Rhoas gestured to the two boys once more – 'they found you, half a day's ride from our castle gates, on death's door. They brought you back and Emera has done what she could to heal you. I understand the feeling of waking in a place you do not expect to be, so I will look past these last moments of your behaviour, but I'm afraid I do have some questions for you.'

Azraelle was older than she could have expressed to them, even if she remembered exactly how many years it had been. Yet this mortal king still managed to make her feel shame at his words. She had overreacted, come barging into a room ready to take on anyone who looked in her direction, and he still showed her nothing but compassion.

'You found me?' Azraelle looked past the king to where his two sons stood.

Xadrion nodded tersely, watching her – surveying her as only a trained commander might. He was examining her, looking for her weaknesses and strengths. His gaze had Azraelle shifting in her seat, the unfamiliar feeling brimming in her chest at the sight of him.

'Fennhall,' Azraelle said, sifting through her memories, trying to place the location. She had knowledge of the mortal realm given she'd had to navigate it each time she ferried a soul, but the names of the kingdoms were always changing as they rose and fell. 'We're in Thesadel?'

'Yes, that's right. Thesadel, and I'm King Rhoas of Thesadel. Why were you on the brink of death on my kingdom's doorstep?'

Azraelle knew the truth would not do here. It went against everything in their laws to talk to mortals about their existence. While it wasn't uncommon for the gods to visit the mortal realm occasionally, it was not allowed to highlight their presence. Of course, there were the occasional ones who thought to allow the mortals to worship them, to provide them offerings and their virgin daughters, but they were never allowed to stay on this realm for long once discovered. The offspring created from Azraelle's kind and the mortals were abundant in this realm, but they were still mortal so the balance of Destiny was never tipped too far either way.

'I don't remember,' Azraelle answered.

'You remember nothing?' Xadrion questioned, disbelief written in his expression.

'I remember pieces,' Azraelle clarified. The shudder that went through her was only half pretend when flashes of the years spent in Zeus' confinement pushed to the forefront of her memory. No, the truth would not do, but she could easily summon the memories of her pain to provide the element of truth to her words. 'I don't remember how I got here.'

'Who caused your wounds and left you for dead?' Rhoas pushed.

'Some… men. Took me from my home and kept me locked up. I was… young when I was taken.' Azraelle didn't even believe herself – she was normally a much better liar. She knew she needed to create the illusion of specifics to keep from having to give any real answers. If she were a child when she was taken, she had a reason to not give them a name of her made-up home.

Emera's hands left Azraelle's back and with their absence went the calmness her magic made Az feel. It wasn't like Azraelle's magic, but it reminded her what it felt like to have that power nestled inside.

'I'm sorry for what I did to your guards,' Azraelle said, trying to pull the conversation in a different direction. 'I don't think I killed any of them.'

'You didn't,' Gabe confirmed from his guarding stance at the doors. He watched her, the insult she had caused him obvious in his expression.

'I am sorry for the hassle I have caused you, and I deeply appreciate the help you have given me in my healing. If you let me leave, I promise you will never have to see me again.' Azraelle hoped that this could be it, that they'd let her walk out the front door and never think of her again. She had to go, had to find her way back to the Underworld, to Nyx, so she could recover her powers under the protection of her mater.

'Where would you go?' Ilyon asked, finally speaking. There was a calmness to his eyes, one that showed he wasn't scared of her; he wasn't even wary of her presence anymore. Unlike Gabe and Xadrion, Ilyon was ready to believe the front Azraelle put out and had immediately gotten on board with trusting her. 'You were abducted from your home when you were young, probably within our kingdom if your final location is anything to go by, which means that whoever did this to you is out there. Plus, you're not fully healed. You won't survive out there by yourself. You could stay, heal properly and work with us to find whoever did this to you.'

Azraelle didn't get the chance to object before Rhoas spoke once more.

'My son is right, of course. I can't let someone in your condition out into the streets, with nothing to her name. And it is within my authority that I need to track down who did this. Without you, I have nothing to go on. So, you will stay, Emera will continue treating you and when you are up to it, there are a few things I think I will need your help with,' Rhoas said.

Azraelle didn't see the point in arguing, not when her plan could easily be adjusted. She was sure it wouldn't be so hard to sneak out of the castle. Besides, she had been there for weeks it seemed, unconscious, healing and weak, and Zeus hadn't found her. No one had found her as far as she was aware. For whatever reason, she hadn't been tracked while healing in the castle; maybe it wasn't urgent for her to leave right away. Maybe she could get enough strength back to make her passage to the Underworld safe.

Azraelle made herself look smaller, weaker. She hunched herself inwards, letting part of her weight rest on Emera behind her.

'That's incredibly kind of you, your majesty,' Azraelle said. 'I am already so indebted to you for your assistance thus far, but you are right – I am in no position to turn down a safe place for a little while longer.'

'I would not allow you to turn it down regardless,' Rhoas said. 'Ilyon, help Emera return Azraelle back to her rooms. Gabe, track down some quarters for Azraelle to stay in while she remains here. She will move to her own rooms once Emera deems her stable enough. Xadrion, wait here a moment, would you?'

And just like that, the room that had fallen into conversation was swept into action once more. Ilyon approached Azraelle – no fear evident in his behaviour as he wrapped an arm around her torso – and hoisted her up while supporting most of her weight. The touch against her back and scarred body made Azraelle wince but she was glad for the contact. Emera walked on Az's other side, not touching her again while Ilyon seemed to have her under control. Azraelle felt the hollowness of Emera's magic suddenly, walking right beside her but so far from reach.

As she was ushered from the room, Azraelle took one last look at Xadrion where he stood beside his father, the beauty of him striking her all over again. She would need to get it together when around him, and fast. Whatever it was he was summoning from inside of her only meant trouble.

Gabe pushed the doors open and disappeared. Before long, Azraelle was back in the rooms she had awoken in, Ilyon gently laying her on the healing bed. He looked at her as if he wanted to stay, wanted to keep talking with her, but one glance from Emera sent him away.

Azraelle wanted to get straight into planning her escape, finding where she could leave the castle from, but as soon as her head hit the pillow, the full force of the day hit her. She was still healing, still nowhere near recovered and she had just spent her first few hours from waking getting into a physically demanding fight. No, for now, Azraelle would sleep some more.

THREE

XADRION

Xadrion felt an unshakable rage for days after the woman, Azraelle, had woken up. If he had to have imagined anything upon her wakening, it wouldn't have been the events that followed. Hearing the commotion outside the doors, followed by the proceeding fight, Xadrion had stayed embarrassingly rooted in place.

The way she moved through the room, not a single soldier successfully landing a hit on her, had left Xadrion speechless and gawking. Hearing her story, imagining that there were men in their kingdom who were treating women the way she had clearly been treated, had only intensified his anger. He could tell instantly that Azraelle hadn't given them the full details, her half-truths evident in her hesitations. But then again, it *was* a lot for them to ask her to reflect on the obvious torture and trauma she must have experienced.

Despite everything, Xadrion still felt nothing short of impressed that she had managed to fight the way she had – after weeks of unconsciousness and however many years of torture, she still managed to move faster than any of them. He really shouldn't have been surprised that his father also noticed her talent, but it didn't stop the anger that followed what his father said once everyone else left the room.

I'm going to offer her a permanent place to stay when she's healed enough to decide, Rhoas had told Xadrion. When Xadrion asked what for, his father pursed his lips together, preparing for Xadrion's reaction before he even said the words.

She's going to be your next trainer.

The screaming match that followed lasted longer than Xadrion had pride to admit. Yes, he knew he needed a new trainer – he had after all surpassed the teachings of all who had been given that position thus far. And yes, she had incredible talent in hand-to-hand combat, as she'd very clearly displayed to everyone in that room. A small part of him was curious to her teachings, was interested in learning the footwork she displayed for the brief moments of the fight in the throne room. And yes, he knew where his hurt ego was coming from. There were women in many different combat positions throughout Thesadel's ranks, both mage and soldier positions alike, and Xadrion had proven himself against every one of them. But this woman could barely stand. Still, Rhoas had seen something in her that convinced him she would be enough of a challenge for Xadrion to warrant being his next trainer.

The fighting against his father ended up being pointless, as he knew it was from the beginning, and he had left the room like a kicked pup, skulking away with a tail between his legs. He knew the anger he felt wasn't Azraelle's fault, but he hadn't visited Emera's rooms to check her condition since that day. In fact, now that Azraelle was awake, Xadrion hadn't even seen Emera around.

Days passed this way before his father called on him once more.

'How is Lady Azraelle's condition?' Rhoas asked, seated behind his desk.

'Is Emera unable to offer that report?'

His father's mouth thinned to a line in disappointment. Xadrion's behaviour was less than impressive to him, yet Xadrion still wanted to lash out in the faint hopes that the whole situation would be avoided.

'One would think that as the future king to this vast kingdom of ours, you would be taking every chance you could to help your citizens and ensure their wellbeing,' his father said. 'You will find a time to meet with Lady Azraelle today. Emera also will need to be present. I will find it extremely upsetting to find that I must walk myself down to ask for Azraelle's help in your training. You will request her assistance, assuming Emera's clearance of her health, and you will begin taking a vested interest in tracking down those that are responsible for the harm done to the woman you saved.'

So, it was decided, and now Xadrion had a deadline. If he didn't speak with Azraelle today, his father would, and that would end up even worse for Xadrion. Once he left the study, he stalked the castle hallways for some time before he finally decided to head in the direction of Emera's rooms.

His knock went unanswered, not a single sound coming from inside the rooms. Of course, this only served to irritate Xadrion further. Without much other choice, Xadrion slid to the ground beside the door, resting his arms across his knees. He would wait for their return – surely with a barely back from death patient they wouldn't have gone too far.

Maybe he would get lucky and Azraelle wouldn't want to stay. She'd been insistent on her first day up, seemingly determined to get out of Fennhall that very day. Maybe she would reject the offer and leave them. He'd done enough at this point, surely. He'd found her, got her back to the castle, back to Emera and saved her life. He didn't owe her anything else.

It wasn't long before there were footsteps in the distance, approaching his direction. He heard Emera's voice first, comforting and calm.

'You managed the walk well today,' Emera said.

'It's getting easier,' came Azraelle's voice. She was quiet and reserved in her manner of speaking. She sounded different now that she was calm, a familiarity in her tone already developing when she spoke to Emera.

'Your back has bound together again so you should be able to start doing some light exercises to help you get moving again if you wanted,' Emera said.

'Thank you,' Azraelle responded. 'Your magic is… soothing.'

'I imagine it's both pleasurable and painful to feel its presence when your own is depleted,' Emera said. Silence followed for a moment too long. Xadrion eagerly listened to their conversation, his intrigue piqued. Finally, a soft laugh broke the silence. It wasn't joyful, or happy – merely surprised.

'I suppose I shouldn't be surprised you could sense it,' Azraelle said.

The two women came around the corner now, Emera holding firmly onto Azraelle's elbow and supporting part of her weight as they walked. Emera looked like she was opening her mouth to say something else when her eyes landed on Xadrion, pushing himself to his feet now that they were in view. Azraelle's gaze followed, settling on him leaning against the wall.

'Prince Xadrion,' Azraelle greeted, a polite smile on her lips. Her eyes flickered from him to a point to his left, as if she were struggling to make herself look his way.

'Xadrion,' Emera said, not including his title the way she always made sure to in public. 'What are you doing here?'

'I came to see Lady Azraelle.' Xadrion thought Azraelle's smile turned mocking, her eyes meeting his a little more often. 'And you. I came to ask a favour.'

'Whatever it is, I would love to hear it. But please, let's go inside. I need to sit for a while,' Azraelle said. Emera supported her as they brushed past Xadrion, pushed the door open and led the way inside. He followed them in, watching as Emera settled Azraelle into one of the chairs around a small table.

The two women seemed so comfortable with each other already after their few days of cohabitation. Azraelle didn't eye Emera in the same way she watched Xadrion. She never turned a suspicious look in Emera's direction, not like the one she now kept fixated on Xadrion.

Emera gestured for Xadrion to take one of the remaining seats around the table, bringing over a jug of water and some cups.

'So, Prince Xadrion. What is your favour?' Azraelle asked once Emera had also settled into a chair at the table. He had been so entranced in the women's conversation, so interested in the things they said when they thought they weren't being listened to. Now, faced with the purpose of his visit, Xadrion could not release the tension from his jaw. He knew her fighting ability, but here she was tired and exhausted from a walk around the castle hallways. That was who was supposed to train him – if she even agreed to it.

All these thoughts swirled through his mind, convincing himself of the inability of this woman to train him, and yet it was her who was looking at him as if she held the power between them. She was watching him as if she knew he would rather be anywhere else, that he didn't often ask for favours, as if she could see the vulnerable position that he felt he was in. The piercing gaze of her black eyes was mocking. It took a moment too long for Xadrion to look away from those eyes, the darkness in them so intense that Xadrion truly couldn't tell if there was another colour that lined them.

'You have combat experience?' Xadrion asked Azraelle. There were so many holes in her story. She had been taken young, but no one learned how to fight like that as a child and retained the memory throughout all those years. She had to have trained for years, had to have taken the time to master her craft.

'Yes,' Azraelle answered after a slight moment's hesitation. She looked cautious now, not sure where he was going with his questioning. That, or she was avoiding her own holes in the story she had provided.

'Look, there's a lot of unanswered questions, I'm sure, for everyone. You clearly have some things you need resolved and as your experiences represent a threat within Thesadel, we would like to offer you help,' Xadrion began.

'In exchange for what?' Azraelle queried, still cautious.

'You're not seriously asking for an exchange to help find who did this to her?' Emera asked, her disgust at the idea evident in her expression.

'No.' Xadrion stumbled over himself to speak. 'We would never hold justice for those criminals from you in exchange for you doing anything. We're invested in helping find who is responsible regardless.'

'I don't mean to be short with you, *Prince*, but is what you're wanting to ask me really that difficult for you to express?' Azraelle asked.

Xadrion's anger boiled, frustrated mostly with his own inability to simply speak what needed to be spoken. Azraelle watched him, which had Xadrion shifting in his seat. In the throne room on that first day, she'd barely glanced at him for longer than a few moments at a time. Sitting so close to her in Emera's rooms and having her stare Xadrion down left him feeling uncertainty.

'King Rhoas would like to offer you a permanent place to stay. Your rooms are being organised as we speak. And there would be money for the work we could offer you,' Xadrion said, noting for the first time the clothes Azraelle had been dressed in. Gone was the dressing gown she had worn while unconscious; instead, Xadrion recognised an old dress of Emera's. It hung loose on her, Azraelle's undernourished state doing nothing to help fill the fullness of Emera's measurements. The emerald pendant sat nestled against her chest, sitting atop an exposed criss-crossing of scars marking her skin.

'What work would you offer me?' Azraelle asked, pulling Xadrion's gaze back to her face from where it had settled on the exposed skin of her chest.

'Instructing. Me.'

Silence took over the room. Emera stared at Xadrion, bewildered. Azraelle blinked, once in shock and then a genuine humour-filled smile crossed her face. She laughed, the sound kicking Xadrion's anger up to a whole new level.

'You want me to train you to fight like me?' There was nothing specific she was doing that Xadrion could pinpoint but somehow her words felt mocking.

'In exchange for accommodation, a salary and a position,' Xadrion said through gritted teeth.

'This is from the king's request, and not yours?' Azraelle asked, eyeing him closely. Xadrion got the distinct impression that everything he had said, everything he had done whilst around her until that point, was being neatly stored away in her memory to be used in her own analysis of him.

'Yes. But it would be an honour to learn from you.' He was angry, but he also knew how to be courteous and if she said yes, courteous was what he would need to be.

'She won't be ready for some time,' Emera interrupted. 'Azraelle has only just begun being able to walk herself.'

'How long until you think I would be ready?' Azraelle asked, an eager glint in her eye as she turned to look at Emera. Xadrion added this to his own observations of Azraelle, the eagerness that she displayed to move and train. She may have been looking at him mockingly, but she genuinely desired to train.

'At the rate we're progressing, with the treatments every day, I'd give you another two weeks before you can start wielding any kind of weapon, let alone engage in combat,' Emera answered.

'Well, it would seem we still have some time to think on this,' Azraelle pondered. 'Might I request some time to consider? Simply as I have suddenly found myself with some version of the future that I wasn't entirely prepared for, and I would very much appreciate being able to think things through.'

'The king, I believe, would like an answer soon, but I'm sure he will allow you time to consider the offer.'

'Would you let the king know that I would like to visit him to discuss the particulars of this agreement? Not today, of course, I fear that walk was enough, but if he can make time for me in the next few days, I would be greatly appreciative.'

Xadrion gave his agreement, and with nothing else to be discussed until her answer was provided, he excused himself from the two women and left the room.

He was not far from the rooms when he ran into Ilyon.

'How is she today?' Ilyon asked.

'Up and walking. She seems in good spirits,' Xadrion answered.

'I'm heading over to show her to her new rooms, so if you need her she'll be in the west wing from now,' Ilyon responded. Xadrion stepped to the side of the hallway, allowing Ilyon to pass by. The west wing, Xadrion noted to himself, was where the royal rooms also resided and usually were only offered to honoured guests. Rhoas, who had seen Azraelle all of one time, seemed to have assigned her a great deal of respect already.

Xadrion made his report to his father, who was pleased with Azraelle's consideration, before he returned to his rooms. Emera didn't come that night, despite the routine they'd previously held. It wasn't that unusual, but he hadn't seen her since Azraelle had woken. If a few more days passed, Xadrion decided, he would find her himself.

FOUR

AZRAELLE

It hadn't taken long for Azraelle to realise she enjoyed Emera's company. Emera was quiet more often than not but she laughed easily and seemed to have an unspoken understanding for when Azraelle needed the time to sort her thoughts. The comfort of Emera's presence had Azraelle feeling like she could speak, like she could verbalise what she was feeling in any moment, especially after no sign of Az's magic resurfacing after the weeks that had passed. The two of them had fallen into comfortable living while Az was gratefully staying in Emera's rooms. Nonetheless, she was grateful when Ilyon arrived shortly after Xadrion left that day.

'I've come to show you to your rooms,' Ilyon said, a lazy grin resting on his features.

It was that grin that made Azraelle decide she very much liked Ilyon also. He was already so different to his brother Xadrion; in fact, they almost couldn't have seemed any further apart despite the similarities in their appearances. Azraelle hadn't seen Xadrion yet without his hair bound in his braids, while Ilyon had never come to her with a single binding in his long hair. His eyes were comforting, the colour a reminder of the wood of Eviria's mountain trees.

Azraelle was tired from the walk she and Emera had taken around the hallways, but she was so eager to have her own space once more that she didn't want to delay. There were some things she needed to figure out, and she couldn't do that with Emera watching her closely.

Emera helped Azraelle stand, indicating for Ilyon to support her other side. It would be a slower walk than what she had managed earlier, but neither Emera nor Ilyon made her feel as if they were in a rush. Slowly, Ilyon began to lead them down the hallways once more, heading to the west of the castle.

The limitations of this body had been of increasing frustration since she awoke. Walking was not something she had thought would ever cause her such trouble. And flying... well, she still hadn't let herself think too long about the wings that were now gone from her back. Azraelle had to stop the thoughts from breaking down all the carefully crafted control she had every time she sat down and didn't have to account for their presence. Or whenever she dressed each day in the garments that didn't have nor need a placement for her wings. Azraelle couldn't think about it, not when there was so much she needed to figure out – especially establishing just how vulnerable her position was within this castle.

It took the trio at least double the time Az assumed it would have normally taken to walk to the new rooms the king was gifting her, and she had to pause several times before she could continue. But when they got there, the walk felt worth it. It wouldn't be far for Emera to travel each day and eventually it would be nothing for Azraelle to travel on her own, but the rooms were beautiful.

Coming in through the door, the first thing that greeted Azraelle was a beautiful entryway with décor made of almost exclusively wood. She was thankful for the castle's aesthetic, reminding her nothing of the cool marble that Mount Olympus was filled with. The first room held two lounge chaises facing each other, with vases of flowers and artwork lining every wall. Through one of the open doors, she noted the washroom, and through the second was the bedroom. Pushing into the bedroom showed possibly the largest bed Azraelle had ever seen, which was surprising given the luxuries she had indulged in over her years.

Emera stayed standing by the front door while Ilyon strolled right in to lounge on one of the chaises as Azraelle explored.

'This is beautiful, thank you,' Azraelle said to Ilyon as she came back to the main room.

'There will be someone who will come assist you in the morning and night, especially while you are still recovering, to help you change and tend to your rooms. Emera will also be able to visit you here but having someone else will help free her up once more while you still need a bit more help,' Ilyon said. 'Other than that, the rooms are yours to use as you wish.'

Ilyon left after making sure she had settled in, but Emera still stayed, hovering by the door. Once Ilyon had gone, Emera closed it behind him and came to sit on the lounge.

'Have you felt any of your power begin to return?' Emera asked, concern evident in her expression. Azraelle grimaced at the reminder of what she was missing. She wasn't entirely surprised that Emera had managed to detect the absence of her power. Emera hadn't pushed her for an explanation as to why it was missing or for any answers on what happened to Azraelle over the last years. She was grateful – it meant one person she hadn't been forced to lie to. Az couldn't reveal who she was – she definitely couldn't reveal that she had been tormented by Zeus for Chaos only knows how long. She couldn't even remember what gods this area of the mortal realm worshipped and how acceptable it was to wield magic. She assumed, given that the king himself had his own personal seer, that magic was accepted, but there was only Emera who Azraelle had encountered so far.

'Nothing yet.' Would her power even come back? Were her wings gone forever? She had no idea and had no emotional capacity to think too deeply for the answers to those questions.

'When you are healed further, I would like to suggest some of the more… intensive methods for regaining your own power. If you don't see any change before then,' Emera said. Azraelle smirked, knowing exactly what those intensive methods were. Emera looked nervous, as if the idea of suggesting this to Azraelle had taken a great level of effort.

'With you?' Azraelle lounged back in her own seat, attempting to look casual as she did so, but still wincing as her back was stretched. Emera's face went red and her eyes widened in embarrassment.

'I mean, yes. No, I don't know,' Emera stumbled. 'There are others who we could source. There are those who specialise in the pleasure houses for regenerative properties, so maybe someone there. I… I could do it. I'm always happy to help.'

Hm. Pleasure houses. Yes, pieces of this part of the mortal realm were beginning to piece together in Azraelle's memories. They did have a tolerance for magic, bordering more closely to living with it than neutrally amongst it, despite the surrounding kingdoms not being so accepting. The idea of going to a mortal pleasure house didn't immediately leave Azraelle with a positive taste in her mouth.

The immortals were the source for the existence of magic, in both the immortal realms and this one. The idea that the regeneration of magic was possible through physical connection no longer surprised Azraelle, although she was sure it still left the mortals with confusion towards *why* exactly it was able to heal. It linked closely to one of the big differences between mortals and gods. Whether it was the boredom of their eternal life, or simply an encoded part of their biology, Az didn't know where it originated from, but the sex drive of the gods was considered… exceptional. And so, it only made sense that somewhere at the beginning creation of magic, the casting of restorative magic was linked with something immortals spent a significant period of their life doing. There were few of Az's kind who she hadn't spent a night or two with over the millennia in the attempt to curb those desires.

Azraelle hadn't been with mortals before, not ones still dwelling in the mortal realms at least, but she knew the restorative element was a lot more effective if done with someone else with power. While Azraelle didn't know where or how it had originated, she knew that the restoration came not purely from engaging in intimate activities with someone, but instead through the process of linking the power's together through the physical linking of bodies. When two – or more – people were experiencing that level of intimacy between each other, it allowed for magic to transcend the borders of the individual bodies and to provide a true soul-level connection.

'I will consider the method you are suggesting. But know that I don't invite to my bed anyone who does not want to be there. I will not use you for that service, not for something that should be as pleasurable for you as it can be,' Azraelle eventually answered. Emera blushed and instinct told Az that this wasn't something Emera had lightly suggested.

Azraelle breathed deeply, trying to tap into the heightened senses that came with being immortal. It wasn't so easy without her power to enhance it but the faintest scent of Emera's arousal scented the air. Emera was attracted to her.

It was a dangerous game interacting with mortals in that way. Although, Azraelle wondered with her powers non-existent if the risks would be as likely as they usually were. Mortals who had been unlucky enough to catch an immortal's eye in that way were usually left worse off from the encounter, one way or another. Whether it was from an unwelcome gift nine months later, or from an adoration curse that kept them seeking the immortal for most of the remainder of their life, it usually had some devastating effects.

'As you wish,' Emera stuttered, standing quickly. She bowed her head slightly and left Azraelle's rooms. Azraelle would have felt bad over Emera's embarrassment except for the knowledge that it was better for Emera in the long run to have nothing like that to do with Az.

Azraelle spent the remainder of that day resting, exhausted from the day's activity. When she finally found herself truly alone, she caught her anxiety building. It was the first time she'd felt truly alone in… well, ever. In Zeus' cells, she was constantly monitored while the visitors had been a daily occurrence. Before that, Azraelle had been surrounded by the Ravens. She'd been by herself at times, of course, though someone was always within a shout's distance from her. The longest time she'd been alone was when she was retrieving a soul, something Azraelle had often dragged out for the solitude it offered. The loneliness from before the Ravens did not originate from being by herself but rather… no, Azraelle definitely didn't have the emotional capacity to think back to those early years of her existence.

For now, she was alone. Yes, Emera and the others were close by, but these rooms were hers and she had absolutely nowhere to be and no reason to leave them. The unfamiliarity of that had Azraelle jittery for the first few hours alone in her new rooms.

As promised, a lovely lady by the name of Darlene came to her rooms that night to help her bathe and dress her in nightclothes. She arrived with a small stack of fabrics, which she took great care hanging in the large wardrobe in the bedroom. Darlene had brought a few more nightgowns, as well as a few simple dresses. Nothing extravagant, mostly simple gowns of one colour with some gentle patterns around the necklines and sleeves. All the same, it was a kind gesture and made Azraelle feel very welcomed in her new rooms.

The next morning Emera returned and set about the regular routine of their usual morning. Emera spent some time working her magic into a gentle massage on Azraelle's bare back, and demonstrated some of the basic movements she encouraged Azraelle to do morning and night if she could handle it.

'I know it may be improper of me,' Azraelle began, 'but do you think you could assist me in speaking with the king today?'

Emera agreed, stating that she was aware of the king's schedule and that he should be free at that moment if she wished. Darlene arrived and helped Azraelle dress in one of the plain dresses – the colour a faint peach. Azraelle was sure that with her own pale skin, it would leave her looking completely washed out, but there were no darker fabrics amongst the dresses that had arrived.

Emera slowly led Azraelle through the halls, keeping their arms linked to support Azraelle's weight if she needed. Already, the walking was feeling easier than it had the day before. Healing was a slow process, but Emera's magic was keeping her progressing at a steady pace.

They eventually reached a simple brown door, which was opened upon Emera knocking to reveal a large study. Bookshelves lined all walls and in the centre was a large wooden desk, with the king seated behind it. Upon looking up from what he was working on, Rhoas smiled at the two women before beckoning them inside.

'Ah, Lady Azraelle. Xadrion reported you were interested in paying me a visit to further discuss my offer. Please, come and take a seat.'

Azraelle walked in and took the seat, Emera following suit until Rhoas continued to speak. 'Emera, would you mind giving Lady Azraelle and I some time to talk privately? I believe I heard some commotion earlier of a broken something or other from one of the training sessions. It would ease my mind to know you had attended to it.'

Azraelle knew Emera saw through the king's small lie, but she bowed regardless and left the room, sealing the door behind her. Gone was the distrust present on that first day in the throne room. It seemed Emera had complete trust in leaving Azraelle alone with her king now. It left Rhoas looking directly at Azraelle, a genuine smile crinkling the outer corner of his eyes.

'Lady Azraelle,' he began.

'Please, I'm not a lady. Azraelle is fine,' Az interrupted. The use had seemed ironic to her at first, but as more people continued to refer to her that way it left her wishing they wouldn't. She was no lady. She wondered if she held any title anymore.

'Azraelle it is then,' Rhoas corrected. 'How are you settling in?'

'Wonderfully, thank you. My rooms are amazing, and everyone has been more than welcoming,' Azraelle answered.

'Even Xadrion?' A sly grin marked the king's expression. So, he knew that Xadrion had an attitude and that Azraelle seemed to be one of his least favourite people she had observed him interacting with. She hadn't seen much of him, mostly just glimpses through windows as her and Emera had walked by. Emera had spoken highly of him but to her he had seemed... angry. She wished she had the strength to peer into his mind for just a moment to see what his problem was. Xadrion's anger felt nearly tangible when Azraelle did find herself in the same room as him, as if it were a pot that could boil over at any moment.

'He's been fine. I'm greatly appreciative of his help when they found me,' Azraelle said. Emera had told her the story of how they had found her, the way she first appeared when she was dropped into the healer's rooms, recounting even how Xadrion had visited her every day while she was unconscious. Funny, given once she was awake, he had only visited the one time.

'He is hard to swallow at times, but he has a good heart,' Rhoas said. 'He is, for the most part, prepared to take over the protection of Thesadel and its citizens when the time comes, but he does still have some more to learn. This is what I was hoping you could assist with. He has burned through his previous trainers, picking up what they teach him faster than I can procure new ones. I fear I have run through everyone in my kingdom, and those of our neighbouring allies who are willing to visit.'

'It's very kind of you to consider me in this way, though I'm just not sure I'm the right person for the job,' Azraelle replied tentatively. 'I'm not sure of my plans for the future, now that I have this future to think of.'

'I understand this all must be a very troubling time for you. You have some time before you can even travel though, surely, given your injuries?'

'Yes, but after that. I'm not sure if the people who held me might find me again if I stay here, in this area,' Azraelle said, the words not quite a lie. Rhoas watched her closely, letting the room fall into silence while he did so. She didn't know why no one from her kind had found her yet. Zeus probably would have assumed she were dead, or at least no longer a threat.

But her family, her friends, her Ravens – surely at least one of them had begun looking for her. The guilty verdict professed by the Moirai, one of Az's own sisters, was probably responsible for some level of that. One found guilty of altering Destiny the way Az had been... well, there would be consequences for those who chose to interact with her once more. All the same, she still felt like someone would have found her if they could, anyone who would have been willing to hear her out. The feeling of abandonment settled strongly in Azraelle's gut.

'They can't find you here,' Rhoas eventually answered.

'You don't understand,' Azraelle began before Rhoas' next words pierced straight through whatever she was about to say.

'The castle is warded against those who might track you.'

Azraelle sat straight in her chair and blinked once, confused. Warded. Not many wards existed that could block tracking magic. Mortals with magic had some ability to track, but not a strong one – nothing that would cross more than the span of a kingdom. All the wards that Azraelle knew of were tailored against immortal magic. Was the king suggesting that this castle had been warded specifically against her kind being able to track within its walls? Was the king suggesting he knew more than he should?

'You have wards?' Azraelle asked tentatively, testing the waters.

'We have wards. Put in place decades ago by a... close friend. Emera was taught to maintain and uphold them, refresh them as needed. This is one of her primary roles she provides for us,' Rhoas answered.

'Why would you require wards around this castle?' Azraelle was pushing, looking for that last confirmation of what she was beginning to suspect. The king knew enough about her kind to know how to defend against their prying eyes. But why?

'The why is a story for another time. The question you're dancing around asking, I will provide you the answer. We keep the wards up to keep the gods out,' Rhoas said.

Azraelle was stunned, silent. Rhoas was smiling at her, as if he genuinely found her reaction amusing in some way. Az didn't speak; she felt like she couldn't. How could this mortal king know anything about the gods?

'Who put the wards up?' Azraelle asked, breaking the moment of silence that followed.

'Someone who wanted a place of protection for herself very much,' Rhoas answered.

'Protection from who?' She needed to hear a name... or anything.

'From the evil I assume left you with those gashes down your back, the only one who has the power to send someone tumbling to our realm from that realm above ours,' Rhoas said. 'Zeus.'

Azraelle's eyes widened, unable to mask her shock.

'Xadrion found you lying in the dirt, in the centre of a clearing that had never previously been there. He didn't think too much of it, didn't think past getting you here and getting you healed. But I put it together. There's not much that leaves an impact on its surrounding area like that, not much that leaves injuries like the ones on your back, as if you had something giant ripped from you. My friend… she never had wings. But she told me of them, of the ones who did,' Rhoas explained. More silence. Azraelle could barely order her thoughts.

'Do you know who I am?' she eventually rasped. Who of her kind had found their way to this mortal realm and trusted this mortal king for protection. And why?

'I do,' Rhoas answered. 'My friend told me stories of some of your… siblings. Ones who were kind to her, who had helped her over the years. She told me of you once, long ago – goddess of Death and so much more. She told me of your task in our world, how you carry those to their next paths. She told me of you once, fifteen years ago, on the last night I ever saw her.'

'She knew me?' Azraelle whispered, her chest feeling as if it were about to break open.

'She told me of the boy you saved and what it had doomed you to from doing so,' Rhoas answered.

It had been an exceedingly long time since Azraelle had felt the feelings that bubbled inside her now. Even in Zeus' cells, tortured and beaten daily, she had never let the desire to cry overtake her, had never let a single tear fall down her face. Yet right here, in this mortal king's study, her throat was burning and her vision was blurring. He knew – knew exactly who she was and what had been done to her. And he wasn't afraid, he wasn't pushing her out of his home. In fact, he had welcomed her and taken care of her.

'It wasn't the boy's time to die.' Azraelle tried to swallow down the burning in her throat.

'I know,' Rhoas said. And with that, the tidal wave broke through. Azraelle's chest felt like it was cracked in half, her heart heavy as if an anchor were tied to it. Heaving sobs wracked her chest. In a far-off place, she felt her hands grip the chair beneath her so tightly the arm pieces crumbled apart in her hands.

Gentle hands came to touch her shoulders, but the king didn't speak. He let the emotion wipe through Azraelle hard and fast. It took only moments for her to feel as if she had expended every tear she could, empty once more. Composed once more. The gentle hands left her shoulders and Rhoas moved back to his chair. Azraelle's head was thumping from the pain of crying, and the strain of trying to process what had been told.

'I don't know what happened after that. My friend was unable to visit again. She warned me that Zeus was battening down his hatches and would pull his people around him. She warned me she wouldn't be able to see me anymore. She told me you had been tricked, that you were paying for the crimes of your brother, protected by your mother. But she told me that the wards would protect me and my own,' Rhoas explained. 'With you inside the castle walls, Zeus will not find you. He will not be able to see you here. It does mean that no one else will either so if someone else were looking for you, they would not be able to find you. You could leave, and allow them the chance, but this would also allow Zeus to find you once more.'

Azraelle pondered his words. That explained why no one had come to see her. Why not even one of her Ravens or her siblings had come. She'd never deluded herself into thinking that her mater would come – her mater who had not entered the mortal realm for... a very long time. Az didn't think even the loss of one of her daughters would be enough to change her mater's mind about that. Again, that feeling of abandonment hit her hard. Az had no children of her own, had never found one of her kind she wished to make that commitment to, but she wondered if she would have made that same decision as her mater if she had.

Az had no idea if Zeus would be looking for her still or if there was now a bounty on her head for her guilty declaration. If someone found her here, well... there was no nice way to put it. She was fucked.

'It would appear, King Rhoas,' Azraelle said, 'that your castle is the safest place for me right now. As for what the future holds, I still don't know if I can guarantee you that, but I'm going to need some time to collect myself. It will take me a decently long time to return to my full strength, if that is something I can return to at all anymore. And I am currently not able to return to my realms, not without the threat of someone handing me in.'

Rhoas smiled, despite the heaviness of their conversation.

'Does this mean you will accept my offer? Train my son while you heal and while you find your way out of this predicament you are in. If you leave us in the future, I will hope that you do find your way home one day. But for now, stay with us,' Rhoas said.

'Your son may be a bit of an asshole, your majesty, but he will be an excellently trained asshole.'

FIVE

AZRAELLE

It was going to take some time before Azraelle was ready to take up Xadrion's lessons. Emera had said two weeks, but by the end of the first week, Azraelle was feeling restless and bored.

'I need to move, even if I'm just instructing. I won't push myself too far,' Azraelle promised Emera. Her back didn't need the bandages anymore and her wounds were closed fully. The scars left behind from her wings were ghastly, and Azraelle took great care to wear clothes that covered the length of them. It wasn't that Azraelle was ashamed of scars – she'd lived her whole life proud of the wounds she bore on her skin – but she didn't need any more attention paid to her by the citizens of Fennhall than she was already getting.

In the past week, Azraelle had spent her time becoming familiar with the layout of the castle on her walks. She could now comfortably lead herself around, and the walks had stopped expending her entire day's energy. On the agreement that she didn't really need mortal currency, the king had instead granted her access to his tailor, who had provided her with an entire wardrobe. It had taken most of the week for them to make what she requested, but her wardrobe now was filled with clothes more to her liking. Az had included dresses, as she knew it would be useful to blend into this mortal realm, but had also demanded her own assortment of shirts and trousers. She would need them to train in, but she also just generally preferred them. Dresses hadn't been a regular outfit of Az's since her years as a child, many millennia ago.

The castle inhabitants eyed her curiously whenever they spied her on her walks, dressed in pants and a shirt, and the guards always stood further to attention when she was near, but for the most part, Azraelle didn't feel anything aimed towards her from the people of Fennhall besides their nervous glances.

'It's only been a week,' Emera said.

'I know. But I think the outside air will only help me at this point. And there's no risk of reopening my wounds. The worst that will happen right now is some exceptionally sore muscles,' Azraelle retorted.

'You're not going to give up until I clear you, are you?' Emera said, smiling at her. They were sitting in Az's room, each lounging on their own chaise. Emera had stopped by after she'd spent the morning attending to some minor ailments in the city surrounding the castle and the two women had quickly passed the last hour in conversation.

'I definitely won't.' Azraelle's own smile felt halfway genuine in Emera's presence.

'Have you felt any return of your magic? I'd feel a lot more comfortable knowing you could be channelling that to your own healing during the day,' Emera asked.

Azraelle ground her teeth in frustration. Not at Emera, but at the fact that another week had passed without a single trace of her magic. It shouldn't have disappeared when she was thrown from Mount Olympus. The wings had been torn from their connections, which explained their permanent absence, but the magic was hers. It would always be hers. Yet, if what Emera had told her about the condition she had arrived at the castle in, Az was sure it had to do with how close to dying she had come.

Through inbuilt instinct, magic could channel itself into keeping its wielder alive on Death's door. It could let itself entirely feed into the body, doing its best to fix whatever harm was happening. In truth, Azraelle had probably only survived because of her magic's last attempt to keep her alive as she fell.

'You would have sensed it if it was returning, I'm sure,' Azraelle quipped.

Emera pursed her lips as she watched Azraelle across from her before she stood and came to sit on the same lounge that Az was seated on. Hesitantly, as if cautious of Azraelle's reaction, Emera reached her hands across and took hold of one of Az's. Emera had touched Azraelle an endless number of times by that point – she'd had to for the healing – but this was different. This was tender, and affectionate.

Azraelle didn't speak, only continued to watch Emera as she seemed to have some internal battle within herself.

'Let me help you,' Emera breathed, slowly closing the distance between their two bodies. Emera's hands moved from Azraelle's, moved to her face and gently cupped her cheeks. Every movement she made was slow, as if she were giving Azraelle the time to pull away at each shift.

Slowly, she leant forward, her hands gentle on either side of Az's face. The warmth of Emera's magic brushed against her cheeks, followed shortly after by the feeling of Emera's breath on her lips. Azraelle's eyes closed of their own accord, the feeling of Emera so close left her unable to think straight. It was a bad idea; in fact, it was a terrible idea. But that magic was so soothing, so warm. And Emera's breath was so close to her now, and she smelt so fresh and inviting that Azraelle couldn't break through her own thoughts.

With her eyes closed, the feeling of Emera's lips finally brushing against her own was nearly overwhelming. Her lips were soft, and questioning, as if asking permission for every movement they made. The contact had Azraelle letting out a deep breath, as if the tension was being lifted from her with the physical contact.

Flashes of the harshness of physical contact within Zeus' cells crossed Azraelle's mind, but each of them was swept away under the gentleness of Emera's touch. Each memory that surfaced reminding Az of the brutality that had been inflicted upon her body was pushed from her mind as Emera's lips moved across Azraelle's. So many had used her body as a means of delivering pain, but Emera kept all of the panic from that at bay.

'I can help you,' Emera whispered, her lips moving against Azraelle's. Bad idea. Such a bad idea. But when Emera moved to kiss her again, Azraelle let her, and then let her deepen the kiss. Emera's hands moved from Azraelle's cheeks, down until they were holding her shoulders, no… pushing her shoulders. Her mind was so clouded that Azraelle let herself be guided down, Emera moving above her now. Their tongues were dancing together, Emera's lavender scent washing over her.

Once Azraelle was lying down fully, Emera moved her lips, brushing down her jaw to kiss beneath her ear, slowly making a trail down Azraelle's neckline until she reached the collar of her tunic. Not once did Emera's soothing magic stop flowing wherever Emera touched Azraelle.

Azraelle could feel her body reacting, feel the desire awaken within her. It had been a long while since she had been gifted with touch for pleasure. Before the cell… well, she'd never been one to shy away from contact with others.

Emera's lips left a trail of heat wherever they went, and Azraelle's desire began to pulse intensely. The light butterflies in the depth of her abdomen, the tingling at that so sensitive bundle of nerves. Oh, she wanted this from Emera. She would happily have Emera's lips across her skin, would be happy to give her hours' worth of pleasure in return.

One of Emera's hands moved to Azraelle's thigh, the other reached gently to cup her breast over her shirt. Emera's fingers moved gently over her nipple, eliciting a quiet moan in response.

It was the moan that shocked Azraelle enough to open her eyes. She couldn't do this. Regardless of how much she wanted it – how much she needed it – Emera was mortal, and Az did not take mortal lovers. It was *never* a good idea. Gently, Azraelle moved her own hands to clasp Emera's wrists, pulling them from her body. She instantly missed the contact but knew she could push through until she was thinking clearly once more.

Emera looked up from where she had lowered herself, her eyes questioning. When she saw Azraelle aware and watching her, it was as if she could read Az's mind.

'Emera,' Az whispered, moving so she was half sitting once more. Emera went to pull away, the embarrassment at Az's rejection evident on her face.

'I'm sorry, I should have asked,' Emera said, making a move to get up. Azraelle didn't let go of her wrists, pulling them gently so Emera was forced to turn back to her, their bodies still pressed closely to each other.

'You asked,' Azraelle whispered, locking her eyes with Emera's. 'You asked every step of the way and I said yes.'

'Then why?' Emera asked, her voice hushed as she remained looking confused at the rejection.

'It's just not a good idea.'

Something akin to anger flashed behind Emera's gaze, the embarrassment now nowhere to be seen. Az couldn't give her a reason, not one that she would understand. There were no reason two mortals shouldn't indulge in that relationship together, no reason that would have dire consequences. And that's what Emera believed Az to be – mortal. But she wasn't, and there were dire consequences.

Emera didn't push the subject, for which Azraelle was endlessly grateful. Despite being the one who had ended the contact, the sudden lack of Emera's warmth made her heart pang in loneliness. That type of contact with another person… it was something Az had been missing since she had first been captured.

Emera left to return to her daily tasks, leaving Az to her own devices. Once she managed to calm herself down once more, an activity that involved a full head dunk under the cold water in her washroom, she did her exercises, and then spent a good while trying to channel down to feel even a breath of her magic. Where there used to be that pool of strength within her, there now existed a deep, dark well – empty of even the smallest drop.

Eventually, Az made her way out of her rooms and through the hallways of the castle. Emera hadn't exactly given her an answer, what with being side-tracked by their intimate moment, so Az decided to assume it would be fine for her to begin her duties with Xadrion. She had heard the training rooms from her own room and was sure she would find him there. It didn't take her long to leave the heavy castle walls, cross the paved courtyard and come to the large stone barracks where she heard weapons clashing inside.

Standing outside the barracks, Azraelle was reminded vividly of what it felt like to be standing outside a different building – one that elicited the same sounds from within. The sounds that came from the Ravens as they trained were faster and harder than mortals could ever manage, but the familiarity of the sounds left her feeling vulnerable.

Nakir, who was Azraelle's Second, would be taking care of the Ravens in her absence. But that guilty verdict hanging over Az's reputation left her feeling worried for the future, for the future where she may never get to return to her legion. Azraelle had led them for many millennia – since the moment of their conception in this existence. She had trained them, lived with them, loved them. And now it had been many long years since she last saw them, ever since that moment with Edda before Zeus' carefully laid trap.

Azraelle missed them.

'Are you going in?' Azraelle turned to see Ilyon approaching, a grin plastered on his features. She was sure that he spent most of his days smiling or laughing. It was comforting to know that a person capable of such happiness existed.

'I am,' Azraelle answered, aware of how she must have looked with her hand frozen above the handle to the door. Ilyon gently nudged her hand away, taking the role of opening the door.

'I know the deal was that you would train Xadrion,' Ilyon said, 'but do you think you could have the time for both of us?'

'Of course,' Azraelle answered, as they walked in together. She tried not to take notice as eyes shifted in her direction. The last time a lot of the people in that room had seen her up close would have been the first day she woke – the day she interrupted their ceremony and left a few of them in the infirmary. Emera had assured her that they had all woken with nothing more than a bad headache, but Azraelle still felt guilty.

'I mean, obviously you have to make the time for Xadrion first, but maybe I could come to you after or before? I don't mind getting up early, whatever works for you.' Ilyon was babbling. Azraelle found it charming in its own way, the way he kept stumbling over his words trying to make justifications for his request. She wondered why he hadn't been included in the deal in the first place. Xadrion would be taking over the kingdom – so it made sense that he would receive the training of a crowned prince – but it was a smart decision to have the same treatment provided to both sons. From what she'd seen around the castle so far, Azraelle got the distinct impression that Ilyon was largely left to his own devices.

'Ilyon,' Azraelle interrupted, a small chuckle escaping her as she watched him stop talking mid-way through a word and look at her with doe-eyes. 'I'll train you. Don't worry about it.'

Ilyon grinned, seemingly happy with her decision, before pointing through the crowded room to where Xadrion stood with his eyes fixed on Azraelle.

Even from across the room with dozens of people between them, the moment she locked eyes onto Xadrion, she felt the now almost familiar feeling in the depth of her chest. Every time she'd seen him through a window over the last few weeks or heard his voice in a room she'd passed on her walks, something inside her had responded. Az didn't know what the feeling was trying to signal to her, but she had been doing her best to avoid being caught unaware by his presence so as to avoid feeling it. The few times she had tried to push to the source of the feeling she was reminded with a sudden pang of pain in her mind that she shouldn't be doing that.

Of course, it frustrated her to know there was something locked inside her own mind, some part of her that she was being denied access to, but it had been that way for centuries. Whatever it was Azraelle couldn't remember was guarded well enough in her own mind that even with the mastery of her mind it had remained hidden for hundreds of years. She hadn't even been able to piece together who had created the block in her memory.

The main room of the barracks was large enough to accommodate the few dozen men and women who were training at that moment. Many were watching her out of the corner of their eyes, demonstrating a weak attempt to look as if they were still sparring. Some partners had weapons, others simply had wrapped fists and pads. There were people on their own doing strength circuits around the outer edges of the room, and benches lined one wall where a handful were clearly taking a breather. Those ones in particular did not make any effort of pretending they weren't openly gawking at her.

Xadrion was watching her but had clearly been involved in some conversation with his two companions beside him. Azraelle moved from the centre of the room, knowing he would come to her when he was no longer preoccupied, and found herself standing next to a handful of weapon racks, each containing an assortment of wooden and blunted blades for training.

Blades weren't her desired weapon, although the length of her lifespan meant she was fortunate to have trained enough to be considered an expert by mortal standards at all the options displayed on the racks in front of her. Over the millennia there hadn't been more than a handful of times where the Ravens second purpose – to be a serving army – had ever been required, but they still kept their skills sharp at all times. Azraelle's magic was always her chosen weapon, the havoc she had been capable of reaping far beyond what a single sword could ever hope to accomplish.

Xadrion finally removed himself from the two he had been instructing and cautiously approached where Azraelle was standing. The way he looked at her, the way he approached her, left her unsure as to what he thought of her. He was wary, as it was smart to be, but he had also saved her, and that seemed to be conflicting for him in his mind. The woman he had saved had now been requested to teach him.

'You accepted the offer,' Xadrion said, a statement that didn't necessarily require an answer.

Azraelle picked up one of the swords from the rack, tossing it between her hands. 'Your father can be mighty persuasive.'

'Are you capable? Emera said two weeks,' Xadrion asked, still seeming to be looking for any way out of her following through on her agreement.

In truth, she had no idea how well her back would hold up to what she was planning to put it through. No idea how her mind would hold up either, given every movement she'd ever trained had been accounting for the presence of her wings. Az didn't want Xadrion to know any of that though, didn't want him to see any trace of weakness within her past what he had already seen.

A grunt from a nearby soldier interrupted their conversation as he was knocked from his feet.

Xadrion was fidgeting with his hands, his lips pursing as if he kept deciding against opening them to speak. Again, Azraelle wished she had enough of her power to push into his mind and see for herself what he was thinking.

'Let's start. I want to see where you're at,' Azraelle demanded, throwing him one of the wooden training swords. She beckoned him to follow her to a clear space in the centre of the room, leaving a comfortable distance between the two of them. Xadrion didn't raise his sword.

'You didn't grab a weapon for yourself,' Xadrion said.

'I don't think I'll need one today.'

The flash of rage that passed Xadrion's face gave her a strange amount of satisfaction. His ego was so weaved into the outcome of this fight already, she could sense his tension at not understanding what was happening.

'I would feel better if you had a weapon to defend blows with,' Xadrion said through gritted teeth.

'I'll make you a deal. You land a blow, and I'll grab a weapon. I just need to see if you can make a blow,' Azraelle taunted. Despite the lack of her own power, Azraelle hadn't been completely abandoned by her senses. In that moment, as Xadrion's anger flared Az felt the presence of it around her. She breathed deeply, her senses immediately registering what could only have been described as a storm brewing. His anger was easy to rile, and that was all that was needed to spur him into action.

Azraelle had to hand it to the man – he gave it a fair go. She assumed he would have become clouded by his anger, become reckless and hurried in his movements, but he didn't. He was furious, there was no denying that. She could feel the heat radiating from him whenever they got near to each other, but as soon as he started moving, the training he had clearly received his whole life kicked into effect. He was a skilled fighter. But he wasn't fast enough; not anywhere near fast enough.

Az could see the influences in his fighting, ranging from several kingdoms across this mortal realm. He had managed to find a way to blend them together beautifully. A small part of her mind registered the beauty in his movement, his grace and power. An even smaller part found herself somewhat heated at her admiration of him. No – not him. She was simply still frustrated from the release she didn't allow herself that morning with Emera. It was residual tension.

In response to Xadrion's attempt to hit her, Azraelle made her style centre around fluidity. She was moving around him, his weapon, ensuring that she was never where he expected her to be when his sword finished its planned arc. The longer they danced, the more Az noticed the eyes of others in the room watching them. Watching her.

Xadrion noticed as well; his expression clearly displaying his agitation. He hadn't come close to landing a hit. It really wasn't his fault; by all accounts he was an exceptional fighter. But what mortal could have compared to Azraelle, goddess of Death?

Eventually, Az called a stop to their round. She did her best not to let on that even that exceedingly small amount they had done had left her back screaming at her, desperate for rest. She acted calm and composed, never one to show weakness.

'I don't get it,' Xadrion said between breaths. Azraelle grinned, his anger making her feel more rejuvenated than anything had for a long time. By the end of their fight, the ease with which Azraelle scented his fury gave it a nearly visible presence in the air around them.

'No. You don't,' Azraelle agreed. Xadrion's eyes flashed and the veins in his forearms protruded as he tightened his fists in frustration. 'But you will. I will make you get it.'

She needed to rest. Her back had started spasming and didn't show any signs of stopping. Azraelle took the time to demonstrate to Xadrion the first series of movements she wanted him to practise outside of their lessons together. It consisted mostly of footwork she needed him to be able to complete quickly and efficiently. If he could successfully make it through the routine without falling flat on his face or his ass, at the speed that she demonstrated to him, then he would be ready for the next one.

There were several times Azraelle had to approach him and each time she moved closer the scent of him washed through her. The sweat that was coating his skin enhanced the scent so much that, even without her magic to assist, her senses were overwhelmed. Azraelle needed to get her impulses under control. It wouldn't do her any good to be so at the whim of her desire while surrounded by mortals.

Once Xadrion was settled into his own routine, Azraelle left the barracks, waving back at Ilyon in the corner. He was animatedly throwing thumbs up in her direction, clearly excited that his older brother had been left with no victory to his name.

The only detour to her rooms was a quick stop by the kitchens to grab some bread and soup, which she awkwardly ate as she walked the hallway back to her rooms. Azraelle nearly fell asleep at the table as she finished her food, again in the bathtub, and again as she was pulling on a large comfortable shirt to sleep in, before finally she succumbed to her fatigue as she fell to the bed.

SIX

AZRAELLE

Az wasn't prepared for the dream that swept upon her with sleep. No... not a dream. Azraelle did not dream normal dreams, she never had. Despite the absence of her magic, the dream that found its way to her as she slept was indeed a warning premonition. She'd had them before – as the goddess of Death, she was often offered premonitions of deaths, ones that had required her more than the other Ravens to be the carrier to the next life.

The premonitions usually came with a bit more detail, specifically how the person was going to die, where they were going to die and where they needed to go. This one showed nothing of those details. Instead, Azraelle was left with only one image as she sat awake in her bed, night still holding the sky outside. An image of a man dead in a field of tall grass. His eyes were glazed over as if they were full of ice and a giant burn cindered across his chest.

Why was she receiving this vision when no other form of her magic had come forward? She had no magic and she had no ability to ferry the dead as she had once done. Azraelle played the premonition over and over in her mind, searching for any understanding of what she had seen and why she had seen it. Nothing new revealed itself, no matter how many times she scrutinised the image.

Eventually, with no other alternative, Azraelle went back to sleep. Was this Destiny mocking her? She wouldn't have been able to do anything, would not have been able to hold that man's soul in her hands as she ferried him into the next life, and definitely would not be able to find her way to wherever this man had died in order to do so.

The rest of the night held only restless sleep for Azraelle, so she was grateful when morning finally broke and there became a reason to break out from the covers. Dressing herself in a loose shirt and pants tucked into the leather

51

training boots she had ordered from the dressmaker, she was leaving her rooms just as Darlene entered. Seeing that the task of dressing Azraelle had already been completed, Darlene set about to ordering the room instead.

It was one thing Azraelle was grateful for, despite valuing her privacy. She was an exceptionally messy person; she always had been. Darlene had kept the rooms clean over the last week, never once making her feel bad for the piles of clothes that always found their way to the floor or the never-made bed in the morning.

If Emera was surprised to see Azraelle standing at her door that morning, she didn't show it. Instead, she stepped aside and allowed Az to enter and assume her previously usual position for their morning sessions – one of Emera's couches.

The session was awkward. Emera's angered reaction at Az's rejection in their last session was standing between them and their previously comfortable interactions. Azraelle wanted to ease the tension, wanted to hold her hands and let her know that her offer had been more tempting than she could ever know. Az didn't know how long had passed in Zeus' confinement, but she was certain it spanned over a decade. A decade without another person's tender touch left her wanting it more than she could have ever explained but she didn't know how to tell Emera that she wanted her – not without having to give the reasons behind why she couldn't have her.

'I heard you went to training yesterday,' Emera commented, after at least a half hour of silence had passed.

'I did.' Azraelle didn't dare tell Emera how much it had taken out of her to do so. Today, as restlessly as she had slept, and as early as she had awoken, hadn't helped with the soreness that was spreading throughout her body as each hour passed. It wasn't just her back, but every muscle in her body ached from the fatigue.

'Your back looks fine. I suppose you were right about only needing a week,' Emera remarked shortly. She was pissed. Whether at Azraelle being right or just at Azraelle in general, she couldn't quite tell. Probably both.

'Still no sign of your magic?' Emera asked, through gritted teeth. She was coming to the end of the treatment, her magic slowly fading from Azraelle's awareness.

'No,' Azraelle lied. There was no way she could tell Emera of her prophecy, not when it would involve explaining what it was her magic even was.

The session ended with no relief in the tension between the two of them as Azraelle stood and pulled her shirt back over her head. Emera turned away, and quickly, her cheeks stained with a tinge of red to them.

'Thank you,' Azraelle said and hurried from the room. The blushing had taken a serious stab at Azraelle's self-control. Despite Emera's anger, Az could read the desire, and being able to see it left her struggling to suppress her own. Never mind that with the flush of blood to her cheeks came the intoxicating lavender smell over Azraelle's senses.

The training yards – that's where she needed to be. That's where she would burn her energy. She was one of the first people to arrive, given the still early hour in the day. Az was moving through her own set of warmups when Xadrion arrived. His long hair was tight in its braid, forever pulled from his face. The sheer size of him made him seem every inch a warrior and his beautiful brown skin, and dark features, left his silver eyes shining in their difference. He would make a princess incredibly happy one day to be at his side.

Azraelle didn't stop moving, even as she observed him. Moving and stretching was the only thing that helped ease the back pain she could feel worsening. Still, watching him caused a dip in her pace, the beauty of his form eye-catching as he entered the room. Yes, he would indeed make a princess *incredibly* happy one day.

Azraelle needed to get herself under control. She could feel her lust brimming and close to boiling over. First Emera, now Xadrion. She needed to stop these thoughts about the mortals around her. It would land her in nothing but trouble. And yet her eyes could not leave the broad shoulders and chiselled torso of the man walking toward her.

Azraelle stopped moving only once Xadrion had come to a stop in front of her. She wasn't sure why she irritated Xadrion so much, why he had such a problem with her when he had been the one to take her in, but she could feel his anger again. It was heavy and roiling over him, like a taut rope about to snap.

'Start with the series of movements I showed you yesterday,' Azraelle instructed.

'No sparring today?' Xadrion sounded disappointed. Had he wanted to rematch against her? He hadn't even come close to getting her the day prior; what hope would he have had with one day passing? But then, Azraelle quickly realised, that was exactly why he wanted a rematch. He had lost to her, and that had bruised his ego.

'Not today. You need to do a lot more before we go against each other again,' Azraelle answered. The anger she sensed intensified, if his clenching jaw was anything to go by. She had insulted him. Not intentionally this time, not as she had when she was trying to play with him in their previous interactions. This time, she had only been trying to state how much work he would need.

'Besides,' Azraelle continued on, not wanting to start a fight at the beginning of their session. 'I'm still recovering; it might take too much out of me.' It was a lie; she had been desperate for physical movement and release all that morning. A sparring match with Xadrion would have probably eased it.

Xadrion gave her a look as if to say that he definitely did not believe that.

'Now, come on. I need to see your first series,' Azraelle commanded. She wasn't sure how much of her skill she could teach to Xadrion, not when her skill had been honed over thousands of years and in large part was only a result of her magic's assistance in her training. Xadrion would never move as fast as she did or be as deadly – not as a mortal. But she could teach him more than what he knew.

Xadrion looked like he wanted to argue but seemed to decide against it. He settled into his stance and started the movements.

Two days passed in this same fashion. Each morning, Azraelle would meet Emera at her rooms for their morning healing. She'd head to the barracks, arriving before nearly everyone, and go through her own warmup. Once Xadrion arrived, she would instruct him on different patterns of footwork, almost as if teaching him steps to a dance. She would never say that to him. Something told Azraelle that if she compared what he was doing to a dance, Xadrion's ego would be hit again. Once she spent the few hours with Xadrion, Azraelle would find Ilyon to take him through the beginning of his lessons. After that first day, and after deciding not to do as much physical work with Xadrion, she'd had the energy left over to spend time with Ilyon and not feel absolutely bone-ridden tired. All the same, sleep came exceedingly earlier each night after being up and around all day.

No premonition came to her after that first night, as if Destiny had realised her uselessness in the situation. Why it had even bothered to appear in the first place was a mystery of its own.

It was on her fourth day of training with Xadrion that their now-regular routine was interrupted. She had finished her lesson with Xadrion and Ilyon after that and was heading back through the courtyard of the castle to return to her rooms. Being later in the afternoon, the courtyard was filled with inhabitants of the castle as they strolled beneath the warmth of the sun. Azraelle had found herself amongst the last group of soldiers coming back from the barracks but had only just stepped into the courtyard, thinking of the hearty meal she wanted to get from the kitchens, when panic started to sound from the castle gates.

The sound of several horses moving quickly toward her echoed before three horses appeared, two with riders seated and calling for Emera. On the third horse, face down and slumped over the saddle being pulled by the other two, lay a man. His blonde hair and fine clothes were muddy with blood. Az couldn't see much else of the man's features.

Xadrion appeared behind her, coming from the barracks she had just left him in.

'What happened?' Xadrion barked to the seated riders, his question commanding. The three horses pulled to a stop, and one of the conscious men jumped from the horse and ran into the castle. The other dismounted also, running to the horse that carried the bloodied man as he gave his report.

'We were attacked. I don't know,' the man said, his voice panicked and stuttering.

'By whom?' Xadrion demanded.

'We didn't see. Karlin was riding behind us. We were out near the farm sector, coming back here, when we heard his scream. By the time we even turned around, he was on the ground,' the man answered. As he spoke, Xadrion pulled on the bloodied man, hoisting him seemingly effortlessly into his arms. As he did, turning the man to be face up, Azraelle caught a better look. And nearly stopped breathing.

The man's eyes were frozen open, glazed over as if they were glass or ice. On his chest, a burn had torn through the front of his leather armour and tunic beneath, leaving a blistering mess on his chest. It was the exact man she had seen in her dream nights ago.

'We just threw him on the back and ran. There was no one else around who could have done it,' the first man was babbling. Emera came rushing from the castle, running straight to Xadrion and putting her hands directly onto the unconscious man. Time seemed to slow at that moment, as Emera sought her first initial diagnosis. Azraelle knew what she would find, knew that the man in Xadrion's arms was already dead.

Despite the panic around them, Xadrion seemed in control. In control enough to be able to pay attention to what was going on around him, to pay attention to Azraelle and to her distinct lack of panic. He was watching her, the dead man in his arms between them, Emera's presence fluttering to the side. It felt as if Azraelle were cemented in place, and like Xadrion was somehow rooted with her. Around them was chaos, noise and panic in every direction, but the two of them alone stood with no movement. Xadrion's iron eyes didn't leave hers until Emera gently pulled her hands from the man and placed one on Xadrion's shoulder.

'Prince,' Emera said, using Xadrion's title for the first time Azraelle had heard. 'There's nothing I can do for him.'

Azraelle didn't even blink at the words.

'I don't even know what could have caused injuries like this,' Emera said.

Someone jostled into Azraelle's shoulder. Broken from the frozen trance she had found herself in, Azraelle turned on her heel as fast as she could, left the group in the courtyard and pushed through the castle doors. Once she was inside and alone, she began to run. She ran through the hallways, listening carefully for any other footsteps and ensuring she ran in the opposite direction. It led her a very roundabout way, but eventually she found herself panting and heaving inside her rooms, her legs burning from the effort.

She had received the premonition days ago, days prior to the man's death. That never happened. She always got the images as they were occurring, as a sign that it was time for their soul to be ferried. And they had always come with the details required for her to find the target and escort them to their next path. She saw this days ago, and with so few details she wouldn't have been able to help even if she did have her magic. Why did Destiny see fit for her to learn this knowledge earlier than it came to pass?

Azraelle felt useless. Her magic hadn't even flickered for the nearly three weeks she had been awake. She had no way to get to her Ravens and no way to find any one of her siblings. There was no way her mater would dare to find her. And her wings. Gone.

No tears came, but the feeling inside her was inescapable.

The moment with the king when she had sobbed was not a usual occurrence for Az, but it had been somewhat of a relief of pressure for her. Now, it seemed, she was back to her original method of coping – no tears. There were only giant, painful cracks inside her body as if the emotions inside were taking their own swords and slashing her with it.

In the endless time she had lived, all the time with her wings, she had never once taken them for granted. They felt like the greatest part of her; they gave her freedom and power. And now they were gone. She wanted them back, but she would at the very least settle for the return of her magic. She craved something familiar and warm to comfort her in this strange circumstance she found herself in. Would she ever be able to return home? Would she die as her pater had done so many years ago? Would it be a true end, or would she be granted the gifts of her immortality? She prayed to Chaos itself that... that what? That it would be a true end? She couldn't tell in that moment what she wanted.

Azraelle heard nothing from the own cacophony of her mind while she knelt in the middle of her room, palms face up on her knees. Chaos had never listened to her, had never dared allow her to glimpse the presence she so desperately sought. Why should it have been any different in that moment? On her knees, palms exposed and head bowed as if awaiting a sentencing, Azraelle couldn't have been weaker. Why would anything have chosen to bother with her, let alone Chaos?

'You knew he was dead?' came a voice, ringing through the crashing in her mind. Azraelle's head snapped up, whipping to face the doorway to her room. Xadrion. Of course he had seen her; of course he could tell she already knew the man's fate.

'What?' Azraelle snapped, her voice quieter than she would have liked. She was weak. So fucking weak.

'You already knew he was dead. You didn't even react,' Xadrion said, stating it now rather than questioning her.

'I suppose.'

'How could you have known?' Xadrion asked. Azraelle didn't answer – couldn't answer. There was no answer she could give him that wouldn't land her knee deep in shit. Az barely managed to shrug.

And then, with her head bowing from the shame of her situation once more, came something unexpected. Contact. Her shoulders felt it first, and then a firm grasp settled beneath her arms and hoisted her up. Hard enough that her feet instinctively sought the solid ground beneath her and suddenly she was standing.

'Did your magic tell you?' Xadrion asked, moving to stand in front of her. His eyes, silver and piercing, met hers.

'I don't have magic.'

So, he had overheard the conversation with Emera the other week. She'd wondered what he had heard as she rounded the corner with Emera but had decided that playing unfazed would be the best approach.

'You don't need to hide it. You're safe with it here,' Xadrion said.

'You don't understand,' Azraelle said. 'I don't have magic.' Silence fell over them. Xadrion's gaze never left her face, her own gaze looking anywhere else. She was Azraelle – bringer of Life, goddess of Death, deity of Resurgence – and yet, before this mortal man, she wished once again to be on her knees facing Chaos' absence rather than having Xadrion peer at her like that.

'How did you know he was already dead?' Xadrion asked, breaking the silence.

'The blood,' Azraelle lied. 'There was so much of it, on him and his clothes. But the horse didn't have any. He was dead before they put him in the saddle, with no more blood left to pump.'

'Very observant,' came a voice that was not Xadrion's. Emera. Xadrion stepped away from Azraelle and turned to face her as she entered the room.

'How are the other men?' Xadrion asked.

'Untouched, it would seem. Someone only wanted Karlin dead,' Emera answered. Xadrion moved away from Azraelle completely, leaving her alone in the middle of her room.

'I have an appointment with Azraelle. Could you excuse us?' Emera asked, politely.

'Will you come find me after?' Xadrion asked, his voice dropping in volume significantly, as if he didn't want Azraelle to overhear. It sounded almost intimate the way he asked her. Not at all like he was asking her to visit for a report.

'I have a lot to do tonight, Xadrion,' Emera answered. There was silence for too long, and then footsteps. Azraelle listened as Xadrion's heavy footsteps left the room, leaving her and Emera alone.

Where Xadrion's touch had been strong and firm, Emera was much gentler as she came to face Azraelle and placed a hand on her cheek.

'You left so suddenly, I needed to see if you were okay,' Emera said, concern coating every one of her features.

'My magic is gone. And I'm so afraid it's not coming back,' Azraelle said. How long had it been since Azraelle had ever told anyone she was afraid? No memory of having done so sprung to mind. It was not something she would have ever said.

'I could help you,' Emera said, pleadingly as if she needed Az to consider her offer.

'I can't,' Azraelle whispered, dropping to her knees once more. She would never, *never*, take away a mortal's ability to think for themselves, and coupling with a mortal always risked that. But there was no one around her that she could turn to for that kind of help.

'I've reached the end of my patience with those words, Az.' Emera dropped to her knees in front of her. 'It would help you. I want to help you. You need to tell me a reason I should not be able.'

Azraelle considered, really considered, what she had left to lose. Emera had some knowledge of her world, although she didn't know how deep it ran. She knew enough to maintain the wards; surely, she would have a sense of the things they were designed to protect against. She could tell her just enough, just enough to make her know why it wasn't an option.

'Your wards. The ones around the castle,' Azraelle began.

'How do you know of those?' Emera blurted, a mild wariness to her expression.

'King Rhoas informed me what they were, and that you maintained them. Tell me what you know of why you must keep them up,' Azraelle said. The look on Emera's face had Azraelle doubting if she'd already said too much. Realisation fell over Emera's expression as Azraelle's request hit her.

'You're like her, aren't you?' Emera asked.

'Her?'

'The women who taught me the wards. She visited the castle enough that I got to know her very well as she taught me. She told me of her kind,' Emera said, her voice no louder than a whisper as if she were afraid someone would overhear. 'She told me of the gods.'

Azraelle could have almost sighed from the relief that lifted from her chest. She knew. She already knew.

Who was the mysterious woman who had shared so many immortal secrets with this mortal kingdom? What was it about Rhoas and Emera, potentially others who roamed this very castle, that had made one of Az's own kind tell them anything? Rhoas had said the woman knew Azraelle, but Az could think of no one who would have dared, or even who cared, to do such a thing.

'Yes, I am like her,' Azraelle said. The freedom of being able to openly admit it had Az feeling giddy.

'But what does that have to do with us not being able to be together?' Emera questioned.

'It is risky, incredibly so. For you,' Azraelle said. 'Being with someone like me can change the way you think. It can make everything you do, everything you feel, be centred around me and what you think I might want.'

'How is that possible? King Rhoas seems fine,' Emera said.

'King Rhoas?' Azraelle asked, dumbfounded. It took her a moment longer than she would have liked to piece together what Emera meant. 'You mean to tell me he was *with* this woman?'

'All the time. She was his queen,' Emera answered, reaching her hands forward to hold both of Azraelle's. He didn't seem to be under any infatuation curse in the times she had spoken to him. It was usually more obvious that they were influenced if they were.

'Who in Chaos was this woman?' Azraelle asked.

'Her name was Hera.'

SEVEN

AZRAELLE

'Hera?' Azraelle repeated, sure she hadn't heard correctly. Emera nodded, puzzled at Az's reaction. 'Hera has been in this castle?'

'Not recently, not at all. The last time she came I was a child. She taught me and the others training beneath her the means to uphold the wards. Eventually, the others all ended up stationed elsewhere, so it fell to me to take the role once my mentor passed on,' Emera answered. She thought for a moment. 'It's been at least fifteen years since she last visited. She was his queen, but she couldn't stay at the castle permanently. They were able to keep her absences unnoticed for the most part, but she was definitely Rhoas' lover.'

'His lover? Hera was his lover?' Azraelle asked. Everything within her scattered in confusion. Hera, who had sat so quietly at Azraelle's trial, never once even lifting her gaze to look at her. Hera, who Azraelle had once spent time with centuries ago, long before the war between their two families. Hera had been one of the only outsiders approved by Az's mater to even interact with Azraelle, though not to see her powers. Hera had a life here, away from Zeus, and hadn't been back to it for fifteen years.

Azraelle knew that was the timeline now, knew it had been fifteen years of imprisonment in Zeus' torture chambers. After her capture, Zeus would have rallied Mount Olympus around him. It would have been tightly monitored, whoever came to and from Mount Olympus. Hera wouldn't have been able to leave, wouldn't have been able to come to the mortal realm to visit her lover. Fifteen years Zeus had taken from Azraelle. Those invisible blades inside her felt as if they had started swinging once more.

'Yes. How come Rhoas is not impacted the way you say I would be?' Emera pushed.

'It's not a guaranteed, but it's something I can't risk,' Azraelle said.

'That doesn't sound like your choice to make,' Emera said quietly.

Azraelle whipped her gaze to Emera, shocked at her words. 'Not my choice?'

'No, not to take the risk or not. If I am here, on my knees in front of you, offering this knowing the consequences that could happen, you do not get to deny me that choice,' Emera said.

'And if I do not want to?' Azraelle retorted. Emera watched her; their hands still clasped together.

'Do you not want to?' Emera asked, shuffling forward on her knees. She moved her hands to rest on Azraelle's thighs, her thumb and fingers spreading around them in a way that had Azraelle's mind instantly blank of all thoughts except those hands where they were.

'I-I,' Azraelle stammered, not able to get any words out. She did want it, wanted it more than anything. Fifteen years, no magic and her wings gone. She needed it.

It was answer enough for Emera, who swept forward and closed the distance between them. Her lips landed on Azraelle's, moving against them effortlessly. Azraelle took hold of Emera's waist, pulling her even closer until their bodies were pressed fully against each other's. She kissed Emera in return, more desperately than she had perhaps ever kissed anyone. Lavender overwhelmed Azraelle's senses, Emera's warm breath sweet as it mingled with her own.

It was exactly what Az needed. Emera deftly pulled Az's shirt over her head, breaking their lips apart for only a moment to do so. She pushed gently on Az's shoulders, lowering her to the carpet she had been kneeling on. Az didn't mind; she didn't even want to stop long enough for the time it would have taken them to move to the bed.

With her back to the ground, Emera hovered above her, both hands on either side of Az's shoulders. Moving from her lips down to the hollow between her jaw and ear, Emera nipped at her gently and then moved lower still. She travelled the path of her jawline, down her neck and past her collarbone until Az could feel warm breath on her bared breasts, the sensation delighting every nerve in her body.

The moment Emera captured Az's nipple in her mouth she arched her back, to offer more of herself, as much as Emera would take. Emera moved to her next nipple while her hands deftly undid Az's pants, tugging them down. Azraelle raised her hips to assist, but Emera pushed them back down before breaking her mouth from Azraelle's skin.

'Don't move, don't think. Let me pleasure you,' Emera said, glancing up at Az from beneath her lashes.

'Emera,' Az pleaded, desperate for the touching that had stopped while Emera had been talking. Emera smiled, sweetly despite the things she was doing to her, and lowered her head once more. The trail of kisses continued their downward path, pausing around her hip bones, Emera's teeth grazing gently on them as they did so, and then continued on. When she was finally low enough that Az lay above her, completely exposed, Emera's breath became all that Az could focus on.

Emera was right there, right where she needed in that moment. Her breath was gentle on Az's exposed body, warm, and yet still cool against her arousal that had gathered in expectation. A single finger moved to trace the skin around her, coming closer and closer to where she desperately needed to be touched. Az's hips bucked once more, and Emera laughed gently at the pure need Az was displaying.

'Tell me you want me to,' Emera said, every word tickling with her breath.

'Yes, please,' Az said. 'I want you.'

Emera's finger moved in, tracing right up until it settled on that small bundle of nerves. The moment her finger made contact Az released a lengthy moan. Fifteen years without a single loving touch, and now one moment of it had Az nearly breaking. Emera didn't give her time to get her senses together; instead, she lowered her mouth to close her lips over the sensitive apex of nerves, suckling lightly with gentle swirls of her tongue. Her fingers moved lower, a single one sliding in, leaving Az bucking her hips again, wilder and desperate.

It surely wasn't long, not more than a minute, of this rhythm before Az felt herself building. The lower base of her stomach began to knot, and her toes curled against the carpet beneath her. Emera knew exactly the pressure to apply with her tongue, how fast to move her single finger to give exactly what Az needed.

As Az came closer and closer, Emera switched to a second finger, curling both inside her slightly until Az couldn't think or see, merely respond. A final punch of tightness encompassed her body before an overwhelming and shattering release swept through her, causing Az to cry out from the sheer pleasure. With her cry came something else – something very small, which Az believed she could have imagined, especially as once her orgasm started to die away so too did the small feeling she had sensed. She had felt a flicker, just for an instant, inside her. Not from her lower stomach, but rather from that well she had searched inside herself so many times these last few weeks looking for any sign of her magic.

Emera didn't stop, not until the wave had been ridden to its final moment. When Az finally was able to uncurl from her pleasure, Emera looked up with a smile.

'I felt that,' Emera said, moving back up Az's body to look her in the eyes. 'I felt you.' Azraelle could have convinced herself she was imagining it until Emera said that. Emera had felt her as well – had felt her magic – and she wasn't looking at her the way people, the way even many of her own kind, usually did when they felt her magic. No, Emera was looking at her as if she were as attracted to her as she had been a moment ago.

Az couldn't help herself then. It was as if the floodgates had opened, and every need for this comfort from the last fifteen years came barraging forward. She took hold of Emera, flipping the situation so that it was now Emera beneath her and hurriedly pulled Emera's own clothes from her body. Her body was heavenly. Her figure was full – her breasts and hips the most of all, but even her waist and thighs provided purchase for Azraelle's hands to hold.

Az would have liked to take her time, kissing her way down Emera's body as Emera had done for her, but she couldn't fight past the urge to feel Emera around her fingers, to taste her on her tongue. She needed everything this woman had to offer her. So, Az lowered her own head, ravishing upon the lovely woman scattered on the ground beneath her and didn't stop until Emera came to her own release. From the first, came a slower pace, one that allowed Az to build back up, edge Emera from one brink to the other until a second orgasm wracked Emera's body.

Somewhere along the way that night, they found themselves on the bed, taking turns in pleasuring the other, until they both reached their final orgasms together.

With each explosion of pleasure, she felt the small flicker. It wasn't back; it would take its own time in returning to her once more, but at the very least Az was reminded who she was – *what* she was. Her power would return to her. She would get through this, one way or the other. Her power would come back.

Emera didn't stay the night. In fact, she made particular effort to point out that if she had been affected by being with Az, she would have asked to stay the night. It did ease Az's mind to see her still behaving very much like herself, not yet seeming to be under Az's influence.

That night, Az slept better than she could remember and managed to sleep long enough that she was stirred awake by Darlene.

'It's good to see you are getting some rest, my lady,' Darlene said, after she had gently shaken Azraelle awake. Darlene had brought with her a plate with a warm breakfast that Az gratefully dug into once she had seated at the table in the main room. Darlene used the rare opportunity of Az still being in her rooms to fuss around her, and as Az ate her breakfast, Darlene brushed gently through her long hair until every tangle had been removed then proceeded to braid it. She was quick with her fingers and was done before Az had finished eating.

'King Rhoas has requested you to pay him a visit this morning,' Darlene said.

Azraelle wasn't surprised; she hadn't seen the king for a few days, and there was still much to discuss. Ilyon and Xadrion had been spending a lot of their time scouting the nearby area for any indication of the fictional men who had abducted Azraelle, pointed in a false direction by Az herself. Rhoas was allowing the use of resources to facilitate the lie, but she was sure he would want to know if there were any progression in her plans.

Once she finished eating and finally allowed Darlene to help her dress in her regular loose shirt and pants – despite Darlene's objections that she absolutely *must* wear a dress in the king's presence – Az headed in the direction of the king's study. The guards standing posted beside the door opened it immediately for her, revealing Rhoas seated behind his desk. Azraelle offered a small curtsy, the movement unnatural, to which he smiled and gestured for her to take a seat.

'How are you settling in?' Rhoas asked.

'Very well, thank you. Your staff and accommodation are greatly appreciated. They have been more than welcoming,' Azraelle answered. She wasn't lying. While there had been initial suspicion surrounding her violent outburst upon first awakening, her presence in the barracks and walking the halls with Emera had been changing that. No one really looked at her anymore as if she were anything other than what she seemed like – a girl who had been rescued by the prince and had been traumatised enough to react poorly upon waking.

'And how is training going? I hear you have been taking lessons with Ilyon also,' Rhoas said.

'I have,' Azraelle responded. 'I have the time and he's an eager student. Both your sons are doing well so far. There is much I feel I can teach them.'

'Will you be sticking around to see through their training?'

'I will, at least for now,' Azraelle said. 'Being protected by the wards is offering me the comfort to heal. I do think I will need to leave the protection when I am feeling up to it, at least long enough to contact someone. I don't know what is happening outside the mortal realm right now.'

She didn't necessarily need to leave the wards to try to contact someone but Az imagined when making first contact she would need as few barriers in her way as possible. Whoever she could contact would need to be able to see her well enough to connect, at least to begin with, and Az didn't want to risk the wards blocking any potential connection.

'Would you try to reach one of your siblings?' Rhoas asked, leaning forward in his seat. He was intrigued at the idea of her, Az realised, and her siblings. Az didn't know who she would reach out to – anyone who was listening would be a start – but which one of her siblings would actually be able to help? Many of them had moved into their spirit form, but those that hadn't she had not seen for some time. The closest would be those who had settled into the Underworld – they would be most likely to hear her call. But would any of them come, with her guilt likely announced to all the Pantheons – Olympus, Atlantis and the Underworld all?

The memory of the Moirai standing opposite her in Olympus sprung to mind. Not only did she have to consider who would or wouldn't be able to hear her, but could she even trust her own siblings to keep her presence hidden? If the Moirai, who Az would have previously declared the most trustworthy and honest of all her siblings, could stand and announce her guilt to their enemies, could any of them be trusted?

'I will try, but I don't know who may hear me,' Azraelle answered eventually. 'Why did you not tell me it was Hera who protected this castle?'

Rhoas' eyebrows raised in shock.

'I suppose I was trying to keep her safe,' he answered after a short moment of stunned silence.

'From me?' Azraelle asked. 'Why would she need to be kept safe from me?' Rhoas looked uncomfortable, as if he were struggling to find the words. 'Is it because you're worried I hold something against her for not helping me? Or for standing by Zeus' side as his wife?'

'She does not stand by his side,' Rhoas defended.

Azraelle felt her anger stirring, tried her best to suppress it, and failed incredibly at doing so. 'She does, and you are a fool to think otherwise,' Azraelle snapped. 'Yes, she may have visited you occasionally, enough to grant you one, maybe both of those sons of yours I would wager, but she has stood by Zeus for near eternity. And when you are nothing in the ground, she will stand by him for eternity onwards.'

'She does not stand by his side,' Rhoas repeated, anger flaring in his expression for the first time Azraelle had seen. 'And don't bring my sons into this.'

Azraelle felt like a sullen child, not knowing what to do or say except for pout and fold her arms across her chest. She wasn't angry at Rhoas; she didn't even think she was angry at Hera. She was just angry. Everything she had known for as long as she could remember was gone. There were a lot of people Azraelle knew she could direct her anger towards, but none of them were here or would be anywhere near her perhaps ever again.

'You know she's as much a prisoner as you ever were,' Rhoas said, his voice softening now at Azraelle's silence.

'I know,' Azraelle eventually admitted. For she did know. Hera was Zeus' wife, but it was never a willing agreement. It had been a direct order from the king of the Titans, Cronus himself, that had ordered it. It was Demeter who was Zeus' real partner. The majority of Zeus' demon spawns, Apollo and Artemis included, were from his union with Demeter. As far as Az knew, Hera had only offered Zeus one child – Athena – and of course the unborn baby who had caused the entire mess between their two families.

If nothing else, that was what had been the catalyst for everything that had happened since. Az's brother, Hypnos, had told her of it once. Hera had watched her firstborn grow under the direction of Zeus, the result being Athena, goddess of Warcraft. She grew to be lethal and currently held command of a good portion of Zeus' armies. As Hypnos tells it, once Hera realised she was pregnant once more, she panicked. She had sought Hypnos' assistance in a reckless attempt to send away her unborn baby without Zeus' knowledge.

And Hypnos, the stupid fucker, had agreed to it, as infatuated as he was with Hera. Of course, nothing went according to plan. Zeus discovered the plot and began the hunt of Hypnos. Hera's baby ended up not surviving, which Zeus felt was a direct result of Hypnos' interference, and thus began this obsession with hunting their family. It didn't help that her mater had offered shelter and protection to Hypnos, allowing him escape from any and all consequences of his actions.

Az's pater would have never allowed it to happen. If Erebus were alive at the time and by her mater's side, he would have been tough but fair. Hypnos may never have been able to agree to help Hera in the first place and maybe Az's entire family wouldn't have a target on their back. But Erebus wasn't here, wasn't anywhere at this point. He was in that in-between, the place that wasn't true death but served as close to it as an immortal who died could get. One day, Erebus would return. In the meantime, Az's mater, and by extension Azraelle and the rest of her siblings, were weakened. Which was exactly what Zeus had been trying to determine with his torturing. He didn't know if Erebus was here or there, and it made all the difference to whatever Zeus was planning.

'Xadrion and Ilyon,' Azraelle began. 'Do they know?'

'No. They know Hera, of course. I had married once, a long time ago, but she died in childbirth and neither survived. Hera was able to be around at the start, enough for them to know her and understand her to be their mother,' Rhoas answered. Azraelle noted the glaze that overcame Rhoas' expression as he reflected on his time with Hera. He loved her.

'And what do they think has happened to her?' Azraelle asked.

'They believe her to have died. Only Emera and I know the truth, but Xadrion and Ilyon believe she died on an outing from the castle,' Rhoas replied.

'I'm sorry, for Hera. I can tell you loved her.'

'Love. I love her, still. This isn't the end, and I know that one way or another I will see her again. In this world or the next,' Rhoas said.

'I hope you do.'

EIGHT

AZRAELLE

A calm overtook Az's life for those next few weeks that she hadn't felt for a long time. Training progressed with Xadrion and Ilyon at a slow but decent pace. With the help of Emera's regular healing, as well as the extra sessions they got in most nights – among other things – Azraelle felt her back heal. Not fully, because that would have brought with it a brand-new set of wings.

Ilyon had taken to Az like an adoring puppy. He hung on every word she said, every lesson she gave him, and before long, Emera, herself and Ilyon regularly began spending time together around the castle. He was funny and kind. Azraelle watched the show he put forward to everyone and saw so far through it she wondered how no one else had. As vain and spoiled as he acted, he couldn't have been any further from either. He was incredibly generous and he laughed, a lot. He was a happy person and Az couldn't help but let some of it rub off on her.

Xadrion had begun to tolerate her more easily, it seemed. As Azraelle had healed and become increasingly competent at actually instructing him through her own movements, he settled more easily into respecting the position over him he had offered her. He was progressing quickly, his movements getting faster, and they'd managed to have some decent parries – even if Azraelle was still only giving him a fraction of what she was able.

Xadrion never spent time with the small group Az found herself surrounded by. He had appeared at Emera's door a couple of times, but upon seeing either Az alone, or with his brother, he eventually stopped appearing. Meanwhile, Emera had shown no hints of being influenced by the physical contact with Azraelle.

'My mother wrote me,' Emera said, as Ilyon and Az lounged across the same chaise in Az's room. Ilyon was lying down with his head across Az's thigh, a

67

movement that Az had quickly become accustomed to from Ilyon. Emera sat opposite them, flicking through the pages of the letter she had just mentioned.

'Is that a happy or sad thing for you?' Az asked. They had never really talked much into their family or personal lives. The time with Emera was spent mostly healing, tumbling in a bed, or in comfortable silence while reading. She'd not mentioned her parents until then. Azraelle had been grateful for it; it had meant less situations requiring her deceit. Despite the openness now present between Emera and herself, there was still much Az knew she couldn't tell Emera directly, for everyone's safety.

'Happy, I hope,' Emera answered. 'She's thinking of coming to visit. My father has fallen ill but should be strong enough to travel and she's hoping I may be able to help. It's been a long time since I've seen them. We kind of fight a lot, but I think I'm excited to see them.'

Ilyon was watching Emera as she spoke but turned his head to rest deeper in Az's lap as he looked up at her.

'Have you ever been curious to find your parents again?' Ilyon said. It felt like Az's lies were going to keep piling up, but that was just a consequence of staying amongst mortals. She'd been at the castle and conscious for over a month now, had been telling her false stories for the entire time. Emera looked at her with as much curiosity as Ilyon did, despite knowing the abduction story to be a lie.

'There's no one out there for me to find,' Azraelle answered, keeping her expression and tone as neutral as she could. 'My family is dead. I was an orphan when I was taken.' Lies. So many lies. Ilyon couldn't know, and as much as she enjoyed spending time with Emera, it was a bad idea to tell her the extent of *who* her family was.

'I'm sorry,' Ilyon said gently. 'My mother is dead too.'

The king's words echoed through her head, the secret adding to the ever-growing pile. Az ruffled her fingers through his hair playfully before gently hoisting his head so she could move herself from beneath him.

'Who feels like some fresh air?' Az asked, moving to stand by the window. It was only midday and it was a rare day off from training. Xadrion had some gathering of sorts with some of the higher-ranking guards and the king, and Ilyon had decided against his symbolic presence being necessary.

'A ride?' Ilyon asked, jumping to his feet. 'Absolutely!'

'I actually have a lot to get done today, as nice as this has been so far. You two go ahead and enjoy the day,' Emera said. She kissed Az's cheek and ruffled Ilyon's hair in a similar manner before leaving the room.

Ilyon's excitement was palpable. As they walked from the castle doors to the stables built just beside the main entrance gate in the defensive wall of the castle, Ilyon chatted endlessly.

Ilyon's horse was magnificent, but where his was light, the mare that was lent by the stable for Az was as dark as night. She was stunning and rode comfortably, never once resisting Az's guiding nudges on the reins.

Ilyon and Az rode side by side through the stone gates of the defensive wall and took the fastest route out of the surrounding city. It was the first time Az had left the boundaries of the castle, and she was curious as to how far the wards would protect. She'd honestly wanted some fresh air when she'd suggested the ride but she was also anxious to attempt to contact one of her siblings. Before she'd been taken, Azraelle hadn't seen her six living sisters for years, but her four remaining brothers – Thanatos, Charon, Hypnos and Momus – had all been settled in the Underworld. It was one of them who would be most likely to hear her.

Az didn't know if her power had returned enough to try what she needed. For fear of burning out while it was slowly returning to her fully, Az hadn't attempted anything. Her ability to blend into the shadows around her had failed so spectacularly on the first day she had awoken and since then even her trials to do so had left her with unremarkable results.

'So,' Ilyon said, interrupting the comfortable silence that had fallen over them while they rode. They had made it well outside the city boundaries easily enough and were moving casually through well-travelled paths lined with forest either side. Az looked to Ilyon to see the cheeky grin that was plastered across his expression, his eyes glinting deviously.

'Yes?' Azraelle questioned, her own tone humorous. Something about Ilyon made her feel like she could smile again, as if everything would be okay. He reminded her of when she was younger, much younger, with none of the usual concerns that plagued her.

'You and Emera?' Ilyon said. 'When did that happen?'

Az laughed. They hadn't been overtly affectionate in front of him, and when Ilyon left at the end of each day, Emera would usually go with him, only to return later that night alone. Still, she wasn't surprised Ilyon had pieced it together.

'A few weeks ago,' Azraelle answered.

'She's very lovely,' Ilyon commented. 'Xadrion must be pissed.'

'Why would Xadrion be pissed?'

'Up until you got here, he and Emera would spend their nights together.'

Ah. The way Xadrion had asked if Emera would come find him after, all those weeks ago. The way he visited Emera's personal rooms but would quickly leave when there was other company inside.

'I think who Emera wants to invite into her bed is her own decision, Xadrion be damned,' Azraelle said.

Ilyon laughed. 'I don't disagree with you. And I doubt Xadrion really knows if anything is going on between the two of you, but he has become particularly cranky as of late without the regular visits. Pent up, one might say,' Ilyon said, with a cheeky glimmer in his eye.

'Oh, please!' Azraelle chuckled at Ilyon. 'He's the crowned prince of Thesadel. I'm sure that man can find endless bodies to warm his bed.'

'I don't believe for a second that Emera doesn't have some super special talent in that particular area,' Ilyon joked.

'I would never dare to make a comment on that!'

Both of them succumbed to laughter. Their horses, unbothered, simply continued on their casual pace.

Eventually they came across a clearing with a small pond to one side and Az and Ilyon dismounted upon reaching it. They tied their horses up and moved to sit in the grass. Az sat cross-legged, and Ilyon sprawled across the grass with his head in her lap. He was so young, only just eighteen, she had discovered in the recent time she'd spent with him, and yet he was significantly larger in his frame than Azraelle. He wasn't broad and defined, not in any way like Xadrion was, but rather was tall and lithe. He was muscular and defined but his muscles seemed more tuned towards grace and agility, rather than strength and force as Xadrion's were.

'I'm glad you decided to stay,' Ilyon said with his eyes closed.

'Mm?'

'That castle was getting boring,' he said.

'Boring even for a prince with the title but none of the obligation?'

'With my father always working and Xadrion as the heir, it doesn't leave me with many official responsibilities to fill my time with. Xadrion and I used to spend more of our time together, but it's just been me for a while now,' Ilyon answered.

'And what did you do to pass the time?'

'Just because I'm not the crowned prince, doesn't mean I don't get my fair share of bodies to warm my bed,' Ilyon joked. His eyes remained closed as he spoke and Az found herself absentmindedly stroking through his hair. It was so long and smooth, always free, and down compared to Xadrion's tight braids.

Az got the distinct impression that if he could have, Ilyon would have begun purring as she continued stroking his hair. Eventually the soft sounds of contentment turned to gentle snores. Once he was asleep, his rumbles were the only sound breaking the silence of the area, as well as the occasional horses sniffling or hoof shuffling.

The sun was gentle as it broke through the trees surrounding them. In another life, Azraelle would have been purring herself at the feeling of the sun spreading along her wings, but this was not that life, and her wings were not here to feel the warmth. Before she could dwell too long on their absence, she decided it was time to try to signal one of her siblings.

Easier said than done.

There was a particularly useful ability the gods shared that made communication across the realms infinitely easier. It usually worked better when it came from within a family, and it worked best between two lovers, but it wasn't unheard of to be able to happen between any combination of gods. If both parties were thinking intently of the other, it acted as a signal. A connection could be achieved between each person that allowed for some exchanging of words, even images if the connection was strong enough. It depended on a lot of things and was unpredictable at best. But it was the only way Az could think to make contact.

There was just one problem that surpassed all the others: there was no way her siblings would by chance be thinking of her in that moment. That was where the magic came in.

Azraelle closed her eyes and settled into the calmness of the surrounding clearing. Turning inward, she looked to where that well existed within her and peered down. It had once been brimming with her power, overflowing in its strength. Now, it barely registered as a small puddle in the bottom of the well.

Azraelle could do endless things with her magic at full strength, but she'd always had a closer affiliation to her powers of Death over everything else. Despite the temporary peace she had settled into as of late, Death was still the easiest for her to turn to, so coated was she in it. Azraelle knew the weakness she felt kneeling on the carpet that night begging for Chaos to listen had never really gone away, even if living among the mortals as she had been brought a sense of ease. Death swam over the weakness inside her as if it were sampling a dish. Yes, she had gotten close to dying herself, and enough of it still lingered that Death settled over her like an old friend.

Az was surprised, but pleasantly so, when Death responded to her summons. She'd been worried there wasn't enough of her power back to cast that thread. Her magic responded as if it had been waiting for her command for a while now, ready for action at any given moment. The Underworld was so intricately linked to Death that, as well as being the closest physically to the mortal realm, it was also the most relative to her power. She sent that thread in the general direction of the Underworld, hoping it would work to open any of her brother's minds to the idea of her.

Once she was satisfied the signal had been sent, Azraelle cast her mind slowly in the direction of her siblings. She moved through them one at a time, giving a long moment after each in the hopes that one of them had received her signal.

Azraelle?

Azraelle's hands clutched at her chest, as if to soothe a physical hurt. If

Azraelle was the goddess of Death, it made sense that the person who had received her signal was also Death – that is, the very personification of it.

Thanatos?

Where in Chaos have you been?

It was so very Thanatos that Az felt the tears spring up once more behind her closed eyelids. The two of them had always shared something that Az never had with any of her other siblings. Perhaps it was because they both knew what it was to be touched by that cold hand of Death. Perhaps it was that they were born closest to each other, Thanatos only a few hundred years older than herself. Perhaps it was that their appearances had marked them so close to each other – with their stark white hair – or that they were thought to have been soul-twined from the moment Azraelle was born.

Long story. Short version: Zeus.

Zeus decreed you guilty of tampering with Destiny's thread. The Moirai themselves backed up the claim. They reported that you were downcast to the mortal realm and died as you fell, Az. The fall should have killed you. What did you do?

Az could hear the worry in Thanatos' voice. It was as bad as she had feared. There was no way she could leave the mortal realm right now, not when the moment she did she'd be locked back up. For now, she was assumed dead. For now, she could take advantage of the safety that offered her and remain undetected for a little while longer.

Not dead, Az replied. *Didn't die from the fall, although I think I nearly did. I'm being warded for now. I don't know why the Moirai is backing Zeus' claims because that boy's destiny was not supposed to end. I checked it first, Than, of course I did. I checked the thread, and he was supposed to live.*

Why would the Moirai declare that you had altered the path of Destiny?

Your guess is as good as mine, Azraelle answered. Ilyon's snores stopped echoing in the background of her notice.

I have to get back to the wards, Than. I'll signal you again when I can. I know it's a lot to ask, but I can't come home until this is resolved. I need you to look into what's happening, find out what you can on your end. I need you to get me out of this.

Of course, Az. I'll look into it. Don't wait so long to signal next time.

Azraelle could have wept openly after contacting her brother. Any of her siblings would have done, but for it to be Thanatos made Az feel instant relief. As complex and confusing as Az's relationships with the rest of her family had been over the eons, Thanatos had been a hard defender of hers and had always made all her problems feel smaller. Maybe they really were soul-twined like everyone had said.

'Az?' came Ilyon's sleepy voice. His eyes fluttered open and he looked up at her. 'Was I out long?'

'Not very. Come on, let's head back.'

NINE

XADRION

It had been over a month since Azraelle had burst through those doors and fought their guards, yet despite the rocky beginning things seemed to be settling very smoothly. Xadrion was not making progress in their training at the rate he wished, but the daily sessions had left him aching in muscles he didn't even knew he had. They didn't even spend their time working on the offensive manoeuvres; instead, Azraelle drilled him mercilessly on footwork and speed.

You don't need to be stronger, Azraelle had said to him during one of their sessions. *You have clearly more than enough muscle. But you need to be able to move that hulking size of yours out of the way faster.*

It was such an innocent comment for her, one specifically targeted to his training, but Xadrion had been unable to stop thinking about it. The idea that she was looking at his body in any way made him feel nervous, despite knowing she was watching him every time she critiqued his form.

In the month that Azraelle had been up and around the castle, she had completely altered from the perception he had of her initially. It had been somewhat difficult to shake the image of her as the defenceless, injured woman who lay unconscious in the road, but once Azraelle had healed completely, she had beaten that image so far out of his mind. Every time Xadrion entered the barracks for his own training, Azraelle was already there doing her own. During their session together she took every opportunity to match herself against him in their drills, as if she wanted the workout herself. Once they were finished, she would walk to Ilyon and complete as long and gruelling of a session with him as she had just finished with Xadrion. She was unstoppable. Her endurance was like no other he had ever seen.

Ilyon had taken to her almost instantaneously. Outside of their training sessions, he would find the two of them spending time together, often

73

accompanied by Emera. Xadrion was happy she was fitting in so well, of course, he just hoped that Ilyon wasn't following his typical pattern of behaviour – that being attempting to fuck anything that moved. Ilyon had caused his own share of scandals amongst their court by bedding princes and princesses alike, ruining reputations of many who visited Fennhall as diplomats. Xadrion let himself ponder the thought briefly, wondered if Azraelle would want Ilyon in that way.

Maybe Xadrion's mind was just stuck on that train of thought because of the absence of late-night visits from Emera. Yes, there were others who frequented his bed, but even Xadrion had to admit that Emera provided exceptional companionship. He hadn't seen Emera properly since Azraelle had woken up that first day and while initially that didn't seem important, it felt as if something had changed between them the more weeks went by.

Xadrion reflected back to the night he had entered Azraelle's chambers, the day Karlin had been ridden back through the gates already dead. That alone was mystery enough considering they still had not determined how Karlin could have been killed. The burn across his chest obviously was what had done it, but how had someone snuck up to the group of three men, burned Karlin hard enough and fast enough to kill him, and then gotten away unseen before the other two men had even turned to find what had happened? None of it made sense. And no answers were being brought to light.

The events in Azraelle's room following that had also haunted Xadrion's mind.

I don't have magic, Azraelle had repeated to him. He'd heard the conversation with Emera; he knew that Azraelle's magic was absent from healing. But the way she had spoken it sounded broken, as if the idea of her magic returning was hopeless. After seeing her strength return over the weeks, to see her in that moment kneeling on the ground looking so exhausted by her existence had left Xadrion feeling... something.

All these somethings he was feeling, he had gotten no closer to understanding what they were in the weeks that had passed. He wasn't angry toward her anymore, although she had somehow discovered how to rile him up during their sessions. Despite the seemingly ever-present anger that skittered beneath Xadrion's skin, no one called it to the surface as effortlessly as Azraelle's remarks. The brutal training was a nice distraction, leaving Xadrion so tired that he often didn't have the energy remaining to be irritated. As much as the constant exhaustion was wearing him down, he would take it any day over the anger that had settled over his daily life. He would give anything to not feel like his skin was the only thing stopping him from exploding.

Emera had dismissed him that night in Azraelle's rooms. She'd responded to his question to visit her with a solid, undeniable no and Xadrion had not found Emera alone since that moment to ask her again. He needed to talk to her. He needed to know where they stood, and, if they were done, he needed to know how he hadn't realised it was done until it was already over.

A sharp pain lanced across the back of Xadrion's head, interrupting his train of thought. He grimaced, bringing his hand up to rub where it now throbbed, to see Azraelle standing in front of him with her practice sword dangling between her fingers of one hand.

'Where the hell is your head?' Azraelle demanded, disappointment evident across her features. Right. He had been halfway through a session with her when his thoughts had run away with themselves. There were a lot of things on his mind lately, and this wasn't the first time he'd found himself lost within as he tried to work through them. The feeling of that something he was feeling was unsettling him, and he'd desperately been trying to solve what it was he was actually feeling.

'You didn't need to hit so hard,' Xadrion snarked, the throbbing in his head still present.

'Oh, I'm sorry, *Prince*. I'll be sure to send out the message to not hit you so hard to those who may one day face you on the battlefield,' Azraelle said, her mocking tone making his title sound like a joke.

'That's not what I meant,' Xadrion snapped. Azraelle knew how to press on his anger, and even though he knew she was right, he still took the bait. 'Don't worry about it.' With his dismissal, he lunged forward again, hoping to catch her off guard, noting the sword lazily hanging between her fingers.

Faster than Xadrion could track, Azraelle's hand whipped the training sword back up to an easy deflection of his swing. She barely looked like she broke a sweat as she easily swatted away his hit. Xadrion wasn't even surprised it didn't work. He'd seen her reflexes often enough by that point to know that the feigned looseness in her hand wasn't something that would stand in her way of being instantly ready to defend. In fact, with the speed of her reaction, Xadrion wondered if she had been holding the blade like that to specifically elicit this brazen attempt from him.

'Come on, Xadrion. That was a poor effort.' As angry as the criticisms made him, she was right. Then she was on the move. Faster than he could see, Azraelle began to advance forward, swinging repeatedly at him from all angles. It was purely luck that he managed to block the first couple of strikes, but as he was pushed onto the defensive and her sword kept coming down, Xadrion knew he was about to get absolutely hammered.

He knew the only way out of that would be to break the cycle, remove himself from her arc and then strike back as fast as he could, in the small hope that it would switch him to the offensive. Azraelle was grinning as she pushed Xadrion further back, her footwork faster than he could follow. He had seen the manic grin on Azraelle's features only a handful of times, usually when he managed to keep up and give her a rally of strikes to parry. There was something about the clash of their weapons that put Azraelle in a better mood.

At the exact same moment that Xadrion decided he would try his manoeuvre and break off to the side, he heard Azraelle's voice.

'Chaos help me,' she murmured, and for the briefest of moments he watched as she stumbled over her own feet. Xadrion seized the opportunity, stepping easily out of the range of her next hit and arced his own sword around, angling it directly at the side of her body. This time, he didn't hold back. His training sword connected with Azraelle's shoulder, with as much force behind it as he could muster. Azraelle had already been stumbling, and the hit sent her almost flying to the ground.

He'd done it. He'd actually caught her.

Azraelle didn't move from her crumpled position on the ground. He'd only hit her shoulder, so there was no reason she shouldn't have been moving. And yet, she wasn't. No sound came from her.

What had happened? Azraelle had never once stumbled in her footing, never shown a single misstep. But before Xadrion had even struck her, she had already been going down. What could have thrown her so badly?

Xadrion dropped to kneel beside her, the image in front of him a stark reminder of the first day he found her. She was curled in on herself, that strange, white-coloured hair of hers dragged through the dirt much the same as the first day. The only difference was the lack of blood. The day Xadrion had found her she had been so bloody he genuinely believed she wouldn't survive the ride back to the castle.

'Azraelle?' he asked, gently rocking her back so that she unfurled. Her body was completely slack, and she rolled to her back with a thud in the dirt. Xadrion noted the glimmer of her silver necklace beneath the neckline of her shirt as he rolled her. No expression lined her face as her eyes remained open and staring. But not aware – they seemed glazed over. She didn't respond to him, so Xadrion gently took hold of her shoulder, giving it a shake. He was just about to call to someone around them to get Emera when Azraelle finally responded.

Her breath quickened, and her eyes snatched onto her immediate surroundings.

'No,' she whispered, suddenly registering Xadrion kneeling beside her with his hand on her shoulder. He didn't see what happened next, only felt the different points of pressure as Azraelle managed to throw him to his own back. One moment she had been lying on the dirt beneath him, the next his wrist had felt a sharp jolt of pain. He'd been pulled forward off his already tentative centre of gravity, and then all at once Xadrion felt the wind knocked out of him as he was left staring up to the roof above.

Azraelle had tossed him, so quickly he had no chance to even detect it was about to happen. He gasped for air, finding none and his vision started to blur. He couldn't even tell which way was up, could only feel an ache through his back and lungs, a strange pressure against his neck and a gripping pressure around his waist.

'Xadrion?' Azraelle breathed. The pressure on his neck disappeared, and as he gasped again, breath finally began to fill his lungs. Above him, he could make out Azraelle's blurry face watching him with concern. Her braid was hanging over one shoulder, and despite himself, Xadrion found himself unable to focus on anything other than where it lightly brushed against his neck.

As the ability to breathe returned and his mind started to clear, his situation became more apparent. Azraelle sat atop him, her legs straddling either side of his waist. They had held him still with such pressure he didn't realise she'd had that level of strength, but their grip was beginning to loosen. It had been Azraelle's hand across his throat, but now that too had been removed. The pressure had disappeared, but Azraelle made no move to get off him.

'I'm so sorry, are you okay?' she asked, still peering down at him from above. He wasn't. He felt winded and it was taking more willpower than it should have to keep his vision from blacking out and from allowing himself to pass out. He moved his hands to grip something, anything to remind himself where reality was and to give him something solid to keep him grounded there. Scrambling for something, Xadrion initially found nothing but dirt until his hands found the source of the faint pressure against his sides – Azraelle's thighs. There, that was reality.

'Xadrion, please answer me. Tell me you're fine,' Azraelle pleaded. How long had he been silent for? It was taking him longer than it should have to come back from the winding he had received. He hadn't truly felt Azraelle's strength until that moment, and it was something he would not forget anytime soon.

'I think I'm okay,' Xadrion managed to rasp. His voice felt hoarse, not surprising given his throat felt like fire. Azraelle's gaze dropped to his neck and her brows pulled together in concern.

'I'm so sorry,' Azraelle muttered, making a move to lift herself from Xadrion, as if she couldn't bear looking at him splayed beneath her. At the feeling of the pressure leaving his sides, and her thighs slipping from his hands, Xadrion squeezed hard.

'Wait, please,' he said, his throat still burning. Azraelle hesitated, looking concerned, but stayed where she was situated on top of him. 'I'm trying very hard not to pass out and feeling you against me is helping.' He couldn't believe he'd let the words slip from his lips, his vulnerability on full display for Az as he tried to get his bearings back, but in that moment he didn't care. Her touch was helping. Where her thighs met his palms and his sides, he felt the warmth reminding him which side of the blackness meant staying awake.

Where her braid rested against the exposed skin on his neck, he felt tethered to consciousness.

When he finally felt like it had passed, and there was no longer any threat to passing out, Xadrion tried to shift his body slightly and grunted in pain.

'That was something,' Xadrion said.

'I'm sorry. I don't know what happened. I didn't realise it was you,' Azraelle said. Slowly, Xadrion let go of Az's thighs and put his elbows beneath him to push himself to a sitting position. Az didn't move, which only resulted in her straddling flush over his lap, her face suddenly much closer to his.

'I think I'm good now.' Xadrion's vision swam as the intoxicating scent of Azraelle washed over him, reminding of a fresh winter breeze. Despite the pain that lanced through his entire body, and how his throat burned, he still felt himself cracking a smile at the expression that shot across Az's features. She looked down to see their bodies pressed together before she quickly pushed against his chest and scrambled backwards off him. Blush rushed over her cheeks.

As Xadrion pushed slowly to standing once more, Azraelle stood at an awkward distance away, her hands fidgeting in front of her body and her eyes nervously darting between him and the ground.

'I'm going to need some explanation of what the hell just happened,' Xadrion said. A glance to their surroundings showed nearly everyone in the room paying attention to them in some way, some more than others trying to disguise their interest by continuing their activities half-heartedly. Azraelle looked uncomfortable as she opened and closed her mouth several times in an attempt to try to speak. Xadrion closed the distance between them, cautiously, and gently took hold of the crook of her elbow. He steered them both outside and around the corner, removing themselves from any peering eyes, and found himself alone with Azraelle in a narrow alley between the barracks and the next building over.

'Now, talk,' Xadrion said.

'Your neck,' Azraelle said, her gaze never meeting his eyes. Xadrion didn't know what his neck looked like, but he could guess. It felt raw still and burned where Azraelle's hand had grabbed him. He was sure that if he were to look, he would see immediate bruising. Azraelle didn't seem able to drag her gaze away from his neck long enough to give him an answer.

'Hey,' Xadrion said, gripping her chin gently and tugging her head up, so her gaze had to follow until she was looking directly at his face. 'Don't look at it, just tell me what happened. You looked like you were unconscious, and obviously when you came back you didn't even recognise me, so tell me.'

Azraelle met his gaze finally, her eyes locking onto his. Xadrion could read the meaning behind her eyes – could see the intense remorse she was feeling for what she had done. But in that moment, despite every ache that echoed through his body, Xadrion didn't care. She had been going down before Xadrion had started to take his swing at her. What had caused her to fall that way?

'My magic has been returning,' Azraelle eventually answered, her voice barely loud enough for him to hear despite the closeness between them. 'Sometimes it makes me see things, warnings almost. One of them came on as we were fighting, and it blacked out everything else. When I came to, I didn't know who you were. It just... I felt your hand on my shoulder and I panicked.'

Xadrion could tell she was still panicked and imagined what it must have felt like for her to wake to hands she couldn't place. In the month she'd been there, Azraelle hadn't given them many details about how her captors had treated her, but given the condition they'd found her in, Xadrion could only imagine. Had she often woken to unfamiliar hands?

'What kind of things does it warn you about?'

Her magic was coming back. The last time they'd properly spoken, she'd insisted she didn't have it, insisted that it was gone. Azraelle shrugged and crossed her arms over her chest. The action made her look small and withdrawn, despite the most recent tussle indicating that she was anything but.

'It shows me death,' Azraelle whispered. 'It shows me someone dying.'

Silence fell between the two, then as if she could no longer stop herself – as if she no longer wanted to stop herself – Azraelle kept talking.

'I saw Karlin's death days before it happened. Usually, I can see it clearer, more detailed, so I can understand who it is happening to and where. With Karlin, I didn't get enough to know what was happening. I only pieced it together when I saw them ride in with him dead on that horse a few weeks ago,' Azraelle said.

'That's how you knew he was already dead?' Xadrion asked. She nodded. Xadrion had seen many examples of magic over the years, more even than just Emera's. He'd heard of prophets – had even heard of a few who had some credibility – but it still took him a moment longer than he liked coming to terms with Azraelle's new information.

'I'm sorry for not telling you.'

'What did you see this time?' Xadrion asked. He'd kept his hand firmly grasped beneath her jaw, keeping their eyes locked. Azraelle didn't flinch from the contact and Xadrion found himself lost in the darkness of her eyes suddenly. They were black, dark as any eyes Xadrion had ever seen. Eerie almost, and yet strangely comforting.

'I saw a girl. A child. She was burned exactly as Karlin had been,' Azraelle answered. 'I don't know where. I can't make it out clearly... can't see it well enough to know where it is. I just see a bell tower. It's big and made of these big, black stones. But there was nothing else around it.' Dread settled deep in Xadrion's gut.

'When is this going to happen?'

'I don't know. I don't usually get so many days warning as I did with Karlin. Usually it's that day,' Azraelle said.

Xadrion knew the location she was describing. It would only take them half a day's ride to reach the single bell tower in the hidden clearing. Xadrion shuddered to think of that place again; he hadn't gone there since he was a kid. The tales of the place had given him enough reason to never want to go back there ever again.

'Go get some weapons, real ones this time. I'm going to get Ilyon. Meet me at the stables,' Xadrion said.

'What are we doing?' Azraelle asked.

'We're going to the bell tower.'

TEN

AZRAELLE

Azraelle knew she shouldn't have said anything. Of course Xadrion was going to try to prevent the death. Xadrion wouldn't see that death was the natural way. Death was inevitable. Yet she had opened her mouth and told him what she'd seen. The premonition, followed by the tussle with Xadrion after, had left her mind scattered and she simply had not thought before she told him.

The image of her finger marks across Xadrion's throat was branded behind her eyes forevermore, even as she approached the stables now fully kitted with gear. Over her pants she'd strapped two daggers, one to each leg, and there was another strapped beneath her shirt against her ribcage, just in case. At her side, tucked into its scabbard, was an ordinary blade she'd taken from the barracks. It wasn't of great quality, but it was metal, and it would cut.

Not long after Azraelle arrived at the stables, Xadrion and Ilyon rounded the corner. Three horses were prepared – Ilyon's pale mare and the black one Azraelle had ridden when she contacted Thanatos included – each with a pack of equipment tied onto the saddle.

'How far exactly is this place?' Azraelle asked.

'Half a day, maybe a little more. We'll have to camp somewhere, and I've packed some rations. I've let the king know where we're headed and he has approved us to leave,' Xadrion answered.

Half a day, each way. That left the three of them outside the protection of the castle wards for over a day. Especially if they camped the night. And that wasn't even accounting for Xadrion making them wait if the little girl wasn't already dead when they got there.

Ilyon looked more serious than he ever had, which meant Xadrion must have already filled him in on what was happening. Azraelle dared a look towards Xadrion, afraid to see the marks around his neck, but he'd changed into a collared shirt hiding most of them. Still, she spied some of the bruises peeking out from above the collar. Xadrion caught her eye, gave her a look as if he knew what she was looking at and subtly shook his head.

'Don't worry about it,' he whispered to her when he passed by her, keeping his voice low enough that Ilyon wouldn't have heard. She did worry about it. Regardless of Xadrion's mother, he still seemed completely mortal. Azraelle could have absolutely broken him had she not gotten to her senses when she did, and there would have been nothing he could have done to stop her. She'd let herself get complacent around the mortals. If she became too comfortable, she would end up hurting one of them, or more.

'The bell tower gives me the creeps,' Ilyon admitted as they all mounted and began their journey through the city beyond the castle walls. Despite his dark skin, Azraelle swore she saw his face pale.

'Why?' she asked.

'We used to spend time camping on some nearby grounds when we were younger, and we found the clearing one day by chance. Even as kids, something about setting foot on the ground just seemed wrong. I don't remember much as I was much younger, but I remember the feeling of being close to that ground,' Ilyon answered. 'Xadrion told me the stories he was told from some of the nearby locals.'

'They're just ghost stories meant to scare children,' Xadrion grunted.

'Maybe. Still, a place designed for the gods to come down and deliver sentences feels like a place that should be avoided,' Ilyon said.

'It was one of the gods' chosen gallows?' Azraelle asked, her heart feeling as if it had frozen. If it truly was, and not just said to be in legend, then they really would be tempting fate by going there. Xadrion wouldn't let her turn them around, she knew that much for sure. If she tried to get them not to go, he'd just go himself.

'Again, it's just a tale,' Xadrion said.

They cleared the city and rode in tense silence. Azraelle was content to let it stay that way; she felt like she needed time to work things through in her mind anyway. What strength would she even have if something did happen at the bell tower? The two princes at her side would not be able to handle themselves if they ran into one of her kind, and everything in Azraelle told her that she wouldn't be able to handle it either. Her power had only just started returning.

Once they cleared the castle wards, Azraelle sent out a signal to Thanatos. If on the off chance he was thinking of her, it would be nice to hear his voice again. He didn't respond, and she didn't want to use what power she did have to send him a stronger signal. She'd keep her mind open to him as she rode, but for now that would have to be enough.

'You okay?' Ilyon asked from beside her. Xadrion had pulled ahead so he was leading the way, leaving Ilyon riding side by side with Azraelle.

'What did Xadrion tell you?' Az asked.

'He told me about your magic and what you saw,' Ilyon answered. 'You could have talked to me about it, about Karlin. Magic isn't feared in our kingdom.'

'I didn't know if it would come back fully.'

'And has it?' Ilyon asked.

Azraelle got the distinct impression that Xadrion was listening. He was still ahead of them, but he had slowed his horse to be a little closer, and she could have sworn he'd angled his head slightly to hear them better.

'Bits and pieces. I can feel it getting stronger again, but I don't know if it'll return to what it was.'

'Why do you think it disappeared in the first place? Was it something to do with the group who abducted you?' Ilyon asked.

'I… uh, no. I had it while I was with them, even though they repressed it. From what I understand,' Azraelle began, tentatively, 'it's something to do with how magic reacts when it's wielder nearly dies. In the same way that if we are suffocating, we try desperately to gasp in air, magic will expel itself to the last drop in the attempt to keep its wielder from dying.'

'And when we found you, they had hurt you so badly that your magic needed to use itself to save you?' Ilyon asked.

'It would seem so,' Azraelle said.

'Do you not remember?'

Az didn't want to tell him the truth. She remembered everything – the entire fifteen years. She remembered the way Zeus had her magic gagged, the way she couldn't summon it no matter how hard she tried. She remembered the torture. She remembered every single face that entered that damned cell of hers, as well as every instrument she'd had used against her.

Most of all, Az remembered the feeling of her wings being torn from her back and the feeling of hurtling through the space between Mount Olympus and the mortal realm. Such a fall, and yet she'd somehow survived. No wonder Zeus believed her dead. By all accounts, she should be. Had her magic really been strong enough to spare her from death after that fall?

'I remember a lot of it. But no, I don't remember the final day. I don't know how I came to be in your paths,' Azraelle lied.

Xadrion turned enough in his saddle that he met Az's eyes. He looked at her with narrowed eyes and an expression that made Az feel like he knew she was lying. Somehow, it seemed, he could hear that it wasn't the truth. But no – that couldn't be. There was no way he would be able to tell. She was just feeling guilty for lying to Ilyon, someone she considered her friend.

But then again, did one lie to their friends like this?

'I'm sorry,' Ilyon said.

'What for?'

'That any of it happened to you,' Ilyon responded. 'It's not fair.'

'Mm.'

Silence descended upon the group once more. They rode for a few hours in the silence before Azraelle noticed the sun beginning to wink out below the horizon. How late in the day had they left? She couldn't remember what time they'd left the castle, or maybe they had made a slow pace, but it was getting dark earlier than she realised it would be. Xadrion noticed as well, and he pulled his horse to a halt.

'We have to make camp. There's no use trying to find our way in the dark,' Xadrion declared. He led them off the main road and down a much smaller, narrower path. 'We're lucky, we made it close enough to our old lodge to be able to find it again.'

Xadrion led the way along the narrow path, only large enough for them to ride one after the other, and by the time they reached the old stone building darkness had completely fallen.

'We haven't come here in years,' Ilyon said. 'I'm surprised it's still standing.'

The building barely looked to be standing, in all fairness. After tying the horses up with some food and water for the night, the three of them made their way inside. It was small and coated in dust, comprising of a single room with a small food preparation area. A dining table and chairs, a large double bed and two smaller cots were the only furniture in the room.

'At least it's shelter,' Az remarked. 'Why did you stop coming?'

Xadrion and Ilyon exchanged a look, one that seemed private and strangely intimate. It was the most affection she'd ever seen the two brothers show each other.

'We didn't keep camping here once our mother died,' Ilyon eventually answered. Guilt burned through Azraelle as she evidenced their grief. Would they ever find out they were grieving for a mother who wasn't dead? She was surprised Ilyon held so many memories of her, given how young he would have been the last time Hera was able to visit. Fifteen years ago he would have only been three, while Xadrion himself would have been ten.

'I'll make some dinner,' Ilyon said. 'Take the bed, Az.'

Azraelle looked to the large bed, with the two cots pushed against the opposite wall. The cots were small, designed for one person only. Now with both the brothers easily clearing six feet tall, their legs would undoubtedly hang from the edge.

'That seems stupid. You won't fit,' Az said, gesturing to the cots in front of them.

'I'll take the cot,' Xadrion said, giving the larger bed a mournful glare.

'I'd rather a cot as well.' Ilyon's expression mirrored Xadrion's exactly.

Of course, Azraelle realised, there was a reason they wouldn't want to sleep in the bed. The last time they had been there the bed would have been shared by Rhoas and Hera, with the two as boys taking the cots.

The beds were incredibly dusty, so she set about taking the covers outside and bashing them against the wall while Ilyon made dinner. It didn't need to be clean, but whatever she could get rid of would be better than nothing. By the time she came back inside, one of them had lit small oil lamps around the room. She remade the beds and then sat at the old dining table to eat the cured meats and sliced bread Ilyon had laid out.

Xadrion fell onto his cot first, rolling so that his back was facing Ilyon and Az, and made to fall asleep. His legs did hang off the end, and only because he was on his side did his shoulders fit well enough. Ilyon took the other cot, his long limbs spreading awkwardly over its small size. In the large bed Az took she couldn't even reach both sides at one time.

Ilyon seemed to have a special talent in falling asleep whenever he wanted. Within moments of his head settling into the pillow, he was snoring softly. Azraelle had a much harder time. She was so panicked over what they were going to find at the bell tower the next day that she wasn't sure sleep was even going to come to her.

As silence fell across the room save for Ilyon's snores, something caught her attention. The sound of someone asleep was easy to distinguish from someone who was awake. In the silence that filled the single room, Azraelle could feel the tension coming from Xadrion's cot. His breathing had not slowed, had not relaxed – Xadrion was not falling asleep.

With nothing else to focus on, Azraelle found herself tracking his breathing, listening to the speed with which it went in and out.

'Xadrion?' Az whispered into the darkness. Silence followed, so long that she thought either he hadn't heard her, or maybe that she was wrong.

'Yeah?'

His response was so quiet, she thought it almost sounded like the wind whispering outside.

'Are you okay?' she asked. Slowly, Xadrion shifted on the cot, rolling so that he was facing back toward her.

'It's too small,' he responded. And yet he had spent the better part of an hour trying desperately to fall asleep there, determined to not come near the bed. Azraelle slid from the bed, her bare feet padding gently over the wooden floors. She could feel him watching the shadows she cast as she moved closer to him and as she came to his cot, he sat up.

'Come on,' she said, reaching her hand forward. It took her a moment in the darkness to find her target, and her hand landed on his shoulder first. She dragged her touch down his arm until she felt his fingers, which she linked between hers.

'I can't,' he whispered.

'I know. But you can. It's a bed. I know what it symbolises to you, but we're going to look past that. For tonight, it's a source of rest that you desperately need. Tomorrow, we can look at what the bed means, but for tonight it is just a bed,' Azraelle said. She didn't know if it would work; she had no idea the kind of comfort that worked for Xadrion. But he needed the rest, especially if things didn't go smoothly tomorrow.

Whatever part of it landed, she didn't know, but it seemed to work. Xadrion stood and let her lead him back to the bed.

'You sleep there, I'll take the cot,' Az whispered, turning to head to his now abandoned cot once Xadrion had sat on the edge of the bed. His fingers tightened on hers and he pulled gently.

'It's big enough for us both, and a lot more comfortable than that thing,' he argued, pulling hard enough now that she would have to actively resist if she meant to still walk toward the cot. She didn't resist; instead, she let him pull her down until she was laying, with Xadrion next to her.

With the two of them, there was significantly less space than it had been with just her, especially as Azraelle tried to keep some distance between herself and Xadrion. Still, she felt the presence of his shoulder right next to hers. She tried not to pay attention to the fact that wherever he neared her there was heat – scorching heat. His familiar storm-like scent filled her senses and the eerie familiarity of Xadrion washed over her.

Azraelle had done well over the past months to ignore the way her attention focused on him each time she was in his presence, as if there was something constantly pulling her in his direction. She'd kept herself from openly staring at him, kept herself from being too close in proximity that the feeling of him enshrouded everything. Now, in the dark, shoulder to shoulder, it was hard to resist. His scent, his presence, it all pressed into her mind as something inside her screamed that he was familiar, that he was somehow *same* and known by her. As this all registered at once Az felt the now familiar feelings of fear and desire fill her, the two somehow existing at once within his presence.

'Your magic has been returning,' Xadrion stated, his voice rough in its whisper beside her ear.

'Mm.'

'Has Emera been… helping with that?' Xadrion whispered.

'Yes,' Azraelle admitted, knowing what it was he was really asking.

'That makes sense.'

'I didn't mean to come between you and her,' Az admitted. She'd felt guilty about it since Ilyon had told her they'd been together before she arrived.

'We weren't anything properly. We just spent time together. I wouldn't have cared if Emera had other lovers at the same time, but I suppose that was her decision to make,' Xadrion said.

Azraelle rolled from her back to her shoulder, adding a little more space to the bed. She'd turned towards Xadrion and could vaguely see the silhouette of him against the dark. He shuffled, copying her position until they were facing each other. Gently, and slowly to let him know that she was moving, Az moved her hand up to touch his neck. She touched where she knew the bruises would be and despite the gentleness, she still heard him wince when she found them.

'I'm sorry for what I did to you,' Az whispered. She could feel his breath on her nose. It hitched slightly as her fingers traced the bruises. Az knew she would never forget the image of her hand wrapped around his throat, crushing it with such ease that the bruises had been there as soon as she'd removed her hands.

'You didn't know what you were doing,' Xadrion breathed.

Healing had never been a strength for Azraelle. While most of her kind had their special talents, healing was nearly a universal ability amongst anyone who wielded magic. There were those like Emera who had honed the craft and who were far more skilled at it, and then there was Azraelle. In all the years she'd been alive, her power had been used more in taking life than giving it back. As the primus of the Ravens, it had never been her responsibility to follow behind and help with the healing, but rather to lead from the front when the situation demanded it.

Azraelle took her time peering into her well again. Maybe it would be a mistake given what she could possibly be walking into tomorrow, but something didn't feel right about Xadrion bearing the marks of her violence against his throat. She pulled up the traces of her power and envisioned them travelling from her fingertips onto Xadrion's skin.

'You don't need to,' Xadrion whispered. He must have felt her power, which meant it was working, even if just a little.

'Shh. I'm focusing.' But it didn't matter, his words had broken through her concentration and her magic sputtered out. When she tried to summon the healing once more, nothing responded. Whether the bruises were gone, she'd have to wait until the morning to see.

'I'm not strong enough still,' Azraelle mumbled.

'It's enough,' Xadrion whispered. Their faces were so close now, she hadn't realised her head had bowed closer to his as she'd been focusing. His breath no longer tickled her nose, but rather her mouth. The urge to shuffle to see just how close they were overtook her, and when she moved slightly her nose brushed against the tip of his.

Azraelle's fingers still trailed Xadrion's neck and his breathing hitched each time they moved slightly.

'If you wanted to try for the neck again in the future I wouldn't mind. Just stop *before* it's completely crushed,' Xadrion said, his voice barely audible but laced with desire. The suggestiveness of his words broke the spell that had been upon her. When had she allowed for them to come so close together?

'Go to sleep,' Azraelle grumbled, hurriedly turning so that her back was to Xadrion. Free of the warmth of his breath upon her, Az finally started to feel her mind clear. She didn't let herself think on how much she *wanted* him to touch her as they lay there.

Azraelle was not a shy person, not when it came to who she invited in and out of her bed. In the world of the gods, it was just another way to pass the time, but Az knew it meant more for the mortals, and it was something she needed to be more careful about. Xadrion was probably the safer option compared to Emera when it came to the impact she could have had on them, given he was descended from Hera. Yet he felt far from safe.

As she made the pointed effort to stay facing away from Xadrion in her attempt to fall asleep, Xadrion let a hushed chuckle stir the air near her ear, which of course resulted in goosebumps running quickly over the bare skin of her arms and the back of her neck.

There was no way she would ever give him the satisfaction.

The night passed and eventually morning came. Azraelle managed to get a few hours of sleep, but she had been right in her guess that she would not wake rested. As morning broke, the air was crisp with cold and she buried deeper beneath the blankets. More than anything, Az did not want to get up and face going to that bell tower.

As she nestled further into the blankets, Az felt herself brush against the body behind hers. Right – she was not the sole inhabitant of said blankets. Warm breath tickled her ear, reminding her vividly of last night. As soon as her body came in contact with Xadrion's beneath the covers, his hand moved to rest heavily over her hip. His breathing still indicated he was asleep, and yet... Yes, his fingers were tightening their hold, digging firmly against her hip, and pulling her towards him.

Azraelle knew she should have gotten up, thrown back the covers and made a run for it, but she couldn't make herself. His grip was firm and in an instant, he had her pinned against him, her back to his chest. After a moment, Az resolved herself to getting out from his grip and made to shuffle out of his hold when her hips brushed back and found something prominent and hard pressing against her ass. Fuck.

Her mind scattered and she could barely think straight at the feeling of Xadrion's hard length pressing into her. Too much of her responded, her arousal instantaneous. She should move. She needed to break the contact and get away from him but so many nerves in her body were telling her to stay.

'Are you imagining what it would feel like to have me buried in you?' Xadrion hoarsely whispered straight into her ear. He was awake. And aware.

'You wish.' Azraelle finally found the strength to rip the blankets from her and jumped from the bed. She was lying, Chaosdamned she was lying through her fucking teeth. That was exactly what she had been imagining.

Standing now, Az faced the bed. Xadrion was perched with his head resting in his palm, propped up on his elbow, and a cocky grin on his face. The marks around his neck had faded somewhat, although not completely. He knew she was lying, knew that those were the exact thoughts that had filled Azraelle's mind.

His arousal was glaringly obvious from where she had thrown the covers back. As she stood in front of him, Xadrion's eyes dropped below her neckline and settled on her breasts. Nothing impressive by any means, barely even noticeable through loose shirts most of the time, and yet now his gaze was lingering. A quick glance showed what it was he was looking at – the shape of her nipples, hardened by the cold, noticeable through the fabric of her shirt.

Az crossed her arms quickly over her chest, turning once more from him and hurried to the pile of their bags. There was a thick leather jacket that she pulled on to brace against the cold before she even dared to turn back once more.

'Wake your brother. We need to get back to the castle as soon as we can. Let's get today over and done with,' Az said. Xadrion was still giving her that fucking cocky grin, pushing Azraelle's irritation through the roof. Despite reading exactly the impact he was having on Az, Xadrion obeyed her commands and walked to Ilyon's cot. He gave Ilyon a quick, hard shove out of the bed.

'Hu – what the fuck!' Ilyon exclaimed as he was sent flying from the blankets and crashing to the cold wooden floors.

'*Lady* Azraelle has deemed it time to get moving,' Xadrion said, the title sounding mocking on his lips. What a fucker.

ELEVEN

AZRAELLE

Xadrion had declared the final distance would need to be hiked, given that there was no actual pathway that led through to the bell tower. They had a quick breakfast, leaving their possessions at the lodge except for the weapons now strapped back into their positions.

For the first time in longer than she could remember, Azraelle was nervous. She'd faced war before, faced battles before, but never without the security of her power. Yet as she tried to peer into her well to see what she had in reserve, she found it glaringly empty. Her powers would not save her today. And Xadrion and Ilyon… well, they were in even more danger than she was. They would be defenceless if the threat they were hiking toward was one of Azraelle's kind.

The hike took less than half an hour, and as they approached, Xadrion signalled to proceed with caution. They quietened their steps and kept themselves to the protection of the trees camouflage.

Xadrion was leading the way, and as they got closer, he ducked down to find cover amongst some bushes. Ilyon, and then Az, followed his lead and perched behind enough shrubbery to keep them hidden from the clearing that was now in front of them.

Ilyon had been right about the feeling he described when approaching the clearing. It was marked by power. Az knew that the mortals had incorporated certain locations into legends without knowing why it was they were doing it. Usually, the locations marked where the gods had come to the mortal realm and expended a significant amount of power. The mortals referred to them as gallows, which was fitting given the locations usually were marked by the deaths of a large number of people.

The clearing in front of them was no different. She couldn't read the energy, not as she once may have been able to. But it was strong, and Az knew it had been the final ground for a large number of mortals, even maybe some of her own kind.

The clearing was still and silent. Everything around them seemed untouched, with no disturbances except their own to be noted. The bell tower stood like a looming figure in the very centre with its distinct black stones, and at the base was a small hole through which she saw the rope that pulled the bell at the top.

There was no sign of change for a long time after they arrived. Maybe the girl had already been killed, or maybe it would still be several days before she would pass through. Either way, Az knew she had to try to convince Xadrion to give up on this hopeless quest.

A few hours passed and Azraelle was preparing herself to begin her attempt to convince Xadrion to turn them back, when something finally changed. It wasn't noticeable at first, and Azraelle was sure Xadrion and Ilyon wouldn't have been able to detect anything. Despite the silence, being in the middle of a forest brought with it less discernible sounds – birds chirping in the distance, insects buzzing around, even animals traipsing across the forest floor.

All sounds had stopped. No birds, no insects, no animals. Something was coming.

Xadrion's head cocked slightly, as if he were listening intently. Maybe he *had* noticed. Maybe he was more observant than Azraelle gave him credit for. Az strained her ears harder, listening for any sign of the approaching danger. Finally, in the distance, the sound began again. Not the sounds of the animals this time, but rather the sound of a panicking run across forest floor. Branches snapped and above birds scattered into the sky, following the path of the sound.

Bounding through the foliage to their right came a baby doe. It was stumbling to each side as it attempted to make it across the clearing. On its side, just above its hind leg, Az could see blood coating its fur.

The doe ran to the bell tower and attempted to hide behind it before the image in front of her began to shift. Where the doe previously had cowered behind the tower, it began to transform. The doe shimmered and morphed until, instead of the baby doe, there sat a girl, curled against the brick of the tower. Az didn't need to look closer to know it was the girl she had seen in her premonition.

Az could barely blink before Xadrion was pushing from their hiding place and sprinting across the field to the girl.

'No!' Az barked after him, but quickly Ilyon followed suit. The girl had been chased, that much was clear. And if she had magic, odds were whoever was chasing her was someone with their own. Az didn't move – couldn't move. She stayed hidden, watching as Xadrion and Ilyon ran to the girl. Xadrion was in the process of hoisting her into his arms when the girl's chaser entered the clearing.

Chaosdamned.

Why the fuck was Deimos there?

'Well, seems my baby fawn has attracted some attention,' Deimos drawled. Deimos was sauntering in their pace, barely looking like they were paying attention to the world around them. Az knew the carelessness was an act, knew Deimos was more observant than most could ever hope to be.

Before her capture Az hadn't seen Deimos for a long time. In fact, last she'd heard, Deimos' sibling Phobos had gone missing, and Deimos had set about finding them. But once, only once, she had heard Deimos' voice, clear as day through her cell wall on Mount Olympus. Azraelle's fear spiked; the knowledge that someone who could reveal her presence back to Zeus was so close caused her heart to quicken.

Xadrion settled the girl back to the ground gently, tucking her back behind the tower. His lips moved silently in a quiet whisper to the girl before he turned to face Deimos with his sword drawn.

'She's just a child,' Xadrion said. 'Leave her be.'

Ilyon was a mirror of Xadrion's stance. Still, Az found she could not make herself walk from her cover. They were going to get themselves killed and she had no power to stop it. If Deimos made that decision to snap their necks, it would be done before she could do anything about it.

'Nothing is ever what it seems, boy,' Deimos responded, who had been lazily strolling toward Ilyon and Xadrion. Midstride, Deimos shifted into their alternate form. Both Phobos and Deimos had the ability, something they'd inherited from their mater, but it never ceased to amaze Azraelle the speed that they transformed. They had two forms, one of a man and one of a woman, and as far as Az could tell they each had no preference for either.

Where Deimos' male form had previously stood, with their hulking size and angled face, there now stood their feminine form. Ilyon gaped, but Xadrion had enough sense to look unfazed at the sudden change. As quickly as Deimos had shifted, they shifted back until they were once again in their masculine form. It was a cocky display of power, something Deimos had always revelled in, something designed to instil a deep fear in the two mortals opposite them.

'We won't give you the girl,' Xadrion said.

'Like you have a choice, boy,' Deimos sneered. Their lazy stroll became purposeful, and they launched into a leap so fast Az knew Xadrion and Ilyon would not be prepared. The only reason they both weren't immediately dead was due to the fact that Deimos had struck with no weapon. Instead, they struck with their fist, knocking Xadrion clean upon the jaw before Xadrion had time to bring his arms up to block.

Xadrion went flying halfway across the clearing, leaving Deimos to turn and face Ilyon. Az desperately peered into that well within her, trying to summon anything that she could but all she found were sputtering sparks that would do extraordinarily little against Deimos. Without her power, her combat ability, as impressive as it was to the mortals, was a puddle compared to Deimos' ocean.

To Ilyon's credit, he didn't balk when Xadrion went flying. He stood his ground, and without the element of surprise on Deimos' side, Ilyon managed to parry for longer than Az expected. Xadrion took moments to recover, jumping to his feet and running to his brother's defence with his sword drawn. Deimos hesitated slightly before the next strike against Ilyon, as if deciding which of the two would warrant his attention more.

Ilyon, seeing the hesitation, lunged forward. He drove his sword in a straight thrust, burying it deep into Deimos' thigh.

'Hm,' Deimos said, pausing in their step. Deimos looked to their thigh, Ilyon having already ripped his sword back out and dropped into a defensive position. As Deimos looked at the wound in their leg, at the blood that poured and began to coat the grass around them, no pain crossed their features. Instead, Deimos seemed fascinated by the sight of the wound on their body. 'That'll do for now.'

Deimos' final punch against Ilyon came with devastating effect. Where Deimos had been toying with the brothers until that point, Deimos finally wielded their power – fire. It coated their fist, sizzling on impact to Ilyon's face, and sent Ilyon crumpling to the ground. Without pause, Deimos whirled to meet Xadrion's approach, stepping out of the way of his swing easily enough, and threw a jab at Xadrion's throat. It sent Xadrion down, gasping for air.

Deimos followed Xadrion down to lean next to him, finally pulling a dagger from their thigh and pressing it against the skin of Xadrion's neck. Az should have done something. She should have shown herself, should have at least tried to talk Deimos down. But Deimos was hunting the girl, and there was a total of one person who Az knew had the power to demand Deimos do such a thing – Zeus. In that moment, Zeus believed Az to be dead, and everything in her told her it was best to keep it that way. She could only hope Deimos didn't feel the need to end the mortal lives of Ilyon and Xadrion. Was Azraelle's survival worth it? She didn't think so, but someone needed to be able to unveil what Zeus was doing.

Deimos didn't make the final strike against Xadrion. Instead, they peered at where their dagger lay against Xadrion's throat. Deimos lowered their head, dropping closer to Xadrion's neck and sniffed, long and hard.

Az knew in that moment she was doomed. Xadrion was half unconscious, fighting hard as it was to keep his eyes open, so he simply lay beneath Deimos as Deimos pieced together what the scent was that lingered on Xadrion's neck.

Az's magic, used last night on that exact spot, would still be fresh across Xadrion's skin. It may not have been so bad, except Deimos had been around

Azraelle, had trained with her on so many occasions in the past and would no doubt have no trouble placing where they remembered that scent.

'Is this one yours, dear Az?' Deimos called, standing from their kneeling position and turning in a circle to peer around the clearing. Deimos didn't see where she was hiding, so rather than revealing herself by responding directly, Azraelle attempted to send her response to their mind. If Deimos' thoughts were trained on her like they seemed to be, the message would go straight through.

Don't kill them.

'Well. He's going to be very unhappy to hear that you're still alive and well,' Deimos said. Deimos had heard her but was taunting her to speak aloud.

He. The very mention of a 'he' gave Azraelle all the answers she needed. Deimos was working with Zeus, and if Deimos told Zeus that Azraelle was there that day, her months spent hiding would be for nothing.

Please.

Deimos picked up Xadrion's sword and pressed the tip of it against Xadrion's chest.

'Come out, Az. Let me see you, or I will push this blade through this little pet of yours,' Deimos taunted. The fact that they hadn't already done so made Az hope that she could talk her way out of this. It depended entirely on how generous Deimos felt like being, but there was nothing else to lose and she had to try.

Azraelle stood from where she had been crouched; Deimos' gaze moved to her as soon as she revealed herself.

I'm here. Don't kill him, please.

'I won't, for now.' Deimos was smiling at her, which did nothing to ease her nerves. It was malicious and wicked, not open and kind as Deimos had once been towards Azraelle, so many years ago.

Take the girl, I won't stop you. But leave them. They don't need to be brought into this.

As if Deimos suddenly remembered what they were doing, they sent a single bolt of fire in the direction of the cowering girl. Xadrion made a noise, almost like he could rally to the girl, but it didn't matter. The girl's magic had been expended and no one was left to defend her. Deimos' fire bolt hit where she was crying, sending her sprawling to the ground, face down.

'She had to die, Az. It was the only way,' Deimos said, refixing their attention back to Azraelle. She was closer now, standing only a few paces from where Deimos hovered above Xadrion's prone body. Ilyon lay further behind them, still completely unconscious.

'I'm thinking maybe I don't have to do any more killing today,' Deimos said. 'And maybe, it's very possible, I don't remember seeing you here.'

And in return?

'In return? Hm,' Deimos pondered. 'Can't it just be out of the goodness of my heart? I mean, we are blood.'

Blood means nothing if you are working for Zeus. What do you want in return?

They were blood, but one of her own sisters had already betrayed her against Zeus, and this was an even more distant connection. Deimos and Phobos had been born from the union of her brother Thanatos with his wife Aphrodite. Az was closer to Thanatos than anyone and everyone else, and Aphrodite had always welcomed her in the past, but Deimos and Phobos had both spent many years away from Thanatos and Aphrodite. While there had never been any bad blood between them and Az, she wouldn't trust them to align with her in the way Thanatos would. As well as the fact that Zeus was technically Deimos' grandfather, Az had no reason to trust them.

'Yes, you're right. It is too much to risk his wrath for nothing in return,' Deimos said, their smile cocky. 'A favour, then. I'm not sure what, but you'll owe me one.'

And in return, you'll leave them unharmed, and won't tell Zeus that you saw me, or that I'm still alive?

'That's right. You'll stay presumed dead, these boys of yours will live to see another day and you will owe me a favour,' Deimos agreed.

Deal.

Deimos smiled, dropped Xadrion's sword to the grass beside Xadrion's body and strolled away from the ruin they had created. Azraelle felt the surge of Deimos' power reach for her, its touch like a warm caress over her body. The deal's power settled over her skin.

'Oh, and Az?' Deimos said, turning to look at her once more over their shoulder. 'You really need to take a closer look at that one.' Deimos pointed directly at Xadrion, gave a wink and, in the blink of an eye, was engulfed in flames as they disappeared. The only sign that they had been there was a small ring of scorched grass, the two brothers prone on the ground and the dead girl slumped behind the bell tower with a giant burn across her chest.

Whatever Deimos was talking about, Az didn't give herself time to think about it. Instead, she ran to where Ilyon lay as he still had made no noise to indicate he was alive. Xadrion was coughing as he regained his breath and was attempting to push himself to a kneeling position.

Az knelt beside Ilyon and placed her ear above his lips. She felt warm breath tickle her ear, providing instant relief with the knowledge that Ilyon wasn't dead, just unconscious. However much of Deimos' power had been added to the punch, it hadn't been enough to kill Ilyon. Az stayed kneeling beside Ilyon until she saw his eyes fly open. He gasped for air and threw himself into a sitting position to take stock of his surroundings.

'It's okay, you're fine. Just relax,' Az soothed. A burn marred half of Ilyon's face, his cheek already blistered and twisted. Az could tell he was in pain, but Ilyon held himself well against it, a silent grimace all the expression he let himself betray. Behind her, Xadrion approached the bell tower and the girl who was dead at its base.

'How could you let her be killed and do nothing?' Azraelle turned to find Xadrion staring directly at her, the dead girl at his feet and a rage burning behind his gaze. 'You could have stopped it.'

'There was no way, Xadrion,' Azraelle seethed, pushing herself to stand.

'You could have fought.'

'Are you fucking serious? If I had fought the way you did, we all would be dead right now,' Azraelle said, filling her voice with as much ice as she could. 'Need I remind you, both you and your brother were on your backs within a minute. Which could have been avoided had you not gone running from the bushes at the first sign of movement.'

'She needed our help,' Xadrion growled.

'The girl was dead anyway. If you had observed the situation for more than a single moment, you would have seen that for what it was. You wouldn't have walked straight into the path of what was trailing her and nearly gotten the both of you killed.'

'Maybe if you actually tried instead of cowering,' Xadrion said. He was pissed, his eyes betraying his pure, unfiltered energy threatening to spill out.

'How dare you accuse me of cowering? He would have killed us all had it not been for me,' Azraelle yelled. Xadrion fell silent, watching Azraelle with more judgement in his eyes than she had ever seen from him. He paused, as if he were trying to collect himself before he spoke again.

'Was a little girl's life not worth trying?' Xadrion asked quietly. That seemed to be the important question to him. Xadrion was willing to judge her entire existence based on what she would have sacrificed for a mortal girl. Az wondered what he would think of her if he knew just how many mortal girls she'd ferried to their deaths.

'No.'

Azraelle didn't quieten in her answer. She believed in her choices, especially given her complete lack of any substantial magic. As she stared him down, a faint crackle of energy surrounded Xadrion. She blinked to clear her eyes, but the energy was gone. Az put it down to her imagination. If he had power, surely she would have sensed it by that point. If Xadrion had inherited anything from Hera, it would have manifested already.

'Can we just get out of here?' Ilyon asked from behind Az. Azraelle turned to see Ilyon watching their fight. He looked bruised and beaten, and the half of his face was covered in a gruesome burn.

'Great idea,' Azraelle said, throwing a pointed glare in Xadrion's direction before storming back the way they had come from that morning. She paused long enough to offer support to Ilyon as they both began walking.

'I'll meet you there. She deserves to be buried,' Xadrion said.

'Fine.'

Azraelle didn't turn back again.

The walk back was slower, given Ilyon's injuries, and it ended up taking twice the duration it had from the morning. When they did make it back to the small cabin, she took Ilyon straight to the large bed and helped him in. Azraelle paced as Ilyon fell into sleep quickly despite his pain. What little magic she could summon she directed into Ilyon's cheek, barely noticing any improvement.

Once she'd expended what energy she had remaining, Az moved on to taking care of the horses. She tracked down more water for them and moved them to a field with more grass for them to graze. She was in the process of brushing them down when Xadrion arrived, perhaps an hour later than Ilyon and Az had stumbled back to the cabin.

Xadrion made to storm straight past where Az was standing with the horses, as if he had decided he was going to ignore her, before she heard him stop completely. Az didn't turn around. If he were going to talk to her, he would have to make the first move. She wasn't going to make it any easier for him. He had no idea what he was talking about and the fact that he'd yelled at her for not fighting made her see red.

'They knew you,' Xadrion said, his voice barely audible.

'Yes.'

'They were with the men who kidnapped you?'

'Yes.'

'That makes sense.'

Azraelle whirled to face him, seething with anger.

'Why?' she demanded. Xadrion turned to face her but didn't say a thing. 'Because it was only okay for me not to fight if I was traumatised by who was in front of me? Because if it hadn't been someone who recognised me, but who surely still would have killed all of us, then I should have gone down swinging?'

'Better that than hiding,' Xadrion snarked.

'No, it's not,' Azraelle snapped. 'Dying a heroic death only means something if you accomplish something with your death. Going down today would have achieved nothing.'

Xadrion looked like he wanted to say so much more, but he opened and closed his mouth several times with no words, as if he couldn't quite figure out what it was he wanted to say.

'What did it mean when they said you were blood?' Xadrion asked eventually.

'What's it sound like to you?'

'I found you, Azraelle,' Xadrion said, coming to stand in front of her. 'I saw the state you were left in, those wounds on your back and the scars that cover the rest of your body. You mean to tell me that your own blood stood by and let that happen?'

'The world doesn't make as much sense as you thought it does, huh?' Azraelle quipped. 'Not everything is so black and white, Xadrion. There are a thousand shades of grey in between. That girl's life and what it meant to fight for her, that was grey.'

'Just because you didn't know what it was to have someone fight for you, doesn't mean it is at all acceptable that no one did. That girl deserved to be fought for. We may never agree on that, but I don't regret trying,' Xadrion said.

'Great, you can go to sleep with a clean conscious. At least you get to sleep tonight, thanks to my actions, might I remind you,' Azraelle said. She stormed inside, eager to get away.

Ilyon didn't wake for hours, which meant they were forced to spend another night in the cabin while he recovered enough to travel again. Xadrion eventually made his way back inside and set about making food.

As night fell, Azraelle made a pointed move to settle into the cot that Xadrion had initially attempted to sleep in the night before. There would be no intimate touches between the two of them that night. No, Azraelle was determined to let Xadrion know he had crossed a line.

It wasn't about Az's made-up tale of her kidnapping and the false idea that no one ever fought for her. Her premonitions showed her people who were supposed to die, they always had. Az didn't have the ability to look into the thread of their destiny to confirm it anymore, but she was sure it would have been both Karlin's and that girl's time. Destiny couldn't be altered that way without consequences and Azraelle never would have even tried.

It was ironic then that she still found herself with a death sentence over allegedly doing exactly that. Even if that boy all those years ago hadn't been destined to die on that day. The Moirai had made the decision to announce Azraelle as guilty, and so long had passed that Azraelle was beginning to wonder if she had misread the threads of his destiny. Maybe she really had altered his course.

Ilyon woke only long enough to eat before quickly going back to sleep for the night. His cheek would need to be tended to by Emera, but Azraelle tried once more before she went to bed to provide some healing. Xadrion shared the bed with Ilyon, but much the same as the night before, he didn't sound like he could fall asleep. Azraelle didn't offer him comfort, not again.

She had gotten too comfortable among the mortals. Today was a stark reminder of how different she was to them; how different she would always be. She could never tell them the truth of her story, could never hope for their understanding, which meant there would always be this barrier between them.

Deimos had nearly ruined everything, nearly revealed too much about who she was while Xadrion lay aware.

In the darkness of night, Xadrion became a different person to during the day; a more vulnerable version of himself. The first night in the cabin he had been so open with Az, she'd found it hard to resist touching him. They had lain within each other's comfort, so close their breath was one. She had grazed his neck, allowed their noses to brush and allowed him to hold her in the morning for longer than was ever a good idea. When night fell that second night, Xadrion softened once more. After hours of silence, Xadrion finally was the one to break it.

'My mother, her name was Hera,' Xadrion whispered from across the room. 'She used to bring all these kids into the castle and let them feast in a grand event. Every week there was that group of kids – all the orphans in Fennhall – eating like they had never eaten before. She would have fought for that girl today. I don't always know the right thing to do, not when it comes to helping others, but I like to think about what she would do and let that be my moral compass.'

His admission hung in the air, followed by complete silence once more. Azraelle didn't want to give in, she didn't want to let him stop dwelling on her being angry with him. But when the night unfolded this version of Xadrion, Azraelle found herself having a tough time keeping him shut out. Especially as she was reminded of the knowledge she kept from him about Hera, and how she could never tell him the truth.

'You can keep trying to be good, Xadrion,' Az replied quietly into the night. 'But don't cast judgement on me for how my actions differ from yours.'

'You're right,' Xadrion said.

As Azraelle found herself drifting to sleep that night, she could have sworn she heard an apology whispered across the room.

TWELVE

XADRION

Xadrion couldn't find the words to talk to Azraelle again the entire next day. They travelled back to Fennhall tight-lipped with Ilyon and Azraelle following behind Xadrion. Occasionally, the two shared their own words but he was never brought into the conversation. When they returned to the castle finally, Ilyon went immediately to Emera to see to his burned cheek and Azraelle fled the stables as soon as they'd handed over their horses.

Xadrion went to his father's study to report back.

'How did your venture go?' King Rhoas asked when Xadrion was seated across from him.

'We didn't save the girl,' Xadrion admitted. 'She was being hunted by this man, or thing, I don't know.' Xadrion told his father of what he had seen, how the man had shifted forms and back again, as if it were the most natural thing in the world to have occurred.

'A shape shifter?' Rhoas asked.

'Magic, I think. They wielded fire in their hands, I saw it,' Xadrion said. 'Ilyon took a burn to the face but is being treated now.'

'And Azraelle?'

Xadrion didn't know how to explain to his father all he had learnt these last two days. Since waking, Azraelle had been silent on the details of those who had abducted her, meaning they had made no progress in tracking them. Laying on the ground as that person stood with Xadrion's own sword above his chest, he had heard them say such things.

Azraelle hadn't spoken, hadn't even uttered a word, yet it seemed as if the other was responding directly to her. More secrets, it seemed.

'I think they knew Azraelle, they mentioned something about being her blood,' Xadrion finally said. 'They mentioned another man, someone who thought Azraelle was dead. They said something about forgetting to mention that they'd seen Azraelle there, and that we would be spared in exchange for a favour from her.'

'What kind of favour?' Rhoas asked.

'They didn't say, just that they would call it in at some point,' Xadrion explained.

'And you're certain they mentioned that Azraelle was blood?'

'Yes.'

Rhoas fell silent, crossed his arms over his chest and tucked his chin into one of his palms. Xadrion got the distinct impression that he was being kept from some vital information.

'Why would one of her relatives have played a part in the torture she was subjected to?' Xadrion asked. His anger had been white hot following the fight in the clearing. In his attempt to source where it was coming from he'd said things to Azraelle he regretted, but it felt wrong to show her where a lot of his anger had stemmed.

The way Xadrion had found her that day on his path, her back bearing wounds greater than any he'd ever seen, had left him with nightmares. He'd seen glimpses of the two large scars on her back peeking through over the last month, mainly when she'd move in a way that rode her shirt up, or in the last few days at the cabin when he'd accidentally glimpsed her washing herself in the small pond behind the cabin. He'd only seen her back, and the scars that remained left him feeling gutted. It was what had driven him to say something to her last night, something to get them back on good terms once more. He didn't want to be responsible for her feeling such anger, not when she'd already endured so much torment.

Rhoas was watching Xadrion as he moved through this series of thoughts, seemingly determined to let his question go unanswered. It appeared Rhoas was weighing up the benefits of his words.

'What are you not telling me?' Xadrion eventually said.

'I think it's Azraelle's place to say,' Rhoas said. 'But, as my heir, I think there is essential information for you to know.'

'What does Azraelle have to do with me being your heir?'

'I haven't been entirely honest with you or Ilyon in my motives behind asking her to stay,' Rhoas answered. 'The training she can offer is invaluable, and I think what she has to teach you will go a long way when it comes to the challenges you and Ilyon will face in your future. But if I'm going to be letting you get further into her world, going on these missions to save these people she sees, I think you need to be more prepared.'

'Prepared, how?' Xadrion pushed.

'Azraelle isn't like you or me,' Rhoas said. 'Her magic, it isn't even like

Emera's. There are things that I think you need to hear from her, and those I cannot tell you. But what I can tell you is what I've heard. There are legends of Azraelle, legends in places you wouldn't even know to listen. Her premonitions are part of her magic, you already knew that, but that's not all. The legends describe her as nearly immeasurable in her power, although most stories are fuzzy on the details of what exactly her powers are. Azraelle's legend claims her as someone even the gods can't compare to.'

Xadrion didn't know what his father was talking about. They'd never had a particularly religious family and talk of gods hadn't played a large part in their upbringing. Xadrion had faint memories of Hera telling him stories as he fell asleep – stories of the gods and goddesses who ruled in other realms. They'd mostly been adventure stories, sometimes romance, but he could barely remember most of the stories given that he was only ten the last time his mother had ever told him one.

'The gods aren't real. And her power – I've seen her try to use it – it's basically gone,' Xadrion interrupted.

'Maybe. All the same, she is the girl from the legends I spent years listening to, and she was dropped practically on our doorstep. As you said, her magic is gone, and I think there's no way that could ever be considered a good thing for this world of ours,' Rhoas said. 'I'd heard of the people who took her, heard that she had been taken – betrayed by her own family – and I think the world has been a worse place for it since.'

'How could you possibly have heard any of this?' Xadrion said.

'It doesn't matter, not really. But if that girl really is everything the legends say, and she has found her way to us, I think there is more to happen in this story. And for whatever reason, it seems you and Ilyon are a part of it,' Rhoas said.

'But why would her family have handed her over like that?'

'Who knows why anyone does anything? Power, maybe. Fear of the man they gave her to, most definitely. The legend I heard tells that it was as payment for one of her brother's crimes, in the hopes that her life might pay for what he had done,' Rhoas said.

She was only a kid when they had handed her over, yet somehow she still had these legends circulating about her. Xadrion felt disgusted when he imagined Azraelle as a child, getting handed over as payment for her family's crimes. How had she spent all those years paying for them?

'You realise you're giving me more questions with every answer you give me, right?' Xadrion said, his agitation growing.

'I know. There are gaps in what I can tell you, things that are entirely her story to tell. But don't let her shut you out,' Rhoas said. 'The premonitions she's seeing, there has to be a reason. Make sure she keeps telling you of them, they will be the clues to the beginning of this story.'

Xadrion didn't think Azraelle was going to tell him about any of her premonitions ever again. She had seemed so unwilling to go to that first one and had buckled only when Xadrion had made it clear he would be going regardless. For whatever reason, Azraelle wasn't valuing the lives she was seeing, wasn't seeing the importance of trying to save them, and Xadrion knew she would keep the future premonitions from him to keep them from that danger again.

But what she had described had come to pass, and with enough time for them to have potentially changed the outcome. Didn't she see that was everything?

Xadrion didn't understand his father's intentions, especially when it felt like nothing made sense even with the added information. No matter how Xadrion prodded, his father had become resolved to saying no more, saying it was Azraelle's story to tell.

More frustrated than ever, Xadrion eventually left his father's study and headed upstairs to his rooms. Hours passed before a knock sounded at the door and, when he went to answer, he was surprised to find Emera standing at the entrance.

'I came to check if you were okay,' she said. Xadrion stepped aside and allowed her to walk in.

'How's Ilyon?'

'He's resting. He'll have some scarring for a while, but I think with continued treatments I should be able to make it disappear,' Emera answered. 'Azraelle told me you got knocked around a bit. Can I check you?'

'Suppose so,' Xadrion said, moving to lounge across his couch. Emera approached and knelt in front of him, placing her hands gently on his arm. Xadrion felt the threads of Emera's power course through him, as if they were scanning him for any lingering injuries.

'Everything looks fine, but your neck?' Emera asked, eyeing it closely.

Xadrion hadn't looked himself in the mirror yet, not since before he'd left the castle two days prior. When he had caught a glimpse of himself at that point, the bruises around his neck were so immediately black that he had made the decision to put on a coat that covered as much of them as he could manage.

Xadrion flashed back to Azraelle lying beside him in that bed, her hands gently on his neck. Every time she'd looked at him since, her eyes had immediately dropped to where the bruises were, and Xadrion could read the guilt behind her gaze. He was worried that every word out of her mouth would have been some apology for having done it. It had hurt more than anything Xadrion had ever physically felt when her hands crushed his throat, but he couldn't live with being looked at with such pity.

Azraelle's magic was so unlike Emera's healing magic, even though she'd barely had enough to offer him. He wasn't surprised he still had the marks around his neck as witness to what Az had done to him, not with how little magic he'd felt from her fingertips to his skin.

'Can you make the bruises go away?' Xadrion asked.

'I can.' Emera moved her hands to his neck and a cold pang settled through Xadrion's chest at the touch. Only two nights ago he'd had Azraelle's hands against his neck in much the same way, yet it felt so different to him now to have Emera touch him.

Azraelle pissed him off. She made him angrier more often than anyone else he interacted with, and yet since she had approached him on that cot and trailed her hands down his arm to link her fingers in his, he also had not stopped imagining what it would feel to be touched by her again. So much so, that even with Emera beside him once more he could barely remember what any of it had felt like with her.

Yet it was Emera who now got to be touched by Azraelle under the cover of darkness. Those few stolen moments in that bed would likely be all Xadrion would ever get. Especially given the anger Azraelle seemed determined to throw at him.

'I'm sorry I haven't visited you,' Emera said.

'Don't apologise for that. You and I never owed each other anything. I understand why you don't want to anymore,' Xadrion replied. And with that, it felt like a very hollow ending to a relationship that had served the both of them for so many years. Xadrion knew they'd never developed feelings for anything further and knew that one day when he had to follow through on his royal obligations, or when Emera found someone she could love, it would have ended. It still saddened him that it had.

Emera finished her healing, pressed a light kiss to his cheek, and eventually left him to his own thoughts. A quick look in the mirror showed the bruising completely gone. At least he wouldn't have to see the guilt in Azraelle's eyes when he found himself facing her the next day in training.

It turned out that Xadrion had nothing to worry about when it came to Azraelle looking at him the next day in training. When he arrived in the morning for their regular session, she was there already doing her usual warmups for herself. It didn't seem to matter how early he got there; she always beat him to it. Ilyon was there also, his cheek red and raw but looking much better than it had the day before.

'I'm putting your lessons together,' Az declared to the both of them. She didn't once meet Xadrion's eyes. And so, the lessons changed. Ilyon and

Xadrion trained together, and where Azraelle went after that, he didn't know. Ilyon's face healed quickly and the only peace of mind Xadrion received came from Ilyon himself telling him that he still spent most days with Az and Emera around dinner and for a few hours after. He couldn't give Xadrion more comfort, however; even Ilyon didn't know where she went between their sessions and dinner.

Xadrion was no stranger to sparring with his brother. They'd trained together often over the last decade at least, and it gave him a chance to match himself against someone he had a chance of beating. Ilyon was taking on Azraelle's lessons as well as Xadrion, which added the element of an equally matched partner to train with.

Weeks passed that way as summer came to its end. The trees were shedding their leaves, and the landscape generally became more auburn and browner in its colour than green and vivid. Xadrion liked this time of year and the way it made the world look. He tolerated what came with it – an increase in social commitments and more visits from diplomats and their courts to Fennhall.

'Did you hear Princess Romina is going to be visiting with the Gaewethian ambassador?' Ilyon said one day as they faced across from each other in the barracks. Azraelle stood off to the side, her arms folded across her chest, sidestepping around them as they moved. Her eyes were homed in on their forms, scanning Xadrion and Ilyon for any sign of breakdown.

'I heard,' Xadrion grunted, throwing a smooth arc with his sword toward Ilyon, who blocked it easily.

'Father is throwing a ball to celebrate their arrival,' Ilyon said.

'I heard that, also.'

'Who is Princess Romina?' Azraelle asked, the first conversation she had responded to with anything other than barked orders in Xadrion's presence.

Ilyon dropped his sword and Xadrion took the same cue. The two brothers took a moment to even their breaths and wipe the sweat from their faces. They had been going for some time and were about due for a short break anyway. He looked to Azraelle as Ilyon answered.

'Princess Romina of the neighbouring kingdom, Gaeweth. Xadrion spent a summer there once and rumour has it the princess has been smitten ever since,' Ilyon said, waggling his eyebrows at Xadrion. Azraelle's head whipped to look at Xadrion, and as much as he wished it weren't wreathed in anger, Xadrion could have wept at the first time their eyes met in weeks.

Her anger didn't make sense and Xadrion was left to wonder why it felt like her gaze was attempting to burn a hole through him. What could he possibly have done to upset her now?

'Are you going to the ball?' Ilyon asked Azraelle, not seeming to notice the tension hanging between the two of them. Azraelle once again turned from Xadrion and met Ilyon's gaze.

'I suppose,' Azraelle said, giving him a small smirk and nudging his shoulder gently with her own. 'Want to be my date?'

Ilyon grinned, wide. Hot, vivid anger pushed against Xadrion's skin, threatening to spill over at any moment. Azraelle looked at him then, concern clear on her expression, as if she somehow sensed the rage that had overwhelmed him.

'Emera as well, we can go together!' Ilyon agreed. Ilyon moved to jab Azraelle's ribs in jest, and she broke her gaze from Xadrion's to quickly manoeuvre them until she had Ilyon in a headlock. Az tussled his hair playfully before tossing him back in Xadrion's direction.

'Very well,' she said. 'For now, get back to work.'

An instant later, she was back to observing their movements with hawk-like intensity, speaking only when their training required it. Xadrion's anger didn't settle and for the rest of the session he was overwhelmed by the feeling of barely contained fury.

The silent treatment from the last few weeks had worn Xadrion down to his last nerve. Maybe he'd said some things that were uncalled for, maybe he had passed judgement on her as she had said to him, but surely it didn't require being this distant. And still, the mystery of where Az disappeared to between those training hours and dinner time was a constant thought of Xadrion's.

Training ended for the day, and Xadrion had nearly resolved to go about his business as usual when he watched Azraelle leave the barracks. Anger swarmed in, and determination to find out what she was doing settled over him. Before he could realise what he was doing, he was following her from the barracks, doing his best to remain hidden from view.

Azraelle walked straight from the barracks, past the stables and out of the main gates to the castle walls. She stayed on foot, to Xadrion's relief. He would not have followed her so easily if she had chosen to take a horse.

She was easy enough to follow through the city below, her white hair like a beacon as she weaved through the crowds. The city people seemed to clear a path for her, and Xadrion noted the glances she received as she moved through the streets. Xadrion kept his head down. As he followed her through the city he was suddenly thankful for his father, for always enforcing he wear his royal clothes when visiting the people. With his head low and dressed in his training clothes, he easily blended into the crowds.

Azraelle walked until she left the confines of the city and didn't stop for the better part of an hour. By the time they came to a stop, Xadrion trailing as far behind as he could without losing sight of her completely, they were deep into the woods that surrounded the city. Azraelle perched herself on a large rock with her legs crossed and Xadrion crept as close as he dared without her detecting his presence.

Still, she seemed unaware enough to allow Xadrion to get close enough to see the features on her face and her closed eyes as she sat on the rock. Her brows were pinched together, her hands clasped in her lap. Long moments passed and Azraelle didn't move, didn't even make a sound.

Maybe she just wanted time to her own. Xadrion was beginning to feel bad for intruding when she spoke at last.

'Where in Chaos are you, Thanatos?' she said, her voice quiet. Chaos. It was the second time Xadrion had heard her use that word, the first when she'd experienced the premonition in training. It was unfamiliar to Xadrion, her words giving no insight into where Azraelle must have taken that from. Az dropped her head into her hands. And then, as if something inside her couldn't help but boil over, Az buried her face into the crook of her elbow and loosed a scream.

It didn't consist of words, only a broken cry that was barely muffled by the presence of her elbow covering her mouth.

When the scream died out, Xadrion made to take a step forward, not entirely sure what he would do but unable to fight the need to be closer to her. A branch crunched beneath his feet and Azraelle looked up, turning to face him fully with her eyes narrowed. Nothing but anger simmered beneath their surface.

'What are you doing here?' she asked, her gaze like shooting daggers.

He had no answer that would sound good out loud. There was no excuse to cover the fact that he'd followed her.

'I'm tired of you being angry with me,' Xadrion admitted, being as honest as he dared.

'So, you followed me to tell me that? To what, to make me talk to you?' Azraelle spat.

'Pretty much.' Xadrion shoved his hands into his pockets in his attempt to not fiddle with them.

'Gods, you have the nerve.'

'Who is Thanatos?' Xadrion asked. The name sounded so familiar to him, but he couldn't place where from.

'What?'

'You said the name Thanatos. Who is he? And why are you out here waiting for him?' Xadrion asked.

'Don't be ridiculous,' Azraelle said. She was trying to evade the question, her eyes now suddenly looking everywhere but to him, as if she were desperate for a distraction to appear.

'Why won't you look at me? Why won't you speak to me?' Xadrion asked, filing the question away for a later time. He had a feeling he would get nowhere if he pushed, so he resolved to return to his original intention of following her – to get her to finally speak to him.

'I don't know what you're talking about,' Azraelle said.

'That's bullshit, Az.' He closed the distance between them, the anger at her indifference finally boiling up and over. She let him approach. If she didn't want him getting close enough to her, didn't want him to touch her, he would have had no chance at doing so. She had evaded his grasp countless times in training for Xadrion to know that was true.

Yet, Az kept her gaze down, lowered to his feet, as he approached and came to a stop in front of her. He grabbed her chin, gently despite his anger, and tugged it up so that she was forced to look at his face. She met his gaze, her black eyes somehow reminding Xadrion of cold ice. Beyond her eyes, Xadrion could see what was pushing her so far, what had pushed her to burying her face in her elbow and releasing a scream that had sent the goosebumps spreading down his arms. She wasn't just angry; she was absolutely consumed by rage.

'Tell me,' Xadrion commanded. Azraelle continued to glare at him, fierce enough that Xadrion began to question if this gaze were any better than her avoidance of him. The way she watched him made him feel like melting on the spot and never bothering her ever again.

'No one is coming for me,' Azraelle whispered. Her eyes never broke in their anger, but her lips quivered as she muttered the words. The fact that she had spoken left him unsure what to do next. Her own expression appeared shocked at the words that had slipped from her lips, evidently surprised at herself for speaking to him in the first place. 'After all I did, no one is coming.'

'What did you do, Az?' He'd moved his hands now to hold either side of her face, his head bowed enough that he could maintain eye contact with her.

'I didn't give him what he wanted. I kept their secrets. I paid the price. Why is no one coming now?' she whispered.

Xadrion thought back to the tale his father had told him those weeks ago. A girl, given over to a man in payment for her family's crimes. What had she been subjected to because of those crimes?

'Who would come for you?' Xadrion asked, gently. She'd said her family was dead that day they had ridden to the lodge. She'd told Ilyon that there was no one left for her. A lie, it seemed. How much had she lied to them to avoid telling the truth of her capture?

'My brothers, maybe. I guess I hoped,' Azraelle answered. 'Never my mater, I know, but maybe Thanatos.' *Mater.* Not a word for mother that was familiar to this kingdom, but one he recognised. And Thanatos, again that name prodded at his memory with its familiarity.

'Why aren't they coming?' Xadrion asked.

'It's better that they don't. But now I'm stuck here and in this form,' Azraelle said, her own hands gesturing to her body roughly. She seemed to be collecting herself once more, returning to her shielded thoughts. Soon, Xadrion knew, she would return to finding the exact right words to say that conveyed nothing but logic and coldness. In no world would it have been better for her to be left without the aid of her brothers, but she was accepting it as the natural rule of things. Just as she had accepted that little girl not being worth fighting for.

'What form?' Xadrion asked, her phrasing bringing with it further confusion. It wasn't the right question. Xadrion could practically see the guards slam back into place, blocking him from her vulnerability. He didn't want to see the walls, not when he had pushed so far. Not when she was speaking to him again. She'd begun pulling her face from his hands, but he gripped her harder and recentred her gaze back to his.

'Don't hide, Azraelle. What form are you stuck in?' Xadrion pushed, bowing his head lower so that his gaze was level with hers. He didn't know what she meant, couldn't piece it together, but something in him knew it was this line of questioning he needed to follow.

An image flashed across Xadrion's memory of the figure in the clearing, switching between their forms with magic. Xadrion's father had said Azraelle's magic was on another level... Was she able to alter her form in a similar way? Was she trapped in this one because her magic had abandoned her?

For whatever reason, despite Xadrion's belief that he'd lost her in that moment and that she was done with speaking to him, Az softened once more before him. She met his gaze and brought her own hands up. In the same way Xadrion was cradling Az's face, she placed her hands on his cheeks. Her touch was timid and gentle, so light at first Xadrion felt more the shifting of air around him than he did her touch.

In a way like no woman had ever touched him, Azraelle's fingertips brushed his cheeks softly. Somehow, miraculously, the ever-present, all-consuming anger he felt dissipated at her touch and he felt calmness unlike any he'd felt for months.

'You don't want to know, Xay,' Az breathed. Her breath tickled his lips, her fingertips gentle. The fondness of his name from her lips sent prickles over his arms and he couldn't stop the pleasant shiver that overcame him.

'What form are you trapped in, Azraelle?'

Xadrion felt something inside his mind. It was gentle and felt like it was unsure of itself as it prodded against the edge of his thoughts, as if it were requesting entrance. Everything inside Xadrion told him to let that prodding sensation in.

As he did, embracing its entrance into his mind, Azraelle pushed herself to her toes and leant forward. It didn't take much to close the distance, but as the presence infiltrated his mind, Az's lips covered his. It was feather light, and Xadrion had every intention of leaning in and deepening the kiss when an image appeared behind his closed eyes.

The presence in his mind was Az, he realised when her voice echoed into his mind.

This form.

And then she was showing him what she couldn't seem to say aloud. In his mind, an image of Az appeared, but it wasn't as she was standing in front of him now. All of her features looked the same, her eyes that same darkness and her hair the same white. But there, spread out behind her, the length of her whole body on either side, were wings. They were black as night, black as her eyes, and all-encompassing as they flared behind her.

Her wings were probably the most marvellous things Xadrion had ever laid his eyes upon.

The image disappeared and Azraelle rocked back on her heels, breaking their kiss. The absence of her lips felt like the absence of air.

'The wounds on your back… that was where they were?' Xadrion asked. He took hold of her hands, linking his fingers between hers.

'Yes.'

'The people who held you hostage, they took them from you?'

'Mm.'

'If your magic returns, can you bring back your wings?'

'I don't know.'

'Can I kiss you again?' Xadrion couldn't keep himself from looking to her lips. He wanted to feel them once more. After their night in the cabin, the way she felt pressed against him as they'd slept and the feeling of sharing the same breath as her, imagining what she would have been like to touch, and taste, had occupied an embarrassingly large amount of Xadrion's thoughts. Now that he'd had such a small glimpse of that touch, and after the gifted kiss she'd just given, he craved more.

Azraelle, however, seemed to not feel the same way. She pulled her hands from his grasp and stepped out of his reach.

'The kiss helped to strengthen the connection I needed to show you the image. It meant nothing more,' Azraelle said. It felt like she'd pulled his stomach through his throat, thrown it to the ground and stomped on it until it was in pieces between them. He couldn't even begin to formulate a response.

'I'm heading back, feel free to follow me again,' Azraelle snapped before she turned and strode back in the direction of the castle. She set a cracking pace, one that had them back to the castle in significantly less time than it took for them to get there.

Az refused to speak for the entire walk and Xadrion felt himself needing the silence to process everything that had just happened, so he let her keep it. She'd had wings, and now she didn't. He had no idea what that meant about who or what she was. Xadrion assumed it fell somewhere in the category of how that figure at the bell tower had transformed between genders. It didn't make it make any more sense, but at least he could lump the two together.

Her magic was returning; it had to have been for her to be able to put that image in his mind. More than that, she'd felt like an actual presence in his head, with a physical representation probing for entrance. Reflecting on the bell tower, had that been how the figure had responded to her even when she wasn't talking? Was she speaking into their mind as they spoke aloud?

More confronting than all of those thoughts put together was the idea of how the wings were no longer there. When they'd found her, she had two gashes running the entire length of her back, exactly where the wings would have stemmed from. They had been forcefully removed, damaging enough that she'd taken weeks to even wake up and longer still to recover.

When they returned to the castle once more, Azraelle left Xadrion immediately and disappeared through the hallways. He supposed he was back to being ignored.

THIRTEEN

AZRAELLE

That was so fucking stupid. Azraelle had no idea why she had been so stupid. Seeing Xadrion standing behind her had shocked her enough to set her off her guard and then he had been so gentle with her, coaxing her in all the right ways to speak to him, that she'd given in.

She hadn't told him everything, not even remotely close. But she had shown him that image of her with her wings, and that had been too much. It wouldn't immediately reveal what she was to him, not unless he already had some level of understanding of her kind, but it was still too risky.

The kiss was the stupidest part of the entire thing. She wasn't lying when she said it helped her strengthen her connection, and a few weeks ago she would have needed the physical connection as well as the mental one in order to communicate images into someone's mind that way. But her magic had been growing over the last few weeks, and she had enough to not have needed to do that. He had no mental defences and had already accepted her into his mind. Yet as she'd stood there, his face so close to hers and his palms so warm upon her face, Az had given in to temptation.

For the remainder of that day, the feeling of Xadrion's lips was impossible to push from her thoughts. She had dinner with Ilyon and Emera, and when she was alone after with Emera, she found herself fidgeting. Why did she feel so bad for what she had done? What she had with Emera was nothing exclusive; in fact, Az had never held an exclusive relationship in her entire existence. But she was meddling in mortal's lives, and it was a much riskier game when it came to their emotions. She knew mortals held a different attitude to intimacy than the one she had been raised in, tending to lead more monogamous lives than her immortal kind. Az was content with her previous lifestyle, but she was also incredibly aware that she was living off the generosity of the mortal king and causing strife within his home by toying with anyone's emotions was a sure way to lose that privilege.

'Come to bed, Az?' Emera said, standing in front of her and offering her hand. She couldn't take the hand that was offered. She had been with Emera since the lodge of course, but that felt easier to dismiss than it did the kiss from that afternoon.

'Are you okay?' Emera asked, settling instead beside Az on the couch when she showed no sign of moving. Emera took hold of Az's hand and pulled it into her lap.

'Today, I showed Xadrion an image of something. In his mind,' Az explained.

'Okay?' Emera said, confused. Emera had been helping her over the last few weeks, specifically with practising with her magic now that it had been returning. Part of that involved her speaking into Emera's mind, so it wasn't something she would have thought to be a big deal, Azraelle supposed.

It was different with mortals, the ability to speak into their minds. While it was possible for a conversation to occur between her and another of her kind, as she had done with Thanatos, over any amount of space so long as the train of thought was maintained, that only worked because Thanatos had the ability to hold up his end. As Emera – and Xadrion, despite Hera's heritage – were mortal, the line didn't stay open. Az could use her magic to put thoughts and images into their minds, but it was nearly impossible for them to communicate in return.

'I kissed him, to help,' Az admitted. There was a moment of silence as Emera processed what she'd said before her gentle laughter echoed through the room.

'Azraelle,' Emera said, running a thumb over the back of her clasped hand. 'You are an immortal, and I am mortal. I am under no delusions as to what that means for the future of us together. I am also under no delusions that you wish to have only one lover. I can only imagine what it must be like to have lived as long as you have, and the loves you must have encountered. I do not request or expect to be the only recipient.'

'But you stopped seeing him when we started spending this time together.'

'That was my own decision that I made for my own reasons. You were a catalyst, Az, but not the reason I ended those interactions with Xadrion,' Emera said.

Azraelle kissed her then. Whatever she had done to deserve someone so understanding, Az would never know. But in those weeks, months now, since she had been cast from Mount Olympus, Emera had been a figure she desperately needed. While it was selfish what she took from Emera, and how little she was able to give back, unless Emera herself expressed the desire to stop, Az would be unable to keep herself from the woman.

'I don't know if I have ever experienced love in the way you mortals do.

I wonder if having all the time in existence laid out before you keeps you from feeling emotions as strongly as those with limited lifespans do,' Azraelle admitted. Her words weren't entirely true or false. She knew many of her kind who had tied their souls to another and loved so fiercely that their passion could have consumed worlds. Azraelle didn't think herself so cold but every time she contemplated the idea of admitting to love, that strange block in her mind seemed to tell her no.

'You haven't loved anyone?' Emera pulled back slightly to look at Az's expression.

'I… I think I have. There are some who I have cared for deeply and a lot I would have died for. But love, as the mortals do, I don't think so. I have never known someone who has sparked such an intensity in my emotions that I would do half the things I've witnessed mortals do for love,' Az answered.

She thought of the one person who had ever come close, the one man who lived even now in the Underworld whom Az had spent the centuries with. Hades' own son, Zagreus, had been part of Azraelle's life for as long as she could remember, their childhoods closer together than even Azraelle's and Thanatos' were. When they finally reached maturity, it had been a natural evolution for them to blow off the physical steam with each other. Nyx and Hades had supported the match, and Zagreus and Azraelle had spent centuries trying to establish just what it was between them. When everyone around them said it was love, for some reason neither had been capable of declaring it. Every time Az had thought she could finally do so, could finally lean in to the love Zagreus would have provided, that pain in her mind would stab so fiercely it would inflict an ice-like sensation through her veins. Zagreus also had never seemed able to declare it, and so they'd let the centuries pass with only the physical comfort spoken between them.

'That's sad,' Emera said. 'An eternity as you've lived and no one who you would love in that way. I don't believe living forever could come with a reduced capacity of love – that seems like an even greater sadness than not having found love. I'm sure you just haven't found your person yet.'

This was one of the greatest joys Azraelle could have ever been given in that moment – the presence of a friend who she was able to be transparent with. The fact that she didn't have to lie about who she was, that Emera had already known of the immortals from her interactions with Hera, allowed Az the comfort to be herself and voice the things that were eating away at her.

In the weeks since her and Emera had started spending time together, after Az was finally able to admit to Emera that she was not mortal, they'd spent a lot of time talking. Az didn't need her back healed anymore, so instead of that regular time dedicated to healing, they had been exploring each other's magic. Az was finding her footing with her own and even was helping Emera to enhance and refine hers. But in the time they had been doing that, the two had spent a considerable number of hours talking.

Azraelle would tell Emera most of her recent life, from her role within the Ravens to the boy she had saved from death. She'd told of being confined on Mount Olympus and the verdict that had been passed down on her. She'd told Emera of the time she'd managed to speak to her brother Thanatos. Az had even told Emera of her premonitions, and how the little girl had died at the hands of Deimos.

Since she'd told Xadrion of the little girl, and the way it had resolved after that, Azraelle had decided it wouldn't be a good idea to tell him about the next premonition she received. It had only happened a few days prior, and Az had been losing sleep over it since then, but she didn't want to face another death. Especially given she still wasn't powerful enough to do anything about it. She'd told Emera, and Emera had not expressed any judgement on her for deciding to keep it to herself.

'Now, come to bed,' Emera said, gently running her thumb over the furrow in Azraelle's brow.

Emera didn't stay the night; she never did.

And so, they fell back into their regular rhythm. Azraelle trained Xadrion and Ilyon in the morning, straight after her own workout. She was getting stronger again, the muscles that had withered during her imprisonment were developing once more. She'd begun to see the corded definition in her arms and shoulders, her legs once more feeling strong and sure beneath her. She felt her strength return with the weight, and a nearly insatiable appetite ravaged her every meal time. To feel strong once more in at least one facet of Azraelle's life had done wonders for the hopelessness she had come to feel.

After their session, Azraelle would leave the castle, ensuring that Xadrion didn't get it into his head to follow her again, and made the attempt to contact Thanatos once more. She'd signalled him once her magic was strong enough, yet still there was no contact from him. After she returned to the castle, she would dine with Emera and Ilyon, spend a few hours privately with Emera, and then she would sleep.

Things continued this way until autumn had fully settled across the kingdom and the ambassador's party from Gaeweth arrived, right when Ilyon had explained they would. Rhoas, Xadrion and Ilyon were the head of the receiving party as they pulled in with their carriages and horses, but a lot of the nobles from within the castle and even the castle workers lined the entrance to welcome the visitors. Azraelle had been granted a spot to stand only a few steps back from where the royal family stood. Rhoas had made such a show of bringing Azraelle into his immediate trusted circle that, after the few months that had passed, the people of Fennhall had stopped being surprised to see her by the sides of the king at dinners, or walking the halls with the princes and Emera. Now, she stood nearly in line with the royal family to receive noble diplomats from their neighbouring kingdom.

The arriving party was fairly large in size. There were probably twenty to thirty people who travelled with them, ranging from what must have been the favoured workers of the travelling nobles, all the way through to the nobles themselves. Azraelle tried to pay attention, but the breath felt like it had been punched from her the moment the princess Romina climbed from her carriage.

Azraelle had never seen a more beautiful woman in all the years she'd lived. Romina wore an immaculate white gown, with a gold bodice. Her hair was golden brown, smooth and glistening in the afternoon sun. A red sash was pinned to the shoulder of her dress and curved her body to create a contrast of colour to her outfit, and she moved as if she was the very embodiment of grace.

Romina's gaze locked straight on Xadrion, and she'd rather have taken a sword to her chest than be forced to see the way their eyes met. Azraelle knew she had no right to think that. This princess was exactly who Xadrion was supposed to exist for. He was the crowned prince to this kingdom and Romina was the princess to another. Their union would be celebrated by both kingdoms as a blessed day in both their histories.

Still, Azraelle wanted desperately to punch *anything* in that moment.

As soon as the party, the remainder of which Azraelle barely noticed, were inside the castle walls and being seen to, Azraelle slipped away as fast as she could. With the returning of her magic, she'd found it easier to play with the shadows and had begun to experiment with moving unnoticed once more. It hadn't been highly successful as of yet, but she kept trying.

Azraelle found herself alone in the barracks knowing she wouldn't be discovered for some time there. Lessons were done for the day, and most of the castle would be partaking in the celebratory feast for the arriving party. There was no one around to watch her as she took up a position in front of one of the training dummy's, no weapons in hand, and began to attempt to beat the crap out of the inanimate object.

Yes, Azraelle was facing an unprecedented event in her life that she never thought she'd have to face. She was estranged from her kind, both familiar and Raven alike, with no wings and barely any magic to her name. She'd been exiled from the immortal realms, the threat of death keeping her from returning. Yet despite all of that, Azraelle was usually in much better control of her emotions.

In this mortal realm, surrounded by these people, there were just *so many feelings*. Having to face any of them was enough to have her considering risking a return to the immortal realms as soon as she was strong enough, guilty verdict overturned or not.

'What did that dummy ever do to you?' came a voice from behind her. Unfamiliar, confident and teasing.

Azraelle whirled to see a single man standing nearby, leaning casually against one of the posts in the centre of the building. He looked older than Azraelle by mortal standards, maybe in his early thirties, but there was something in his eyes reminiscent of a much older soul. He carried a sword in a scabbard at his hip and wore a decadent set of heavy armour. His hair was wild and blonde as it framed his face, kept out of his eyes by a thin elastic band.

'It looked at me wrong,' Azraelle replied, to which the man in front of her gave a genuine laugh.

'Very well, then. I'm sure it deserves it,' the man said. 'The name's Tolemus.' Tolemus approached where Azraelle was standing and pushed his hand out between them. Azraelle clasped his hand and gave it a firm shake.

'Azraelle. You're with the party from Gaeweth?'

'Commander general of the armed forces for Gaeweth. Kind of a nothing title during peace times,' Tolemus responded.

'I wouldn't call commander general a nothing title,' Azraelle responded. She'd seen the level of responsibility Gabe – Thesadel's commander general – had placed upon him. For Tolemus to share the same responsibility must have taken serious commitment on his part.

It was enough information for Az to identify the man in front of her. Ilyon had non-stop talked about Tolemus when he'd discovered he would be part of the group coming to visit Fennhall. He was a man of legend, had led Gaeweth to victory in a war against their neighbouring kingdom Luzia five years ago that many had thought they were doomed to lose.

'High praise, coming from the woman who trains the princes of Thesadel,' Tolemus said.

'You've heard of me?' Azraelle asked before she could stop herself.

'It took all of five steps inside this castle for the workers to note your absence, and not long after for them to eagerly tell me the stories of you beating prince Xadrion to his ass when I asked,' Tolemus said.

Azraelle grinned, the smile feeling foreign on her face after the last few months. Tolemus brought out her desire to laugh, much in the same way that Ilyon did. Already, she felt like she would get along very well with this foreign general – very well indeed.

'I suppose my reputation precedes me,' Az remarked. 'Don't believe everything you hear.'

'So you aren't a witch?'

Az smirked, the rumour one she had herself heard. She'd never done magic in front of anyone, but after the first day when she had awoken and intruded upon the ceremony, taking out a decent portion of the guards present, there had been no stopping the rumours spreading about her, no matter how accepting the castle now was of her presence.

'Well,' Azraelle drawled, 'I never said that.' It wasn't exactly the truth, but still, not outright denying her magical abilities, even though jokingly, felt liberating.

Tolemus unbuckled his scabbard, looping it over a nearby bench. He peeled the heavy armour from his body, leaving a simple outfit much the same as what Az was wearing – a tunic and pants. Darlene had tried dressing her in a gown that morning for the reception, but Az didn't see the point in pretending to be some lady in their court. She would never be that.

'Care to take me on?' Tolemus asked. He rolled his neck, audible pops coming from the action, and stretched his arms out in front of him. 'I could use some movement after those tireless days of travel.'

'Sure.' She'd vented most of her frustration on the dummy by that point anyway; surely, she'd be able to focus enough on pulling her punches now that she'd calmed down. Plus, she genuinely enjoyed fighting. It was one of the main things she missed about the Ravens. Their training together had always been full out, she'd never had to keep herself in check for fear of hurting any of them. Since being in the mortal realm, Azraelle hadn't had the chance to really push herself.

They fought with their fists and their feet, and it took all of two seconds for Azraelle to realise she was facing a different sort of opponent. Where Xadrion and Ilyon were still learning to keep up with her, Tolemus' speed and strength came significantly closer to matching Azraelle's.

He dodged her tentative punches as if she were moving at a snail's pace, and as she pushed herself faster, he somehow managed to keep pace.

'Show me what you can really do, Azraelle,' Tolemus goaded, throwing a combination of punches in her direction. She dodged smoothly, all except the final move that knocked her straight across the jaw. Azraelle reeled, surprised.

Xadrion had broken through her defences once, when she was falling into a premonition, but that didn't hurt even half as much as Tolemus' punch did. He was *strong*. Azraelle whipped back into a defensive stance and allowed a true smile to spread across her features. Yes, this was exactly what she needed. However it was possible, Tolemus was not someone she had to hold back with.

Azraelle let herself loose, unleashing the speed and strength she had kept tied down for nearly three months now. She let herself throw her all into her punches, Tolemus successfully dodging most of them. She landed a few solid hits, but where she'd expected it to knock him out cold, Tolemus simply refocused back into a defensive stance and came back at her.

Tolemus was grinning, much the same as Azraelle was. They must have looked absolutely wild, the manic glint in each of their eyes mirroring perfectly as they tussled in the dirt, the grins only increasing each time one of them managed to land a hit. Az didn't know how she knew it, maybe it was the grin that told her, but she knew that Tolemus was getting as much relief out of this mock fight as she was.

She had no idea how long they fought for, but at some point, Tolemus simply stopped fighting and collapsed to the ground, exhausted. Azraelle followed suit, laying on her back on the dirt floor beside him. She glanced sideways at him, found him looking at her with that distinct manic energy behind his eyes, and simultaneously they both fell into laughter.

They would have looked a mess. She could feel where Tolemus had knocked her successfully and saw evidence of her own hits marked as bruises over Tolemus' jaw and arms. They were both breathing heavily, gasping for breath between their laughter, and ended up coated in dirt as they rolled amongst it. Az had not felt this carefree in… ever, maybe.

'Well,' Tolemus said, once their laughter had finally died down. 'I suppose my first question for you is, what is a goddess like you doing teaching some mortal princes how to fight?'

Azraelle looked at him, really looked at him as he asked her that question. He'd pieced it together, quickly, which meant Tolemus had some previous knowledge of her kind. He knew that there was no way her strength and speed was that of a mortal. And Az could tell that Tolemus' strength and speed was made of the same stuff that hers was. He didn't seem completely like her, but perhaps closer to her kind than to any mortal she'd met.

'Just wasting time, I suppose,' Azraelle answered. 'And what of you? You clearly aren't mortal, not fully anyway. What brings you to being a commander general?'

'I am mortal, in all the ways that count. Not like you enough to be granted access to your realms, but enough like you that I stand out amongst the mortals. Demi-god, my grandmother referred to it as,' Tolemus answered.

'On your mother's side, or your father's?'

'My father's. My mother was mortal, but I couldn't tell you much of her. Grandmother only told me stories of my father, Achilles,' Tolemus answered.

Interesting. She'd heard the name. He was dead now; Azraelle had heard of him, but not of the woman who had sired him a child. And Tolemus' grandmother would be none other than Thetis – goddess of Water – a distant sister to the Titan rulers, Cronus and Rhea. Thetis was older even than the rulers of the immortal realms, Zeus included.

'Where is your grandmother now?' Azraelle asked.

'She died, a few years ago,' Tolemus answered.

Dead. Did Tolemus know that there was always the chance for his grandmother to return? With the gods, death was rarely permanent. Usually, it involved a period of time of regeneration before they could return to their physical bodies. In mortal years, the regeneration time could span centuries. But when you were immortal, what did it matter when a few hundred years were lost here and there?

In the rare occasion that it was permanent, it was hard to predict why. Destiny had its hand in that, Az assumed.

'The mortals here, they don't really know about me,' Azraelle said, tentatively.

'I see no harm in me keeping that secret.' Yes, Azraelle decided, she really liked him. Tolemus felt trustworthy. 'Have you expended enough of whatever got you so pent up?'

'I believe so. Let's go join the festivities,' Azraelle said. Tolemus hoisted his gear in his arms and Azraelle took some to help him carry it rather than have to put it all back on.

Together, they left the barracks and walked back to the castle. They stopped at the guest rooms long enough for him to drop his gear off and for both of them to freshen up before they went to the main hall. Azraelle had looked at their appearance in a mirror in Tolemus' rooms and knew they would be catching attention when they joined the celebrations, no matter how well they cleaned up. Bruises lined both their faces but they remained smiling, despite the pain that was beginning to rear itself across her face, and surely Tolemus' as well.

They entered together and Azraelle found herself overwhelmed at once with the sounds from within the main hall. Tables had been lined out to accommodate both the residents of the Fennhall castle, as well as all those who had travelled with the Gaeweth party. Two seats had been notably left absent on the table that held the royal members of both kingdoms, clearly intended for Azraelle and Tolemus.

Eyes turned to them as they moved through the room, glancing between both their faces and noting the bruises that coated both. Curiosity burned behind the gazes that watched them.

From the main table, Xadrion looked as she entered with Tolemus. She was smiling, genuinely, for the first time in a long time, but at the flash of emotion that swept Xadrion's features, her smile faltered.

Princess Romina sat beside him; a hand casually placed upon Xadrion's elbow as she had been laughing at something he'd said. Rhoas and the man Azraelle assumed to be the ambassador sat opposite Xadrion and Romina, while Ilyon sat on the other side of his brother with Emera by his side. The two empty spaces sat across from Ilyon and Emera. Azraelle held no title within this kingdom that should have ever granted her that privilege. Despite Rhoas knowing who she was, there was no expectation for him to show any deference to her, certainly not in his own court. Yet he'd begun making space for her in these small ways, like the position he'd granted just behind them at the welcoming line earlier that day.

'Here they are!' Rhoas said gleefully, as Tolemus and Azraelle approached, sliding into their seats. The main course was already well under way and a plate was quickly placed in front of them filled with food.

Emera leant back in her chair, raising a single eyebrow at the bruises that coated their faces, while Ilyon sat grinning like a fool opposite them.

'Finally meet your match, huh, Az?' Ilyon joked.

'Close enough,' Az retorted.

Romina looked at Tolemus with a look of distaste clear on her features. Not a fighter, then. Xadrion had become impassive in his expression but his eyes never left Azraelle. She could see his anger seething beneath the cold features of his face, could feel the heat emanating from him. Az had learned the scent of his anger over the last few months, had learned how to pinpoint the exact moment it flared as it filled all of her heightened senses, and in that moment, Xadrion was struggling. So mortal and yet his anger rivalled even the most intense she had been exposed to over the eons. It made her wonder... but no, any power he had should have presented by that point.

'This looks delicious,' Tolemus said before he began shovelling the food into his mouth. Ungraciously so.

Azraelle let the conversation move along without feeling too much like participating in it, digging into her own plate of food ravenously. Ilyon took immediately to quizzing Tolemus on any and everything he could think to ask while Xadrion remained tensely seated. Romina managed to retain some form of contact with Xadrion through the dinner while the ambassador and Rhoas remained deep in conversation about civilities between their kingdoms.

As Azraelle shovelled food into her own mouth, the pain of the hits finally began to settle in and she found herself wincing with each bite. Beneath the table, she felt Emera's foot gently nudge her own.

'So,' Romina said, her gaze finally shifting from Xadrion long enough to take note of Azraelle. 'You are a commander of Thesadel?' Azraelle couldn't stop the laugh that escaped her as she thought of herself as a mortal commander and shook her head.

'Gods, no,' she replied, slipping the mortal language into her speech.

'Then why do you fight?' Romina asked.

'What else might I do with my time?' Az asked, curious to the direction of her questioning.

'As a lady, do you not aim to learn more homely skills, for when you marry?' Romina asked.

'I don't think *Lady* Azraelle is the marrying sort,' Xadrion interjected, throwing a mocking grin in Az's direction.

'But who will provide your protection if you do not marry?' Romina asked, her eyebrows pulled together in confusion at Xadrion's words.

'I believe, my princess, that is the reason as to why Azraelle fights. Why marry when she can defend herself?' Xadrion said. The words were harmless, but the mocking in Xadrion's tone grated her anger.

Overwhelmingly, Azraelle got the urge to punch Xadrion in his fucking smug face.

How dare he mock her at that table in front of these strangers. Her life was not his to judge, and yet it seemed she kept finding herself on the receiving end of that judgement. Whether he was attacking her for not fighting for that little girl or referring to her as a lady with that annoyingly smug tone that mocked every way in which she was not.

'I suppose I'm just not the kind to settle for another's company,' Azraelle quipped. 'If I were to ever marry it would have to be a very special *person* to make me wish to.' She'd emphasised person, not man, as she intentionally and noticeably shifted her gaze to Emera. Cruel, it was so cruel. Emera would know she didn't actually mean to suggest that was the nature of their relationship but Xadrion didn't know that. Azraelle was more than content to let him think otherwise.

Romina did not seem impressed with Azraelle's answers. Tolemus, however, broke the tension with a laugh. He lifted his glass in front of him in a cheer.

'To finding love,' Tolemus declared. Not quite the message she'd been going for, but if it helped move the conversation along, she was glad for it. Tolemus gave a reassuring pat to the top of Azraelle's hand, a move that Xadrion watched like a hawk, and slowly the table moved on to conversation that didn't centre around Azraelle and her potential marrying capabilities.

Still, as the dinner progressed, Azraelle's anger refused to die down. She was pissed at Xadrion for mocking her that way, especially as it seemed like an attempt for him to make clear that he was seeking Romina's favour by doing so. Deafening loneliness coursed through her. Had she really isolated herself so much that she was to serve as a punching bag to bring two people closer together?

For the remainder of the feast, every time Xadrion and Romina exchanged flirty commentary or touches, Tolemus made a pointed move to make some sort of physical contact with Azraelle. Not for a moment did she believe it was because he had any interest toward her.

'I can practically see the sexual tension between you and that delicious, crowned prince over there,' Tolemus whispered, leaning so his lips were awfully close to Az's ear. His breath tickled her and she made a show of giggling and swatting at his shoulder.

'Don't be ridiculous,' Az said between giggles. The scent Azraelle had likened so much to a storm brewing filled her nostrils, Xadrion's anger building with each moment.

'I've seen the tactics of war many times over my lifetime, my dear Azraelle,' Tolemus whispered. 'Love is much the same thing. Let me help you put on a show.'

And for whatever reason, Azraelle let him. They made a grand display of laughing at each other's jokes, though in fairness Tolemus was exceptionally funny. She allowed him to continue with his casual touches and feigned whispers. By the end of the night, Xadrion looked like he was absolutely livid, Azraelle's senses overwhelmed with the storming presence of his rage.

To top it off, Azraelle allowed Tolemus to walk her back to the room, leaving earlier than the others at the table did. As they stood, Tolemus took her hand and strolled casually with her from the main hall.

As soon as the doors closed behind them, they both found themselves overcome with laughter once more.

'That was too much fun,' Tolemus said.

'Thank you,' Az agreed. 'I mean, I think my feelings towards Xadrion border more closely toward complete and total irritation, but it was fun to play that game.'

'Darling,' Tolemus said as they approached her door, 'it's a truly short step from irritation to love.'

FOURTEEN

AZRAELLE

Darlene arrived shortly after to help her bathe and dress for sleep. She took the time to wash through Az's hair, remarking about the level of dirt she had managed to roll in that day before she brushed and braided it.

When Azraelle finally found herself lying in bed waiting for sleep to take her, she found herself unable to relax. How he managed to do it in nearly every interaction they shared, who knew, but Xadrion had left her feeling full of rage as she tried to sleep.

Instead, she spent half an hour pacing her room until she finally decided that she was not going to stand for it. She pulled a more appropriate shirt and pants on and set off through the hallways of the castle. She knew which rooms were Xadrion's from her early walks with Emera, where she had detailed the layout of the castle's hallways and rooms.

From beneath his door, she could see flickering light, as if there were still candles lit. Azraelle knocked once to signal her presence before she pushed the unlocked door open in her anger and strolled in. Xadrion was nowhere to be seen in the first room of his personal suite. The candles were still lit, as if he'd went to bed and forgotten to put them out.

The room was messy, every surface visible covered with stacks of papers and thick bound books. Azraelle immediately started to doubt her actions. If he'd gone to sleep then surely she was standing in a room that she didn't belong. If someone caught her here it would give a very distinct impression of snooping, or of her sneaking out of his rooms in the middle of the night.

A faint noise came from the closed door of Xadrion's bedroom. Azraelle was caught between the feeling that she should leave and the desire she had to investigate that noise. In the end she ended up walking closer, her interest piqued. The overwhelming smell of distant rain and a budding storm had

Azraelle drawing closer, the scents she associated so strongly with Xadrion now captivating her attention.

Since that first day, there had been something deep inside Azraelle that responded to his presence and that moment was no different. She'd been doing her best to not look at him too often, to not let herself feel his heat, for fear of the response he seemed to strike within her. *Something* deep down in her remained ever aware of his presence, his very presence summoning a feeling inside that she had never and could never allow herself to feel.

Everything in Azraelle told her to turn around and not investigate further, knowing what the noises she was hearing meant beyond that door. Despite everything she told herself, she couldn't shake the curiosity that burned through her at the very idea of Xadrion's pleasure. She strained her hearing to try to detect another voice, but the only noise that could be heard was the deep tone of Xadrion's. As she got close enough to his bedroom door, she began to make out the noises more clearly.

He was *moaning*. No other voice filled the room but Xadrion's alone, and yet that was definitely moaning. Now, she knew she really shouldn't have been there. Involuntarily, her mind displayed an image of what exactly he would have looked like on the other side of that door – sprawled in his bed with one hand firmly clasping himself, his strokes she imagined were hard and fast.

Azraelle's own arousal hit her like a wave of butterflies to her lower stomach. The thought of him touching himself like that caused an immediate reaction within her. Her mind drifted back to the outline she'd seen against his pants the morning they'd awoken in the cabin and the feeling of it pressed against her.

'Fuck,' Xadrion said, his voice barely audible from behind the closed door.

The idea of him taking his pleasure into his own hands had Azraelle aching to be inside that room.

'Az,' Xadrion moaned. Azraelle stopped breathing. He was saying her name… thinking of her as he touched himself.

Azraelle felt him in her mind first before she could even peer into his. Her experience with communicating mentally kept her usually from slipping into minds she didn't intend to enter, but Xadrion wasn't practiced in the restraint, should not have even been able to do it. But with her thoughts solely on him, he walked straight past any and all of her defences until he was deep into her subconscious.

He'd been exclusively on her mind and his mentioning of her name indicated to her that she was on his, but nothing should have come from it – not if he were mortal.

Azraelle?

Thinking of me, are you? she taunted, trying to cover for the surprise she felt at Xadrion's ability to link his mind to her own.

Is that why I can feel you?

From inside the room, his moans didn't cease. She could hear his breathing increase in speed, building him to that final moment.

Azraelle took her own steps into Xadrion's subconscious, trailing her mental nails along the barriers of his mind. She was gentle, not wanting to do any damage, but wanting instead to put him into overdrive with his senses.

Fuck, Az. How can I feel you right now? Where are you? Xadrion's breath caught inside the room, a guttural moan escaping him.

In my rooms, she lied. *If you want me gone, all you have to do is stop thinking of me.*

Impossible.

Let me see, Xay, Azraelle whispered, sending a gentle prod into his own mind to show him where to focus his energy. He wouldn't know how to control it, not when it was clearly his first time communicating that way. It took him a moment but with her prodding, Xadrion managed to open the connection between his eyes and her mind.

At once, she could see the surroundings inside his room. Xadrion's eyes looked down at himself and it took everything in Azraelle to stifle her own moan at the sight. She shifted so her weight was leaning against Xadrion's bedroom door and closed her eyes to better focus on the image. The way his hand moved, the hard length it stroked, had Azraelle wanting to touch herself.

Want to see me finish, Az?

Please.

Azraelle dragged her fingertips inside his mind again and through their shared vision, she watched, and heard, as every muscle in Xadrion's body tensed as he gave a final few pumps of his hand. He came hard, the result glistening against the sheets and across his hips, but Azraelle couldn't take her mind's eye from the length held in Xadrion's hand.

And then, she moaned. Aloud. Chaos help her. Their shared eyesight showed him looking toward his bedroom door where Az knew she was standing on the other side. As Xadrion pushed himself from his position on the bed, Azraelle panicked. She turned and ran and didn't stop until she was safely behind her own closed doors, not located too far from Xadrion's.

You should have come in, Az.

I don't know what you're talking about, Az replied, shooting him an image of her safely tucked into her rooms. He wouldn't believe her, but she needed to keep the distance.

I could come give you a hand, Xadrion offered.

She wanted to have him come to her. She wanted to have that time with him under the cover of darkness. Everything in her screamed at her to accept the offer, but to accept him into her bed in that way felt somehow dangerous. She knew if she started down that path there would be no way she would be able to stop. It was already so hard to stop.

I don't want that, Azraelle replied.

Lies. Xadrion's voice was low, a sensual purr straight into the core of her thoughts. *I can see your desires as easily as my own right now.*

While it was Xadrion's first time communicating into someone's mind, he'd gotten the hang of it quickly and Azraelle knew he wasn't lying when he said he could see her desires. She'd felt him in her own mind, easily adapting to the location and taking taunting looks into parts of her she never wanted to show him.

It's not specific to you, Azraelle lied. Xadrion showed her an image of him in the bed at the cabin all those weeks ago, an image specifically from her perspective, with a heavy focus on looking at the form beneath his pants. He was pulling moments from her memory, throwing it back at her as evidence.

Stop me if you want. You just have to stop thinking about me, right? Xadrion teased.

He was right and the smugness she felt emanating from him told Az he knew he was. To break the connection Azraelle just had to make herself think about anything else. But she couldn't, not with her arousal still beating strongly between her legs and her mind's eye showing the image of him in his bed from moments before, saying her name.

I can torment you right back, Azraelle said. She walked into her bedroom and took hold of one of the full-length mirrors, easily picking it up and replacing it so that it reflected her as she took a position on top of the bed. Maybe she had lost her mind, but she wanted the power in that moment and wanted him to know it.

Slowly, she peeled off her shirt and threw it to the ground beneath the bed. On her knees, she emphasised the arch in her back as she pulled her pants from her hips, dropping to her side to allow her to remove the rest entirely. When she was naked, with only the pendant around her neck, she looked herself in the mirror.

I'm on my way, Xadrion said.

No, you have to stay right there. Azraelle gave a warning push to his mind, making him feel the heaviness of her power. If she decided to, she'd be able to freeze him in place. It was part of being able to infiltrate someone's mind but was not a pleasant experience for the person being frozen. Her fingers dragging through his mind had been for a sensual purpose, but the skill of communicating mind to mind had a long history of being abused for torture.

Xadrion didn't make her have to apply more pressure; instead, he submitted to staying in his room, but Azraelle got the image of his hand taking hold of himself once more.

Watch, Az ordered. Looking into the mirror, to give Xadrion's mind's eye the best view he could have, Azraelle slowly traced her fingers from her own chin, down her neck, until she ran lightly over one of her nipples. She pinched it, first gentle and then much harder, her own noises of pleasure filling the otherwise silent room.

Let me come touch you, Xadrion pleaded. She was enjoying his torment too much to allow him to come to her rooms, as much as she wanted that herself. But there was another way she could give him what he requested. In the place he was occupying in her mind, Az took hold of him and signalled where he needed to go.

She shouldn't have been showing him the uses of communicating mind to mind, but her arousal kept her from thinking rationally about any of it. She gestured internally at the part he would need to take control of – the part that would allow him control of her hand that traced her body.

It was crossing the line to the knowledge of how to abuse the power and it was giving Xadrion more control over her than she'd ever allowed anyone to have in the past. But he was inexperienced and if it went wrong, Azraelle was sure she'd be able to override him and push him from her thoughts.

He took to the knowledge easily, his own mental hands slipping over the controls Azraelle had demonstrated to him. Within a moment, her hand was moving again but not because she'd willed it.

How is this even possible? Xadrion asked as he moved her fingers back to one nipple and then the other. It was her hands, and it had felt good when she had done it before giving him control, but now that it was Xadrion controlling her hands, another level of pleasure piled on.

I can explain it to you, or you can keep touching me.

In answer, Xadrion lowered her hand further, seeking that bundle of nerves between her legs. He toyed with her enough that she nearly attempted to throw him out of control just to allow herself the pleasure, but when she came closest to breaking, he finally moved her fingers in to circle lightly over the sensitive apex between her thighs.

Azraelle closed her eyes, leaning her head back in pleasure.

No, Az, keep them open. Watch for me.

Az smirked but opened her eyes and recentred them on herself in the mirror. She was watching him in his own rooms, his physical hands stroking himself firmly, but she was also watching herself through his eyes. The way she knelt with a pillow between her legs and her fingers circling. She ground on the pillow, desperate for any sort of friction, while Xadrion led her other hand up to toy with her nipple.

All of her senses were overwhelmed. The exposure of having someone in her mind with free reign was a vulnerable place to be in, and it left Az feeling particularly sensitive – physically and mentally. Xadrion was adapting to the nuances of being in her mind and in much the same way she had done, he trailed his fingertips down the barriers of her senses.

It wasn't long before the combination of her grinding on the pillow, her fingers completing their circling motion and her nipple being teased while she watched herself in the mirror had her pleasure peaking.

I can feel it building, Xadrion whispered.

I'm close.

Let me see, Az. Watch yourself as I make you finish.

And so, she did. As her lower abdomen clenched, her legs seized and her toes curled. She watched herself in the mirror as the ripples overtook her. As her orgasm finally rushed her, shattering any control she still had over her mind and giving it all to Xadrion, his cry also rang as he finished again.

Her magic, as much as it had ever flickered during these moments with Emera – and even with lovers from her past – had never done anything compared to that moment her orgasm took her. It flared up, the well flooding with her power as it came rushing back to her. Usually, her own hand did nothing to regenerate her magic but in the moment with their minds connected, Xadrion had allowed her that deeper connection that was required. Az marvelled at how only his mental presence was capable of such a thing.

Xadrion had to have felt it. There was no way he'd been occupying that many corners of her mind and not felt the increase of her power. In response to the tendrils of her power once more spearing through her – not at full capacity but definitely more than it had been since she'd woken – something else within her mind responded.

From where Xadrion was steadying himself mentally, something crackled within her. Pure energy bolts reached out to play with her tendrils of power, the two branches of energy leaping amongst each other.

What is that? came Xadrion's voice.

Seems you have some power of your own, Azraelle replied, abruptly. *Good night, Xadrion.*

And with that, Azraelle took advantage of his distraction and shoved him so completely from her mind that his voice was silenced immediately. She scanned her mind, ensuring that there was no sign of him hiding deep in the corners of her subconscious before she succumbed to her panic.

That energy crackling in her mind may as well have been a whip to her face. It was so familiar, so recognisable to her that seeing it within her playing with her own darkness had Azraelle reeling. That energy was pure lightning.

There was only one family she'd ever seen who had power that harnessed energy that way, in that exact same form as what she'd just felt in the deepest centre of her mind. That was Zeus' magic.

Why the fuck did Xadrion have Zeus' power?

Fifteen

Xadrion

Xadrion was left with an emptiness inside him. Only a moment prior he'd had Azraelle's vision playing behind his eyes, had both his pleasure and her pleasure racing through him and had been watching the thoughts she processed within her own mind. The moment she'd finished, Xadrion had been overwhelmed with the feeling of her power sweeping through her mind, encompassing everything that he felt he was.

Something had come from him in that moment of release as well. Where Azraelle's magic looked like tendrils of darkness that swarmed through her mind and senses, Xadrion had felt crackling energy stem from him and rush to work its way through her darkness. The moment Azraelle had detected the crackling energy, he sensed pure panic racing through her mind.

Xadrion could have found out why if he'd been given even a moment to stay. However it was that he was able to link his mind with Azraelle's, he didn't understand, but he'd felt like he knew exactly how to pry deeper. She'd shown him the pathways and as soon as she'd pointed him in the right direction, it had been as easy as breathing to think about what he wanted to do and to have it happen.

But Az hadn't let him stay long enough to investigate her panic. And so, he all at once found himself alone in his bedroom, his now limp dick still held in his hand, and a complete absence of Azraelle's presence. Xadrion could see the pathway back to her mind, could see the exact steps he'd need to take to be taken back there, but where he'd previously walked straight through, there now stood an impenetrable wall.

Seems you have some power of your own, Azraelle had said to him before shoving him out. It didn't seem real, but the feeling of that energy felt like it had born from him. However he'd accessed it, however that was even

130

possible, he'd had some power in that moment. Xadrion tried to reach in and find it once more but found no energy responding to him.

He needed to talk to her – needed to get answers to the questions that were endlessly circling his thoughts – but she'd specifically pushed him out. Xadrion knew he would not even get her in his sight again tonight, not without her inviting him herself.

He didn't sleep well after that. He was caught between two main rivers of thought. The first was his confusion at what had occurred, the power that had emanated from him and how he had managed to communicate with Azraelle through his mind. The second, which occupied far more of his night, had him constantly thinking back on what it had felt like to be as entwined with Azraelle as they had been. Seeing her naked form through that mirror's reflection, watching as her own hands traced those parts of her body that he had only imagined up until that point. Hearing those fucking noises that she made when she was feeling pleasure, pleasure he specifically was giving to her.

Xadrion had felt some form of tension when he was around her nearly from their very first conversation and being in her mind that night told him that she'd felt similar things. It was no surprise it translated across to physical tension when given the opportunity. Yet, Azraelle kept throwing up blocks to get in their way, and Xadrion wondered if that was the first and last time Azraelle was ever going to cross that boundary with him. Anger flared briefly at the thought and yet for the first time in months, his anger felt appeased.

In the moments where Xadrion did manage to get to sleep, he found himself dreaming of a time he long thought he'd forgotten.

Once upon a time, came his mother's voice in his dream. The image that played across the dream was distorted, no distinct images coming through. He saw swirls of white and black, and when his mother's voice spoke, he saw tinges of colour splash across his vision.

There lived a woman who had beauty unmatched by any around her. This woman had lived a long and adventurous life but there was one thing she never felt like she would truly accomplish. She never thought she would fall in love.

Not another love story, Mother. That was Xadrion, interrupting Hera's story. He was young and much preferred the adventure stories.

Yes, another love story. Because, his mother continued, *you have to have the balance. I've told you endless hours of stories to do with Erebus' bravery, and Chiron's victories, but I have not told you of one of the most powerful warriors to exist. Because this love story involves more than just the beautiful woman, but also a general of the Underworld.*

A general? Xadrion's childish voice asked.

His name was Thanatos, and her name was Aphrodite. And this is the story of how their love changed the world.

Hera's voice faded away, leaving Xadrion alone in his dreamscape with nothing but swirling white and black to surround him. Then, all at once, the dream shifted and he was watching his memory from the day he'd followed Azraelle into the woods. Xadrion was watching from above, observing the moment Azraelle had stepped onto her toes and given him that first kiss. That was the moment she'd revealed her wings to him.

Where in Chaos are you, Thanatos?

Azraelle's voice echoed throughout the dream – the words she'd spoken when Xadrion still remained hidden.

Xadrion sat upright in his bed, struggling to get enough air down. The name had sounded so familiar when he'd first heard Azraelle say it but he hadn't been able to place it. The dream reminded him where he had heard it – the tales Hera had told him as a child. After that first tale, he had demanded to hear more of Thanatos. He was described to be the very personification of Death and a loyal member of Hades of the Underworld's pantheon. When Aphrodite wanted to get away from her father, Zeus, she'd run away to the Underworld where she'd eventually met Thanatos.

There was a lot to their story that Xadrion couldn't remember after so many years, but finally he was able to place the name. Hera always spoke of her gods as if they were real, but since she'd died, Xadrion's father had not indulged in any religious conversation. It didn't seem like his father even believed in their existence, despite Hera's belief.

There was no way that the person Azraelle had been calling for could be the same Thanatos. There was no way the dreamworld of Hera's existed, not with its gods and wars and unbeatable powers. Yet, he'd seen so many things since they'd found Azraelle. So many things that would suggest a version of the world existed that Xadrion had no idea about. Maybe it wasn't such a stretch for the truth.

Azraelle had told Xadrion after he revealed himself that it was her brothers she was hoping would come for her. Was Thanatos one of those brothers? Were the crimes Azraelle was paying for her family far greater in size than Xadrion could ever have imagined?

Morning had come, only barely, and Xadrion wanted to find Azraelle and ask her every question that had come to his mind throughout the night. He sent a nudge through their shared connection, following the path that seemed now to be permanently exposed between their two minds, but found nothing but that hard wall blocking his view. She still would not talk to him.

Instead of forcing that confrontation, Xadrion drifted to the kitchens to get something to eat before he headed in the direction of his father's study. With visitors to their castle, his father would take to being more present in and around the throne room, as well as the other communal areas of the castle. Xadrion knew he would wake early to complete the required paperwork in his study before he did so.

Like clockwork, Xadrion found his father bent over some papers, scribbling away at whatever work was needed to be done.

'Morning, Xadrion. You're up early,' Rhoas said, when he looked to see Xadrion standing in the doorway. He gestured for Xadrion to come in and sit, which Xadrion did. Seated opposite his father, he found himself struggling to speak. There were so many questions he had, and he didn't know what his father knew to tell him. Surely Rhoas didn't know anything; what other reason would there be for him not to continue teaching Xadrion and Ilyon about the gods after Hera's death?

'What's on your mind, my son?' Rhoas prompted when Xadrion's silence stretched for too long. There were so many questions circling his mind that he was having a hard time figuring out where to start.

'Has there ever been any power within our bloodline?' Xadrion asked, resolving to just pick a question at random. Any answers at that point would be better than nothing. Rhoas looked at him intently, as if he were trying to gauge where the question had come from.

'Your mother had some abilities,' Rhoas admitted. 'Has something happened?'

'I... I don't know. I think last night I felt the beginnings of something,' Xadrion said. 'Could that have been from Mother?'

'What did it feel like?' Rhoas asked, cautiously.

'It was,' Xadrion began, then paused as he searched for the right way to describe it, 'like energy, pure and unfiltered. It felt like this current of energy sweeping through me. No, not sweeping through me... more like crackling.'

Rhoas frowned and let the room fall into silence. He looked concerned, as if that were the last thing he'd wanted to hear. Slowly, Rhoas folded the papers across his desk into a single pile. He stood and walked to his office door, opening it enough to give some command to the guard who was standing outside before returning to his seat and clasping his hands in front of him stiffly on the desk.

'I suppose I have some stories to tell you,' Rhoas finally said. 'But it involves Ilyon as well, so we must wait for him.'

Xadrion felt nerves settle into the pit of his stomach, uncertainty clouding every one of his thoughts. He had seen his father serious before, but the look that covered his face now was so unlike anything Xadrion had ever seen. His father looked scared.

Moments passed, and eventually the door cracked open. Ilyon entered, rustled from sleep. His clothes looked as if he'd thrown them on and his hair was roughly pulled back into a band to keep its mess contained. Ilyon looked at Xadrion with concern as he approached, taking the second seat on this side of the desk.

'What's going on?' Ilyon asked their father, who was looking tensely between his two sons.

'I have some information that I think is owed to you both,' Rhoas said. 'I have to preface this by saying, I genuinely wished and believed you two would never have to enter the world I have kept from you. But it appears the world has come knocking on our doorstep.'

'Father,' Ilyon said, his eyebrows pulling together in confusion. 'What are you talking about?'

'I have not been truthful about your mother, Hera,' Rhoas said.

'What do you mean?' Xadrion asked, sensing he was so close to some of those answers to the questions that had been dominating his thoughts.

'Xadrion has begun to display some magic tendencies,' Rhoas explained to Ilyon. 'You may have also, Ilyon, though I know I have not made you feel capable of saying anything to me if so. It comes from your mother. She was not who you remember her to be.'

'Where is this coming from?' Ilyon demanded, looking between Rhoas and Xadrion quickly.

'I know you were too young to remember, Ilyon, but your mother wanted you to know. I didn't think it was a good idea, but she insisted on telling you the stories of her people whenever she could. Xadrion, the stories she told you as you fell asleep, the stories of the gods and their lives, they were all true,' Rhoas said.

'What stories? What gods?' Ilyon said, his confusion turning into frustration. Xadrion wished he had patience to give to Ilyon in that moment, as he knew that Ilyon's memory would not have served to remember the stories Hera had once told them. But the answers were right in front of Xadrion now, only a breath away, and he didn't have the patience to lead Ilyon through to the same questions.

'Ilyon,' Xadrion said, placing a hand on his shoulder to focus him. 'Please, let him talk. Azraelle, is she one of them?'

It was the question that burned the most inside Xadrion's mind. While there were a thousand other things he wished to know, knowing what Azraelle truly was seemed like the most pressing to him. He'd seen her wings, felt the capabilities of her power and seen her fight. There was no way she was mortal, not a chance in this world or the next.

'Yes,' Rhoas admitted as he leant forward and clasped his hands together on the desk. 'I have spoken with her and confirmed it to be so, though I'd heard of her long before she ever came to our land. Hera knew Azraelle long ago and told me stories much the same way that she told you stories.'

'How could Mother have known Azraelle? Did they meet when Azraelle was a child before she was captured?' Ilyon interjected.

'She's not as young as she seems,' Xadrion pieced together. 'She's not mortal, right? If she's a god, she's as old as time itself. She wouldn't have been a child before her capture.'

'Not quite,' Rhoas said. 'As Hera tells it, the world began from Chaos. From Chaos was created five beings. They were Tartarus, Gaia, Eros, Erebus and Nyx. Tartarus and Gaia formed an extensive list of descendants from their union, while Erebus and Nyx did the same. Azraelle is a child of Nyx and Erebus.'

Chaos. The name he'd heard from Azraelle's own lips. The very being who stood at the head of the world, creator of who knew how many gods beneath. Azraelle had been so careful to only use the word when she thought no one was around or when it absently slipped her lips. Was she so ancient she had met the creator of everything?

'I've heard these names before, but I thought they were just empty gods that were worshipped,' Ilyon said quietly. His brow remained furrowed as Rhoas spoke, unable to make sense of what he was hearing.

'Not empty gods,' Rhoas said. 'They all very much exist. But what I have to tell you does not have to do with Azraelle, not entirely. I believe that much of her story should remain hers to share, if and when she chooses to share with you.'

'Where did Mother descend from?' Xadrion asked, desperately trying to organise the pieces he was being given.

'Hera, while older than Azraelle, actually is further removed from Chaos than Azraelle is. Azraelle represents the second generation through Nyx's line, but Hera came from Tartarus and Gaia's line. Her parents were Cronus and Rhea, said to have been the rulers of Mount Olympus for most of time, until they were overthrown by their son, Zeus,' Rhoas said.

'Zeus?' Xadrion said, disbelief at what he'd heard. Zeus had been a prominent figure in the stories his mother had told to him. In nearly every story, Zeus had been framed in a negative light, someone that most of the other gods had attempted to escape.

'This is basically where you two come in,' Rhoas said. 'Hera lived on Mount Olympus with Zeus, but there were some years where she was able to escape his presence and visit the mortal realm. Zeus had a wife, Demeter, who when he was preoccupied with her presence, Hera was able to visit. It was from these visits that you two were born.'

'You mean to tell me that a god came to our realm and chose you, a mortal king, to have children with?' Ilyon asked, disbelief clear in his expression.

'Exactly,' Rhoas said, a sadness in his eyes unlike anything Xadrion had ever seen in him before. Xadrion had been too young to remember much of how his father reacted after Hera's death but seeing the pain in his eyes now, Xadrion could tell he had never recovered from losing her. 'Or at least, mostly. That's how you came to be, Ilyon. Xadrion's story is a little different.'

'Different how?' Xadrion asked, finally beginning to feel hesitation in his search for answers. He didn't think he wanted to hear what Rhoas was preparing to say. Was there a point where he wouldn't be able to come back from the knowledge he was gaining?

'The magic that you felt, the current that swept through you,' Rhoas began, 'that's not Hera's magic. That's Zeus'.'

Xadrion's brows pulled together in confusion, not understanding the information he had heard. It didn't make sense. Nothing made sense.

'Why the fuck do I have Zeus' power?'

His mind was screaming at him, telling him that of course he knew how he had Zeus' power. He shut it down, not wanting to believe it, not wanting to give in to what his mind was telling him.

'The first time I met Hera, she was already pregnant with a child,' Rhoas said. Dread sunk deep into Xadrion's gut. 'She was pregnant with you. Hera had already had one child to Zeus, a girl who Hera had great concerns over. When she became pregnant once more, Hera sought to remove her baby from Zeus' grasp. She visited the realm and through fate, luck or chance, we met and fell in love. I offered to guard her child if she could get you to me. The story of how she did so is a long and messy one, but she succeeded.'

'Zeus is my father?' Xadrion asked, the information taking too long to sink in, the dread deep inside him building, bringing a fresh new bout of anger with it. Faintly, in the periphery of his senses, the sound of thunder cracked in the distance, and behind Rhoas, rain began to pelt against the stained-glass window.

'Yes,' Rhoas said. Xadrion could see Ilyon staring at him from the corner of his eye. He had no idea what to say or how to react. Zeus was his father. And that energy that had crackled through him last night was Zeus' power.

'So, I'm descended from a god?' Ilyon asked, breaking the silence. 'I'm a demi-god?'

'Yes. And you, Xadrion, you're descended from gods on either side. What form that will take for you is yet to be seen, but you are much the same as Azraelle is, though she has at least a few thousand years on you,' Rhoas said.

A few thousand years. At least. She was that old?

'I don't know what to say,' Xadrion admitted. The rain drops hit harder against the window, filling the room's silence.

'You should take some time to think things over,' Rhoas agreed. 'You can, of course, come back to me when you have any questions, and I will do my best to answer them. Azraelle may also be able to offer you both some help when it comes to helping you understand your power.'

'She knows of our mother?' Ilyon asked.

'She does,' Rhoas said. 'She pieced it together shortly after she woke. I would encourage you to seek her out for help. While she's been training you in physical combat, her talent with magic would also be of benefit to you both. Especially if your power is starting to come forward.'

Xadrion didn't know what to say. Ilyon was smiling, somehow ecstatic with all he had heard despite the fact that the very ground they walked on had been turned upside down. The idea that Azraelle knew information about Hera and hadn't told Xadrion or Ilyon made his chest tighten. It shouldn't have hurt so much to know that Azraelle hadn't told them the truth, and yet, it did.

'There is one thing I need you both to consider,' Rhoas said, tentatively. Suddenly, he seemed more nervous than before.

'There's more?' Xadrion said, tired from the information overload he had received.

'Azraelle may not respond well to the information that Zeus is your father,' Rhoas admitted.

'Why would she care?' Xadrion asked.

'Azraelle's story of being abducted for the last fifteen years is not false. She may have misconstrued certain details to you, but she was very much trapped and tortured,' Rhoas said.

'And that has to do with Zeus how?' Xadrion pushed.

'Zeus was the one who trapped her.'

SIXTEEN

XADRION

Zeus, his father, had been the one to torture Azraelle. The one who had taken those magnificent wings of hers and torn them from her body. The power that flowed through him, the crackling energy, had been responsible for the torment of the woman he'd been pleasing only hours before.

Suddenly and all at once, Xadrion understood the abrupt ending to their night. The way Azraelle had reacted when that energy had sizzled between their minds, twirling amongst her own tendrils of darkness, had been a reaction of pure panic. She'd thrown him from her mind in such a rush that he hadn't been able to see much else, but her panic had rung through loud and clear.

'Zeus tortured her for fifteen years – to what end?' Xadrion asked his father – no, not his father. He was no heir of Rhoas, should never have been given the title of crowned prince and yet, Rhoas had given it to him. Had taken it from Ilyon, his natural son, and passed it to Xadrion as if he weren't some other man's child.

'I once told you it was to pay for her family's crimes,' Rhoas said. 'It's not a false version of the story. Her brother, Hypnos, was who Hera turned to when she was attempting to smuggle you out from Zeus' grasp. Hypnos helped, but Zeus detected him in the process. Hypnos managed to escape, which meant Azraelle's mother Nyx could protect him from Zeus' wrath. It started a war between the two families, one that had not advanced on either side until Azraelle was trapped.'

'How did Zeus trap her?' Xadrion asked.

'That is more her story to tell than mine, I'm afraid,' Rhoas said. 'I don't know the full extent of it as a lot of it happened after Hera... died.'

'And why has Zeus not come for me?'

'He believes you died in the attempt to smuggle you from him,' Rhoas admitted. 'He blames Azraelle's family for the death of his child. It was Hera's wish that you remain out of Zeus' sight, so the castle has been warded – which Emera maintains – to keep the eyes of the gods from seeing those within the castle walls. It's what has kept Azraelle safe while she's been here and kept the two of you from Zeus' knowledge.'

'I need to go,' Xadrion said, standing abruptly. His chair scraped back, and he felt he could barely walk from the confusion that swirled in his mind. 'I need some time.'

Rhoas let Xadrion go, while Ilyon remained seated. He would no doubt have more questions for Rhoas, but Xadrion needed to get out. He needed to find air that felt easier to breathe, to find a place where he could process everything that he had heard.

Xadrion didn't think it through, did not establish a plan that he could follow, simply arrived at the stables and prepared a horse. He'd grabbed a sword, as well as a bow and arrows from the barracks as he'd passed but made no other detours as he left the castle. Rain soaked through his clothes almost immediately and it didn't look to be stopping, but Xadrion pushed on. He rode for hours, not thinking too closely about the direction in which he was going.

His entire worldview was shattered.

Rhoas, who he had believed to be his father, was not. Gods, who he believed to be some fairy tales told to children at night-time, were real. Azraelle, the woman he'd assumed to be a lady who'd fallen upon their path by chance, was a god, or a goddess, Xadrion supposed. Zeus, the antagonist in every story his mother had ever told him, was his father, and the man who had tortured the woman he'd come to care about.

Azraelle was not letting him too close, so how much Xadrion may have developed those feelings for her, he didn't really know. But she was important to him. He had seen her pain, her vulnerability, and had been into the dark recesses of her mind. He had goaded her, tormented her for her decision to not fight for the little girl when one of her own family stood across from her. A person who also worked for his father, Xadrion pieced together, and who had been complicit in Azraelle's torture. But also, Azraelle's family, in some way.

Xadrion had fired that crackling energy deep into the corners of Azraelle's mind. It had happened without his control but when it did, it felt like a way that Xadrion could further connect the two of them. By binding their powers together in their minds, Xadrion felt closer to Azraelle than he ever had. To her, it had been a stark reminder of the energy that had once been used to torture her. For fifteen years, Rhoas had said. She'd been held by Zeus for fifteen years.

He may as well have tortured her himself.

Coming back to reality, Xadrion realised he had ridden further than he'd thought, so far that the old camping cabin path had appeared in front of him. He took it, travelling the final distance before dismounting and apologising to his horse who he had ridden the whole way through. Not hard, but it had still been a half day's travel to get to that cabin. He carefully unleashed the horse from its gear before tying it under shelter from the rain, near water and grass.

Xadrion walked into the cabin, stripped the weapons and sodden clothes from his body and climbed straight into the bed. The lack of sleep from the night before, coupled with the stress from that day, had him asleep nearly as soon as his head hit the pillow.

He didn't know how long he slept for, and no dream save for one bothered him. The dream was a door, with nothing else in sight. Knocking came from the other side, followed by a gentle, familiar voice calling his name. He knew the voice; he trusted the voice. Xadrion opened the door and was swept up in the same lovely white and black swirling from his dream with Hera. It swirled about his face and body. No other images bothered him as he slept.

Xadrion awoke when the windows showed nothing but darkness outside. The rain had stopped. He'd slept half the day, and still felt no better for it. Within a moment of being awake, Xadrion felt another presence and heard a slight rustling in the corner of the room.

'So,' Azraelle drawled, 'you give a girl an orgasm and then run off to the woods never to be heard from again?'

She'd come, had somehow found where he had run to and followed him. Xadrion remembered his dream, remembered the white swirling around him when he'd opened the door to that sweet knocking. He'd known the voice, known who it was requesting entrance. And he'd given it to her, giving her exactly what she needed to find where he had gone.

'What are you doing here, Azraelle?' Xadrion asked, pushing himself to a sitting position in the bed.

'Your father told me of the conversation he had with you this morning,' Azraelle replied. 'He said you'd taken off and had no idea where you may have gone to. I got worried when you didn't show up to training.' Xadrion remained silent. 'Ilyon showed up, had quite a lot to say about this newfound knowledge of his. Overly excited, that one. Not at all running off to the woods because of it.'

'The power, from last night,' Xadrion said.

Azraelle stood and walked to the bed. She'd been leaning against the dining table but now Xadrion could see her outline through the shadows as she approached.

'Zeus' lightning,' Azraelle said. 'I know.'

'You're a god,' Xadrion said.

'Yes.' Azraelle was grimacing slightly but continued walking towards him. Every step was slow, as if she had to make herself move forward with each one. She was here, was coming for him, but it did not appear easy for her to be so near to him. Her eyes tracked down his bare skin, roaming down his chest to the blanket that concealed his waist. A grimace flashed across her features before her eyes returned back to his. He saw sadness and also… fear. She was afraid of him.

'You're thousands of years old,' Xadrion said.

'I suppose. I've lost track of time.'

'My father tortured you,' Xadrion stated. The bed shifted beside Xadrion as Azraelle took a seat across from him. She didn't touch him. Instead, Azraelle clasped her hands together and sat tersely on the edge.

'Yes.'

'How can you be near me? I shot his power straight into your mind last night. You have every right to be disgusted at my very presence,' Xadrion said.

'You don't disgust me,' Azraelle said. 'It is not easy to be around you, especially not now I know the power that lays beneath your skin. Not when I still lose nights of sleep over the time I spent locked up there. It is an active effort to separate you from him, one that I may need more time for, but I know you're not him.'

'Why did you come?' Xadrion asked.

'Because,' Azraelle began, 'you are one of my kind. You are an immortal. You're settling into your skin with no one around to help you, and that can be dangerous. And because I imagine Zeus would love to hear of your existence, and I am not in the habit of leaving things out for Zeus to find. You have power, Xadrion. And I want to show you how to protect yourself with it.'

'How?' Xadrion asked.

Azraelle took hold of Xadrion's hand and then smoothly stepped across the bridge between their minds, entering that space where she could read his thoughts and touch his senses.

Your mind is exposed, Azraelle said into his thoughts, running her fingers along the edges of the wall surrounding his senses. Her touch was sensual and delicate. He shivered in response. *Anyone can walk in and do what they want. Mental torture is harder to combat than physical torture and I don't wish to see you subjected to it.*

'How do I protect my mind?' Xadrion asked, his interest piqued. It felt good to have her in his mind, to have her touch his barriers. But torture inside the mind… that was a weakness he didn't want to be exposed to.

In his mind, Azraelle tugged him to the edge of the bridge. She gestured for him to look down it. Despite her presence within his thoughts, the giant wall still stood on the other end of their connection.

You build a wall like that.

'I'm sorry for pulling you out here,' Xadrion said. 'Rhoas told me of the wards that have been protecting us. It was careless of me to leave them.'

'A few days won't hurt. As far as I can tell, Zeus has no reason to believe you, or I, are alive. He shouldn't be looking our way for now,' Azraelle said.

'What about that person, the one who killed the girl? Would they tell Zeus they saw you?' Xadrion asked.

'If they had, I think I may have already heard so by now,' Azraelle said. 'Deimos honours their deals. They have to.'

'Who is Deimos to you? They called you blood.'

'My brother's child.'

'Which brother, Hypnos or Thanatos?' Xadrion asked. He could see her smile through the darkness, a small chuckle escaping her.

'I suppose Rhoas told you more than I realised. Deimos is Thanatos' child,' Azraelle answered.

'And do you have other brothers or sisters?' She had never been so transparent with him. All the secrets she'd kept for so long – it seemed like she was as relieved to be able to speak it as he was to finally hear it.

'Many, but I have not seen them for some time.'

'And Erebus and Nyx? Rhoas told me they were your parents,' Xadrion said.

'They are,' Azraelle said. 'That is an awfully long story. But the short version is that Erebus is dead, or as dead as our kind can really get. He will return to this world one day but not for many years to come. Mater spends her time in the Underworld.'

'Why has she not come to you?'

'She isn't able,' Azraelle answered calmly, though Xadrion didn't miss the way she pressed her lips together and cleared her throat before she spoke. 'Nyx represents night and is one of two remaining direct descendants of Chaos in existence right now. Being that close to Chaos comes with a significant amount of power but also has some catches. If Mater were to step foot on the mortal realm without the presence of Erebus, thousands would die. Her power is hard to maintain on its own, and it is only with Erebus' ability to suppress it that it remains balanced. With him removed from this world, she can't risk mortal lives in that way.'

'That is... incredibly complex,' Xadrion admitted.

'She does the same for him. It's a part of holding so much power at one time,' Azraelle said, and then she laughed to herself, as if she were thinking of some inside joke surrounding it. Xadrion would give anything to hear that sound more often.

'Show me how to build the wall.'

'It's a fairly simple concept, but one you'll have to practise,' Azraelle said.

'You simply have to imagine a wall surrounding this chasm in your mind. When you build the wall, I'll push things toward it, and you must try to keep them out. Doing so will build the wall thicker and stronger, and eventually you will be able to hold out anyone who tries to enter.'

'How did I enter your mind when your wall is so seemingly impenetrable?'

'I was thinking of you,' Azraelle admitted, her shoulders shrugging slightly in the darkness. 'You were thinking of me. It kind of opens up a channel. You only got in because I chose to let you in.'

'And that's why I can't get in anymore, because you don't want me in?' Xadrion asked.

'I think it's best if you stay out from now on,' Azraelle said. 'I shouldn't have let last night go so far.'

Images flashed across Xadrion's memory, a reminder of how far exactly they had gone last night.

'That hardly seems fair, given how easily you step into my mind,' Xadrion said. He took hold of both her hands while running his mental fingers along the outer edge of her mind. She didn't pull her hands away, but she also didn't drop her wall.

'Push me out of your mind then,' Azraelle said. 'Force me to go.'

'And if I want you to stay?'

'Then you will never be able to build your wall.'

'It's so hard to focus when your fingers are brushing my thoughts,' Xadrion admitted. He reached his own hand forward and laid it upon Az's cheek. Her hair was damp as it fell from behind her ear to brush the back of his hand. If she were not going to let him in to her mind, then he would have to settle for breaking her physical defences.

Az's eyes closed when his hand came to her cheek. Her lips parted slightly and her breath quickened. In response, Azraelle's mental fingers ran along the walls of his mind, slow and sensual.

Force me out.

Xadrion didn't want to but learning to build his own wall seemed important to Az, so he tried. He pushed her back towards the bridge that linked their minds, resolving to push her back across it and build up his own wall.

He got her a few steps closer to the bridge when an image flashed across his mind's eye. It was Azraelle, kneeling and naked as she had been the night before looking through the mirror. Xadrion stumbled internally and her mental presence pushed her way back into the depths of his thoughts.

You have to block me out. Don't let me distract you.

'Easy enough for you to say. I can't think when I see those images,' Xadrion said.

Try again. Don't let me get through.

So, he tried again. He pushed her back, taking a firm hold of her presence and rushing her back to the bridge. He made it slightly closer when another image flashed across his mind. Azraelle, watching herself as her hands circled between her thighs. Xadrion stumbled again and Azraelle effortlessly pushed her way back in.

Seriously, Xay. You'll never keep anyone out if this is all it takes to get in.

His name on her lips broke his focus usually, the shortened version she had occasionally called him whispered into the depth of his mind pushed his resolve further away and Xadrion wanted nothing more than to give in to the images and pull her into his arms. Instead, he pushed again, determination setting in despite the hardening he could feel beneath the sheets. Whether she knew the extent of the effect she had on him, Xadrion didn't know, but Az definitely knew what to do to keep him distracted.

Xadrion got her with one foot onto the bridge between their minds when she overwhelmed him. Images of Azraelle flashed so fast through his mind, followed closely by sounds. Moans. Her moans. She showed him the image of herself in the mirror, grinding atop the pillow in a way that had made Xadrion want to be that pillow more than anything. She showed the image of her fingers circling, the moans escaping her lips as she built into her release. And finally, she showed him the image of her orgasm, shaking her body with a fierceness that had made his own finish come the night before.

When the image disappeared, Xadrion was kneeling in the surface of his mind, Azraelle towering above him, nowhere near the bridge back to her own mind.

Push. Me. Out.

And then she slammed endless images towards him. He saw the image of her orgasm ripping through her over and over. He saw the image of her standing outside his door, her arousal dripping between her legs as she listened to him pleasure himself. She saw images of them laying in that very bed in the cabin, his dick hard against her ass and his hands digging into her hips. She slammed him with the images over and over.

Xadrion gritted his teeth and did his best to tune it out. He did his best, which was hard because Azraelle's body was everything he had ever dreamed of touching and tasting, and he was being overwhelmed with it. He pushed, turning a blind eye to as many images as he could. Instead, he stared directly at his feet in his mind as he pushed against her presence.

It felt like hours passed before he saw the threads of the bridge beneath his feet and knew that he had gotten her outside the landscape of his mind. Now he just needed to build the wall. He envisioned one that was similar to hers, a near mirror image of that dark, all-expansive wall on her side of the bridge, and imagined it slamming around the perimeter of his own mind. He gritted his teeth harder, closing his eyes to focus solely on building the wall, and hoped that it worked.

A moment later, Azraelle's bombarding stopped. No more images flashed across his view, no more sounds filled his ears and no longer could he feel Az's presence resisting his push. He looked up, looked back at the space that he had been trying so desperately to push her from, to see he was now standing on the bridge between his mind and hers, but that on either end of the bridge lay a wall.

His wall was not what he imagined it to be. It was not never-ending and black as night and did not seem impenetrable. It was energy, pure and unrefined, crackling along the perimeter of his mind. He didn't need to reach across to it to know it would zap to touch. Across from him on the bridge, Azraelle shrunk away from the crackling wall.

Xadrion opened his eyes and found Azraelle watching him.

'That's good,' Azraelle said. 'You need to keep it up. It will feel tiring to maintain it at first, but you have to keep it going to build your strength with it.'

'What if I want you back in?'

'You can't want me back in, Xadrion. You shouldn't want me in your mind,' Azraelle said.

'That's bullshit, Az.'

'No, it's not,' Azraelle argued. 'You don't let anyone into your mind ever. I shouldn't have done it last night. You don't drop that wall for anyone, even if you think you want them there.'

'Why not?' Xadrion pushed.

'Because the second you have someone you're willing to let in fully like we did last night, you become weak and vulnerable to that kind of attack.' Azraelle stood from the bed quickly, moving away from his reach. 'Zeus – and others – will use that to get exactly what he wants,' Azraelle said. She'd moved back to the dining table, keeping her back facing Xadrion. She put her hands down to the table and leant into it, as if the effort to remain standing was suddenly too much for her.

Xadrion stood and walked towards her, slow and purposeful, the air chill against his bare skin. She tensed as he approached her but didn't evade his touch as he reached his hands out and placed them on her shoulders. He dragged his hands down her arms until they covered hers. Xadrion linked his fingers through hers, his arms partially enclosing her within their grasp, and pulled gently until she rocked back on her heels. Her back settled against Xadrion's torso while her head angled until it was resting against his shoulder. She was a whole foot shorter than him at least, which left her head settling directly into the divot of his bare chest.

Her hair had fallen from its usual braid and was damp against his chest. She felt stronger in his arms than he'd even realised she was. Compared to the first day when he had run with her through the castle, her body like an empty vessel in his arms, she had changed so much. The training they'd been doing, all the training she had done in the hours before their sessions, had crafted her body so that muscles rippled taut beneath her skin.

'I am not weak for wanting you in my mind,' Xadrion whispered, directly to her ear. Azraelle's lips parted as her head tipped back, their bodies flushed against each other. 'And you are not weak for letting me in last night.'

'You don't realise the power you held when you ran through my mind. You don't know what you could have done when I gave you the access to control my body. You had all the power,' Azraelle whispered.

'No, you know that's not true,' Xadrion said. 'You gave it to me and you could have easily taken it from me at any moment you wanted. Giving someone else control is not the same as you losing it.'

'If Zeus finds me again, or finds you, he will be able to use you in a way that he never succeeded at when I was imprisoned,' Azraelle said. She made no move to pull away from him, her eyes still closed as she leant her head into his shoulder, exposing her neck to Xadrion's breath.

'How would he ever use me against you?' Xadrion whispered.

'The things he sought from me when I was his prisoner, I didn't give them to him. He tried and tried for years, *years*, Xadrion. Physically, he could do whatever he wanted. I know what it is to be trained against physical torture. But when someone is in your mind and has control over you in that way, we've never developed tactics to defend against that. Once they are in, it's game over. But Zeus never infiltrated my mind, not even for a moment,' Azraelle admitted.

'You think he could use me to break into your mind?' Xadrion asked.

'I *know* he could use you to break into my mind.'

'Maybe you should practise your own defences against me,' Xadrion said, leaning his head down until his nose rested against Azraelle's exposed neck. Her breath caught and her fingers tightened over his.

'That's not a bad idea,' she whispered.

'I don't think you give yourself enough credit. That wall of yours is impenetrable. I have no ability to get inside it unless you let me,' Xadrion said.

'Maybe you should take another look,' Azraelle said. He felt her switch her attention to that bridge between their minds, where they both now stood between each of their walls. She led him across it, toward her wall, black and long as night. As they got closer, the image of the wall in front of them began to shift. Where there had previously been a wall as thick and strong as ever one could be, there now appeared to be cracks running across its vast surface.

What are those? Xadrion asked into their minds.

That is every weakness I have. Give it a push.

Xadrion looked at the cracks, looked through the cracks. He saw the weaknesses she spoke of – images of Ilyon and Emera laughing, images of an ethereal woman who looked like Azraelle only older, and images of Azraelle flying in formation amongst hundreds of other women. He saw glimpses of a marbled room, blood coating the white walls, and saw hundreds of faces flicker across, their grins more maniacal than the last. Finally, he saw himself.

It felt wrong, like he was invading some part of her he shouldn't be allowed access to. But he followed her command and reached his hand up until it rested over the crack that held the image of him. Gentle, without much force behind it, Xadrion pushed.

Around them, Azraelle's wall came tumbling down in pieces.

When the crashing ended, Xadrion found himself amidst a smoky ruin of black marble with Azraelle's mental figure kneeling in the mess. The image of Azraelle kneeling in her bedroom after Karlin's death came to mind, her palms face up on her knees and looking utterly hopeless. In front of him now, in Azraelle's crumbled mind, she was in that exact position.

This is why Zeus will use you to break me. My connection to Death is what keeps me strong, but my connection to Life – to the mortal realm – makes me weak, Azraelle whispered.

She was defeated, resigned to the weakness she had shown Xadrion, the one she was convinced would bring about her downfall – her connection to mortals. Because she did believe that, Xadrion saw as he peered beyond that shattered wall. Azraelle felt as shattered as that wall looked. Xadrion didn't understand what she meant when she spoke about Life and Death, or how her connection to them could be a strength or a weakness.

All the moments of Azraelle's torture flashed across his view, all the ways in which Zeus had tried to break her over those fifteen years. He saw where every hand had ever touched her, how so many unknown faces had used her body for their own means. He saw all the days Azraelle had left the castle and sent out desperate pleas to Thanatos to answer her, to give her a solution to being stranded on that mortal realm with no family around her. Xadrion saw an image of Az from when she had wings, soaring through night sky with a band of winged warriors behind her, and the abandonment she felt to not have them around her anymore. Deep down, beneath all of that, was a festering ball of resentment that was wound so tightly he wondered if Az had ever actually taken it out to have a look at it. That one, he knew without being told, was her feelings toward her mater, Nyx. Finally, he saw every memory that had resurfaced in her mind the night before, the very moment Xadrion's power had sparked deep within her mind.

Azraelle could not handle him in that moment. It had been unfair of him to ask her to, to ask her to respond to his touches and desires. Her physical strength had convinced Xadrion that she was more okay than she actually was. If he pushed tonight, he would not get the vulnerable and open version of her he had received last night when she'd given him her mind. He would get this shattered version who was only giving him what he craved because she'd resigned herself to the idea that Xadrion was part of her weakness.

'It's time to sleep,' Xadrion said, tugging her to the bed. He sat her down, pulled her boots from her feet and slid in beside her. He held her and eventually she slept. Despite his recent sleep, Xadrion soon followed.

SEVENTEEN

XADRION

The next morning, Xadrion had caught and skinned breakfast for them before Azraelle woke. He would prepare it for them when Az was awake but while he waited, he allowed himself the pleasure of sliding back into the bed with her and pulling her to him once more. His clothes had dried through the night and there didn't look to be any storm on the horizon. It felt rare to be up and about before Azraelle. No matter how he'd tried over the time she'd been at Fennhall, he had never gotten to training earlier than she had.

He would not ask for her body again, not when he could see that she wasn't capable of giving it to him for pleasure. He would wait, at least until he could make sure she felt strong within herself once more. Yet, he wanted her, gods, he wanted her, and he knew that some part of her wanted him. But peering into her mind the night before had made Xadrion see how much she would be resigning if she accepted that desire in her current state.

'I had another premonition,' Azraelle whispered into the cool morning silence. Xadrion kept his hold around her, content to let her speak at her own pace. 'I had it over a week ago, at least. I think it's too late; the person is dead. I should have told you.'

A week ago, Xadrion may have been mad hearing that. He would have thought her a coward and probably stormed away in some attempt to make her feel responsible for the life lost because she'd said nothing. Now, he was thankful she had made the decision to tell him. Az had kept so much secret and would have continued to keep that secret if she didn't feel like being honest. Maybe it was the beginning of her deciding to fight.

'Do all gods get the premonitions, or is that just you?' Xadrion asked.

'As far as I know, it's not everyone. Thanatos, our older brother Charon, and myself are the only ones I've met who have had them. We owe a special responsibility to Death. The premonitions usually serve as a message that our services are needed but I don't know why I'm still getting them when my powers aren't strong enough to do anything,' Azraelle answered.

'How do the premonitions tell you what Death needs to be done?' Xadrion asked. Xadrion felt unnatural referring to Death as if it were a person, but as Azraelle talked more he came to realise she perceived it at least as a present entity. It left Xadrion with the distinct impression that any questions he may think to ask would barely scratch the surface in exposing this new immortal world's answers.

'Usually mine show me souls I need to help pass from one life to their next. Charon's and Thanatos' were different,' Azraelle said.

'So, you were Death's deliverer?' Xadrion clarified. 'You carried people from this world when they died and took them to their next life?'

'It's... a lot to explain but yes, that is the core of it. I had a lot of help to carry out the role, but I think that position may have fallen to someone else now,' Azraelle said, evasively.

Xadrion let her dodge the question, not wanting to push her so far that she shut him out again. Her temper had been one to match Xadrion's and despite the recent illusion of peace between the two, Xadrion didn't trust in it lasting. For now, he resolved to take in as much of her as she would allow. As he realised the bubble they existed within during that moment, he tightened his arms around her as they lay alone in the cabin together. At any moment he feared the bubble would pop and this new side to Az and all the knowledge she contained would be shut to him forever.

Endless images of her were on repeat in his mind, but he kept pressing them down and away. This was the first time he'd truly been alone with her and he was not going to blow it by trying to feel her up. As much as it *was* a nagging thought to do so.

Instead, Xadrion ran one of his palms across her back in a soothing gesture. He'd thought it a harmless gesture, forgetting the scars that covered her. His hand brushed over ridged skin that travelled the length of her back. First one scar and then the other. The image of Azraelle's wings flooded his memory, followed quickly by the very first time he'd seen her, her back slashed and bloody as she'd been cast into the dirt.

The skin was healed but would the wings ever be? What had it meant for Az to have had those magnificent wings and now to feel their absence every day? He knew she was struggling with it; she'd expressed it to him that day he'd followed her. Maybe he could have looked into her mind to get the answers to all these questions but it felt intensely wrong to enter her mind at will, especially when she seemed to be struggling so heavily with putting her wall back up.

'Will you tell me next time you have a premonition?' Xadrion asked.

'I don't think there is anything we can do to prevent them, Xay,' Azraelle said.

'Maybe, but like you said last night, we shouldn't get in the habit of leaving things out for Zeus. If these premonitions are showing people who are being targeted by Zeus, killed by Deimos on Zeus' orders, maybe stopping one of them will give us some answers. Or at the very least make it harder for Zeus to act on whatever it is he's planning,' Xadrion explained.

'Okay, I'll tell you if I do.'

Azraelle pushed herself from his arms then and slid from the bed. She pulled her boots on, as if she were restless to set about the day. She'd always beaten Xadrion to the barracks, and he'd never heard of her sleeping in even on the days they didn't train. It seemed Azraelle was not a person who liked to sit around.

Xadrion followed her up and set about cooking the rabbits he'd caught for them. After they'd eaten, Xadrion was outside tending to the horses – his and the one she had ridden to join him – when Azraelle emerged from the cabin, her long hair braided down and over her shoulder and a strangely joyful smile evident on her face.

'What's going on?' Xadrion asked. The way she was watching him was almost... playful? He'd never seen that glimmer to her expression before, it made him wish to keep her right there, safe in that place where she was free to be playful.

'I requested a few days off when Rhoas asked me to find you. I figured you would need some time away from the castle, and the ever-looming ball to celebrate the *princess* Romina while you dealt with things,' Azraelle explained as she sauntered toward him.

'And what did you have in mind for those few days?' Images flickered through his mind of ways he would very much like to spend them. He wanted to reach across, straight into her mind, and plant them in there. Since he'd pushed that wall last night and had it crumble down around them, he'd sensed she hadn't rebuilt it, which meant he was free to walk in and do what he wanted, but the thought of it worried him. If she hadn't rebuilt the wall, it wasn't just Xadrion's dirty images she was at risk of.

Xadrion's own wall remained up, though he was aware of the energy it required of him to do so. Her wall had seemed so large and ancient, so unbreakable, that he marvelled at the amount of energy it must have required over her years to keep it strong. How long had she spent building that wall? And how long would it take her to rebuild it?

'I would like to train with you,' Azraelle said. 'Not as we have been doing. You've nearly reached the limits of what your mortal body can push you to do physically, but if we can get that power of yours alive and working, who knows what we'll discover.'

'God-tier training?' Xadrion asked, his own smile creeping across his face. Something about the wild glean behind Azraelle's eyes had Xadrion's excitement building.

'God-ling level, at least,' Azraelle taunted.

'God-ling, my ass,' Xadrion said. He felt both amazed at the easy banter they'd fallen into and slightly insulted at being referred to as a god-ling.

'I know the location is tinged with some bad feelings but I'd like to suggest we head to the bell tower. It's a place of power and your power will likely respond to it, much the same as how it woke to play with my magic,' Azraelle said.

The idea of stepping back into that clearing made Xadrion feel uneasy, especially when he thought of the little girl's body he'd buried just outside the borders of it. They hiked the distance to the clearing in silence and when they emerged, there was nothing that indicated any sign from the last time they'd been there. He'd buried the girl but had done so deeper into the woods as it hadn't felt right to leave her in the ground of the bell tower. There was a slight char on the circle of grass where Deimos had disappeared from but aside from that, there was nothing.

Xadrion felt the presence of the place pressing down upon him.

'What happened here? Why does it feel this way?' Xadrion asked. Azraelle shrugged.

'I wasn't powerful enough last time we were here to read the power,' she admitted.

'And now?'

'I can try. But I'd much rather show you how,' Azraelle said. He felt her then, standing at the entrance to his wall, as if her presence were waiting politely to be let in.

'You can fraction a portion away for me to step into while safeguarding the remainder of your thoughts. I just need the part of your mind where I can show you the images to run you through it step by step,' Azraelle said.

'How do I let it only partly down?'

'Imagine giving me a key, but that the key only unlocks one door. Put the rest of your mind behind the other doors but leave what you want me to see behind the one the key unlocks,' Azraelle instructed. Xadrion imagined what she'd said, locking away everything except for the ability for her to communicate directly to his mind, and then envisioned letting Azraelle step through the barrier.

As soon as she was in, he knew it had worked. Crackling energy safeguarded everything besides that one secured room.

'You're quick to learn the mental steps,' Azraelle commented. 'I wonder if the physical will be as fast when we unlock it.'

Whenever he'd felt Azraelle gesturing to a new place in his mind in the past, it didn't come with written instructions on what would happen. He just followed her blindly, trusting that it was leading to the right place. The messages she communicated didn't form through words but rather appeared as an instinct that she offered him – one that showed him the path to follow.

Az showed him such an instinct as she stood in the caged part of his mind. She showed him what it would look like if he extended his power out, and let it join with the power he felt echoing through the clearing. She showed him the way he could use it to observe the source of the power from the clearing.

I've never seen anything like this, Azraelle admitted into his mind. *It's like you have all the pathways to your power, but none of them have woken up.*

Are all gods usually born with their powers? Xadrion asked.

No, it comes to them in time. But new gods are rare, and I was kept from most of our kind growing up, so I've never really seen the mind of a god who is coming to their power.

But you know how to wake my powers up? Xadrion asked. Azraelle grimaced in front of him, her expression a clear indication that she had no experience having done so. She shrugged slightly.

Not exactly. They usually awaken by themselves, usually at a younger age than you are even now. It may be the castle wards that have kept it suppressed so far, or maybe it is simply not being around others of our kind.

Okay, Xadrion replied warily. *Let's give it a try.*

It can come with side effects, Azraelle warned. *Coming into your power isn't necessarily a smooth process, it often comes with a lot of teething issues.*

Like?

Anger and difficulty controlling the power. I don't remember exactly; I haven't really seen someone else coming into their powers and mine came so long ago. I also had my family nearby to help me through it if I needed it, Azraelle answered.

I'm angry all the time anyway, Azraelle, Xadrion said. He wondered briefly if this was what had been happening to him all along. He hadn't felt so quick to anger for most of his life, but it had been growing in its presence over the last year or so. When Azraelle had arrived he'd felt it grow even more, not in how often he felt it but in the intensity with which it hit him. Had that been his magic's way of trying to make itself known? Maybe if he unlocked it, that anger, which had at one time been so unfamiliar to him, would leave him alone for good.

Xadrion followed the instructions she'd shown him, imagining his lightning dancing with the power as it had danced with Azraelle's darkness. In response, Xadrion felt the power of the clearing as if it were joining with his own and his vision shifted.

Where there had been an empty clearing, he now watched as the environment around them sped up. The birds flittered through the trees so fast they looked like miniature shooting stars. A beam of light centred on the peak of the bell tower and illuminated the entire clearing. It flashed so brightly Xadrion had to shield his eyes, and when he removed his hands to look forward once more, he saw a single figure standing at the base of the tower.

Hera, the figure at the tower, looked around the clearing. Her gaze passed right over where Azraelle and Xadrion stood, as if they weren't even there, and then she walked away from them, leaving the clearing completely.

She was more beautiful than he even remembered. Her skin was radiant in its brownness, her hair tightly braided in thin, neat rows back from her face. She wore a dress that reflected the very colours of the morning sky, and she moved so gracefully. Hera looked exactly as he had pictured her a thousand times from memory, only infinitely more beautiful.

Xadrion took a step forward to follow her when he felt a hard tug on his elbow. He turned to see Azraelle watching him, her brows pulled together in sorrow.

'She's not really here, Xay,' Azraelle said, her hold on him softening. Sadness coated her expression as she watched Xadrion. 'The clearing is just showing you where its power emanates from.'

'Hera is the source of its power?' Xadrion asked, not understanding.

'Not exactly,' Azraelle said. 'The bell tower is a beacon, a signal that allows gods to use it as an established point of travel between the mortal realm and our realms and allows them easier travel. There are others I know to exist, but this must be the nearest one to Fennhall.'

'Can't they just travel between the two realms wherever?' Xadrion asked.

'Yes, but if there's already an established pathway it is significantly easier. Otherwise, it can take an extreme amount of power,' Azraelle said. Azraelle stepped out into the clearing fully, walking until she was standing in the middle of it.

'I need to do something in your mind, and I need you not to panic,' Azraelle said. Xadrion walked to stand in front of her and took hold of her hands in his own.

'I trust you, Az.'

From within the space he'd carved out for her in his mind, Xadrion began to feel her presence moving around. It felt like she was searching, digging through the space, looking for something in particular. The feeling of Az moving through him and her power touching the inner reaches of his mind had Xadrion's skin prickling. Az hid so much from him, and Xadrion knew even after peering into her mind that there was so much more he could come to know about her. But regardless of the distance she kept between them, Xadrion could not deny the physical response his body had to her presence.

Xadrion unlocked the remaining guards in his mind to give her full access. Azraelle would be disappointed, he was sure, but he wanted to feel more of her, to memorise what it felt like to have the essence of her moving through his mind. He needed to feel Azraelle's tendrils entwined with his own power he felt like he needed it more than the very air he breathed.

The swarm of Azraelle's tendrils moved within him. He'd felt them before when his own power had infiltrated her mind and they'd played together, and he'd seen them from the glimpses he got into her mind. Rather than playful, or looming, as they'd once felt to him, they seemed like they were trying to coax something from him. Whenever Azraelle found a pathway within his mind, she sent strands of her darkness down them. In response, Xadrion could feel something within him awaken. With each one she coaxed awake, the pool beneath the surface of his power grew.

Xadrion let her do what she needed, not feeling any of the worry she'd told him he should feel at someone else searching through his mind. Az seemed desperate to make it clear to him exactly what level of damage could be done, and he believed her, but he found it impossible to look at her as if she were a threat.

'There,' Azraelle breathed after at least an hour of silence had passed. Sweat beaded her brow. 'Your power was dormant, as if it had been buried in you somehow. I found what branches I could. Magic likes to interact with other magic, so I sent a little bit of mine through to wake it up. How do you feel?'

'I can feel it,' Xadrion said. Because he did. He could feel the power and it was no longer in flickering moments. Now, it felt like it was growing, had already grown so much. Now, it felt like it could burst from his skin at any moment.

'Imagine letting it out to play,' Azraelle instructed, pulling her hands from his reach and taking several cautious steps away from him. 'Imagine it coming out and coating your skin like a barrier of iron. Imagine it hardening every defence you have. Imagine it lacing every movement you make with extra strength.'

As Xadrion imagined what she was instructing him to do, the air began to crackle around him. Azraelle watched him, cautious at the power that was now emanating from him, but she didn't back away any further. He didn't want to think about how this would feel for her – how every way she coaxed his power out was bringing her one step closer to that which had inflicted so much pain upon her.

He wanted to make sure everything he was doing was okay, but once the power started to wake, it felt so impossible to stop. He felt the way his magic moved to strengthen him, how it remade his body in a way that now no longer felt mortal. Xadrion thought it should have hurt, this remaking, and yet it didn't. It felt instead glorious and unlike anything he'd ever experienced. His senses sharpened, his skin somehow thickened, his muscles felt more ready to explode in action than they ever had. It was like he had stepped into a whole new body, one that was limitless.

'No wonder I never caught you in training,' Xadrion marvelled. Azraelle grinned at him, an edge of madness to it. She looked… immaculate. Everything he perceived was richer. Everything he sensed he registered faster. Az had always been beautiful to him, but the things he noted now left him breathless. The dark of her eyes, the glow of her hair, the corded muscles beneath her skin that she had spent so many hours building before their own sessions.

She was beautiful. Xadrion saw her anew; saw the way the sun cast across her face, causing the sweat in her dark brow to glisten. He marvelled at the contrast of her brow, the darkness of it compared to the shocking white of her long, braided hair. He saw the way the same sun caused the shadows from her full upper lip, and the petite upturned nose to cross her otherwise pale skin. Her lips had the faintest glimmer of moisture, a sight that made him want to capture them in his own.

His eyes showed him everything. He saw the beauty, but he also saw the pain. Every stretch of her skin exposed to the sun was coated in faint white lines, tales of hundreds of cuts inflicted upon her body. Her arms, her neck, even the pale skin of her face was covered with them. He'd never been able to see most of them before, faint as they were.

'Catch me now,' Azraelle said, and then she was leaping at him. They had no weapons – they didn't need them in this body of theirs. She lunged for him and he was able to keep track of her movement in a way he never had before. He saw the way she would move to take a swipe at him and knock him down, and he knew exactly where to move to avoid her. He stepped from her reach, whirling until he was behind where she'd passed him. Azraelle was prepared and already turning back. Her instincts had once been faster than he'd been able to detect. Now, she was still faster than Xadrion, but he could keep up.

They began moving around each other, faster and faster while Az pushed Xadrion to his limits. He didn't think he would ever catch her speed, but when he managed to land that first blow to her he saw how the force she'd taken left her reeling. He would have stopped, afraid to do harm in this new strength of his, but she laughed and simply began moving faster.

Her laugh echoed through the trees; Azraelle consumed every sense he had.

Xadrion had no idea how long they fought for, exchanging blows between them. He began to get a feel for containing his strength in his attempt to not seriously hurt her, but she became something almost untraceable as they fought. At times he would swing for her, confident he would hit, until she seemed to dissipate and blend past him as if she ceased to hold a physical form. By the time he'd looked back to her to check what he'd seen, she was standing there once more smiling at him.

It felt like Xadrion had never moved before, had never breathed, and now he finally could. He found that the steps he took carried him further through the clearing than they ever would have, that the speed he ran got him from one point to another faster. It felt like he'd finally allowed his body to reach its capabilities. Azraelle appeared to feel the same, if her wild grin was anything to go by. She was made to move fast.

Azraelle was only giving Xadrion time to find his footing, he realised. She let the fight go on, let him get his swipes in while giving tactical swipes of her own, until Xadrion started to feel confident in his moves. When he had gotten the hang of it, after what very well must have been over an hour of back-and-forth hits, Azraelle switched the dynamic. He aimed for her, his fist passing straight through that strange corporeal mist she became, and she appeared behind him. He began to turn to her but he was too slow. She was so fast. By the time he'd realised what she had done, Azraelle had leapt onto his back, manoeuvred her elbow beneath his chin and thrown her weight forward, rolling over his shoulder until he was slammed on the ground with his head firmly held in a headlock in the crook of her elbow.

He could get no air down and he reached up to tap her elbow, signalling his resignation. She released him immediately, her laughter echoing across the clearing.

'I thought you were into choking,' Azraelle taunted. He remembered those carefree words he had muttered to her that first night in the cabin, the night after she'd choked him so badly his neck had bruised. She'd slammed her defences up as soon as he'd said it that night and he'd instantly regretted it. Now, it seemed, she was ready to joke about it.

'Pretty sure I said to do it up until crushing my throat,' Xadrion joked back, pushing himself from his back so that he was sitting across from her. She was on her knees in the grass, her skin glistening with sweat from the workout. He'd never seen her really sweat before. Her braid had tussled so that strands fell out and framed her face. This was the most carefree he'd ever seen her, and she'd never been so breath-taking.

The realisation that they'd been fighting for longer than he thought hit him as he looked to the sky. Or the very process of activating his magic had taken longer. Either way, the sun had disappeared below the tree line and the sky was filled with magnificent streaks of orange and yellow, purple and pink. They'd been in that clearing *all day*. His body was tired but not as tired as it should have been after spending the majority of the sunlight fighting.

Azraelle stood, offering her hand down to help him stand. Xadrion took it gratefully, letting her lead the way back to the cabin. When they arrived, Xadrion tended to the horses as Azraelle moved to the rear of the cabin where a small pond of water was. He'd watched her through the cabin window once, watched her dip into its surface to wash the day from her body. He hadn't seen anything, nothing further than the scars that lined her back. It had been those scars that had him looking away the first time.

Now Xadrion knew if he followed her, if he tempted her to let him join her in the water, things would happen that he wanted more than anything. He knew she'd let him, had seen it in that carefree attitude she'd demonstrated the entire walk back. Azraelle had even hummed as she walked, a tune he didn't recognise. Whether she realised she was doing it, or if it were an absentminded decision, he couldn't quite tell.

Xadrion didn't follow her.

Az gave a great impression that she was in a much better place, even seeming happy, but Xadrion knew that level of hopelessness he'd seen the night before didn't disappear in one day.

He didn't question her. Seeing the light-hearted version of Azraelle was a nice change, and he didn't want to be the one responsible for bringing her back into sadness once more. Instead, he tended to the horses, bathed once Az was done and made them dinner with the remainder of the catch from that morning. By the time they'd finished eating, both of them collapsed into the bed weary for sleep. Xadrion could not prevent himself from pulling her in as he drifted off, pressing her as close to him in his arms as seemed possible in that moment. A peaceful sleep overcame him.

EIGHTEEN

AZRAELLE

They decided it was time to head back the next day. Azraelle knew it was the safest decision but dreaded the idea of returning to the castle and leaving the freedom that had showered her the day before. She had not felt as liberated as that in a long time. Fighting with Tolemus had been the closest thing, but Tolemus was only a demi-god and she could not push the limits of her physical skills as far as she had with Xadrion.

They'd left early but set a carefree pace and the horses ambled slowly side to side. It would take longer to reach the castle at that pace, but neither of them seemed to care.

'You mentioned Nyx lives in the Underworld. Did you live there, too?' Xadrion asked as they rode.

'Yes, and no. I lived in a realm within the Pantheon of the Underworld. Nyx lives within the House of Hades,' Azraelle began. Azraelle didn't want to tell him everything, not when so much of where she resided had been kept a fiercely guarded secret for as long as it had existed. Eviria was her home, a place she had crafted for herself to escape the solitude she'd had enforced upon her for the beginning centuries of her life. Its secrets were protected to keep her Ravens safe and to keep the army for being used for any unsanctioned purposes.

'Hades?' Xadrion interrupted, seemingly unable to stop himself from jumping in.

'Yes. Your uncle, I believe,' Azraelle said. 'What did Hera tell you of the gods?'

'I only remember parts of stories. Not enough that anything makes sense.'

'Chaos is the creator of everything, but it was Nyx and Erebus who created the god's realms as we know them – Olympus, the Underworld and Atlantis. When the realms were created, it fell to the children of Chaos to monitor them.

Eros quickly disappeared and has not been seen since, while Tartarus and Gaia made the eventual decision to leave their physical forms to give more to creation. Erebus and Nyx were left to govern the realms,' Azraelle explained.

'Cronus and Rhea rose to power together, but when their sons – Zeus, Poseidon and Hades – overthrew them, Nyx ultimately made the decision to allow them dominion over the realms. Zeus gained Olympus, Poseidon gained Atlantis, and Hades was handed the Underworld. Nyx remained with him, assisting Hades in the significant task of handling the dead. Over the millennia, Nyx committed many of her own children to the House of Hades.'

It was the longest Azraelle had talked in Xadrion's presence for. He was silent now as he listened, his eyes keeping on her as they rode. He looked entranced.

'Charon and Thanatos directly serve Hades. The rest of my siblings are spread through many realms, but as part of my responsibility to Nyx and to Death I was given command of one of Death's armies – the Ravens. We lived in Eviria, a hidden realm within the Underworld,' Azraelle said.

'You were a commander?'

'I was their primus, commander to them since their very inception. They were all fierce women, souls who had died and chosen to forge themselves into something new. Nyx gifted them to me as an army that could help with my tasks as one of the hands to Death. We lived separate to all, and only visited other realms when our duties required it,' Azraelle answered.

'Do you miss them?'

'Terribly.'

Azraelle fell into silence once more and Xadrion let her.

Occasionally as they continued to ride, Azraelle tested his mental barrier, showing him ways that he could strengthen it and build it higher. Xadrion took the cues on board and adapted easily to what she offered.

Azraelle did whatever she could to think about anything other than the fact that her own shield was not back up. She could not rebuild it and did not know what to think about why. That shield had been present in her mind for thousands of years… since the moment Thanatos had taught her the means to build it when she was a child. She'd crafted it, the wall a very reflection of who Azraelle thought herself to be. Tall and long, dark as night itself, and completely laced with shadows. She had imagined something so impenetrable, so opposed to any sort of weakness, that she could never be harmed.

She supposed it made sense that it had crumbled at this point in her life. She had weaknesses now, and a lot of them. Maybe she always had, but now they were staring straight at her and she had no choice but to confront them. That wall had been built without the idea of any weaknesses being present. It had no chance of standing strong now that its internal fractures had come to light.

Thanatos would be so disappointed in her.

Sister?

Azraelle blinked, her eyes shifting to look at Xadrion beside her. They rode casually, in one of their moments of silence.

Than? Azraelle asked. *Where have you been?*

I'm sorry for not answering you. I've been looking into what we spoke of. He'd carefully avoided answering her question. It seemed Azraelle was not going to get an answer as to why she had been ignored for so many weeks.

And?

Nothing, Thanatos answered. *If Zeus has been the one responsible for altering Destiny's thread, and not you, he has carefully hidden any evidence.*

Could you not find the boy? Azraelle asked.

It has been over fifteen years since you brought him back, and no one was with you to evidence who he was, Thanatos answered.

So, what does this mean for me?

I have sought an audience with Hades, Thanatos answered. *I believe I can get him to agree to let you seek asylum in the Underworld from Zeus. But he is going to need some sort of proof. You need to find something, anything, that creates any sort of doubt over Zeus' decree of your guilt.*

How in Chaos am I meant to do that?

Maybe you can find the boy, Thanatos answered. *I will continue looking on my end and try to follow the other beginnings of leads. But I don't know how much time I will have, Az. I've been getting some concerning premonitions, and it has been taking more and more of my time to answer to Death's responsibilities.*

Thanatos didn't need to outright say why it was harder for him to fulfil Death's responsibility; Azraelle knew it was because she was no longer sharing his burden. Charon, their other brother also affiliated to Death, acted as the ferryman into the Underworld, but Azraelle and Thanatos had always had to split the soul retrieving between them, as well as their other tasks. Now, Than was by himself and the workload would be swarming him, even with the Ravens likely at his disposal.

I'm getting premonitions still, Azraelle admitted. *I don't know what they mean, not when I have no power to ferry them right now.* She sent an image of the premonitions she'd received, first Kardin, followed by the little girl and finally the most recent vision she'd had. A man, similar in age to Kardin, with a giant burn lashed across his chest.

I will look into it, Thanatos responded. *Find some evidence, Az, and come home.*

I'll do my best.

With that, their connection died. Hearing Thanatos again made her feel slightly better, although nothing he said had appeased her worries. He had found nothing that would help her return home, nothing that explained how

Zeus and the Moirai had altered the version of events so drastically that Azraelle had walked out with a guilty verdict. Maybe it was enough that he'd gotten Hades to consider granting her asylum. *If* she could find reasonable doubt.

Azraelle looked back to Xadrion and found him watching her intently.

'Without your shield, I can sense when you're using your magic,' Xadrion said. Azraelle pursed her lips, frustrated. She was so exposed, so vulnerable, without her shield.

'I was talking to Thanatos,' Azraelle said.

'And?'

'No answers.'

'What is he looking into for you?' Xadrion asked. Right. She'd never actually told him that story.

'It's a long story,' Azraelle said, hesitant.

'We have hours before we reach the castle again,' Xadrion said, indicating the long and empty road ahead of them. Azraelle let the silence hang over them, pondering the newfound openness she felt comfortable displaying and the conversing that felt so easy suddenly with him. She sighed and resolved to his line of questions.

'When I was caught by Zeus,' Azraelle began. There really wasn't harm in it, she supposed. Xadrion knew everything else, nearly. 'He kept me imprisoned, but not without means. If he had have just taken me without declaring a charge others of our kind would have forced my freedom. He needed to do things lawfully.'

'Rhoas said it was because you were paying for your family's crimes, for Hypnos helping Hera to smuggle me away from Zeus,' Xadrion said.

'Yes, that was his true motive. I was a pawn for him in the war against my family,' Azraelle agreed. 'But the rest of our kind, they don't condone the war between our families. He would have needed further proof of crime. I was charged with altering the threads of Destiny, which is essentially the highest crime you can commit as a god. There are rarely any consequences for the killing of mortals, but there are times when Destiny marks someone's path and if we are personally responsible for it being changed, we face extreme repercussions.'

'Extreme, how?' Xadrion asked.

'A death. It's not permanent, not usually for our kind. When we die, we go to the Chaos realm where we spend time, centuries usually, being reborn. But sometimes – rarely ever but enough to scare our kind into fearing it – sometimes the god never returns. Maybe it's Destiny has decided their path is up,' Azraelle said.

'Did you alter the threads of Destiny?' Xadrion asked. Azraelle turned and scowled at him, anger rising quickly at the genuine uncertainty behind his question.

'Of course not,' Azraelle said. 'I would never.'

Xadrion looked remorseful immediately, as if he hadn't realised that asking the question was such an insult.

'I was ferrying a soul,' Azraelle continued. 'But when I read their threads, it wasn't their time. So, I brought them back.'

'You can just bring people back?' Xadrion interrupted.

'Yes,' Azraelle said. 'It's not quite that straightforward, but yes. To do so without Destiny supporting me would come with a severe price, one I wished never to have to pay, although it would seem I am anyway. I brought them back because it wasn't their time and Destiny's threads told me so. Only, Zeus caught me when I was returning to my home and charged me with doing so.'

'And you were found guilty?'

'Somehow, yes,' Azraelle admitted. 'One of my sisters was there, acting as a witness against me. She has a... special means to understand Destiny, and she announced my guilt for all to see.'

'Why would she have done that?'

'I don't know, genuinely,' Azraelle answered, her own pain at her sister's betrayal like a fresh knife to her stomach.

It needs to be this way. Forgive me. The Moirai had said that to her, standing before her in front of Zeus' dais. Why had her sister felt it was necessary to deem Azraelle guilty, knowing she would be cast down? Azraelle should have died, by all accounts that fall should have killed her. Why had it not? How could her own sister have had a hand in what should have been Azraelle's death?

'So, Thanatos is looking into how you were framed?' Xadrion asked.

'Yes, but he can't find anything.'

'What would be evidence enough?'

'Maybe if I could find the mortal who I brought back,' Azraelle said. 'I had the ability to read Destiny's threads, and it hasn't returned to me yet, but maybe if I could find them and read their destiny then I could show that I did not alter the threads.'

'How would you find them?' Xadrion asked.

'*That* is the question without an answer,' Azraelle admitted. She had no idea how she was going to find the boy. He wouldn't be a boy anymore, at least, but if anything had happened to him, if he were dead, then so was her chance to show her innocence.

Xadrion let them fall back into silence, leaving Azraelle alone to her thoughts. They returned to their natural state of existing side by side, as they finished the remainder of the journey back to the castle.

Upon their return, it was as if they had stepped back in time. The open flow of conversation suddenly seemed stiff and jilted once more, as if they were both realising the people they had been out there at that cabin were different than who they could be in the castle. They still had roles to play, even if Xadrion's entire worldview had shifted. Xadrion had not asked Azraelle for more intimacy since the night they'd shared their minds. Had he realised that very thing? Did he see that they couldn't be any more than what they were?

'You should go find your father,' Azraelle said, when Xadrion looked like he was about to open his mouth and say something to her. 'He's worried about you; he'll want to hear that you got back safely.'

Xadrion eyed her but gave a slight nod in agreement.

'Very well. Back to training tomorrow?' Xadrion asked.

'Absolutely,' Azraelle said. She waited until Xadrion had turned and left before she released a large sigh – of exhaustion or relief, she couldn't quite tell. Her journey to bring Xadrion back had gone well. She'd retrieved him, as she promised Rhoas she would, and had managed to find the pathways to give him access to his magic. He'd taken to using it like he'd been born to do it.

But a small part of her was still worried. Not about Xadrion, but about Ilyon. As a demi-god, it would be unclear how his power might represent. It would be difficult for him to find it out on his own, but with her help he might be able to adjust easier.

Azraelle returned to her rooms and changed out of the clothes she'd been stuck in for two days. Hearing from Rhoas how Xadrion had left, and after what he had heard, she had worried. If he were out there alone and in a panicked state anything could have happened. She'd left to follow him immediately, his sleeping mind giving her the access she needed to find where he was.

Azraelle bathed and changed before heading back out. She was combing her hair through her fingers as she moved through the hallways towards Emera's rooms. One knock had Emera's door swinging open to reveal her standing looking scattered in the doorway. Her panicked expression disappeared almost as soon as she saw Azraelle. Behind her, fast asleep on the couch, lay Ilyon. Azraelle had meant to find him after, but now it seemed she'd found both in one place.

Emera threw her arms around Az and squeezed her tightly. If she wasn't blessed with greater strength, it very well may have crushed her.

'You can't do that ever again,' Emera chastised, pulling her in by her hands. Emera kicked Ilyon's foot, causing him to sit up hurriedly, his hair a nest around his head. Azraelle smiled at the sight.

'Xadrion?' Ilyon asked.

'He's fine,' Azraelle answered. 'He thought he'd try to bury his troubles in the woods. But he's back now.' Azraelle noted the blanket that hung over the back of the couch, wrinkled as if it had been used recently. Ilyon's shoes and a dirty shirt of his lay abandoned beside the couch. Had Ilyon spent the night here while they waited? Azraelle smiled at the thought of the two of them together, both building each other's panic through their own.

'How are you?' Azraelle asked Ilyon, shuffling in to sit next to him on the couch. She ran her fingers through the mess of hair, trying to detangle it as a means to distract herself.

'I'm fine!' Ilyon declared. 'I told Emera what Father told us, but it seems she already knew a fair amount of it.'

'Speaking of,' Azraelle began tentatively. 'There's probably more to the story that you both deserve to know. Xadrion and I had some discussions around it, and it seems like something you all need to be included in.'

Az told them everything she had told Xadrion. She told them of the boy whose destiny she was charged with altering, the capture she'd suffered at Zeus' hands, the way that she had been cast down and subsequently found by Ilyon and Xadrion. She explained about what Thanatos had told her, the way forward to clearing her guilt, and finally she told of unlocking Xadrion's power.

'I want to continue training with you both, but I think the lessons will need to be altered. We need to find a more secluded area, one without witnesses to what we'll be doing. But I think I can help you both when it comes to realising your power,' Azraelle said.

'I think I have some to add to this story,' Emera said. Both Ilyon and Azraelle turned to look at her. 'I worked with Hera when I was a young girl and learned from those above me who had learned from her. Her power is one I understand well. I don't understand Zeus' power, which makes sense as to why I never felt any detection within Xadrion. But I have sensed Hera's magic within you, Ilyon.'

'You have?' Ilyon said. His eyebrows pulled together in his confusion but his eyes lit up.

'Just the beginnings. I can sense healing magic more than others, which I've felt within you,' Emera said. Chaos help her. Azraelle was practically useless when it came to teaching healing. She could barely manage it herself, let alone show someone how to do it.

'Well,' Azraelle said, 'I suppose this means you're coming to training, Emera. Ilyon is going to need you to teach him.'

'Why not you, Az?' Ilyon asked.

'Because Az's power isn't designed to heal,' Emera answered for her when Azraelle hesitated. It wasn't that she was ashamed of her power's capabilities, but it had been some time since she'd had to explain the nuances of different magic. 'It wouldn't know the difference between stitching someone up and pulling them apart.' Emera was joking, and her tone was light as she said it, but she wasn't wrong. She didn't know how to heal, not in any way that really mattered.

Her magic had been designed to cater for Death more than Life. It had always interested her how heavily she leaned one way, despite her affinities including Life and Rebirth also. Az supposed it was that Death had always been the more dominant force in the world and so had taken up more of her time, leaving her needing to adapt her magic to that more than anything.

'That is badass, Az,' Ilyon said. He was smiling, unaware of the depth of truth behind Emera's assessment of Azraelle's powers. Death was powerful and, indeed impressive, but it was also destructive and dangerous.

'Maybe, but not entirely helpful right now. At least it means you get to look at Emera's face rather than mine every day,' she joked.

They spent some time catching up with each other, the conversation drifting away from magic and gods and anything out of the mortal realm. Ilyon began raving about the play he and Emera had gone to see the night before, but quickly the conversation turned to the man Ilyon had been ogling on stage that Emera had to drag him away from at the end of the production. It was light-hearted and made Azraelle laugh as Emera recounted the amount of effort she had to put in to drag Ilyon away. It was something Az had noticed about Ilyon as well, the way he managed to find at least one beautiful person in each room he entered to make eye contact with and attempt to flirt with. Ilyon was beautiful as well, and a known prince, so he'd never had any issues the few times Az had observed him doing so. He would do *very* well among the immortal realms when he eventually found himself there.

They arranged to have dinner brought to Emera's rooms, but Az's thoughts drifted away in contemplation.

'I'll be right back,' she said as she stood and rushed from Emera's rooms. Az jogged through the hallways, the movement feeling good after she'd spent half the day riding and the other half lounging in Emera's rooms talking. It didn't take her long to reach the guest wing. She knocked on Tolemus' door, remembering which one he was in from the night they'd trained together and freshened up in his room.

Tolemus opened the door, dressed in a plain tunic and pants, no sign of his station visible. Though he smiled when he saw it was Azraelle, she couldn't help but notice his first expression had been one of sadness. All light but one candle had been extinguished in his room and a plate of untouched food sat beside a half empty wine bottle on the table. Tolemus moved to step back to invite her in.

'I was actually hoping you'd come join me,' Azraelle said, gesturing her chin back down the castle hallway. 'I'm having dinner with some friends who I think you would really enjoy the company of.'

'Well, that sounds like just my kind of thing,' Tolemus said. He followed behind her without question as they made their way back to Emera's rooms.

'How did your trip go with that prince of yours?' Tolemus asked as they walked, a sly smile on his face.

'If you're implying I was anything other than a perfectly behaved lady on the trip, I would say that you have sorely misjudged me,' Azraelle said, jokingly. He hadn't misjudged her in the slightest, of course. Azraelle had not held out from intimacy so long as she had done with Xadrion. And now, with the small taste she had offered him, it seemed he was done with his advances. It was definitely for the better, Azraelle reminded herself.

'I'm sure you are quite a lady,' Tolemus said. 'I was sad to see you go. We're here only for another week, and it has been quite some time since I have been around one who understands my life.'

'I have quite the surprise for you, my dear man,' Azraelle said. They'd reached Emera's doors, which she pushed through as if they were her own. Inside, Emera and Ilyon were still sitting, their gazes shifting to Az as she entered with intense curiosity. When Ilyon saw Tolemus standing behind Az, his eyes widened.

Az closed the door, pulling Tolemus over to sit with them.

'In the spirit of sharing secrets,' Az said. 'Tolemus, I think you and Ilyon have more in common than you realise.'

'What's going on, dear Azraelle?' Tolemus said. Ilyon was looking at her, eyes wide as if to ask her what she thought she was doing. It *was* a risk, she supposed. But Tolemus had seemed instantly trustworthy, which was a feeling she didn't get from many people. She didn't know how to put into words what she wanted them each to know about the other, without having them panic at the thought of the other knowing.

Azraelle formed an image in her mind, showing the way she and Tolemus had fought that night in the barracks, the way he'd moved at a speed no mortal could have done. She followed it closely by the image of her and Xadrion and the way their power had twined amongst each other playfully in the clearing the day prior, and finally she finished with an image of Ilyon as she imagined he would look wielding the healing magic of Hera's. She pushed these images, one after another, out towards Ilyon, Emera and Tolemus. She was pleased to see Tolemus had a barrier around his mind, but when she politely requested access, he granted her enough for her to place the images.

'The princes are demi-gods?' Tolemus said into the sudden silence.

'You're a demi-god?' Ilyon said almost simultaneously. Ilyon became an instant ball of energy, pushing Azraelle away from where she had dragged Tolemus to sit and took her spot so swiftly she barely registered as she found herself suddenly sitting beside Emera instead. Before Tolemus had time to collect himself, Ilyon was throwing question after question at him.

Despite the overwhelming energy of Ilyon, Tolemus smiled and did his best to answer Ilyon's questions before he had more thrown at him. Azraelle smiled as she watched, settling back into the couch, and resting her head against Emera's shoulder. She linked her fingers through Emera's as she watched the situation before her.

There would be a lot to work to be done. Ilyon and Xadrion needed a lot of training, Tolemus would have to leave in a week and Azraelle had to figure out how to find evidence to present to Hades. Surely another premonition would come sometime soon. She would have to face what that meant, and probably what Xadrion would be asking her to do by stepping in to attempt to prevent it. But for now, in that moment, she could be content with this little slice of normalcy she'd found.

NINETEEN

AZRAELLE

When Azraelle woke the next morning, she was leaning awkwardly across Emera's couch, her head resting on Emera's shoulder. The empty plates of their dinner remained scattered on the table where they'd left them the night before. Emera was snoring softly beside her and across from them, Ilyon was sprawled on the other couch. On the floor between the two, the small table that was there having been shoved off to the side, Tolemus lay face down. They'd all fallen asleep there, so entranced in their conversation with each other that none of them had managed to make it back to their own rooms.

Tolemus was snoring, heavily, and Ilyon had never looked so ungraceful as he did in that moment, long limbs sprawled every direction. Azraelle smiled as she slowly manoeuvred herself out of Emera's grasp and tiptoed over Tolemus' head to get outside the tangle of bodies. After the discussion last night, Azraelle was eager to make a start on their plans. Ilyon and Emera needed to learn how to craft their shields, and they needed to spend the time to wake Ilyon's magic.

She wanted to give them all she could offer, wanted to help them realise their own magic and teach them how they could defend themselves with it. Whatever would happen to her in the future, Az didn't know, but these people – these new friends – were better with their magic at full strength.

Despite her restlessness at wanting to start, Azraelle couldn't bring herself to wake them. She was an early riser; in fact, she rarely slept full nights at a time, so she took to going to the kitchens to grab them breakfast. As she did, Azraelle passed the open door to Rhoas' study. It was early, but Rhoas had often been the other early riser in the castle when she'd ventured into the hallways each morning.

Azraelle knocked gently before pushing it further open. Rhoas looked up at her, a warm smile on his face.

'Hello, Azraelle,' he said. Azraelle dipped into a polite curtsy in acknowledgement before moving further into the room.

'Did Xadrion find you yesterday?'

'He did,' Rhoas said. 'I appreciate everything you did for him. He returned surprisingly adapted to the news.'

'He's level-headed,' Azraelle agreed. 'I think he needed time to process more than anything. I just stopped by to let you know I'm going to be starting some magic training today and was wondering if you had any property that is… private enough to not draw attention to us as we do so.'

Rhoas chuckled, then said, 'Yes, I imagine that kind of training becomes a great deal more destructive than what that barracks should be watching. There are some old stables that no one really goes near anymore. That part of the castle's grounds fell into disrepair some time ago and hasn't been fixed since.'

'That sounds perfect.'

Rhoas gave her instructions on how to get there before he stood with sudden seriousness, the air around them seeming to become immediately more tense.

'I am glad you felt comfortable enough to open up to Xadrion,' Rhoas began. 'He reported to me much of what you told him, and your current plans to look into your premonitions.'

'But?' Azraelle asked, sensing where his hesitation was coming from.

'I have worked extremely hard to keep those boys out of the eyes of your kind, specifically to keep Xadrion from Zeus. I am worried, obviously for my son's safety, both of them,' Rhoas said. 'I don't want them to know that Hera still lives.'

'I haven't said anything to them.'

'I know, and I'm thankful,' Rhoas said. 'If they knew she was still alive, that their mother was out there in the hands of that monster, I don't think anything would stop them from marching straight to Olympus and demanding her back.'

'And you are content to leave her there?' Azraelle asked, not trying to sound challenging but curious as to how Rhoas himself had accepted leaving her there.

'I live in agony over it every day,' Rhoas admitted. A pain flashed behind Rhoas' eyes that told Az he was telling the truth. 'I cannot fathom what she is going through at his hands and imagining so leaves me with many sleepless nights. But Hera sacrificed everything for those boys, and I cannot let it be in vain.'

'I understand,' Azraelle said. 'For what it's worth, I agree that keeping them from Zeus' hands is the best option. Though, I do worry it will create an irreparable rift between you and your sons when they find out, because they will eventually find out.'

'I hope that day comes when Hera herself returns to tell them,' Rhoas admitted.

Azraelle curtsied once more, excusing herself from his office, and continued on to the kitchens. Her shadows had begun showing themselves to her once more, the darkness they offered becoming an increasingly tempting song. Falling into that mist had been as easy for her as breathing and not having that ability to pass without a trace had left her feeling especially vulnerable. Now that the shadows were returning, she could feel herself relaxing more with each day that her power grew.

Azraelle let herself get swept into that darkness as she walked, let the playfulness of her tendrils wrap around her as they tussled her clothes and hair. Chaos, she'd missed that. Flying was her favourite form of travel, but there was something about feeling the very essence of her shift into a mist-like state and be dispersed into the world around her that was irreplaceable. She couldn't do anything physical in the mist-form, it was purely a means of getting from one place to another but it was relaxing to let everything go and just drift.

She let go almost entirely, enough so that when she turned a corner on the way back, she had all but passed around someone before she realised what she had done. The body she had dispersed around stopped moving behind her, and Azraelle decided to commit to the shadows completely. Maybe if they didn't see her at all they would think they were imagining things.

Before her, watching her shadows retreat into the corners of the hallway, stood Xadrion. He was smiling and eyeing the tendrils as if he knew exactly what they were.

'You think I wouldn't recognise it was you, Az?' Xadrion asked. Azraelle let herself settle back into her physical form and leant her shoulder against the wall with her arms folded across her chest, the bag of food she'd scored slung in the crook of her elbow.

'How did you know?' she asked, unable to stop her own smirk.

Xadrion moved toward her, coming to a stop so close to her body she felt her breath catch. He lazily placed a hand forward until it rested on Az's protruding hip. Where his fingers settled, she felt the heat emanating. He tightened his hold, pulling her slightly closer to him until Az's thigh settled against Xadrion's own.

'I would recognise you in any form you held,' Xadrion breathed. Az couldn't get enough air in. The way he was standing there, looking at her, left her immersed in his eyes and movements. It would be so easy to lean up, just as she had in the field that day, and catch his lips in hers.

In the corner of her mind was Xadrion's presence, standing on the bridge that linked them but not stepping into the boundaries of her mind. His eyes never left hers as his mental presence seemed to peer *at* her mind's space. Rather than step across as he so easily could have, Xadrion frowned and released his hold on her waist, taking a notable step away from her.

One look had been all it took for him to see it was not her that he wanted. He had looked at her mind, not even bothering to step in, and had seemingly decided he was not interested. Azraelle's stomach sank, but she kept her expression as contained as she could. This was why he was so bad for her. He didn't even want her, not in the way she wanted him, and Az still couldn't shake Xadrion from her mind. Still, she couldn't rebuild those walls around her to keep him out. Azraelle did not have space for another weakness, one that would certainly make itself known if he had actually wanted her.

'I was coming to visit you. I think we need to start with Ilyon's training immediately. I'm just worried our sessions will now require us to leave the castle's wards to go undetected,' Xadrion said, as if he had something stuck in his throat.

'Come on, I've got it all figured out already,' Azraelle said, trying to add the iciness to her voice so as to appear unaffected by their brief moment of contact.

She led Xadrion the rest of the way through the hallways until they reached Emera's rooms. Azraelle felt heat beneath her skin at her embarrassment, at how easily she was sure he'd read her. The dynamic between them had shifted and he now held the power over her emotions.

When Azraelle led the way into Emera's rooms, Emera was awake and sipping on some tea with Tolemus. Ilyon was sprawled in the exact same position Az had left him in. Azraelle couldn't pull her eyes from Xadrion as he looked around the room, taking stock of Ilyon sleeping and the pillows that scattered the ground where Tolemus had slept.

'Tolemus is going to be training with us,' Azraelle said. Tolemus looked towards them, a smile on his face more genuine than she had seen him display in others presence and gave a little wave to Xadrion. 'He's much the same as Ilyon, so I think it will be useful for them to match against each other. Emera also will be helping, as she understands the elements of Hera's power more than I ever could and would be able to assist with his learning.'

Xadrion said nothing but gave a slight nod of confirmation. He hadn't stopped scanning the room around them. Azraelle placed the food on the counter and walked to where Ilyon was sleeping, snoring, and gave his shoulder a gentle shake. With a feeling of affection – and fondness – for Ilyon that resembled the way Azraelle imagined it would feel to care for a younger sibling, she swiped his hair back from his face as his eyes began to open.

Azraelle was the youngest of her siblings, and Thanatos who was next before her had already been old enough that Azraelle had never known what it felt like to have a younger sibling to grow up with. In fact, Azraelle had not been allowed to be around many others besides Thanatos and Zagreus as she came of age, which had been one of the biggest contributing reasons behind her initial fleeing to Eviria with the Ravens.

'Morning,' Ilyon grumbled. He stretched his body out, limited by the couch's length, and pushed himself to a sitting position. Several joints popped in release as he shifted and stretched, while his hair remained an absolute mess about his face.

Azraelle laughed as she ran her fingers through his hair, doing what she could to tame the wildness. With her fingers still in his hair, her gaze shifted back to where Xadrion stood in the doorway, his eyes seeming to watch every move she made. Azraelle could've sworn she saw that flickering of rage behind his eyes, a look he'd given her more than a few times. The familiar scent of an approaching storm filled Azraelle's senses, the fresh smell of rain so at odds with the anger she felt from him. The air crackled around Xadrion, and for the first time now that she knew he had power behind his anger, Azraelle was concerned. How long could he go with his magic pushing his anger before he exploded? Perhaps for the first time also, Azraelle felt herself worried at the thought of how easily he felt anger towards *her*.

After the couple of days they'd spent alone at the cabin, she had assumed they would return on better terms. Yet, as soon as they'd rode into the stables on their return, the energy had shifted between them once more and it seemed they were back to normal. Or at least Xadrion was. Azraelle didn't know how she could forget the intimacy of his power brushing against hers, or of his mind within her own. As much as the lightning came with its struggles for her, mainly in its reminder of everything she suffered at the hands of Zeus, Xadrion's lightning had somehow seemed as if it were trying to comfort her through that suffering. Like it was trying to prove to her own darkness that it was different energy, and that it wouldn't hurt her in that way.

'Come on, Ilyon, time to start training,' Azraelle said, pulling his hand gently until he stood in front of her.

As a group, they ate the breakfast Azraelle had brought back with her before they each broke off towards their individual rooms to get changed from the clothes they'd slept in. They agreed to meet in the courtyard outside the entrance doors. Xadrion still did not comment on everyone having stayed in Emera's rooms last night, even as he stormed away to wait at the agreed location.

When they had all reconvened in the courtyard, Azraelle led the way to the stables Rhoas had detailed to her. Ilyon and Tolemus walked at the rear of the group, Xadrion in the middle, while Emera and Azraelle led the way. She could hear Tolemus and Ilyon chatting animatedly and the idea of them getting along so well made her heart sing. There was no way this peace was permanent, at least not for her. The future would undoubtedly hold more than a few challenging times, but for now she was feeling calm.

'The old quarters?' Emera asked as she pieced together where they were heading toward. They were away from any buildings by that point, the stretch of land between the castle and its buildings and the older grounds was empty except for the gardens that they now walked through. Az could see the few abandoned buildings from the moment they entered the gardens and knew immediately they would be perfect for what they needed.

'It's far enough away that no one will hear us when the fighting becomes more unnatural for the mortals to watch,' Azraelle explained. 'We need space, and a lot of it, but we need privacy more than anything if the princes are going to keep their powers hidden.'

'And what of yours? You also need to keep yours hidden,' Emera said.

'I'm sure half the castle already thinks I'm a witch,' Azraelle said, and Emera laughed. Azraelle was under no impression that the people in the castle completely trusted her after her initial outburst, but she had reached a place of comfortable cohabitation with them that was easy enough. Still, Az knew they watched her whenever she left her rooms, and particularly as she had been training the princes. 'But yes, it isn't a safe idea for me to reveal the extent of my magic. It's frowned upon for mortals to be told of my kind.'

'Frowned upon?' Emera prodded.

'I mean, there are gods who have taken it upon themselves to descend to the mortal realm and set the mortals to worshipping us. I wouldn't be surprised if you'd heard more than a few stories spread by my kind about their own heroic tales. But yes, it is frowned upon,' Azraelle explained. 'To reveal our kind to a mortal is a sign of great weakness, either vanity or love.'

'Love is no weakness, Az,' Emera said, frowning at her as they continued walking side by side.

'Not to mortals, maybe. But for immortals it's different,' Azraelle said. 'When we are immortal to so much, invincible to nearly anything that might harm us, having someone who you love can be used against you.'

'Has that been done often?' Emera asked. Azraelle knew it had. Many of her siblings had given themselves over to Chaos, opening themselves to leaving their physical bodies, because the ones they had loved had been killed over and over to get to them. Even Thanatos and Aphrodite had faced perils because of it, with Aphrodite being Zeus' daughter. Zeus had tried to use her an endless number of times to reach Thanatos, to take his revenge against Hypnos and Nyx. If Aphrodite weren't so stubbornly in love with Than, it may have worked.

'More than a handful of times,' Azraelle admitted. 'Too many have been lost because of it.'

By that point, the group had reached the series of abandoned buildings. Az scanned until she found the one with large sliding doors that opened to a room with stables lining each wall. On the other end of the room was another large door, which, when opened, revealed an oval room large enough for their purposes. Az imagined it would have been used for the horse's training, the size more than large enough for the large animals to run at full speed.

The floor was compacted dirt and there was nothing lining the room except for old leather items and pieces of equipment in the occasional pile.

It would work perfectly.

'Tolemus, can you run Xadrion through some moves? I'm going to need to work with Ilyon a fair amount today,' Azraelle said. Tolemus grinned, almost maniacally, and jogged into the centre of the room with Xadrion. They had no weapons – they wouldn't need them. Xadrion and Ilyon knew how to fight with swords, and weapons would become a part of training once again, but for now they needed to understand how they could rely on their magic.

Azraelle pulled Emera and Ilyon to the barrier of the room and sat down in the dirt with them. Spending the few days with Xadrion had allowed Azraelle to figure out possible pathways for waking up their magic. It had taken her some time with Xadrion to find all the pathways she had but doing it with Ilyon that day did not take anywhere near as long. It helped that Ilyon didn't have any barrier in his mind yet to keep Azraelle out.

It was the first thing she had to fix. She spent most of that morning speaking directly into Ilyon's mind, showing him to build his wall and strengthen it over time. Azraelle wasn't surprised to see the shape of his wall when it formed – a perfect replica of the wall that surrounded the giant castle of Fennhall. Where Azraelle's had been black darkness, and Xadrion's was lightning crackling, Ilyon held an impenetrable stone wall.

Tolemus' wall also didn't surprise Azraelle. She knew of his grandmother, Thetis, and her affinity to water. It made sense that Tolemus' wall was a thick sheet of water with a current designed to wash away anyone who tried to push through.

Where Xadrion was adept at his mind work, Ilyon was next level. Az was surprised by that, considering Xadrion had the full powers of the immortals, while Ilyon shared only some. It didn't do anything to stop him, not after she woke his passages up. He crafted a wall so quick and strong that Az felt again wary at her own inability to bring hers back.

From the other side of the room, interrupting her thoughts, swearing echoed from Tolemus and Xadrion. Well, actually it was only Xadrion who was swearing, loudly. Az looked over just in time to see Tolemus practically pick Xadrion up and throw him across the room. Xadrion flew more than a few body lengths before he went crashing to the ground.

With his magic strengthening his skin and strength, Xadrion sprung to a crouched position and was leaping back at Tolemus before any time had passed.

'You're done,' Xadrion grunted as he launched himself back to Tolemus, slamming a shoulder so hard into Tolemus' chest that they both went flying to the ground. It quickly descended into a brawl on the ground. Even from the distance Azraelle stood at she could feel the air in the building begin to crackle, the current of Xadrion's power getting swept away as his adrenalin built.

'Do we stop them?' Emera asked from where she was now working with Ilyon. It turned out Ilyon had a significant healing affinity, which Emera had excitedly been trying to show him the ropes of.

'You keep going, I'll handle the brutes,' Azraelle said. Ilyon offered her an apologetic look as she turned to walk towards the brawling men. Az jogged to where Tolemus was now pinned and made out his expression of concern as Xadrion towered over him. She'd never seen Tolemus look genuinely worried, which made Az concerned for how much pressure Xadrion must have been applying.

As long as Tolemus had held his power for, it was nothing compared to the full strength of an immortal, which Xadrion now was. Given Xadrion had spent the entirety of his life studying combat, combined with his newfound power, Tolemus had never stood a chance. But Xadrion should have been restraining himself. Azraelle began to run to reach them, her panic building. Why was Xadrion not stopping?

'Xadrion, back off,' Azraelle called as she reached the two men on the ground.

Azraelle reached out as she got behind them and moved to yank on Xadrion's shoulder. If he was aware of his surroundings, it should have been the only thing necessary to snap him back to resting and get him from atop Tolemus. It didn't work. Xadrion seemed determined to rain down throws at Tolemus. Azraelle tugged harder, her panic climbing at the cuts that were quickly appearing across Tolemus' face from Xadrion's strikes. Tolemus tried to struggle, tried to push Xadrion off, but nothing was working. Azraelle threw all of her own strength into pulling Xadrion back.

Faster than she had ever seen Xadrion move, he defensively swung to face Az. Azraelle only had time to take in Xadrion's prepared crouch before the first blast hit her.

Lightning.

Cold, hard lightning rocked through her body, sending her flying across the space and slamming into the dirt so hard she was winded immediately. The air rushed from her, pain spreading through her ribs and down every limb.

Lightning, there, in her body.

Every memory of the fifteen years sprung to the surface, despite the months she'd spent pressing them away. Where packed dirt had once been beneath her, the feeling of cold iron now spread below her. She was right back in that cell again, with that electric current pulsing beneath her skin. She felt the burns, the heat, the way she had smelt her own skin sizzling wherever the lightning had touched her.

'Azraelle?' came a voice. The familiar vibrations of the voice had her blood singing for the present. But, Azraelle couldn't see anything, couldn't think of anything except for the current that ran through her body, no longer just a memory.

'Azraelle, please, be okay,' the voice spoke again. And then she felt the hands on her. Those cruel hands that had touched her so many times in that cell of hers. They were back, and they were on her shoulders, then her arms, then her face. Azraelle let loose a wild scream, lacing it with every image of death she could summon, and flung her power at those hands. They would not touch her like that, not ever again.

Azraelle felt the tendrils come to her call, aimed at the hands that had been holding her face only a moment prior. A yell came from nearby, one of pain and shock. The hands had left, and where there had previously been lightning, she now felt hollow.

Above her, Azraelle could see the roof of the dilapidated building they'd spent their morning in.

Breathe, Azraelle told herself.

She was not in the cells. That was not Zeus' lightning.

Azraelle rushed to face the yell she heard, seeing an image that left her reeling. Ilyon and Emera were running toward them, Tolemus stood between her and Xadrion, who was prone behind him. Tolemus was facing her, crouched with his once discarded sword now raised and ready but his eyes pleading with her. Az looked straight past him to where Xadrion lay on the ground, her tendrils slicing at him over and over. His eyes were glazed over, his body arching off the floor. That image of his body with her shadows over him buried itself into her core and snapped her awake. All at once Azraelle knew what she had done to him.

Az pulled her power back to her as fast as she could summon it and felt her tendrils readily obey. The images of death she'd conjured and shot at Xadrion's mind had broken straight through his shield, or he had let her in, and had been tormenting him with the sights as he lay in the dirt getting slashed at by her darkness.

As soon as the power returned to her, Xadrion pushed himself to his hands and knees and retched. Tolemus continued to stand guard between them as Xadrion heaved. Ilyon and Emera hesitated between the two for a moment like they didn't know where they needed to be before Emera decided Xadrion needed the most immediate help and ran to reach him.

What the fuck had happened?

Xadrion finished retching. No one seeming capable of moving. When nothing else was coming up, Xadrion finally looked up and locked his sights straight onto Az. He looked… sorry, maybe. His eyes were bloodshot from the heaving and he was still struggling to gulp down air. He stood, hesitantly getting to his feet, pushing past Emera and Tolemus, and came straight to kneel beside her.

'Are you okay?' Xadrion whispered in a panic. 'I didn't know it was you, Az. I couldn't tell where I was.'

Azraelle tried to speak, tried to comfort him in some way, but she couldn't make herself form words. She couldn't pull herself completely from that cell she'd occupied for so long, the methods of torture that had been employed against her. Instead, she stared blankly at Xadrion. Her tongue felt like lead in her mouth, unable to move.

'Azraelle, please be okay,' Xadrion pleaded. She was kneeling, unable to pull her gaze from him as he knelt beside her, seemingly debating whether it was okay to touch her or not. He finally made a movement, extending his hands toward Az as if he would offer physical comfort. Az flinched away and scrambled to her feet.

'I can't,' Az finally managed to choke out before she gave herself over to shadows, morphing into her mist-form within a second. She could see the chaos she was leaving below her, the way Ilyon and Emera watched the shadows with fear, how Tolemus watched them with sadness, and Xadrion… she didn't want to try to piece together what Xadrion's expression meant.

Az darted away, leaving the abandoned stables completely. She found herself drifting, not back toward the castle they'd walked from that morning, but instead further away. She continued through the series of abandoned buildings until she reached the outer castle wall. Azraelle silently slithered up and over and continued using corners and buildings to provide shadow as she moved outside of the city completely. She didn't stop until she knew she was outside the bounds of the castle wards.

Azraelle fell to her knees as she shifted back to her physical form. No tears were coming, they hadn't since she'd broken down in Rhoas' study when she'd first arrived. Instead, Az gratefully welcomed the familiar feeling of sharp strikes across her insides, as if there were a sword tearing at her internally.

Azraelle had felt the lightning, sure as day, hit her and send her flying. When she'd moved to pull Xadrion from Tolemus, Xadrion had struck at *her*. He'd thrown his lightning at her so hard she'd ended up halfway across the room. It had been Xadrion touching her, Xadrion's hands on her face trying to pull her back from that place she'd gone. And it was Xadrion who she had thrown her magic at in a panic.

It took the better part of an hour for Azraelle to finally drag herself fully back to the present. Feeling Xadrion's lightning strike her had impacted her more than she thought it would. Looking down at her shirt showed her the burn that had ripped straight through it, settling into her skin where the lightning had entered. She had known they would have to start practising with their powers soon enough, but Azraelle was hoping to have a bit more time to mentally prepare for feeling the lightning once more, maybe even to teach him to pull back in time to avoid any serious injuries.

The pain of the burn across her stomach hit Azraelle with more force and she doubled over on her knees.

As Azraelle was struggling to settle herself back into reality, she felt something gentle enter her mind. With her walls still down, the presence was in her mind for the shortest of times, taking a quick glance around before it disappeared. Azraelle recognised that presence, knew the probing it was doing, and so sat back and waited for them to find her. They knew exactly where she was and there was no point in panicking. The pain of the burn continued to grow until it was almost intolerable.

Azraelle heard them before she saw them. Gusts of wind pushed toward the ground, rustling the treetops and sending the forest floor scattering every way. The gushing beating of wings, wings that had been so alike her own, sounded as their owner flew to where Azraelle had stopped.

Azraelle was surprised they'd managed to find her but was not surprised at *who* had found her. Descending from above, her white wings giant as they spanned the length of the area Azraelle had found herself in, came Nakir, Azraelle's second.

After so long without seeing her – without seeing any of the Ravens – Azraelle felt the tears build up in her eyes. She would not let them fall, *could* not let them fall. It was not a vulnerability she wanted to show to Nakir.

Nakir was one of the most beautiful women that Az had ever seen and probably ever would. Her hair was so long and dark, the complete opposite of Az's stark white hair. On the battlefield they had stood as a contrast to the other but always fought side by side. Azraelle tried not to pay too much attention to how beautiful Nakir's wings were, how equal to Az's own they had once been.

'I knew it,' Nakir whispered, before she dropped fully to the ground and pulled Azraelle in for an embrace. It was so uncommon for them, this form of physical contact. Hundreds of years Nakir had been Azraelle's second, for thousands of years before that they'd been fighting together. They did not hug.

But it seemed Nakir needed it, and Azraelle sure did, so she embraced her old second in return, wincing at the pain that lanced through her abdomen with the movement.

'How are you here? Why are you here?' Azraelle could feel the tears springing further but still choked them away and refused to let them fall.

'I knew you weren't dead,' Nakir said, finally pulling from their hug and extending them so that Az was being held at arms lengths from her, Nakir's hands on Azraelle's shoulders. Her wings were folded down, but each was at least as long as Nakir was tall, so they were always visible even when tucked behind her.

'How did you find me?' Azraelle asked. She was grateful Nakir was there, but now there was the risk that others weren't far behind.

'Thanatos let me know there was something in this area I should be looking for,' Nakir answered. 'I kind of put together what the something was.'

'You came looking for me?' Azraelle asked, unable to hide the shock from her tone. She had missed Nakir, as well as the other Ravens, more than anyone else in her period of containment. For so many thousands of years they had been her family, the women she rode into battle with on the rare occasion that their force was needed, and the women who helped her carry out Death's purpose.

'Of course, Az,' Nakir said. Not Primus. No, Azraelle would not be referred to as primus again. The reality of that hit her hard and Azraelle swallowed back the lump that formed in her throat. She was found guilty, banished to death, and Nakir would have taken control of the Ravens in her place. This was the new primus. Nakir was not here to take Azraelle home. She wouldn't be allowed, not when there was still a death sentence over Az's head, and the crime she had been charged with was of greater offence to the Ravens than anyone, given their particular role in ensuring Destiny's pathway was honoured.

'I didn't do it,' Azraelle blurted. 'The boy, I didn't alter his destiny. I read his threads first and they extended so far beyond that point. He had hundreds of years, Nakir. *Hundreds* while he was only a child. I didn't bring him back lightly.'

'The Moirai declared against you,' Nakir said. Nakir was tense now, as if they were reaching the point of her visit. Gone was her friend and second, in front of Az now stood the primus of the Ravens – Death's Hand.

'She said it needed to be this way,' Azraelle said. She still didn't understand her sister's intentions, doubted she'd live long enough to find out at this rate. 'She asked for my forgiveness and then declared me guilty across all of Mount Olympus. I don't know why she declared against me.'

'You cannot come back with such a charge,' Nakir said. 'I could be content to pretend you had died in that fall, but you know many of our kind won't. For what you did for me, I would not reveal you. But you cannot return.' Nakir made a pointed glance at where Azraelle's wings no longer were. Azraelle pushed the reminder from her mind, not willing to face what it meant for her wings to be gone, if she ever managed to remove the guilty verdict placed over her.

'Thanatos believes that if I can find the boy, I can prove that his thread was not altered. At least enough to cast doubt over my sentence long enough to have people stop wanting me dead,' Azraelle said.

'That could work,' Nakir said. 'Can you track him from what you remember?' Azraelle shook her head.

'My magic is not fully back yet, not at the level I need it to be at. I think I would recognise him if I were near to him, but if he is far away, I don't remember enough to find him once more. The time I spent on Olympus before the trial has left me disoriented from all that happened before,' Azraelle explained.

'I could search our records,' Nakir suggested, her face showing her dread at the thought. 'It might take me a while – a long while, given the state of them, but there has to be something in there about him.'

'Of course,' Azraelle said. 'But you cannot let anyone know you are looking. Simply find the information on him, return and give it to me. I will find him. You are too traceable and until I have the boy, I need him to remain from the watchful eyes of those who would harm me and mine.'

'I know how to be stealthy, Prim – Az,' Nakir said. Azraelle pursed her lips at the near slip-up, the ache settling deep over her chest at the reminder.

'I know you do, Nakir,' Azraelle said. She closed the distance between them once more, folding her own arms around Nakir's body and holding her tightly.

'I know it will not be the same if I return,' Azraelle whispered. 'I do not wish to take all you have earned. I just wish to be able to return to my family, and I am so grateful for your help in doing so.'

Nakir squeezed her gently then released the hold completely.

'I have to go. It is too risky to stay much longer,' Nakir said. 'Get back inside wherever you've been hiding. I will find what you need and return here when I have it. Thanatos will tell you when I'm on my way.'

Azraelle nodded, but Nakir was already unfurling her wings. Nakir pushed up, the area around them being caught in the updrafts of the wind, and the echoing boom of her wings pushing her up left Azraelle's head reeling.

Nakir had come for her. Not even Thanatos had been able to do that. Nyx never could. No one ever would have. But Nakir had done it.

When Nakir was gone, Azraelle finally succumbed to her tears. She had not been abandoned, not as hopelessly as she had felt before. Maybe, after all this, she would still hold a place in the Ravens. They were the family she had surrounded herself with all those thousands of years, and the idea of not being able to be with them once more hurt her more than most other thoughts. But... her wings. She could not fly with the Ravens if she could not fly at all.

Interrupting her thoughts, the crash of footsteps moving through the woods broke the silence. She had just enough time to wipe the traitorous tears from her cheeks, definitely not masking the sight of her crying, when Xadrion's presence scanned out toward her, trying to find her exact location. He settled on her and a brief moment later, Xadrion himself appeared.

He stopped as he entered the clearing and watched Azraelle as if he were waiting for her to give the approval of his approach. He would let her lead the conversation that was to follow.

TWENTY

XADRION

Xadrion had never seen Azraelle with tears in her eyes before. In the months she'd been there, Az had never displayed any significant moment of sadness besides when he found her in her room after Karlin's death. Seeing her on her knees, the hopelessness over her expression that day, had left Xadrion feeling concerned for what that level of hopelessness did to a person. He'd since peered enough into Azraelle's mind to see exactly what it did to her.

Now standing before him, he could see Azraelle with tears brimming. Xadrion couldn't stop his eyes shifting to look at the singe across the front of her shirt and the burn that he could clearly see across her abdomen. The burn he had given her. But he hadn't known it was her, hadn't even known it was Tolemus beneath him.

The power had been boiling within him all that morning and he'd been looking forward to working some of the pent-up energy out in training. He'd been so consumed with the power that lined every move he made that Xadrion didn't even realise he'd lost control. He didn't notice the moment the energy took over, the moment he merely became a conduit.

When Azraelle had pulled him from Tolemus, his power had raged and all it registered as was someone standing between his power and its target. The lightning had left his fingers before he'd even known what had happened, as simple as if he'd been swatting a bug. Turning around and seeing Azraelle flying through the air, hearing the horrific thump when she crashed into the dirt, had snapped him from the trance instantaneously.

He'd felt the presence of her magic before of course and had felt it when she used it for other means but being on the receiving end of an attack from it was unlike anything he'd ever experienced. The images that had crossed his mind, slamming straight through any and all mental defences he'd managed to erect, left Xadrion feeling sick even as he stood in front of Azraelle now in that clearing.

Despite the sickness it had dragged from him, all Xadrion wanted to do was run to Az and hold her in his arms until they were both okay, but Emera had demanded he stood still long enough for her to close the wounds coating his arms and hands from Azraelle's lashes. By the time he could move again, Azraelle was long gone. As if he'd been cut over and over, there now were mostly scabbed over cuts running the length of his arms.

'Azraelle, I am so sorry,' Xadrion said, but didn't move any closer. He didn't know what place she was in, if him even being in her line of sight was something she wanted. He had shot her with the very power that had tormented her for nearly two decades.

'It's fine,' Azraelle said, not looking at all like it. For someone already so pale, the absence of any colour in her cheeks had Xadrion worried. 'I just needed time to recollect myself.'

'I don't know what happened, Az. Truly, I wasn't present in my mind. It was like the power had taken over my body.' He wanted to explain himself, wanted for the tension between him and Az to be gone, but knew that she had every right to not want to see him. Azraelle's brows knitted together and she leant a palm weakly against a nearby tree trunk. The very effort of standing looked difficult for her. How serious was she hurt?

'That happens,' Azraelle said, breathlessly. 'It happens when you are first learning to control it but it usually happens in a much more contained environment. I remember going through a similar thing. I should have planned for it, but it slipped my mind.'

'This is not your fault. I should have been able to control it,' Xadrion argued. Xadrion wanted to move closer to her, but she still had not relaxed towards him and despite the pain he could see in her expression she was still keeping a wary eye on him.

'You couldn't have,' Azraelle said. 'We spend a lot of time training when our powers first begin to represent, but it is done under suppression for that very reason. The power will want to swell up and take over. You need another who can keep you in check while it happens.'

'Can your magic suppress mine?' Xadrion asked.

'Mm, maybe,' Az said. They still stood across from each other, neither getting closer. 'I can try, but it's usually done with someone more intricately linked. Family, or soul-twined.'

'Soul-twined?' Xadrion asked, the term unfamiliar in all that they'd discussed.

'Two gods with two magics that are compatible. Their powers can link them together at times, other times relying on the other's strength. Even sometimes it allows the exchange of their powers,' Azraelle answered.

'Do you have a soul-twined? Someone who helped you through the suppression?' Xadrion asked.

'Thanatos,' Azraelle answered. 'He was able to suppress mine during the period.'

His eyes roamed back down to Azraelle's abdomen, to the stark burn visible beneath the nearly tattered shirt. The lightning burn looked different to any he'd seen from fire. It had blistered and burnt, but somehow it looked like the remaining wound had streaks visible from where the lightning would have flowed. The image reminded Xadrion of vines – pale, ice-coated vines.

Azraelle seemed to feel his gaze, and she peered down at her own stomach, moving to pull as much of the threads of the shirt from the blistering burn beneath. A hiss whistled through her lips as she winced in pain, and she leant her shoulder heavily against the tree for support.

'Let me help,' Xadrion said, taking a step forward. Azraelle whipped back to face him. As she tensed, he paused, long enough for her to note his movements and nod for him to proceed. Xadrion quickly closed the rest of the space between them.

'I just need help getting back to Emera,' Azraelle said. 'Transforming back to my shadows becomes more difficult when pain is tying me to my physical form.'

Xadrion nodded and propped his arm around her waist, gently doing his best to avoid the burn. He supported her weight, light as she was, as they moved back in the direction of the castle.

'I wish I could take it all back, what I did to you,' Xadrion said as they walked. Azraelle peered sideways and up to him, such difference in their heights.

'It is a setback, and one that obviously comes with things I need to work through, but I knew we would have to face it eventually,' she said. 'Your power needs to learn how to work well with others, which means we are going to have to keep training. You can't be afraid to use it because of this.'

'How can I not be?' Xadrion asked. 'How can I pretend everything is fine when I did this to you?'

Azraelle shrugged slightly, her weight shifting more onto him as they walked. Were her eyes drooping? Her steps definitely seemed less sure.

'It's just a scratch,' Azraelle said. It was the impact of that scratch, as she'd called it, that sent Azraelle stumbling on her next step. Her legs gave out beneath her, and she would have fallen completely had Xadrion not already been supporting so much of her.

'Clearly not,' Xadrion grunted as her weight fell completely onto him. He swept his other arm beneath her knees, easily lifting her so that he was carrying her in his arms. She glared up at him but wrapped one arm around his neck. With his own new strength, holding her fully didn't feel taxing on him at all.

'I can walk,' Azraelle insisted.

'Maybe, maybe not. I don't care to see you attempt to make it the rest of the way back,' Xadrion said. She was so close to him now, her face so close to his own. Xadrion had to keep himself from looking down at her, for fear of not being able to pull his eyes away. He needed to keep his eyes on the surroundings, on the path in front of him as he walked, but the image of her in his arms kept calling to him.

Azraelle scoffed but relaxed in his grasp. When Xadrion shifted her too harshly, it elicited small gasps of pain and as they kept walking, she seemed to be doing her best to keep the sounds of pain from coming out at all. She'd travelled in shadow form all this way, clearly not even registering the pain of the injury at the time, but now that it had hit her it appeared to be intensifying.

Azraelle pressed her face sideways, directly into the muscles of his chest, and beneath her breath uttered, '*Anathematizo.*' He'd never heard the word before but he got the distinct impression Az was cursing.

Xadrion could feel Az's magic begin to shift around her, a soothing feeling emanating from beneath her skin. Across her abdomen small wisps of those black tendrils whispered around the burn, darting across it.

'I'm not great at healing,' Azraelle said, 'but I think I can do enough to not pass out until we get back to Emera.' They'd crossed the city entrance by that point and there were bustling people moving about them. Azraelle had gone straight over the castle wall but to get back in, they'd needed to detour around to the gates.

Xadrion picked up his pace, reaching the castle wall as fast as he was able. He felt her shaking in his arms as if a coldness had settled deep within her.

Emera was waiting in the courtyard when they got there, Ilyon anxiously pacing behind her. They rushed inside, the scene resembling the very first day Xadrion had brought Azraelle back to the castle. They took her instead to Azraelle's rooms and Xadrion laid her across her own bed. He hadn't been in this room more than once, the day Karlin had died. Xadrion didn't know if he could count the time he'd shared her mind and watched her pleasure herself on that very bed, or more when she'd given him control to pleasure her.

Had that really only been four days ago?

It was a different image now, seeing her lying on her bed with the burn he had given her. Emera cut the shirt straight up the middle, taking the time to gently pull the loose threads from the blistering wound on Azraelle's stomach. Emera draped a fresh cloth across Azraelle's chest, keeping her shielded while she was treated, and the ever-present emerald pendant laid across Azraelle's neck.

Xadrion stood back, giving Emera the space to move around as she needed. Azraelle didn't pass out or make a noise, even as it seemed the pain had become almost unbearable. Instead, silent tears fell over her cheeks. That image of Azraelle crying would haunt Xadrion for the remainder of his days, he was sure.

'Ilyon, you can help. Come here,' Emera ordered. Ilyon came closer until they were both standing over Azraelle. Emera took Ilyon's hand and placed it over Azraelle's abdomen, on a rare patch of unburnt skin. 'Think about channelling your energy into her, as if you want to wash away all the pain and suffering, as if you could undo what has been done.'

Emera placed her own hands over Az, and then both Ilyon and Emera bowed their heads and set to working. It was slow to begin with, and at the first instance of magic swirling the room Azraelle's eyes flickered to where Xadrion stood in the corner. They held him there, never leaving his own while Ilyon and Emera worked.

Tolemus arrived at some point and came to stand beside Xadrion but didn't say anything.

Xadrion didn't know how long had passed before Emera and Ilyon stopped working. When they released their hold on Azraelle and stepped back, Az finally broke the gaze she'd held since the healing had begun. Xadrion moved forward, needing to see how bad the damage was. Where there had been a blistering burn, there now was a knotted twisting of red scarring that lined her abdomen. Now that it was clearer Xadrion could see the point of entry his lightning had taken, sitting more to one side than the other. While there were many other smaller scars across Azraelle's skin Xadrion had become accustomed to seeing, now seeing a new one caused by his own power, the guilt overwhelmed him.

'With a few more sessions we should be able to get the scarring right down,' Emera said.

'Thank you,' Azraelle said quietly. She looked at Ilyon beside her and reached over to squeeze his hand gently. 'You did so well, Ilyon.'

The tenderness in her voice took Xadrion by surprise. It wasn't what she should have been talking about. Azraelle should have been yelling at Xadrion for his recklessness and everyone should have been fussing to take care of her. Instead, Azraelle seemed disengaged, as if she were not even aware of what had happened to her.

Xadrion couldn't help himself. He wanted to see past the impassive expression she had settled into while they healed her and the distinct lack of tone she was displaying for them in that moment. He needed to make sure she was really okay. Xadrion pushed himself towards her mind, hoping to get even just a glimpse from the outside to comfort him that she was fine. When he got to the edge of that bridge between their minds, preparing to take that look inside, he found he could not.

Azraelle's eyes met his, surely sensing Xadrion lingering on the boundaries of her mind. Where for the last couple of days there had been no wall, now something had taken shape. It hadn't been there when he was searching for her only a matter of hours ago; he'd used her mind to find her location. Now, after she'd held his gaze for the duration of her healing, it seemed she had managed to piece something together.

It wasn't the wall it had once been. No longer was it as tall and long as the eye could see, and no longer did it even seem to be in the form of a wall. Instead, when Xadrion looked at the beginnings of the shield around Az's mind, it looked like how he imagined it would feel to be floating in the middle of an endless night sky. Between the bridge and Az's mind was a chasm that opened to expansive nothingness. Not even black, just void. Xadrion did not want to know what would happen if someone tried to step into that chasm.

Azraelle had been rebuilding her wall as she had held his gaze.

'You can all leave now and stop fussing so much. I'm fine, just let me rest,' Azraelle said. She pushed herself from the bed and pulled the covers around her naked chest. She gave gentle shoves to Ilyon and Emera to send them toward the door. Tolemus seemed content to stay beside Xadrion, or so it seemed as he had followed Xadrion closer to the bed.

Emera looked like she was going to kick up a fuss, but Azraelle gave her a look that warned her against such actions and even Ilyon looked hesitantly between Az and the door.

'Can we get you anything?' Ilyon asked.

'No, honestly. I'm fine. I just want to sleep by myself for a while. I'll see you all at breakfast,' Azraelle said, letting an effortless smile come through. Xadrion didn't have to be able to peer into her mind to know that was forced.

'And the ball tomorrow night, will you still join us?' Ilyon asked, trying to stall the forced eviction of the room.

Azraelle laughed. 'Of course, who am I to stand up my dates?' she responded. Ilyon seemed appeased at her laughter and left the room with Emera. Tolemus took hold of Xadrion's forearm and gave him a gentle tug.

'I know what you may want to do,' Tolemus whispered as they moved. 'But let her have some time. Talk to her tomorrow.' Xadrion wanted to do anything besides leave her room in that moment. He wanted to make sure she was okay, that he hadn't done irreparable damage to both her and the relationship he had started to feel budding between them. He needed to make sure that she wasn't so lost in her own thoughts that he would lose her forever.

She had started building a wall. That was a good thing; Xadrion hoped so at least. It meant she was willing to start trying again, willing to protect herself from whatever might choose to hurt her. But she'd done so while staring directly at him, as if she were memorising exactly what she perceived as her weakness and examining how best to accommodate for it in her shield.

Xadrion let Tolemus pull him from Azraelle's rooms, though he wanted to stay. Azraelle needed time, he knew that, and if he stayed, he risked pushing her even further from him. Emera and Ilyon left together, heading back in the direction of Emera's rooms.

'I'm sorry,' Xadrion whispered to Tolemus.

'What for?' Tolemus responded, surprise evident in his raised brows. They began to walk down the hallway. Xadrion at least did not have a direction.

'For not controlling myself in that fight. I could have hurt you like I hurt her,' Xadrion answered. There was silence as they walked, as if Tolemus was deciding how best to answer him.

'I don't blame you, Xadrion, and I don't believe Az does either. I remember when my power came in. The feeling of it building under my skin was intoxicating. I felt like it would be the easiest thing in the world to just let go and let it do what it wished. And I don't even have the full power of the gods as you and Azraelle do, merely some of it,' Tolemus said. 'Azraelle knows that also.'

'If I can't keep it contained, how do I keep it from hurting someone, hurting her, again?' Xadrion asked.

'I think that's something you need to think long and hard about that. I don't believe Azraelle's magic will be enough to keep you suppressed, not when her power is so different to yours. Without someone with power closer to yours, I think you will struggle to be around anyone. And I think you will begin to notice its impacts sooner rather than later,' Tolemus warned.

'What impacts?' Xadrion asked, his panic rising at the unknown that was happening within him.

'The strain it takes to keep your power from unleashing, at least while you are learning the full extent of it, is difficult to outlast. You're going to get to a point where you will feel like you need to explode in order to get some sort of relief,' Tolemus said. 'How angry did you feel today?'

Xadrion thought on the question, reflecting on the rage he had felt all morning. Running into Azraelle in the hallway, touching her hip and being reminded all over again that he couldn't be with her had started it. Being taken back to Emera's rooms where they'd all spent the night, seeing Azraelle interact with such tenderness, and display such intimacy with the small group in the room, had made Xadrion feel rage. Not at the group, and never at her, but at himself. The way he yearned to be the one whose hair she tucked away, who she offered her casual touches to, the way he could not be had made him furious.

He had felt his magic brimming all morning, as if fuelled by the anger he'd felt. But he had thought nothing of it.

'Extremely angry. Am I forever doomed to be filled with rage as I have been?'

'In a way. Being forced to keep that initial outburst in check won't make you feel anything positive, that's for sure. But giving in to the anger could have it coming out anyway,' Tolemus said.

They'd walked up the stairs now, coming to a top level of the castle. They stopped at a window, no one else visible on that floor.

'So, the outburst is inevitable, the only difference being if I can be around someone who can suppress its limitations or not?' Xadrion asked, feeling hopeless.

'Basically,' Tolemus answered. 'But for now, let part of it go. Send as much as you think you can part with safely straight out this window and into the night sky. It's lightning, right? Let it storm.'

A storm. Yes, Xadrion could do that.

When it had stormed in the past, Xadrion had never felt so alive. Ironic, he supposed, knowing everything he knew now. Xadrion nodded and turned to face the window fully. He pressed his hands against the windowsill on either side and imagined what he wanted to happen. All the tension he was feeling, all the worry he felt towards if Azraelle was okay, or if she could ever forgive him, or how he would ever safely be around her if he could not control himself. Xadrion imagined all of that leaving him.

With a single shock of energy, a giant crack of lightning shot into the now night sky. The light illuminated the city for a brief moment, and as if in answer a giant crash of thunder echoed.

It didn't do much, but the power beneath Xadrion's skin did feel like it simmered down slightly.

The storm raged on for the rest of the night.

TWENTY-ONE

XADRION

True to her word, Azraelle came to the common mess hall for breakfast the next morning. Ilyon and Xadrion usually took their meals there as a means of being accessible for the people of the castle, especially as they had the visitors from Gaeweth. It was expected of them to dine with the royal party when possible, specifically Romina and the ambassador.

Emera, Tolemus and Azraelle all entered together, laughter echoing upon their entry. Neither of the women wore dresses; instead, both had chosen to wear pants they could move in and a loose-fitting shirt. At Azraelle's waist was a sword she'd had made for herself, and her hair was braided back and over her shoulder. She was laughing, seemingly pain free from the shot he'd made against her the day before and, as he always was when she entered a room, Xadrion was entranced by her beauty.

Emera, Tolemus and Azraelle all bowed out of respect to the princess before they took their own seats at the table.

'Do you all intend to fight today?' Romina asked, eyeing Az's outfit with no attempt to hide the disdain from her expression.

'Maybe you could join us, Princess,' Azraelle said, the edge of a taunt to her voice. Xadrion sucked in a breath, hoping the princess wouldn't realise she was being baited.

'Oh, no, thank you,' Romina responded, doing her best to look gracious at the offer, but still only managing to look appalled at the idea. 'Will you be joining them, General?'

'I will, my lady. Unless there is another use of me you might have,' Tolemus responded.

'That's fine,' Romina said. 'Please just be back in time to prepare for the celebration tonight. Some particular outfitting is required.' Romina was talking to Tolemus but was looking between Azraelle and Emera, eyeing their clothes. Azraelle smiled, outwardly sweet, though Xadrion knew it was anything but.

'That reminds me, my dear Emera, we must ensure we bathe today,' Azraelle said, that sweet smile still dominating her expression. 'I know we tend to forget how to do those lady things.' Then Azraelle pushed from the seat, having only had the time to take a few bites of the plate she had in front of her, and stormed from the room.

Emera stood, looking from Romina to the doors Azraelle had just hurried through.

'Apologies, Princess, I'm sure she did not mean to be so cruel,' Emera apologised, before curtsying low and following Az from the room. Tolemus gave Xadrion a pointed look, then shifted his gaze down to where Xadrion had his arms laid over the table. Across the left one, Romina had gently placed a hand. Xadrion had not even noticed when she'd done it, so entranced by Azraelle entering as he was.

'Maybe she is lucky she can fight,' Romina said. 'For surely no one could ever handle being married to her. She will need to protect herself.'

'She is not so bad, my lady. I have noticed the social requirements of a lady is very different in Thesadel then they are at home in Gaeweth,' Tolemus said, trying in his own way to defend Azraelle. Xadrion felt shame at not being the first one to stand for her.

'Azraelle is under no burden to marry, should she not wish to do so,' Ilyon said. 'She is as welcome here under our protection as any.'

'Then why does she choose to fight?' Romina asked, still puzzled.

'Sometimes,' Xadrion barked, tiring of the conversation, 'it is not up to us to choose our paths. Azraelle does not reject being a lady because she prefers to fight but fights because she has had no other choice.'

'Oh,' Romina said. It was enough to end the conversation.

Eventually, Tolemus, Ilyon and Xadrion headed to the old stables, and found Emera and Azraelle already there. They were running through basic foot patterns, to which Emera was hopelessly falling over herself in her clumsiness. She was lucky she was a healer and not a fighter.

Xadrion felt his power brimming beneath his skin for the entire training session, but he did his best to push down. Tolemus volunteered to be partnered against Xadrion again, but Azraelle didn't let him.

'I can handle it, Az,' Tolemus argued.

'I'm sure you can, but I need you to work with Ilyon. And I need to try to suppress Xadrion,' Azraelle said. So that was that. Tolemus moved to where Ilyon stood and began to demonstrate different ways he could incorporate his powers into his fighting. Tolemus taught much in the same way Azraelle had that day at the cabin. The two fought so differently and yet they had very similar styles of teaching.

'Can you do it?' Xadrion asked, turning to face Azraelle. 'Are you able to suppress me?'

'I can try, but I don't think it will really be enough to prevent any significant expression of your power,' Azraelle answered. When she looked to him, her eyes never lifted high enough to meet Xadrion's, while her brows pulled together in concentration.

In his mind, Azraelle's familiar presence waited at his mental shield asking for entrance. He opened it, creating the space for her to step into. All over again he was reminded what it felt like to have her in his mind. A shiver ran through his body, heightened as his senses already were with the power simmering within him. Every time she was even near him, Xadrion had to admit to being particularly aware of her presence. And when she was in his mind, closer to him than any physical touch could ever allow, it was a whole other story.

After a moment of her being in that space he created only for her, the beginnings of her magic stirred within him. Tendrils of darkness coiled around the exposed switches in his mind. In response, there was a very slight ease in the tension he felt boiling within him. It was barely noticeable, the urge to give in and release his power still a near overwhelming sense. The only thing that kept him from releasing it was the image that was burned behind his eyes, the one that had plagued him as he slept the night before – the image of the burn covering Azraelle's stomach.

'That's all I can manage,' Azraelle said, disappointed. 'Your magic is too dissimilar to mine.'

'I'm sorry,' Xadrion said. He didn't know what exactly he was apologising for, but he felt the need to anyway. Maybe again for all he had put her through and all she had gone through before.

'It's the way of things. We aren't usually so estranged from our own kind when our powers come in,' Azraelle said. 'I think that's kind of the purpose. If we are so far from our kind when that initial surge of magic occurs it ensures we can be discovered by those who would understand us.'

'Seems like an interesting failsafe,' Xadrion noted. Azraelle watched him carefully as she slowly began to pull her power back to herself, the tendrils leaving his mind. 'Leave them. If it can limit the fallout even a small amount, I will take it.'

Azraelle stopped withdrawing and nodded in agreement.

'I think the darkness wishes to stay anyway,' Azraelle said quietly. 'It's harder to pull them back than it should be.' Xadrion had felt the same thing the night she had let him into her mind. It had felt like their magic was playing with the others; like it was attempting to thread itself together. Xadrion wondered what would have happened that night if Azraelle hadn't forced him out when his lightning presented itself. He knew what his lightning must feel like to her, and yet every time he felt his power entwine with Azraelle's he couldn't shake the feeling that his power was trying to play with hers. They were so dissimilar, but he could have sworn his power was trying to connect with hers. Even as he'd lost control the day before, the lightning emitting from him too fast for him to comprehend, his power had felt like it was trying to latch to him rather than be aimed at her.

Xadrion didn't understand how that could be, how he could even begin to explain the feeling that his power had sentience, but the moment that lightning had struck her he'd heard the wordless apologies whisper from somewhere deep within him.

Xadrion wanted to say something to lead them down that conversation. He would have said anything to encourage them looking into the ways their magic seemed compatible, mostly because he wanted some part of Azraelle to admit they were more to each other than she allowed them to be. Before he could push the conversation any further, Azraelle motioned for him to get ready. Training was about to really begin.

They set about moving, similar to how they had during their time at the cabin. Azraelle poked and prodded from within his mind, showing him the ways in which he could further enhance his moves and strength with the power that simmered within him.

With each strike that Xadrion made, he couldn't help but notice the ripple of tension that ran through Azraelle's body and the grimace that occasionally crossed her expression. For all that she tried to hide it, every time lightning sparked between them her face betrayed her true fear. The pain ran deeper than she was letting on and it was too much to ask of her to face him in that moment. Yet anytime Xadrion tried to bring the training to a stop, Azraelle doubled down, forcing him to either respond or get thrown across the room. He'd learnt the hard way that she wasn't going to let him stop until she was ready – if the broken boards across some of the walls Xadrion's body was thrown against was anything to go by.

When Xadrion didn't feel as if he could stand a moment longer, and Azraelle had a light sheen of sweat coating her skin, glistening in the sunlight that shone through the cracks in the roof, Azraelle let them come to a stop. Ilyon and Tolemus stopped their drills while Emera joined them from where she had been practising in the corner. Azraelle called the end of the session.

Xadrion was exhausted and the power that had been simmering beneath his skin had died down somewhat. He'd managed to keep it contained at least for the day, keeping the events from yesterday from recurring. Yet Xadrion knew as his energy returned, so would the feeling of his power building within him, bringing with it the difficulty of resisting that urge to release everything and let it run freely.

When they got back to the castle, walking as a group, Azraelle quickly left them be and returned to her rooms. Training had taken them through to midday, and the ball was not until sunset, but Azraelle seemed determined not to spend any longer with them upon their return. Ilyon, Tolemus and Emera all went to spend time in Emera's rooms. They invited Xadrion, but he didn't particularly feel like their company either.

Xadrion needed a solution to the building pressure within him, and fast. He could not withstand it on his own, that much both Azraelle and Tolemus seemed to agree. And Azraelle could not help him if the suppression they'd tried that morning was anything to go by. No solution came to Xadrion's mind.

Instead, Xadrion spent the rest of his day catching up on work he hadn't done while he'd run off to the cabin. Everything within him was shifting, and the idea of monotonous paperwork seemed like the only thing that could distract him in that moment. It worked, mostly. Xadrion managed to tune out the thoughts springing to his mind as he worked, long enough that one of the castle's workers came when it was time to get ready for the ball.

Having rough hands pull at Xadrion's clothes and preen over his skin caused the anger to resurface with renewed vigour. The idea of playing court politician was the last thing he wished to do. He didn't want to have to entertain all those people, didn't want to hold another empty conversation with Romina. Didn't want to stand in a room full of people and pretend he wasn't focusing solely on where Azraelle moved within the room. Most of all, Xadrion didn't want another day of Azraelle avoiding being alone with him.

He didn't blame her, not when he himself couldn't stop remembering what the burn looked like gaping and blistering on her abdomen, but he still resented that there was so much that stood between them.

When Xadrion was dressed in his finest jacket and pants, a stark white shirt beneath and the least scuffed boots he could find, he made his way to the throne room. At the top of the room, beside where Rhoas' throne sat, there was a stage with musicians already set up, playing a local song intended for waltzing. As he was announced, Xadrion noticed the room was already filled with attendees. He must have taken longer to get ready than he'd thought. He cringed at the announcement with the title prince before his name, the lie of his heritage one that still went believed throughout the kingdom. He would have to talk to Rhoas about that. Xadrion could not, certainly would not, take away what was Ilyon's by birthright.

Rhoas sat atop his throne at the head of the room and Xadrion made to move straight there. He would be the courtly prince, seated politely by his king's side and greeting all who spoke with him. He could make it through the night. He had to. Xadrion did his best to ignore the itching beneath his skin and the way it felt like his insides were boiling inside him.

Romina approached shortly after he stationed himself beside Rhoas and curtsied slightly to the king. She was beautiful in a red gown he was sure cost more than any dress should have.

'Go and dance with our esteemed guest,' Rhoas muttered to Xadrion beneath his breath when Romina stood expectantly at the bottom of the dais. Xadrion felt the simmering anger at Rhoas' order but did his best to put on a smile and walk down the dais to where Romina was standing. He offered her his hand and led her to the dance floor.

'Xadrion Mescal, you're different to the boy you were when you visited Gaeweth,' Romina remarked when they were settled into a slow dance to match the song he knew to be one of Gaeweth's most popular.

'I am no longer a boy.'

'Yes, that much is true,' Romina said. She looked up at him, her brown hair pinned back with a slim golden circlet atop her head. A princess. It had been an unspoken agreement for many years that they would unite their kingdoms' friendship. But that had been when he was a prince and a mortal. Even if he had wanted Romina, everything would still have changed the moment he learned the truth.

'What of you? Surely you have had your own experiences that led you to your own womanhood during our years apart?'

'I don't know what you may be implying, my prince, but I am a woman in all ways but one. I follow the ways of the gods and live a faithful woman's life,' Romina replied, a faint blush creeping over her cheeks. While Xadrion had not been raised with religion, he was not unfamiliar to the concept. Thesadel was a mixed bag of believers, but Gaeweth was a devout land. They believed in multiple gods, though their names often differed from the names Hera had mentioned in her tales. Xadrion wondered what Romina would do if she knew the very woman she seemed to antagonise the most was one of her precious goddesses.

'You have not loved someone from Gaeweth?' Xadrion asked.

'It is not for me to love,' Romina replied. This was the most honest he'd ever heard Romina be with him. She was the example for how royals were supposed to act. He had never seen or heard rumour of transgressions from her on any part. She would be the perfect wife in reputation. Yet Xadrion could not fathom himself loving her. Even when the woman who had the beginnings of that attention from him spent her nights with others, had probably spent many nights with many others.

'Should it not be for you, though? We all deserve it,' Xadrion said. 'Could you not imagine what it must be like to spend your life in true and complete love?'

'I only hope that the man I am given to is one I can learn to love with time,' Romina answered. So honest. So vulnerable. Open to Xadrion in every way if he could have ever taken it.

Xadrion could not make himself respond to her, so instead scouted the room, noting Ilyon and Emera dancing nearby on the dance floor. Emera was dressed in a beautiful green gown, her red hair like a flame amongst the surrounding colours, while Ilyon was dressed in a very similar outfit to what Xadrion wore. As he searched the room for the one figure he always felt he was watching for, his eyes caught her entrance, as if he knew that looking that way at that moment would let him see what he had most wanted to.

Passing through the doorway, her hair like molten ice around her, was Azraelle. During their sessions, in dirty training clothes with her hair braided away from her face, Azraelle was beautiful. As she was in that moment, entering the throne room, Xadrion nearly fell to the floor at the injustice of her beauty. Her hair was down, framing her face, and long enough that it only stopped when it reached her waist. It looked like liquid the way it shifted as she walked.

She wore a dress, black as night, the cut of it causing Xadrion to stiffen beneath the waistband of his pants and having to focus to push those particular thoughts away. The top had a plunging neckline straight down between her breasts, the skin between covered only in a thin lace that left little to the imagination. In the skirts, Xadrion caught sight of a bare leg, exposed through a slit that ran the entire bottom half, high enough to leave Xadrion both wishing for and dreading a misplaced movement revealing too much of her skin. Azraelle's dress was the opposite of Romina's, which was as elegant and respectable as any princess could be expected to wear. Azraelle was pushing every limit that existed that night with her choice of dress and Xadrion could not breathe because of it.

Beside Azraelle, catching Xadrion's attention as they entered arm in arm, was Tolemus. He wore an outfit that matched Azraelle's perfectly, one that accentuated every detail. Rage boiled within Xadrion at the image of someone else on her arm, someone else being close enough to feel her, to smell her. Someone that was not him.

It seemed Azraelle had abandoned the idea of going with Ilyon and Emera and chosen instead to attend with Tolemus as her date. Too many people were watching their entrance, entranced by the rare sight of Azraelle dressed as she was. Xadrion couldn't blame them; he could not bear to take his eyes from her.

'Maybe there really isn't a lady within her after all,' Romina muttered. Xadrion whirled to face her once more.

'What do you mean by that?'

'Dressing like that, she's doing her best to scare away any appropriate men,'

Romina answered, casting a judgemental glance back at Azraelle. 'I should need to speak to Tolemus about being seen with a woman of her standing.'

'She is not some common whore,' Xadrion growled. 'She carries a high level of respect within this castle and this court. You don't get to cast judgement over her for what she wears and how she passes her time.'

'Prince Xadrion, I did not mean to offend you,' Romina said quickly, meek in her apology. Her eyes betrayed fear as she met Xadrion's gaze, and then cast her own to the floor quickly.

'Azraelle is not a lady, and I should never wish her to be. Not if it means she spends her time thinking solely on how men might perceive her and learning how best to service her husband,' Xadrion said. 'You might do well to take a lesson or two in standing up for yourself.'

Romina was silenced by Xadrion's venomous words. He caught sight of tears brimming in her eyes as Romina looked anywhere but at him and he extracted himself from her once more to stride back to his seat beside Rhoas. He was too harsh, but his anger did not let him turn around and make amends. Romina was a product of the kingdom she was raised in, her beliefs the very thing that kept her reputation intact and her families reign solidified. Xadrion should have held more patience; it had once been one of his greatest traits and yet now with an anger that never let him be, he had found himself so far from his own character. It had been building for the better part of a year, long before even Azraelle had stumbled across his path, and Xadrion could not recognise the man he was now. The noise in the room, the heat of so many bodies pressed against each other, the image of Tolemus' arm wrapped around Azraelle's as they had entered, left him feeling as if his blood was boiling.

He could not get his power to settle.

Azraelle and Tolemus approached, paying their respects to Rhoas, before turning to walk away. As Azraelle's gaze met Xadrion's, she froze, tilting her head slightly at what she seemed to be reading within him. Up close, she was more beautiful than he'd ever seen her. The black of her dress, the plunging neckline, the bare skin he could see down her front, highlighted by the ever-present emerald pendant around her neck that settled between her breasts. As she had half turned, he saw the back of the dress – or the lack thereof. Not even a thin sheet of lace provided an image of modesty. Her back, exposed for all to see.

She had made no attempt to hide the scars that ran the length of her spine. Her hair was long enough to sway across them, covering pieces, but many people around her were looking first to her and then to the scars that plagued her back. And there, visible beneath the lace that dipped low enough at the front, Xadrion could see the twisted skin that still remained from his lightning.

Xadrion felt her step into his mind, crossing into the space he felt he had permanently waiting for her. He let her in willingly, desperate for any sort of connection to her. As his power tried to burst from within, Xadrion felt Azraelle's tendrils move through him, doing their best to suppress the intensity of his crackling power. It worked, enough at least for Xadrion to feel his thoughts begin to return to a semblance of order. Her void eyes locked to his own, her tendrils that had every ability to be devastating were instead soothing through his mind, doing their best to caress the sparks that ignited within him. Even through their darkness, lightning cracked through.

You're losing control, Xadrion. It had been days since she'd last spoken to his mind, since their time at the cabin, and her voice set his nerves on fire.

I can't focus enough to get control.

You must, Azraelle insisted.

Xadrion threw an image at her mind. While Xadrion could see Azraelle's shield was stronger than even the day before, she let the image through. He showed her what he saw when he looked at her, the way his focus was pulled entirely to her.

How can I focus with this?

I'm sure you can push through those particular feelings, Azraelle answered. She sounded so stern, but a slight smirk crossed her lips. Azraelle continued on walking away with Tolemus but she stayed within his mind. Her tendrils remained wrapped around his own crackling energy in their attempt to keep him at bay. It worked enough to calm him down but came with the other dominant feeling whenever he was exposed to Azraelle's magic joining with his own: the sense that his magic was finding its match.

Tolemus led Azraelle to the dance floor and rested his hand gently on her exposed back. His fingers brushed against the first of her scars, settling over the ridge of it, and twined amongst the ends of her hair. They started moving, twirling across the dance floor with an effortless kind of grace. Azraelle had been around for so long, Xadrion was not surprised she had such grace. The way he'd seen her fight had given him every impression that she would be as fluid in all other movements. Tolemus being so graceful was more of a surprise. His fighting style was closer to what Xadrion could relate to – a reliance on strength and force – but the moment they started moving, Tolemus demonstrated a grace nearly equal to Azraelle's.

Azraelle laughed as they moved and, for several songs, Tolemus whispered sweet nothings to her. With every passing song, Azraelle became more entranced by the man standing before her, gazing up at him adoringly and occasionally tightening her hold across his shoulders as the moved. Still, she never pulled her power from Xadrion. Just when Xadrion didn't think he could take it anymore, Ilyon and Emera approached them, and they spent the next few songs exchanging partners until they had all danced with each other.

'That is a dangerous game to play, my son,' Rhoas said from beside him.

'What game?' Xadrion said, his attention never leaving Azraelle.

'Loving a goddess,' Rhoas responded. Xadrion turned to face Rhoas, his whole body shifting to look at him better.

'I do not,' Xadrion declared, the itch beneath his skin increasing.

'Take it from someone who loved such a goddess themselves, you do,' Rhoas said.

'Well, hypocritical of you to say then, considering,' Xadrion countered.

'Indeed, but I say it because of that experience. Loving Hera is the best thing of my life, and also the most painful thing,' Rhoas said.

'Is?' Xadrion pressed. Rhoas didn't speak of Hera often, had rarely communicated to his sons the level of love he had or still held for Hera. Xadrion had always wished he spoke more about her.

'Was,' Rhoas said, quickly. 'It was the best thing of my life. Yet now I must live the remainder of my life without her because of the dangers of her world.'

'Is it better to love a mortal woman, who will still die before the end of my time?' Xadrion challenged. Rhoas pursed his lips, silent for a moment. Xadrion had not come to terms with what it meant to be a god yet and he couldn't fathom living an immortal life. But it gave him something at least to use in such an argument as this one.

'I cannot offer you what is better for you. That is a decision you must make for yourself. I just mean to say it is a dangerous game, especially with one such as Azraelle,' Rhoas said.

'Why especially her?'

'My son,' Rhoas said. Xadrion tried not to pay attention to the sting that now accompanied the familial term, the way he felt his skin itch that bit more with his power begging for release. 'She has been alive for more time than you can comprehend. She has had the world of the gods to pick from when it comes to suitors and yet she still has picked none. The legends of her, the ones who spoke of the power she held and the role she was tasked to carry, they all spoke also of her inability to love.'

'How could they know such a thing?' Xadrion demanded.

'They can't. No one is to know if it's true or not, I suppose,' Rhoas admitted. 'But within her kind, she stands out. Most will either love many at a time, and the remainder who choose to spend their immortal lives with one tend to live and die over and over with that one of their choosing. She has done neither of those things.'

'Legends are half told from made up stories,' Xadrion rebutted.

'I hope you're right,' Rhoas said. 'For I fear you may be too far in to be okay if the alternative is true.'

Rhoas allowed Xadrion to stew within his thoughts after his final words. If he loved Azraelle or not, it wasn't the right question to ask. It meant nothing if they could not be around each other, nothing if he could not be around her without harming her. It meant nothing if she resigned to him because she was resigned to her perceived weakness. Now, being blocked from her mind, Xadrion could no longer check to ensure her peace of mind. He had no idea where they stood, and how okay she was.

Romina did not approach Xadrion again that night, and he did feel bad for the words he had spoken to her. It would be important for him to right that wrong before Romina and her party left in half a week's time. He would do his best to fix it, but not if it meant he had to listen to her say one more word about Azraelle.

Xadrion himself stayed seated beside that throne for the hours that followed. He admired the music, spoke to those who approached, but did not keep his gaze from Azraelle for most of the time. She laughed and danced, more carefree than he had seen her since the cabin, but it didn't feel as earnest. Even the tendrils she left throughout his mind felt like they were echoing her dishonesty to his thoughts. Xadrion was still coming to terms with his own power's sentience but somehow, he felt like even Azraelle's tendrils were trying to communicate *something* to him.

Hours passed in that fashion, but as if a sudden urgency had overtaken him, Xadrion found himself leaving the dais and heading straight onto the dance floor, directly to where she was dancing with Tolemus once more.

'May I interrupt?' Xadrion asked through gritted teeth. Tolemus turned to him, smiled graciously, and offered Xadrion her hand.

'So, he does dance,' Azraelle commented as Xadrion took the hand she kept extended to him.

'I do,' he murmured, stepping closer until their bodies were against each other. His hand slid around her waist, feeling the ridges of her scars beneath the palm of his hand. His other hand lifted their arms, trailing lightly across her wrist, then her palms, then her fingers, until he locked their hands together. With the hand pressed against her back, he pulled her closer until Xadrion felt the warmth of her body through his shirt. Even through her dress, he felt it.

'Where is Romina tonight?' Azraelle asked, one corner of her lips turned up in a smirk. Even though Xadrion knew she was trying to get a rise out of him, something about how she said it made Xadrion know she wasn't actually trying to anger him, as if it was somehow a joke they could share.

'I have not made it my business to know where she has gone,' Xadrion replied. They began moving across the dance floor, slow enough that Xadrion could maintain the contact between their bodies. Above all else, he needed to feel her close to him, no matter if their dancing didn't match the tempo being played.

'She might disapprove of your spending time with someone so unladylike,' Azraelle taunted.

'To which I would say I don't care.'

'You're hard to get a typical rise out of tonight,' Azraelle commented, peering up at him through her lashes with those dark, bottomless eyes.

'I do not wish to be angry with you,' Xadrion said. 'I don't think I could be angry with you in this moment.'

'Oh?'

Xadrion lowered his head until he felt his lips brush against her ear. She shivered within his arms.

'You are captivating,' Xadrion breathed. Goosebumps shot down Azraelle's arms. Encouraged by the response, he nipped her earlobe between his teeth before he pulled away to look back at her face. The depth of the void within her eyes glimmered as she watched him. Her lips had parted slightly and when he pulled away, it took her a moment too long to catch her breath.

'How can one focus on the dance when sweet nothings are being whispered into their ear?' Azraelle whispered.

'What I whisper into your ear is not nothing,' Xadrion said, smirking at the hunger he could see behind her eyes. 'It is everything I truly wish to say.'

'Yet all your actions until this point seem to suggest otherwise.'

'How so?'

'I mean, you see me physically as someone you may be attracted to. But I am not captivating to you, not in any other way. You desire me physically but hate yourself for doing so because you hate who I am,' Azraelle said, as if she were admitting some great thought.

'Is that what you think?' Xadrion demanded to know. He twirled her out as the music called for it, then pulled her back in, bringing their bodies once more to be flush against each other. 'That I hate you?'

'That's what I know,' Azraelle responded.

Xadrion gritted his teeth and felt the power skitter over his skin once more. He had been rejecting any physical approach with Azraelle since the night they'd shared their minds, but it was not because he did not want her. He did not think she was ready to accept him and did not want to accept her attention if it came out of her resignation.

But she had interpreted that as him hating her.

'I could never hate you,' Xadrion admitted.

'I don't believe you,' Azraelle said.

Xadrion twirled them across the dance floor once more, Azraelle effortlessly keeping pace. He leant forward again, his gentle bite now falling upon her exposed neck.

Let me in, Xadrion sent down the bridge between their minds. Azraelle's shield opened enough for Xadrion to step through, showing him a hollowed-out version of her mind. She had created her own safe room in her mind, showing nothing to Xadrion behind the deeper wall.

Once in, Xadrion placed an image he had burned into the core of his memory. He showed her the image of Azraelle, naked atop her bed looking through her full-length mirror. Xadrion conveyed every feeling of attraction he had towards her with that image.

That doesn't prove you don't hate me, Azraelle responded. *That just confirms your physical attraction.*

How could I be so physically attracted to someone I supposedly hate? Xadrion asked.

It's entirely too easy, for gods and mortals alike, Azraelle responded. *What about the times you decided you didn't want to touch me? All the times you remembered it was me who stood in front of you, not someone you actually cared for, just someone you wanted.*

What times were those?

Azraelle showed him her own images. She showed him the moment he had found her in the hallway, half in her mist-form, where he had grabbed her hip out of his desire. She showed him the moment he had let go, how she'd read in his eyes that he did not want her enough to override his dislike of her. She showed him the moment they were in the room afterwards, when she had observed rage flicker over his features at the way she'd brushed Ilyon's hair with her fingers.

That is not me hating you, Azraelle.

It sure seems like it, she responded.

On the contrary, that was me wanting to be the person whose hair you were brushing. That was me wanting to take you right there in that hallway. That was me wanting to be with you in every way but knowing that if I pushed for it, you would give in, and then you would hate me.

Saying those words to her in their minds felt easier than voicing them aloud. They were the most truthful words he could have ever offered her. Because if Azraelle had accepted him in the state she'd been at the cabin, if she'd agreed to be with him then, she would have come to hate him and resent him. There was no doubting of that.

And why would I come to hate you? Azraelle asked.

They were still dancing, eyes intensely locked in the others as they held their internal conversation.

You would come to resent me for making you love. Because for some fucking reason you think love is the biggest weakness of them all, Xadrion answered.

And you think you could make me love you? Azraelle said, her tone taunting, as if she were trying to goad him away from his confessions.

I know I could. His words had been laced with the depths of his desire as they echoed into her mind. Azraelle's hands tightened their holds on where they rested, one in his hand and the other atop his shoulder. Her fingers dug into him, her head angled back in that way that Xadrion knew already after only a few instances of observing it, meant she was aroused.

So, you refuse to try to fuck me because you feel I will fall in love with you and then come to hate you for making me do so? Azraelle clarified, her tone heavily lined with sarcasm.

Don't discredit what I'm saying, Xadrion said. He didn't know what was making him feel so confident in his words. Maybe he'd just gotten so sick of them pretending there wasn't *something* between them. Maybe the anger simmering beneath his skin was making it hard to focus on filtering his words.

Xadrion traced across her back with his fingers. He covered the dimples at the base of her spine, then caressed up until he was tracing her neck beneath her hair. Slowly, he lowered his hands back down, toying with the band at the back of her dress sitting low on her hips.

How cruel of you to withhold your magical dick that makes women fall in love with you, Azraelle taunted. The song ended and she swiftly pulled from his grasp. Her face was flushed and he could see the heaviness to her breathing, but she turned from him, that damned skirt of hers revealing the crease of her thigh and hip as she did so and stalked away.

Azraelle returned to Tolemus where he had been watching them from the side of the room. She took hold of his hand and began to walk around the outside of the room with him. Xadrion was too far away to hear them, but Azraelle had left their minds open to each other, as if she wanted him to listen in on what was happening directly around her.

'Walk me to my rooms?' Azraelle asked Tolemus, her tone suggestive and flirtatious. Tolemus chuckled and allowed her to lead him across the room.

'Of course, my cruel beauty,' Tolemus responded. Xadrion felt indescribable rage as he watched them leave the throne room together, hand in hand. Energy crackled in the air around him and his nails bit into the palms of his hands as his fists clenched at his sides. He debated letting her go, debated letting her win the argument. She wanted him, just as he wanted her, but he had not wanted to push her for fear of her shutting him out completely.

Did it mean anything if she simply replaced him with someone else?

Xadrion would not let it happen. Only a few moments had passed since she had led Tolemus from the room, but Xadrion could handle it no longer. He stormed from the throne room, determined to interrupt whatever he would walk in on to demand some real truths from Azraelle.

TWENTY-TWO

XADRION

When Xadrion burst through the doors of Azraelle's rooms, a demand already on his lips ready to be given, he stopped dead in his tracks. Tolemus was not in the first room; in fact, he was nowhere to be seen in either of the two adjoining rooms, Xadrion noted through their open doors. In the centre of the first room, however, was Azraelle.

She was still in her dress, her bare leg visible beneath the skirt she had slightly pulled back. Azraelle had pulled her hair over one shoulder, letting it flow down to her waist, but leaving the length of her neck exposed on the other side. The way she was looking at him as he entered the room had Xadrion's mind emptying of everything except his lust.

'Tolemus didn't catch your fancy, after all?'

'Mm, not today,' Azraelle teased. At her feet, as if playing in the skirts of the dress were the swirling, dark tendrils. As he took a step forward, he watched as the tendrils reached for him and somewhere deep inside, Xadrion felt his own power spark in recognition.

Yes, he felt it whisper within him. *She wants to play.* The current that swept through him felt similar to a giant sigh of relief, as if it had been waiting a long time to feel wanted by Azraelle's own power.

'Could you give me a hand with the dress?'

Xadrion hardened immediately. He walked to stand behind her and placed his fingers gently over her bare shoulders, running them down the lengths of her arms. He was delighted to see goosebumps trail the path of his fingers.

'You are so cruel,' Xadrion whispered and leant forward to place his lips on the exposed side of her neck. He kissed her there, gently, then nipped at her earlobe. Azraelle leant her head away as if to give him better access to her neck.

204

'I am merely a woman who needs help with removing an elaborate gown,' Azraelle breathed.

Xadrion's fingers traced from her arms back to her shoulders. He took hold of the thin straps of the dress, the two smallest pieces of fabric he had seen being the only thing that kept the dress in place.

'You call this elaborate?' He tugged them down gently, pulling them over her shoulders and sliding them down her arms. The dress, previously fitted so closely to her body, slid down effortlessly with it. The black skirts pooled at Azraelle's feet, her darkness playing amongst the fabric. There was not a single undergarment to be seen.

'That was very complicated,' Azraelle teased as she stepped forward out of the skirts and turned to face him. He'd seen her body before, naked in this way, but that had been through her eyes and a reflection in a mirror. Now, with her standing in front of him, nothing obstructing his view of her, Xadrion couldn't figure out where he wanted his eyes to go.

Her face, beautiful as ever, was always difficult to pull his eyes from. But there, lower, her collarbone caught his attention. Then lower, to the emerald pendant nestled between her breasts, her nipples hardened in the cool air. Lower, lower, Xadrion nearly got caught on the burn that still settled on the right side of her stomach until his eyes found the light tuft of hair that led between her legs. His whole focus shifted from the damage on her body to the beauty of what stood before him.

Xadrion walked around the dress and came to a stop in front of her. Azraelle was half smiling at him as he approached, as if she were daring him to do something. She had no idea the somethings he wished to do to her.

He rested his hands on her hips, his fingers tracing patterns on her skin. The sight of his dark, calloused hands running across skin he'd never thought he'd be given permission to touch nearly knocked away any control he was trying to maintain.

'You are a temptress,' Xadrion breathed.

'Will you give in?' Azraelle brought her own hand up until it rested against her neck, then trailed it down her body, dragging his gaze with it.

'Tell me what you feel for me is no weakness,' Xadrion demanded, one of his hands coming up to grip her chin. He pulled her face up until their gazes were locked. His dick twitched in his pants, but he tried to remain focused, to keep his mind clear. The sight of Azraelle's body in front of him made that nearly impossible.

'Why is that so important to you?' Azraelle whispered. He had to push on, had to ignore how easily he could capture that full upper lip of hers in his own in that moment.

'I do not want a woman who will settle for me, resigned to the weakness it signifies within herself,' Xadrion said. 'You are not weak, Azraelle. And the things you feel for me, they aren't weakness. I will not touch you if you think they are.'

'My wall is back up,' Azraelle said, her breath quick as Xadrion used his thumb to stroke her jaw gently, his grasp still firm.

'I noticed,' Xadrion said. 'That doesn't answer my request.'

'My wall is back up because I am learning how to incorporate my feelings for you into its defence. I've found how I can use the knowledge I have about the things you can make me feel to strengthen myself, not weaken it,' Azraelle explained.

'So, say it.'

'You will not be my weakness. What I feel for you will be no weakness of mine,' Azraelle said. It wasn't exactly what he'd asked her to say, but it was enough.

Xadrion closed the gap between them, lowering his lips until they closed over hers. They'd kissed once in a field many weeks ago. It had been gentle and swift, and Azraelle had distracted him by showing him the image of her wings. This was instantly different. When their lips met, Xadrion felt the sensation of fire burning beneath them. The moment he felt those soft lips of hers against his, Xadrion was overcome with the need to feel and taste every inch of her.

He licked at her top lip with his tongue, which Azraelle parted willingly. Their tongues met and moved together, the taste of her mouth so overwhelmingly intoxicating he didn't think he'd be able to stop kissing her enough to do everything else he wished to do.

Now will you fuck me? Azraelle teased into his mind, without breaking their kiss.

Now I will do everything I ever dreamed of doing, and then I will fuck you.

He moved both his hands to cup her waist, lifting her effortlessly. Azraelle wrapped her legs around her own waist, locking her feet behind him. Without breaking the kiss, Xadrion walked her through the door to her bedroom before placing her gently on the bed, himself now hovering over her. Through the fabric of his shirt, Xadrion could feel the heat emanating from between her legs.

Finally, Xadrion managed to pull his lips from hers. The feeling of being physically separated was not one he enjoyed, but he needed to do other things with his mouth. He needed to let his lips taste the rest of her, to memorise every detail of her that he could. Xadrion moved so that his lips trailed kisses down her neck and over her collarbone.

One arm he kept wrapped around her waist, pulling their hips closer to each other, while the other hand he moved to cup her breast, taking her nipple between his thumb and index fingertip. He rolled it gently, a soft gasp breaking through Az's lips. Xadrion lowered his mouth to capture her other nipple, running his tongue over it and suckling. Azraelle moaned and arched her back to offer him more of her.

Azraelle's fingers moved over Xadrion's, pressing against them so they rolled her nipple with more force. He gazed up at her as she did this, to see her watching him with eyes black as the void chasm in her mind.

'Harder,' she whispered. Xadrion twitched again in his pants and grinned wickedly around her nipple still in his mouth.

'Not a fragile woman who needs help with your dress anymore, Az?' Xadrion taunted, as he moved his mouth to kiss down her sternum. He brought both of his hands to her nipples now, rolling them harder between his fingers. She tipped her head back and moaned in appreciation. Where he had trailed saliva across her skin, he watched as goosebumps rose across the path his lips had taken.

Azraelle grabbed the shoulders of Xadrion's jacket and pushed it down his arms. He let go of her long enough to allow the jacket to be shrugged off and thrown to the side. She reached over and grabbed the back of his shirt, tugging it effortlessly over his head. As soon as the fabric was removed, he put his hands straight back on her, kneading her breasts and toying with her nipples.

Xadrion lowered his head further, kissing tenderly over the scarred twisting of skin that marred her stomach, the place his lightning had entered her body. Guilt swarmed him, but Azraelle buried her hands in his hair and tipped his face up to look at her.

'It doesn't hurt,' she whispered, sensing his guilt in the spaces they still shared within each other's minds. 'Don't stop, Xay.'

Xadrion kissed the skin he'd marked and imagined lacing his breath with pleasure rather than lightning. He imagined following the steps that he'd heard Emera discussing with Ilyon on how to imbue actions with healing and imagined his breath soothing the twisted skin of her scars. Azraelle moaned and tangled her fingers deeper into his hair. He had kept it braided back tightly but Azraelle quickly removed the band from the bottom that kept it all together and ran her fingers through his hair. His hair tumbled loose as her fingers dragged through it.

Xadrion felt the hair fall down around his face and saw it brush over the exposed skin of Azraelle's beneath him. He remembered the feeling he'd described to her, how he had desperately wanted to be the one whose hair she was running her hands through. It felt better than he could have imagined.

Xadrion kept moving downwards, sliding to settle between her already spread legs. She smelt intoxicating, her wetness glistening in anticipation. Xadrion lowered his own hand to release the buckle of his pants, giving himself the space to readjust as his hardened form was practically screaming for release.

He moved one hand back to her breast, cupping it and playing with it, as his other hand slid down to have that first touch with his own fingers. He slid his fingertips straight up the middle, parting the lips before him, and lowered his mouth to capture her between his lips. Azraelle moaned, loudly.

Fuck. Xadrion wasn't sure if he'd only thought it or if he'd cried it into her mind. She tasted amazing. He used his mouth to taste, dropping down occasionally so his tongue could work its way inside her. She had him nearly busting in his pants just at her taste. Keeping his hand tugging on her nipple, harder as she had demanded, Xadrion moved his other hand down to slide one finger in, then two.

Azraelle squirmed, a lot. As he touched her and licked her and tugged on her, it almost seemed like she couldn't stay still. She kept her back arching up and clamped her breast in her own hand while she left her other hand twirled in amongst the strands of Xadrion's hair. She used the leverage she had over him to all but direct his mouth exactly where she needed it to be, pressing his mouth firmly between her legs.

Use me however you need, Azraelle. I want to taste your release, Xadrion spoke into her mind.

Azraelle grinned above him, locking her fingers in his hair so that they gripped him rough. She pulled at his hair, tugging his head sideways, and took control of the situation. Before Xadrion realised she had done it, Azraelle had swapped their positions so he was now lying on his back, but his mouth had not once separated from that sweet taste. Instead, she knelt atop his face, riding against him in the way she needed.

Xadrion moved one hand so he could use his fingers inside her once more, curling them gently, and heard her reciprocating moan from above. As he looked over her naked body above him, the image of her left Xadrion desperate for his own release. As if Az realised this, she arched back, angling her hands behind her body. She used one to lean against Xadrion's chest to support the rocking she was doing over his mouth while the other reached down and slid through the open waistband of his pants.

The moment Azraelle's hand wrapped around him, he nearly came. It took everything in him to keep himself under control, especially as she began to stroke him. First gentle, her pace increased, and her grip tightened, just in the way Xadrion enjoyed.

Azraelle's tension built in every fibre of his being. Whether it be in the space he occupied within her mind or the way he felt her shadows wrapping themselves around his body, lapping at the heat he could feel emanating from beneath his own skin. He moved his free hand up further and settled it loosely around her neck, the cold chain of her emerald pendant twined around his fingers. He used his new grip to pull her weight down towards him, pressing her harder into his mouth. If he suffocated in that moment, he wouldn't have cared.

Azraelle was tensing, her legs tightening around the side of his head, and the sounds that came from her told Xadrion she was close. In the space in her mind, Xadrion ran his mental fingertips across the barrier of her mind.

Finish for me, Az, right fucking now.

Azraelle twitched above him, her legs locking tightly against him, and he felt her stroking pause as she was overcome with pleasure. Azraelle cried out and he tasted and felt the force of her orgasm, coating his tongue. He changed nothing, letting her orgasm ride itself through to the end, until she'd stopped convulsing above him and her hand began to move once more over him.

As she came, Xadrion felt the tendrils of her magic in his mind stretch their grasp as if they were seeking his own power to play with. He gave them the crackling energy held within him and delighted as they seemed to revel in each other's presence, the shadows swooping in and around the lightning that shot through the darkness. Their magic sizzled together as if it were trying to become one.

The taste of her, the feeling of her walls clenching around his fingers, the image of her breathing heavily above him, had Xadrion done with any restraint. He sat up, pulling her with him, supported in his arms practically seated atop his shoulders, and flipped them back around. Azraelle collapsed into the pillows, the white ice of her hair pooling around her. Xadrion stood at the edge of the bed, extracting himself from her long enough to drop his pants from his body fully and take himself in his hand.

Before him, Azraelle kept her legs spread so he could get a full view of her body. She was smiling, wickedly, as her eyes roamed down his body to see the hard form he gripped in his own hand. Xadrion used his other hand to wipe at her arousal that surrounded his lips. He put his glistening fingers in his mouth and sucked all of her from them while she watched.

'Now you will fuck me?' Azraelle's eyes flashed with pure desire where she lay.

'Yes, now I will,' Xadrion said. He grabbed her legs and pulled her towards him, dragging her until she was situated on the edge of the bed. He settled between her legs, resting his knees against the edge of the bed for leverage, and Azraelle locked her legs back around his waist, pulling him in.

Xadrion used one hand between them to position himself at her entrance, feeling the wetness practically grabbing him. He found no resistance to his entrance. When Xadrion rocked his hips forward, Azraelle pulled him closer, allowing him to enter smoothly. She was still clenching from her orgasm, and he could still feel the walls of her tensing inside as smaller waves continued.

Azraelle gasped as he pushed, burying himself fully, and settled into place within her. He didn't move, didn't pull back out or move his hips, simply enjoyed the feeling of being buried as deep within her as he could be. The way she gripped him with her legs, and the angle it put her at, had not even a fraction of space between his hips and hers.

When Xadrion remained still, mostly trying to focus on not finishing inside her at that very moment, Azraelle began to squirm once more.

Please, Xay. Her voice was quiet but desperate. Xadrion grinned at her beneath him and finally started to move. He pulled out, almost so far that he left her completely, and then back in. He started slow, introducing long strides to his movements, and as he fell into a rhythm, he had to force himself to maintain a pace to keep from speeding up to bring him to his finish. He wanted to feel Azraelle for as long as he could withstand it.

Azraelle tensed her legs around him with each thrust in, which pulled him in to the deepest point he could get each time. She rocked her hips as she moved and as Xadrion held his rhythm, she pulled him harder with each thrust.

Do you want it harder?

Azraelle bit her lip and moaned as she nodded. Xadrion obeyed, adding more force to each of his thrusts. One hand gripped her waist, helping to pull her closer each time, while his other hand moved back to circle where he knew her most sensitive bundle of nerves to be. He rubbed her gently, timing to his thrusts, and saw the moment she began to build again. Azraelle didn't close her eyes, didn't look away from him, as he buried himself in her over and over. The desire evident behind her eyes did not diminish.

It did not take long for Xadrion to get Azraelle back on the edge again, her body writhing beneath him as her tension built. Xadrion loved that she was so responsive, that every time he touched her or pushed back in her, she responded with a sound or a movement. Seeing her desire for him had his own desire refusing to yield.

'I'm close, Az,' Xadrion growled as he thrust harder, faster.

Show me how much you've wanted me. Let me feel it.

Where can I finish? Xadrion asked. He knew where he wanted to finish, knew the idea of pulling out of her would go against every desire he ever had, but he needed her confirmation. He needed her to tell him it was okay.

Azraelle's presence in his mind laughed as she realised his concerns.

Our kind do not procreate that easily, Xadrion. Finish where you most desire.

When Azraelle went over the edge again, her orgasm rippling through her, her walls clenching him as he thrust, Xadrion went with her. He buried himself so deep within her, feeling his own pulsing as he came. Azraelle cried out, wrapping her arms around Xadrion's shoulders, and pulled him close. She buried her nails into his back, overwhelming Xadrion's senses by adding the small pain on top.

Her darkness and his lightning played in the spaces within their minds, as if they were chasing each other around in their own pleasure. Xadrion was breathing heavy, Azraelle doing the same with her chest pressed against his and her face buried in his neck. Xadrion's mind was finally calm, after feeling as if it hadn't been for days.

He wrapped his arms around her waist and slid her back up so that they were both lying side by side in the bed. Their legs were tangled together, despite Xadrion having finally extracted himself from within her. He kept his arms around her, pressing her against his chest, and revelling in the feeling of her breathing against his neck. They were both breathing so hard.

It was more than Xadrion could have hoped or imagined, the way it felt lying with Azraelle in that moment. She was so warm against him, so content to stay in his grasp, that Xadrion thought he had to be dreaming.

'That was… amazing,' Xadrion breathed. He ran his hand through her hair, leaning his chin down so he could place a gentle kiss against her forehead.

'It was decent,' Azraelle whispered as she nuzzled into his neck. She sounded like she was trying to be funny, but Xadrion did not want the humour. He had never felt so at risk of rejection as he did in that moment.

'Don't mock me for once, Az,' Xadrion said, his tone serious. Azraelle pushed herself back onto her forearms, so she could look Xadrion in the eyes. Her face was so close, her lips right there. Azraelle's eyes were dark as they watched him, as they seemed to peer straight through him. He'd never had so many questions about his own performance before, but the idea of Azraelle's disapproval made him nervous.

'I have been alive for a very long time,' Azraelle whispered, her tone becoming serious to match Xadrion's own. 'I have had my pickings of all the gods and goddesses of this realm and the next. Not a single one has made me feel the kinds of things you make me feel.' The earnestness of her words had Xadrion dumbfounded. Part of Xadrion knew she wasn't only talking about the physical feelings, but the connection they had begun to form between the two of them.

'It felt like my magic wanted to play with yours,' Xadrion whispered, lifting an arm to stroke her hair away from her face.

'It did,' Azraelle said. 'It can. You let it a little bit, but there is a lot more room to let it run with my own.'

'It heightened the pleasure, somehow.'

'You have no idea how much further we could push that,' Azraelle whispered, her eyes darting down to his lips. Xadrion felt himself hardening all over again at the look she gave him.

'I don't think I'm done,' he said, laughing softly at himself.

'Good, because I am nowhere near finished,' Azraelle said, smirking. Then she climbed on top of him once more.

TWENTY-THREE

XADRION

Azraelle did not kick him out when they had both finally expended their energy. Xadrion's desire had not died down, and he did not wish to ever have to stop, but he knew they had to sleep at some point. He assumed that when they finally stopped, Azraelle would return to her usual distant self and make him leave her be. She did no such thing.

Instead, Azraelle made no effort to remove herself from Xadrion's embrace as they lay together, coated in sweat. She moved once to go to the bathroom but when she returned, she slid straight back into his arms. Once she had settled back in his grip, she rested her head against his chest and promptly began snoring lightly. His heart felt like it wanted to explode.

Xadrion let himself fall asleep, hopeful for the next day.

She was awake before him, Xadrion realised when he awoke the next morning. Of course she was. He had never managed to beat her to training in the whole time she'd been there. Xadrion stretched his arms out to feel for her in the bed, immediately remembering who was supposed to be beside him, but found nothing. He opened his eyes, pushed himself onto his elbows and peered around the room. Her side of the bed was messy and she was not in it.

Xadrion pulled his pants on and walked into the main room. Dressed back in her regular pants and shirt, with a book open on her lap and a cup of tea in her hand, sat Azraelle. Her hair was washed and braided, hanging down over one shoulder. The dress she had stepped out of and left on the floor last night now was nowhere to be seen.

'Good morning,' she said, looking up from her book as he walked in. Xadrion noted with pleasure how her eyes dipped from his face to his bare chest.

'Morning,' he replied.

'Sleep okay?' She was smiling at him and as he approached, she readjusted herself on the couch to make space for him beside her.

'Perfectly, and you?' Xadrion asked. He wanted to check in, make sure she was okay, and they were okay, and that now that the sun had risen and the tension had settled, they would not be going back to how things were. Xadrion didn't think he could handle if she went back to ignoring him.

'Fine,' she said. Xadrion took the seat beside her and Azraelle extended her legs back out, crossing them over his lap. She'd rested the book on her own lap and placed her cup down to pour a second one, which she now offered him. As Azraelle offered him the cup, she couldn't seem to meet his eyes, as if she were embarrassed at the offering she was making. He took it gratefully and rested his arm over her legs while he drank, pulling them close against his chest.

Azraelle folded her book closed and picked her own cup back up, sipping quietly.

'This doesn't have to change anything,' Azraelle said quietly, still not managing to meet his gaze.

'And if I wanted it to?' Xadrion's heart was thumping hard in his chest.

'I wouldn't be opposed to things changing,' Azraelle said. Xadrion put his cup on the small table in front of the couch, then reached his hand out to touch her cheek. She finally looked up and met his gaze.

'I don't want to go back to the way things were,' Xadrion said.

'Okay.' What looked like relief flashed in Azraelle's eyes.

'Okay?'

'Yes, okay. I can't promise you what my future looks like, or yours as you find your powers, or I seek to prove my innocence. But I am happy not to return to keeping away from you,' Azraelle said.

'We'll figure it out. We can take our time,' Xadrion said.

It was at that exact moment that Azraelle's door burst open and Ilyon and Tolemus came barging in. Both took stock of the sight in front of them and stopped dead in their tracks, Ilyon's greeting cry cut off halfway. Xadrion's hand dropped from Azraelle's cheek as he turned to face the sudden noise, and he saw Ilyon and Tolemus grinning like absolute fools.

'Okay, boys, close your mouths,' Azraelle said, pushing herself out from Xadrion's hold. The absence of her warmth hit Xadrion quickly. She stood and walked over to them, grabbing Ilyon roughly under her elbow and rustling his hair.

'Does this mean no more weird tension in training?' Ilyon said, laughing while she had him head locked. Tolemus was laughing also and Xadrion felt none of the jealousy he'd felt last night towards the man. Had it all been part of Azraelle's teasing? The look in Tolemus' eyes as he watched Az was not one of desire. Instead, as Tolemus smiled, he thought it looked like happiness alone that Tolemus felt.

'Shut up, Ilyon,' Azraelle said as she threw him from her grasp and dodged his returning jab in her direction. In the months she'd been there, Azraelle had never shied away from being Ilyon's friend. At first, feeling how Xadrion couldn't take a similar place, it had made him feel frustration watching her so easy-going with his brother. Now, he was grateful for the friendship they had both been able to offer each other. Xadrion hadn't heard Ilyon laugh so carefree and earnestly in all the time prior to Azraelle.

'Xadrion, I'm going to need to ask you to cover up if I am at all supposed to focus on training today,' Tolemus joked, sending him a friendly smile. The way Tolemus looked at him, genuinely looked at him, Xadrion could have laughed at his own stupidity. Even as Tolemus had danced with Azraelle for so many hours the night before, he'd never actually looked at her with even a portion of the desire he had in that moment, even jokingly, directed at Xadrion.

Xadrion laughed, for the first time honestly in a long time, and retreated back to Az's bedroom, where he donned the rest of his clothes.

'I'm going to go change into something more comfortable. I'll meet you guys there,' Xadrion said.

Xadrion left Azraelle to deal with the two children in the room and made a dash to his own room. As Xadrion got further from Azraelle, he began to feel her power pulling back from his mind. He knew she struggled with the suppression even when they were together and as soon as he was out of her room and partway down the hall, he felt her shadows leave him altogether.

Last night, it had felt like he was boiling to the point where he couldn't go back. As he'd felt the anger and jealousy growing watching Azraelle dance with everyone but himself, hearing the way Romina talked about her, he'd felt the small control he had over his power slipping. As soon as he'd been alone in her room with her, it felt like she'd given him an outlet. Getting to touch her and kiss her made him feel like he could breathe beneath the weight of his power once more.

But he couldn't stay buried within her forever, as tempting as that was. They needed to produce a more permanent solution and fast, it seemed. If he reached the point of not being able to control the initial release of his power, and he wasn't isolated from everyone somehow, he didn't know how it would go. Over the last few days, Az and Tolemus had told him of the dangers, and it was the seriousness with which they spoke that made Xadrion know even going far out into the woods and abandoning him there would not quite be enough to limit the consequences of his power.

The only way he could be suppressed enough to really be able to release it all was by having someone with a closer connection to him, or similar powers, nearby. Zeus was the only person he had heard of who had similar powers, but Rhoas had also mentioned a sister. Did she have a similar power as well? Although, Rhoas had also mentioned Hera's concern for Xadrion was *because* of how she'd seen her first daughter turn out. Xadrion had chills just thinking about what that could mean.

'Prince Xadrion?' came a voice from behind him. Xadrion turned and came face to face with Romina. Right, he needed to solve that problem as well.

'Good morning, Princess,' Xadrion responded. 'I was hoping to find you this morning, actually.' Romina looked him over, her face showing disapproval as she perceived the clothes he was still wearing from the night before.

'Why is that?' Romina asked, her voice laced with venom he'd never heard from her before.

'I wish to apologise for my outburst last night,' Xadrion said. 'I... understand how our customs are quite different from yours, and I should have had the patience to explain it to you. Yelling at you like that was not proper behaviour on my part.'

'It's okay,' Romina said, not sounding at all like it was. Even in her anger she knew how to perform, knew exactly what was expected of her as a representative of her kingdom. They'd bonded once over their patience, when he had visited Gaeweth many years ago, but now it stood as a stark reminder how different Xadrion was becoming, perhaps how different he'd already become.

'Please, I will not be able to rest well knowing you have returned to Gaeweth and are hating me from afar.'

'Better to have me hating you from afar than to have to honour the promise between our kingdoms.'

'Is marriage to me something you really can say you desired?' Xadrion asked. Surely Romina was as uninterested in an arranged marriage as Xadrion had been declaring for years. Rhoas had never pushed him, so Xadrion assumed the understanding had been renegotiated. Perhaps it was another thing Rhoas had just not told him about.

'We would have united our kingdoms and brought prosperity to both our lands. It didn't matter to me what I desired. I kept myself prepared for the moment I would see you, Xadrion Mescal – my betrothed – once more and we could solidify what I believed would happen since I met you as a child,' Romina said. 'I can see you did not do the same, judging by the clothes you are returning in.'

'I would much rather see both of us marry for love, not responsibility,' Xadrion said.

'And tell me, do you love the whore whose bed you occupied last night?' Romina's polite façade dropped entirely as they stood alone in the halls.

His power shot to the surface of his skin, rippling beneath the surface in a way he did not feel he could contain.

'Watch it.'

'She can never love you back. Her sins are too insurmountable to be granted the pure blessing of love,' Romina said. Xadrion couldn't see straight, could barely breathe as the energy crackled throughout him. His skin was itching again and he felt like he would explode at any moment.

He could not take it. He was about to lose control in the middle of the castle he called his home, surrounded by his friends and family, Azraelle only a few hallways over. As exhilarating as it had been letting his power run so free last night, it was beginning to feel impossible to draw it back inside him fully. Xadrion knew this moment was different, that even if he had been seated right beside Azraelle her suppression would do nothing. He needed to get out.

Let me free, his power whispered within him.

'Fuck you,' Xadrion spat, and then he turned and ran through the castle from her. He pushed against the energy, willing with everything he had for it to not explode in that moment. He ran through the castle, breaking out to the sunlight quickly. Xadrion wished he had Azraelle's ability to turn into mist and travel free of any prying eyes, but if Xadrion did have any ability to do that, he wouldn't have known. He'd barely scratched the surface with learning what he could do.

But maybe. Maybe he could try. Not shadows, not mist. His magic didn't work like Azraelle's. Instead, it felt like pure energy, lightning embodied. Xadrion ran toward the abandoned castle buildings, hoping to get as far from anyone as possible. He imagined the feeling of lightning coming from within him, imagined it encompassing all that he was and would ever be. He imagined his very essence blending with the lightning he demanded to strike from the sky, and then imagined he could be where his lightning originated from.

In a series of seconds, Xadrion felt the lightning ripple through him time and time again. Each time, Xadrion knew he was moving further from the castle. However he had done it, whatever part of his power he had tapped into, it had worked.

He kept running, constantly moving between his jumps, unsure where exactly he was going. Each time Xadrion felt himself jump to his next location, he was overwhelmed by the cracking of thunder around him and the crackle of lightning.

Xadrion himself became the storm.

He knew only one thing. He needed to get away from people. If he were going to lose it, he needed to be as far as he could possibly be. It still wouldn't limit the damage he could cause, but it was the only thing he could hope to do. It was that or find some way to get in the presence of Zeus, or his sister. It was such a bad idea, a terrible idea even, but Xadrion hesitated for just a moment on the possibility of it.

When Xadrion came to a stop, he wasn't surprised at the location he'd ended up at. In front of him, the only visible structure in the immediate clearing, stood the bell tower. Its power rippled through the clearing, the remnants of all those who had passed through it over the millennia. What should have taken him hours to reach had seemingly taken only moments by storm.

Now, as far from people as he could manage to get, heat emanating from him in waves as he struggled to push back the explosion he could feel growing, Xadrion was desperate. He was sweating, gasping for air, doing his best to keep that power in check for just a little longer. Xadrion realised and processed what felt like the only two options he had within a matter of moments, not able to spend the time he would have wished thinking it through.

The first, he could let it all out right there, but he found himself remembering Azraelle's telling of Nyx. If she were to step foot on the mortal realm, without the presence of Erebus who was able to suppress her, thousands would die. Would he kill thousands in his first uncontrolled release? Xadrion didn't know if he could live with himself if he risked that.

The second, he could use the bell tower in front of him and find a means of contacting Zeus. It risked everything he had come to know and understand. It would reveal his presence, it would put Azraelle at risk, put Ilyon and everyone he loved at risk. But maybe... maybe if Zeus realised Xadrion were alive, maybe it could be possible to end all of this. Maybe if he knew Xadrion was alive it could all be laid to rest.

Yes, his power hissed as Xadrion's blood felt like it was boiling. *I want to be free.*

How could it be possible that he felt his lightning sparking more intensely with each pump of his heart?

Azraelle, Xadrion sent frantically. *I can't contain it.*

Xadrion? Where are you?

Azraelle, please. Forgive me for what I need to do.

Xadrion felt her presence then, felt her frantically searching at his mind, begging to be let in. He let her see, showed her what he knew he needed to do.

Xadrion, don't, Azraelle pleaded, her voice laced with complete and utter fear. Her panic was clear. But it was too late.

There was no other option.

He'd been moving as they spoke, had moved until his hands rested against the stone wall of the bell tower. His power was tearing at him, like it was shredding him from the inside. Using whatever sense of mind he had left, Xadrion keyed into the bell tower's signal, desperately searching for the means to follow the path that was ingrained into its existence. If he could feel how those who had travelled this way had done it, he could copy them.

At the same time, Xadrion sent every urgent message he could straight down the visible pathway he could now see from the bell tower. The pathway was highlighted straight into the sky, disappearing into some invisible realm.

I need help, I need help, I need help.

Xadrion didn't follow the pathway, he felt as if it wasn't allowing him to, like there was a lock in place that he didn't have the means to open. But he still tried, still pushed against it, and sent his desperate urges along it. It was unbearable, the pain that was now crackling over his skin. Xadrion wondered if it was possible for his own power to kill him in the process of release. He couldn't breathe.

Xadrion closed his eyes the moment he felt it was too far gone to resist anymore.

'Let go,' whispered a woman's voice beside him. He couldn't open his eyes, had no idea who had come to join him. He couldn't even speak to warn her to leave, to get out of harm's way.

Xadrion felt firm hands clasp his forearms, felt them squeeze tightly. Xadrion exploded.

He couldn't have imagined what it looked like, but the feeling of it was like no other. It felt like he became lightning, like the energy crackled out of him and was him and surrounded him.

Miraculously, as soon as he stopped fighting, the pain went away. In its place came a pleasure unmatched by anything Xadrion had ever felt before. Xadrion let himself succumb to the release completely.

Finally free from the pain, with the sound of lightning crackling around him and his power flowing from deep within, he opened his eyes.

Around him, the clearing looked to be on fire. Pure energy crackled and the grass surrounding him had been singed black, but the damage went no further than the barrier of the clearing. The trees beyond looked fine, the sky barely visible through the lightning also seemed fine. In front of him, the woman who had joined him and was clasping his forearms stood, grinning.

Her skin was such a deep brown, the shade so similar to Xadrion's. She was dressed in the finest set of armour he ever had laid eyes upon – golden gauntlets, golden boots, all golden. Her hair was tightly braided, fine thin rows of braids streaming away from her face. From her, he saw lightning, just as he now saw and felt it coming from him. Somehow, she stood, lightning flaring between the two of them, completely unharmed.

She had lightning.

Xadrion saw the edges of the clearing now, his power playing and threading among hers. No… her power beating his own back, keeping it contained. She was suppressing him.

When Xadrion felt the power begin to diminish, he had no idea of the amount of time that had passed. It felt like hours but could have been only moments. Xadrion fell to his knees, feeling absolutely spent as sweat dripped over his brow and he breathed heavily. The woman knelt with him. Her grip turned gentle on his forearms, and as Xadrion's lightning sizzled out around them, he could see hers also diminish.

'Well, little brother,' the woman said, 'it would seem there is a lot you need to catch me up on.'

TWENTY-FOUR

XADRION

Little brother? Surely he'd misheard. But yes, she did look similar to him in so many ways. Her skin, her grey eyes the exact match to ones Xadrion had looked into thousands of times in his own reflection pierced him as they knelt across from each other, even the lightning he could still feel simmering within her felt so similar.

'Do you have it under control?' the woman asked Xadrion.

'I think so,' he answered, his voice coming out hoarse. His throat hurt so much it felt as if he'd been screaming.

'Good, because I think it's time you told me how it's possible for you to be standing in front of me right now.'

Xadrion didn't know what answer he could give her. He couldn't piece together who he could trust, couldn't piece together how to keep everyone safe, not when he was so exhausted. If he told her everything, would she tell Zeus everything? As the calm began to settle once more, Xadrion began to feel the consequences of him revealing himself.

'I don't know anything,' he lied. 'Only that this power has recently begun to appear, and I needed to get as far away from everyone as I could. Who are you?'

'Athena,' the woman answered, her eyes watching him intently. 'You're lying. How did you know this was a point of contact to Olympus? I heard your message; I heard you calling for Zeus.'

'You aren't Zeus,' Xadrion said cautiously.

'No, but I share the power that runs through his veins. The power that also runs through your veins, it would seem,' Athena answered. 'He sent me to investigate. He'll be incredibly pleased to hear you're alive.'

'I didn't want to hurt anyone,' Xadrion said. 'I don't want him to know I'm here.'

Athena laughed. It sounded surprised, but also humourless and... cold, somehow.

'Zeus will know it as soon as I return,' Athena said. 'It's not every day one of his sons comes back from the dead. You should come with me, come meet him yourself. Hera will be so glad to hear of her darling boy's return.'

Xadrion felt like the breath had been punched from him.

'Hera's dead,' Xadrion said, his ears beginning to ring. There was no way he'd heard Athena correctly.

'She's not dead, my brother. Not even close,' Athena said, tilting her head slightly. She looked genuinely confused. She was watching him, observing him for any expression he gave away. Xadrion felt the world around him shift, felt as if everything he had known was shifting with it. Hera wasn't dead? How could that be true? Rhoas had said... had he lied?

'She's alive?' Xadrion whispered.

'Alive and well. Come with me to see her,' Athena said.

'I need time... to think,' Xadrion said. He was so tired, so depleted after that release of his power.

Xadrion, don't, came Azraelle's voice, faint into his mind.

'I can give you that,' Athena said. She stood, pulling him effortlessly with her until they both stood facing each other. 'I can leave you to process but, my brother, Zeus will want to meet you. And he will send me down for you once more.'

'Please, do what you can to stall him. I need some time,' Xadrion pleaded. 'Let me come back to you when I'm ready.'

Leaving with her in that moment was not a good idea. He had no idea what would be waiting on the other side. Xadrion didn't even know if he was strong enough to protect the information of Azraelle being alive and well. There were too many uncertainties. He needed to return to Azraelle, to Rhoas. He needed answers to so many questions.

'Very well, little brother. I will see what I can do,' Athena said. 'Your release was contained, you hurt no one in the process, but you have much to learn. Call for me when you are ready to use your powers fully.'

With that, Athena disappeared. He watched the essence of her travel along the pathway from the bell tower, disappearing from sight.

Standing now alone, surrounded by the decimated clearing and blackened grass, Xadrion for the first time in months felt as if the anger that had plagued him increasingly for the past year was finally nowhere to be found. In its place there was nothing but exhaustion and confusion. So much was still kept from him.

If Zeus demanded to return immediately for him, Xadrion needed to be gone. He needed time to process, to contemplate what he had already heard. Hera was alive. Someone, somewhere along the story, was lying.

I'm coming to get you, Azraelle's voice flooded his mind.

Don't leave the castle wards. I'll find you, Xadrion responded quickly. If Zeus came down and Azraelle was outside the wards, who knew what the fallout could be.

What did you do? Azraelle demanded. Her mental voice sounded like straight fire, laced with daggers as she spoke to him. She was pissed. At him.

Xadrion didn't answer. He had to figure out how to return back. He had no horse and the walk would take too long. He was outside the castle's protections and if Zeus did come to the mortal realm, he would find him instantly. Could he replicate the way he had travelled here? It had been impulse rather than anything. He didn't know exactly *how* he had done it.

Xadrion forced himself to focus, forced himself to ignore the dread that was building in his gut. Hera was alive, Azraelle sounded angrier than he'd ever heard her and Zeus, who Hera had warned him so many times about over and over again in her stories, now knew he was alive. He had to ignore all of it to even begin to call his magic to him once more. He looked in, searching for his power.

Before he'd had the release, his power had felt all consuming, like at any moment he would be thrown from control and overwhelmed. Now, the power within him had calmed and it seemed more eager to respond to his direct command. Without much effort, Xadrion's lightning crackled around him, building that storm once more. He imagined it taking him back to the castle, taking him back to Azraelle, and felt it eagerly obey.

Once more, Xadrion became the storm as he moved over the vast land in little to no time. And he could see where he was going, not as he saw when he was in his physical body but in a way that was somehow other, somehow more.

Xadrion headed for where he could feel Azraelle's presence, sparking straight through her window and landing just inside it. Outside, the storm that Xadrion had created continued on.

When Xadrion appeared, he found Azraelle standing on the opposite side of the room with one of the couches between them. Her hands gripped its back and where she gripped Xadrion could see the wooden frame twisting beneath the force. Her eyes caught his entrance immediately, eyeing him warily, as if she knew exactly where he had been going to appear. When his lightning gave a final flicker around him, Azraelle physically recoiled.

She was... scared? Of him, or of his power. Azraelle had told him in the cabin that she would need time to separate Xadrion from the images she had of Zeus, but he hadn't seen her look so frightened around him, even after he'd shot that lightning straight at her.

'Az?' Xadrion whispered, making to take a step forward. She lifted one hand from the back of the couch and held it up, palm facing him. Xadrion stopped in his tracks.

'What the fuck did you do?' Azraelle said, her voice quiet but firm as she still stood on the other side of the room. Xadrion thought back to how it had felt to have her powers thrown at him, showing him all those horrifying images of death as her powers whipped him over and over, and imagined that her voice sounded a lot like that. She was cold, calm, but beneath the façade lay an overbearing amount of power. Somewhere within him, Xadrion's power recoiled at the distance she had created between them.

'I had no choice, Az.'

'No choice?' Azraelle repeated, her eyes squinting at him in judgement.

'I couldn't control it. I needed help to suppress it,' Xadrion explained.

'Then you come to me,' Azraelle snapped.

'It wouldn't have been enough, not this time. I got so angry it felt like it had lit me on fire.'

'Then you let it burn,' Azraelle said coldly. Her eyes blazed, reminding him once more of that iciness despite their black colour. Xadrion couldn't comprehend the words that were coming from Azraelle's lips, the coldness in her disregard for the consequences.

'I would have hurt people, innocent people,' Xadrion responded, trying to get through to her. Azraelle's eyes didn't soften.

Azraelle didn't even hesitate when she said, 'It would have been better that way.'

Surely she didn't think he should have let himself hurt others. Did the idea of Zeus knowing he was alive really seem worse than potentially thousands of innocent mortals being killed by his hand?

'You don't mean that,' Xadrion breathed.

'Don't I?' Az sneered.

'You couldn't possibly mean to tell me you would have preferred if I had have taken out innocent lives, potentially thousands, over going to Zeus – to my real father – for help,' Xadrion said.

'Your real father?' Az stepped back from the couch. Her back hit the wall and, by all accounts, she looked like he'd shot her straight through the gut with his lightning again.

'Is he not?' Xadrion demanded. His own anger was rising, but the feeling of his power remained settled inside him. In fact, rather than flaring as his power usually did when he found himself in arguments, now as he stood across the room from Azraelle, his power felt as if it were trying to pull back further, as if it too were warning him against Azraelle's rage.

'How can you be so fucking stupid?' Azraelle demanded, and then she became a flurry of movement. Unrestrained, Azraelle was *fast*. Where she had previously been pressing against the wall, almost cowering away from him, now she was moving straight for him. The white of her hair, the darkness of her shadows that moved around her, both reminded Xadrion of a fire burning hot and fast. She became barely tangible as she rushed his direction, moving so fluidly and appearing before him in the blink of an eye. Her eyes were ice. Her shadows growing.

'He is not your family; your family was here inside this castle. And you just signed their death warrants,' Azraelle sneered. 'Probably mine as well, if I can't figure out how to get out of here fast enough. You've thrown yourself to the feet of a man who will smile as he tears down everything around you.'

'If he knows I'm alive, that your family was not responsible for my death, maybe I can make him back down,' Xadrion pondered aloud, hoping to calm the force of Azraelle now in front of him.

'You really are naïve,' Azraelle spat. 'Have you heard nothing I've ever said, nothing Hera undoubtedly told you? You *saw* me, Xadrion. You saw the way I was left; you saw into my mind in a way that no one ever has. You saw what he did to me. That is not a man that is reasoned with.'

'I'd like to try. What other choice is there?' Xadrion pushed. Xadrion couldn't decipher his own thoughts towards Zeus. He knew what had been done to Azraelle, recalled all the stories that Hera had told him when he was younger, but there were so many unanswered questions before him. Was it not his right to learn all he could about his real father before he was made to step into this new world of gods? He would not, could not, excuse Zeus' actions so far, but if there was a chance he could facilitate a future where Azraelle did not have to run and where Hera would be safe to return to Rhoas one day, how could he not try?

'I will not be some fucktoy for one of Zeus' sons,' Azraelle said, her words a dagger straight through him.

'You know it was more than that, what we did,' Xadrion pleaded, stepping forward to close the final distance. He made to grab her but before he could he found she had moved completely out of his range. He tried again, only to find her gone once more. He whirled to face her but kept still so she didn't move again.

'Azraelle, please. Last night meant something.'

'It meant nothing,' Azraelle said, her words like straight acid down his throat. 'I am Azraelle, daughter to Nyx and Erebus. I am *the* hand of Death and the wielder of more than you can even begin to comprehend. I will not be threatened by this weakness because of some son of Zeus who wishes to claim that title.'

'Weakness?' Xadrion demanded, his anger boiling within him. 'That weakness you refuse to name, dear Azraelle, is love. Or as close to it as you seem capable of getting. You don't get a say in who you feel that for.'

'Like hell I don't.' And he could see it, could see the way she was throwing down any emotion she'd let herself feel for him. He could almost physically see the smothering she was doing on every one of those emotions.

'Don't do this,' Xadrion warned.

'It's already done, boy,' Azraelle said. Back in front of him was the version of her that had hurt to be around. The one who looked at him coldly, who spoke to him coldly, who made him feel so incomprehensibly alone even when in her presence.

'You aren't a goddess right now,' Xadrion said. Anger rippled through her, and she looked to be building up for a response. 'I hope I one day get to see you in that truest form, but it will never be possible while you are being hunted. I sought Zeus because I felt I had no choice, but I would do it again if it meant the smallest chance of freeing you from your sentence. I would do that for you, Az.'

'Don't pretend that any of this was for me.'

'It is, and for me,' Xadrion said. 'And for Hera.' Azraelle's expression broke from her anger for the first time at those final words, confusion briefly sweeping over her features before she resolved back to her blank façade. He had caught her off guard with that name.

'Why bring Hera into this?' Azraelle demanded.

'Because Athena told me she's alive and if that's true, and she's with Zeus, then I need to help her too,' Xadrion said.

Azraelle did not even blink when Xadrion said Hera was alive. It was not a revelation to her, Xadrion realised. At least not the news of Hera being alive, only Xadrion knowing so had appeared to shock Azraelle.

'You already knew?' Xadrion asked, his voice coming out in nothing but a whisper. He felt as if he could hear his heart physically cracking inside him. If she already knew, she had lied to him. Azraelle shrugged one shoulder, as if she couldn't care less.

'It wasn't my place to say anything,' Azraelle answered, coldly.

'You fucking knew, and you didn't tell me?' Xadrion exploded. He reached for her once more, faster, and actually felt his hands clasp around her shoulders. She was looking up at him, that icy expression, but as soon as his hands were on her, Xadrion could see the panic beneath her eyes. He wanted to shake her.

'Like I said, it wasn't my place,' Azraelle said, trying to sound indifferent.

Xadrion could barely see through the anger throbbing through his veins and his grip tightened on Azraelle's shoulders.

He couldn't shake her, couldn't hurt her, but in that moment, he wanted to break *something*. Before he could peel his hands from her, Azraelle responded to his tightened grip. The shadows around her deepened and physical tendrils formed in his direction. One moment he was holding her, the next he was overwhelmed by the feeling of her power, targeting him in the way it had in the old stables.

He felt pain slice over his skin repeatedly, as if a dagger was continuously plunging in and out of his thighs, his chest, his hands, everywhere. Xadrion cried out, dropping to his knees as the pain swept through him. Azraelle took a step forward until she was towering straight above him, her face hard as she stared down at him.

'I will never be handled like that again,' she said. 'Do not forget who it is you touch when you touch me.' To prove her point, Xadrion felt the spearing of the images for his mind once more, and managed to solidify his defences in time to not let them in. In the stables he'd let them in, willingly wanting a part of Azraelle inside his mind. What she had shown him that day had left him retching everything inside of him back out.

He knew what he would see, what she was talking about when she said that – Death. She was Death, and he *had* forgotten, or perhaps never fully understood. He had thought her weakened, someone who was recovering and healing and would need further care. She was not.

No, Azraelle was not at her full form, but even in this halfway point she was more than he could ever have imagined. She was Death, and thousands of years old at least, and he was nothing to her.

'Please,' he whispered through the slicing, through the pain. Azraelle only scowled at him, then slowly pulled her tendrils back to her as if to show she could have left them there if she wanted. When the last one left him, he couldn't move. He didn't want to move. Above him, Azraelle shifted into her mist form and disappeared from her window, leaving him standing in that room he had felt so at peace in not more than a few hours earlier.

Xadrion lay there, breathing hard through the pain, struggling to catch up with how things had changed so fast in such a brief time. He had gotten her and lost her within the matter of half a day.

Gone, his power whispered around him into the empty room. Xadrion had just done the one thing to guarantee Azraelle being lost to him for good, and yet he wasn't sure it was within him to regret doing so. If part of living an immortal life meant having the same disregard Azraelle held for individual lives, Xadrion wanted no part of it.

TWENTY-FIVE

AZRAELLE

Azraelle couldn't breathe. She needed to go somewhere else – anywhere else – but it was too risky. Zeus did not know of her yet, but he would be looking her way now, looking for anything with power that stepped foot in the area. She would be a signal the moment she left the castle's wards. Azraelle was trapped in the mortal realm, trapped in this tiny castle behind its tiny walls, and she could not leave. Xadrion had well and truly fucked her, perhaps everyone within a day's ride of the bell tower.

Azraelle hadn't wanted to leave, she realised all too late. Not last night, not when she had been nestled into arms that felt safe at the time. Not when she'd felt things stir within her that she'd never once felt. In her exile, Azraelle had naïvely thought maybe she could have found something good.

Now, she really needed to go. She needed to find the boy whose destiny she was accused of altering, use him to bring back her innocence and return to her kind, to the life she had before this one.

Who had she been to ever think that Xadrion's arms were safe when Zeus' blood crackled within him? The more comfortable he got with his power, the more she would have been exposed to it, have felt its searing presence. Azraelle was not ready for that, did not think she could be ready for that for a very long time. The images of that lightning being used to torture her still plagued her waking nightmares.

Azraelle didn't know what to do, or where she could go, but she found herself drifting from her mist form atop the castle roof. She was on one of the smaller towers, towards the back of the castle. It was stone but flat and had a high lip to it that she could crouch beneath to avoid the majority of the wind buffeting that high up.

Around her, the storm was continuing. Thunder echoed through the area, rain pouring down. The lightning had moved further away, crackling off in the distance.

She had to leave and soon. If Zeus found her again... no, she would not allow that. She'd kill herself right there and submit to hundreds of years missing before she let him. Azraelle fingered the pendant chain around her throat as she considered what it would mean to take her own life. She was willing to do whatever it took to keep herself from Zeus' capture once more.

There used to be such comfort from storms. With her wings, it would have allowed her to fly wherever she wished with ease; now it taunted her, reminded her of what was missing.

The wind taunted her for how willingly she had stayed in the castle after falling, dragging from the hidden recesses of her mind everything she had felt content to leave behind for the time being, while she trained and flirted and fucked her enemy's potential weapon. Azraelle had let herself get so immersed in the feeling of Xadrion, and even the friendship of Ilyon and companionship of Emera, that she hadn't wanted to care about leaving. Now, she had to.

Zeus would not find her.

But how would she find the boy and fix everything? It seemed so impossible. Nakir said she'd look for the records, but that only meant more waiting.

Azraelle stood, letting the wind slash across her skin. No one would see her, not up there. She stood on the edge of the tower wall and threw her arms wide. She wished more than anything to feel the weight of her wings behind her, preparing to catch the draft and send her up.

Nothing happened.

Azraelle thought of her siblings – many of whom she hadn't seen for a long time. She missed Thanatos and Charon, even Eris and Oizys, two of her older sisters that she'd often spent time with. They weren't related to Death, not in the way that Thanatos and Charon shared with Az, but Eris and Oizys had always been supportive of their role. The memories of the few in the Underworld she could call friends sent a sharp pang through her heart.

The Ravens, and the little room she'd occupied in the mountains of their realm, Eviria, was a big source of longing at any given moment. She'd been their primus, and they had understood her and her role, even supported her through it. Azraelle wasn't exactly the same as them but close enough that they'd become the closest friends she'd had.

Nyx, settled in the Underworld, she had been content to leave. Her mater wouldn't have been able to come to the mortal realm, not until Erebus was back, which meant it would have been hundreds of years before she saw her again, at least. There were a lot of things she resented Nyx for, things that had always come between the two of them, but would Az really have been okay leaving her mater for this mortal realm for so long?

Azraelle screamed, long and hard into the wind, letting it carry the sound in whichever direction it wished. She screamed until her throat was hoarse and she ran out of breath.

What have I done so wrong to deserve your wrath, Chaos? Azraelle shot the thought out, knowing there would be no answer. Chaos never answered her. Another who had abandoned her without second thought.

It wasn't necessary to be outside the castle wards to speak to Thanatos, at least. She'd only left the castle all those afternoons for the privacy it offered, for the routine of trying to talk to her brother. For whatever reason, the communication was still possible through Emera's wards. Xadrion and Azraelle had done it between the old cabin and the castle several times.

But would Thanatos or Nakir even be able to find something to help her with?

Azraelle didn't know what to do after screaming, so found herself curling up beneath the lip of the tower wall. There was a hatch in the ground beneath her, leading down and into the tower, but she'd never seen anyone actually take the hallways to get there before. Azraelle curled her knees to her chest and pressed her cheek against the cold ground. With nothing better to do, she fell asleep, the rain sheeting down on her relentlessly.

Firm arms slid beneath her, hoisting her effortlessly from the ground. Azraelle stirred back to wakefulness and opened her eyes to see who was lifting her. Looking down at her, a gentle smile on their face, was Tolemus. He cradled her to his chest, taking the stone steps through the door in the tower.

'Come on, little one,' Tolemus said. 'Immortality or not, you can't stay up there in the storm.'

Tolemus had come.

Azraelle rested her cheek against his chest and wrapped her arms up and around his neck. Tolemus pressed a very gentle kiss to the top of her hair. She was drenched, the sound of droplets falling from her body to the ground below echoed as they walked. Where Azraelle came in contact with Tolemus, she could see his clothing immediately get watered through. She must have looked half drowned.

Azraelle let Tolemus carry her all the way back to her rooms; thankfully, Xadrion was nowhere to be seen. Tolemus led her into the bathroom where he placed her gently on the ground against the wall and began drawing water, using elements of his own magic to heat it.

'Come on, you need to warm up,' Tolemus said, gesturing to the ready bath. Azraelle peeled her clothes off, feeling no shame in front of Tolemus for it, and stepped into the water. She was so cold that the water felt like it was burning her but as she started to warm up, she sunk further and further in.

'Can you talk to me?' Azraelle asked, quietly. She needed to hear his voice, needed to hear something that tied her to this version of her reality. Azraelle felt like she was sliding down a steep mountain and there was no way she could come to a stop. She needed a voice to keep her there.

'I wasn't always the commander general for Gaeweth,' Tolemus said after a moment's thought, pulling a seat to sit beside the bathtub. He leant back in it, watching Azraelle as he spoke. 'I grew up with my grandmother, Thetis. My father died when I was young, so I don't remember him at all and my mother was never in the picture. It was just Thetis and I for a very long time. I was blessed with longer life than mortal men, but still Thetis remained more immortal than I ever would be.

'She was so worried all the time for me, so concerned that something would happen, and I would be taken from her as well, that it didn't seem enough for her. She said she would always need more time, regardless of how much we got. So, we went to the river Styx, and she used its powers and her own power over water to give me a truly immortal lifespan, like you.'

Azraelle had heard of the river Styx, had heard of its power. Not many were strong enough to wield it if they could tap into its power in the first place. There was legend that Thetis had used it once before for her son, Achilles. Azraelle had never heard that Thetis had tried it again.

'It killed her, didn't it?' Azraelle brought her knees up to her chest in the bath as Tolemus nodded.

'It worked, I think. But it took her from me instead,' Tolemus whispered.

Azraelle could not even begin to ponder what that meant for Tolemus, what that meant he was. Destiny did not like to be tinkered with, granting the gift of immortal life so rarely, only ever when a new purpose needed to be served or when an immortal never returned from death.

'Do you know what happens when our kind dies?' Azraelle asked, tentatively. His talking was helping her but if she could offer him any peace, she would have done anything.

'I didn't think your kind could die until she did,' Tolemus admitted.

'We can and we do, fairly often,' Azraelle said. 'But it's not permanent. Or at least, most of the time it isn't. There are tales of some who have died and never come back, but mostly we do. It takes a long time, hundreds of years, but it happens.'

'She'll come back?' Tolemus asked, so quietly.

'It isn't my place to speak of Destiny's plan but there's always a chance. You just have to use those years of yours to wait for her,' Azraelle said. He fell into silence, pondering what she had told him. The silence was too much for her and quickly Xadrion's words rang around her once more.

'Keep telling me your story.'

'Well,' Tolemus began, 'after she died, I didn't know what to do with myself. I spent a good many years in a very bad place and decided to join an army, any army I could. It just so happened to be Gaeweth's. I met another when I joined, a man named Nico. He had magic, magic that is remarkably similar to Ilyon's, so I felt as if he understood me to some extent. We grew close over the years and moved up the ranks together.'

'You loved him?'

'Deeply,' Tolemus replied. 'But I only got years with him before he died. Magic, but mortal. He was wounded in battle and didn't survive. It sent me to that place again, losing another I loved. I didn't think I would ever recover. But by that point I was commander general, and it was easy to lose myself in killing the other sides. Trouble came to me when it was peaceful.'

'How did you recover?'

'I don't think I did,' Tolemus answered. 'Meeting you has made me feel less alone, and the princes as well. Ilyon reminds me so much of Nico in his enthusiasm for life that it has made it somewhat easier to bear. Being around those of my kind makes me feel more alive but even after all these years, waking up without him is the hardest thing I have to face every day.'

'I'm so sorry to hear that,' Azraelle said. His story was not uncommon amongst the immortals and the mortals, those who dared venture to the mortal realm for love. It was why she had never spent an extended period of time amongst the mortals for any reason other than her responsibilities for Death. The mortals loved in such a way she was sure she would have gotten caught up in some way by one of them, and she could not bear to love like that.

Her mind darted to Xadrion, to the beginnings of the feelings she'd started to have for him. Even finding one of her own kind had her mourning that lost chance. Because deep down she knew that the chance to love was something she wanted, it was something she had dreamt of for thousands of years. But she couldn't get it out of her mind that it was also the greatest weakness she would ever have.

Nyx, one of the most powerful beings in existence, had shown her that.

Azraelle hadn't known Nyx before a time she was with Erebus, but Nyx was so content to remain removed from everything, to keep her power down and live through the mundanity of daily life. She had never intercepted in wars; the greatest act of passion Azraelle had ever seen her do was in shielding Hypnos from Zeus' wrath. Maybe it was because she loved, maybe it wasn't, but Azraelle had never been able to separate Nyx's disengagement from the idea of love. That idea was only strengthened when Erebus died and Nyx further removed herself.

'I heard what happened,' Tolemus whispered.

Azraelle frowned and pushed herself to standing in the tub. Tolemus passed her a towel and followed Azraelle as she walked back into the main entrance, wrapping the towel around her body.

'He told you?'

'Ilyon did,' Tolemus answered. 'Xadrion went to Rhoas, took Ilyon with him, and demanded some answers. Ilyon said Rhoas admitted to asking you to not say anything about Hera, but that Xadrion was pissed. He didn't leave the castle, I don't think he's willing to face what happens if he does, but he won't let anyone in to see him.'

'Good. He deserves to be alone right now.' Azraelle meant it, wholeheartedly.

He had risked everything. He'd risked his own life, risked Ilyon's. If Zeus was killing people, was sending Deimos to do so, it only meant something bad. It was no mistake that the girl Deimos had killed had power of a kind. Zeus wouldn't be worrying himself with killing mortals, which meant Xadrion had put Ilyon in danger as well, and Tolemus as soon as he had to head back to Gaeweth and leave the castle's protection. All because he didn't want to hurt anyone on his release.

'I will not condone his behaviour to you, not when I don't understand the depths of what you faced at the hands of Zeus. I just… I don't want you to throw away what he might offer you one day,' Tolemus said tentatively.

'He can offer me nothing,' Azraelle said.

'He can offer you everything,' Tolemus argued.

'I had everything I ever needed before I fell. I just have to get back to it,' Azraelle argued.

'I will help you if I can before I go. But please, think about what he faces with all the new knowledge of who he is. You've had thousands of years to develop coping strategies for this – nothing must surprise you anymore. He has not had that opportunity,' Tolemus said.

'Such a pacifist for a commander general,' Azraelle taunted. Tolemus chuckled, the sound lightening her mood instantly.

'Azraelle, I would burn through cities for you for the hope you give me of my grandmother. I would slaughter thousands if it meant getting Nico back. I am no pacifist. But I do believe in love above every other force,' Tolemus responded.

'Love,' Azraelle scoffed, 'is nothing but lies.'

Tolemus frowned at her but did not argue further. They spoke for a while longer that night, drifting towards lighter matters, such as Ilyon's training and how they might find the boy to free Azraelle. No solutions really occurred, and Tolemus was careful to not mention Xadrion's name and she was grateful for him for keeping her mind occupied. Tolemus seemed content to fill the silence with his own voice and stories, something Azraelle desperately needed. Eventually, Azraelle yawned and Tolemus left to his own rooms leaving Azraelle to sleep once more.

When morning came, Azraelle had resolved herself to the icy mask she knew she could play well. She could go to training, could continue teaching Ilyon easily enough. Thinking of giving Xadrion any more knowledge she held made her feel a little less sure, not now that she couldn't break away from the idea of him going and becoming a weapon for Zeus against her family. But she could pretend to remain working with him and not actually allow for any further progression in his training. She only had to pretend for so long; as soon as Nakir came with the information on the boy, Azraelle had resolved to leaving.

Azraelle went to the old wing of the castle early, earlier than most people were awake for. She needed some time with herself, with her own magic, to make sure she remained in control when she had to face Xadrion again. If he knew how much it had impacted her, he would know just how to use himself against her. Azraelle could not bear to expose herself any further.

Even if Xadrion never willingly went to Zeus, once Zeus tracked him down, she didn't have faith that Xadrion would be able to protect the memory he had of her from Zeus' eyes. She could have tried to remove the memories from Xadrion, to use the familiarity she held with his mind to step in, break his defences and purge herself from his mind completely. Azraelle wasn't sure if it would even work, given how quickly he had picked up his defences. If he detected her before she could do it, he definitely wouldn't respond well to the idea and she would only end up in more danger.

No, she couldn't do that. Mortals were easy, but he was no mortal and his shield was no easy barrier. Azraelle's own shield was not strong enough to withstand an attack as it was. She still needed more time to build it, which meant Az needed to be long gone before Zeus even had the chance to glean the information from Xadrion.

Azraelle spent at least an hour in the stables before anyone else arrived. She practised slipping between her shadow form and back. She practised sending her magic to the twisted scar still on her stomach, imagining it clearing her skin and leaving no further trace of Xadrion ever having gotten close enough to harm her. When she checked to see if it worked, she could tell it was slightly better but still very present.

Azraelle practised her footwork, sending her tendrils as strikes as if they were extensions of her arms. She'd missed moving like that, with access to her power. There were some things she hadn't tried yet, either for fear of not being able to or just because they weren't useful for her yet. But the comfort of her shadows and her tendrils was enough to make her feel like herself once more.

Tolemus was the first one to join her. He set to doing his own warmups but close enough that they could still talk.

'The moment you leave Fennhall you're going to be in danger,' Azraelle said as they each moved.

'Yes, I've been thinking about that,' Tolemus agreed.

'I don't know who Zeus is targeting and why, but you're going to basically be a flare as soon as you leave the wards,' Azraelle said.

'I see no way around it. I can't stay here forever. You can't stay here forever. Not even those boys will be able to stay inside the castle walls forever. We have to find a way out,' Tolemus said.

'I could try to mask you with my shadows, but at that point I don't know if that will intensify your presence or lessen it,' Azraelle pondered.

'My current theory is that I will shut down any and all threads of my power when we leave until we are back in Gaeweth. If I can lower my presence, it might let me go unnoticed,' Tolemus said.

'Could you not stay for longer? At least until we figured this out,' Azraelle asked.

From across the stables, the door opened. Ilyon and Emera entered, laughing together at some joke. Xadrion was not with them.

'I do wish to remain here with you. Something is brewing, something bigger than Fennhall or Gaeweth alone. But I must return first and sort out my affairs. Once I officially remove myself from my position, I can return,' Tolemus said.

Azraelle wished he didn't have to leave at all. He didn't have to, not by her rules, but Tolemus was invested in the rules of the mortal realm and the life he had created there for himself. She would not ask him to throw away everything just to remain with her here, not when she didn't think she would be here for much longer anyway. Tolemus could not come with her to the Ravens, not even to the Underworld without risking being permanently kept there. It was better he remained in his life in the mortal realm.

Ilyon and Emera reached them and settled into an easy rhythm of warming up and chatting. No one mentioned Xadrion; Ilyon didn't even bring up Hera. Instead, they let things continue on as normal. Azraelle gave Tolemus a thankful look, knowing it was him who had worded them up. He simply smiled slightly and moved on. Xadrion never showed up.

At the end of their session, all of them had worked up quite a sweat. Even Emera took part in the fighting portion of the session, and Azraelle had willingly shown her the basics and left Ilyon and Tolemus to pair up. The two men were more evenly matched than either of them would have been to Azraelle, and she didn't mind so much the teaching part. Emera was clumsy and only managed to spend the hours working on her footwork. By the end she didn't seem much better and it had the group laughing at her attempts, Emera laughing with them.

'He won't see anyone,' Ilyon said, finally breaking the unspoken vow of silence as they all walked back to the castle. Emera and Tolemus were ahead slightly, and Ilyon had slowed his own pace to match Azraelle's, as if he wanted to catch her in that moment.

'He'll get over it eventually, Ilyon,' Az said, not wanting her feelings towards Xadrion to make things tense.

'I don't agree with what he did. But he needs to train, to get stronger, now more than ever,' Ilyon said. 'If Zeus does find him, does find out you're alive, you're going to need each other.'

'He's deluded himself to thinking he did it for me.'

'I know,' Ilyon responded. 'He… doubles down when he shouldn't. He's always done so. He's stubborn and pig-headed. But he also hasn't known what it's like to be in your world for very long. He didn't even get time to figure out his powers before the threat of him hurting innocent lives was thrown upon him. He hurt you, Az, and I saw what that did to him, the idea that he was capable of it.'

'Well, he's hurt me again.'

'I know. But – and take this knowing that I care for you so very deeply and admire so much about you – you weren't honest with him, or me. About Hera, first of all. I don't care if Rhoas told you not to say anything, you're our friend and friends don't keep secrets like that. But you also shut him out and left him to deal with the rising burden of his power on his own. Yes, you tried to suppress it. But he didn't even know how catastrophic it could be if he did release everything in those woods without calling for help,' Ilyon said.

'I just need time, Ilyon. He's changed everything, put you and everyone you care about at risk. That's without even adding me to the mix. I need to plan for my way forward from this, to try to help prepare your way forward from this,' Azraelle said.

'Fair enough, just don't shut him out for too long. Please,' Ilyon said.

In the silence that followed, a surge of power brushed against her mental defences. The power was as familiar to her as her own, and she recognised immediately Thanatos' signal for her attention. She opened the connection between them, desperate for anything her brother could offer her.

Azraelle, Nakir has some news for you.

Where is she? Azraelle asked.

Heading back to where she found you last. Can you get there?

I can, Azraelle answered. *It's just dangerous for both of us. We can't waste time; Zeus is monitoring the area.*

Why?

Long story. I'll tell you later. Tell her no magic, Azraelle responded.

'Hey, I think I'm going to take a walk before heading back,' Azraelle said aloud.

'I could come with you?' Tolemus asked, turning to face her. Azraelle was already walking backwards away from them.

'No, that's okay,' she said. 'I'd rather be alone right now.' Tolemus didn't look pleased with the idea but nodded and allowed her to turn and jog back to the old, abandoned buildings by herself. When she was out of their eyesight, she shifted into her shadow form and speared towards the barriers of the castle, then the city and out into the woods. What would have taken at least an hour to travel by foot took mere moments. Azraelle worried it still wouldn't be fast enough.

She could bring Nakir into the castle to hide their signals, but Nakir would already be being tracked. It would practically lead Zeus straight to the castle to take her any further. Azraelle only hoped she could mask her own power well enough for Zeus not to notice her as well.

Azraelle arrived at the small clearing where Nakir had first found her, finding the Raven leaning a shoulder against a tree, her wings tucked in tightly behind her. Nakir's beautiful black hair was free and flowing, her skin golden in its glow beneath the sun.

'Why is Thanatos warning me against magic?' Nakir asked by way of greeting.

'Zeus is surveying the area. I don't want him to be able to pinpoint us quickly,' Azraelle explained. Nakir looked concerned but nodded and quickly walked towards where Azraelle stood. Nakir had become her second for a reason and part of it was because she held a no-nonsense attitude when it was required. She'd been one of Azraelle's closest friends, providing some of the main moments of laughter while she was with the Ravens, but when business was occurring Nakir was only serious.

'I found him. The records were… not easy to find. He'd never been reassigned to you; the records still indicated that Edda was the one responsible for his ferrying. And it was marked as being completed without a problem. Someone has altered the records, Az,' Nakir said.

Azraelle pursed her lips in consideration, not at all surprised. It hurt her to know it, but it didn't surprise her that Zeus had managed to find someone from within the Ravens to assist in his plan that day. Had it even been Edda herself? No, surely not. She wouldn't have been so stupid as to be the one whose name was attached.

'When I return with the memories, we'll scour the Ravens for whoever betrayed our cause. For now, I need the information on the boy,' Azraelle promised.

'Good news. He's on this land. The bad news is we can't find an exact location. The last known place was near the city of Balmoral in Luzia,' Nakir said.

'And his name?'

'Naxos,' Nakir answered. Azraelle knew where the city was Nakir had mentioned. While she didn't spend extended periods of time in the mortal realm, Azraelle had visited it countless times to perform her duties, which had left her with a good understanding of most of the kingdoms and lands. Luzia was on the other side of this land, nearly as far from Thesadel as you could possibly get without crossing the ocean. To get all the way there, to buy herself enough time to find Naxos without being found by Zeus, Azraelle was going to have to be extremely lucky.

'Thank you, Nakir. Your help means more to me than I can put into words,' Az said.

Nakir half smiled and looked like she wanted to say something more but instead clasped her lips together to form a thin line. She offered her hand, a sign of respect and admiration and Azraelle gripped Nakir's forearm tightly in response, feeling Nakir's strong grasp on her own. With the familiar gesture, Azraelle felt her chest begging to crack open and let the emotion out.

'I hope to see you among the mountains in Eviria once more. Make sure it happens,' Nakir said.

'I will see you soon, Primus,' Azraelle said, releasing their arms. 'Now go, before this punishment falls to you as well.'

Nakir looked like she wanted to hesitate, but Azraelle knew her training wouldn't let her. Nakir was a soldier in that moment and knew that no more could be said. She bared her wings behind her, flexing them wide before letting them sweep her up. Azraelle did not wait long enough to watch her go. Instead, she turned to her mist form and darted back to the castle wards as quickly as she could.

She needed a plan, and fast. But something else was troubling her suddenly, something Ilyon had said to her in their session earlier that day. Friends don't keep secrets. It had reached the moment where Azraelle needed to decide what these people were to her. If she left and did not include them in the truth, she was effectively saying she was making her move to leave them behind. As pissed as she was at Xadrion, Azraelle found herself struggling to believe that was the move she wanted to make.

Ilyon had been so warm to her, had brought her so much joy in the small time she had known him. He'd felt like a younger brother, a feeling Az had never had before, not with her being the youngest of her own siblings. And Emera had given her companionship when Az definitely hadn't deserved it. She'd made Azraelle feel more mortal than she had any right to feel, something Azraelle genuinely thought of as a blessing. Tolemus was someone who had offered her trust immediately, someone who she felt could understand the pain Azraelle felt on the inside most days.

Could Azraelle truly let them all go that easily?

TWENTY-SIX

XADRION

After Xadrion had blown up at Rhoas, dragging Ilyon to hear all that was said, he hadn't left his rooms. The night passed and morning had come. Xadrion couldn't stomach going to train with the others. He was already feeling unsure of everything around him and the idea of showing up not knowing if Azraelle would even look in his direction made him feel sick. She had been so angry the night before, so angry he didn't know if she'd kill him or ignore him the next time they saw each other.

Like a coward, Xadrion had decided he didn't want to face her. Ilyon knocked on his door three separate times that next day, each time begging Xadrion to let him in so that they could talk. Xadrion didn't want to face any of it. There suddenly felt like too many problems ahead of him and no solutions to be seen.

Firstly, Hera was alive. His mother was alive and stuck on Mount Olympus. Whatever Xadrion felt towards Zeus, he had yet to figure out, but every option he'd thought about was so heavily influenced by the feeling of needing to get to Hera. To save her, or be with her, it didn't matter.

Secondly, Azraelle had a target on her back and Xadrion had practically let Zeus take ten steps closer to getting to her. If Zeus found Azraelle before Xadrion could find Zeus and convince him to leave her and her family be, he would never be able to forgive himself.

Lastly, the one that Xadrion could not get out of his mind despite the severity of his other two problems, was the idea that Azraelle may never wish to speak to him ever again. The night of the ball had changed everything for him. No… affirmed everything. The moment he had woken the next day he'd been so afraid of Azraelle turning away from him, of her offering him only one night and then never getting to be near her in that way again. Within a day, Xadrion himself had made sure that happened.

Night came again. Xadrion was reading at his desk when another knock sounded at his door. He made no move to get up, no move to let Ilyon know he was even in the room. He was still not ready to face anything.

'Xadrion, please, come out.' Ilyon's voice echoed through the door. Xadrion did not move. After a moment of silence whispered voices echoed on the other side of the door. Not just Ilyon, then. Xadrion wondered who else had come to try to pull him from his state.

'There's news we need you to hear,' Ilyon tried again. Still, Xadrion did not move. Xadrion was happy to wait on his side of the door in silence until Ilyon left. He was happy to stay right there, until the next voice spoke.

'If you don't open this door right now, you may find yourself without a door very soon,' Azraelle called through the door. Her voice was like a dagger to his heart, the urge to see her instantly overwhelming. Her presence left Xadrion reeling. Her voice was still harsh – he could hear the malice she felt towards him even in those words – but she had spoken to him. Xadrion needed to know why. He hadn't even managed to push himself to a standing position when the door opened.

Swirling in the frame of his doorway, Azraelle's tendrils were threaded through the lock on his door and filling the air around Azraelle on the other side. Behind her, Xadrion could see Ilyon, Emera and Tolemus. The moment the door opened to reveal either side of the door to the other, Azraelle fixed her expression into a glare. She pulled her tendrils back to her and they began to play between her fingertips as she walked into the room. The three behind her followed her in.

'I was coming,' Xadrion managed to choke out. Azraelle shrugged as if she couldn't care less. Emera, Ilyon and Tolemus moved to take a seat on the lounge chair in the room, while Azraelle stayed standing notably on the opposite side of where Xadrion stood. She sent her darkness back to his door to close it behind them before the tendrils returned to her fingertips. She made no move to send them away. Xadrion had never seen her keep them around so casually.

'What's going on? Why do I need to be part of this?' Xadrion asked.

'Because these three insisted that you be a part of it.' Azraelle glared at the three sitting on the couch. Ilyon was looking at Xadrion, Emera did her best to not let Azraelle see her cower beneath the glare, and it was only Tolemus who met her glare and held it. He did not turn away until Azraelle dropped her gaze, letting him win the unspoken contest. So, Azraelle was not the one who wanted him involved.

'You need someone who can help you in the field, Az, and none of us can,' Emera said, cautiously.

'Field? What's going on?' Xadrion asked, feeling entirely left out of what was happening.

Azraelle folded her arms across her chest, looking every bit like she didn't want to say a word. Tolemus rubbed his temple between his thumb and forefinger and let out a large exhale, as if he'd grown tired of Azraelle's stubborn behaviour already.

'Azraelle has information regarding the boy she was charged over.'

Xadrion snapped his attention to Tolemus at the information then to Azraelle to gauge her reaction. She was still not looking at him.

'That's great news. Where is he?' he asked.

'His last known location was in Luzia, in the capital Balmoral. It's weeks of travel and outside the castle wards. Azraelle is insisting she can get there and back in much less time through her particular form of travel, but that leaves her alone while she does so.'

'I am more than used to completing tasks like this alone.' Azraelle unfolded her arms and picked at her nails, displaying her disapproval for Tolemus' caution.

'I don't care, my dear angry one,' Tolemus responded with surprising tenderness. 'I will never agree to sending you out by yourself right now. And if you even tried, I would walk out these castle wards right behind you, unprotected.' Something in Tolemus' voice made Xadrion sure he would do it. Azraelle's glare did not leave her face the entire time Tolemus spoke, but at his last words Xadrion could see the flicker of worry behind her eyes.

'So why does this include me?' Xadrion asked.

'You've recently discovered your own ability to travel faster than we can. You are the only one who would be able to keep pace with her. It would ease all of our minds if you accompanied her and provided backup for any potential encounters which could come up,' Tolemus explained.

'Of course,' Xadrion breathed without a moment's hesitation.

Azraelle flinched as if he had physically hit her. She was not excited at the prospect of travelling with Xadrion, that much was clear, but it would mean she would have to address him at some point. Xadrion knew he would have agreed to anything in that moment just for the chance that he would get to be in her presence once more. To get the chance to try to plead his case with her again.

'You're both going to have to be as fast as you can. If you are out there for too long, if you are even in the wrong place at the wrong time, he is going to find you,' Tolemus warned.

'I have an idea that might help you with that,' Emera said. 'Maybe.'

'Anything you can suggest is worth it,' Tolemus said.

Xadrion tried to catch Azraelle's attention, anything to have her look at him just once. She seemed committed to looking anywhere else.

'I've been thinking about the spells Hera taught me to maintain the castle wards,' Emera said. 'I think I may be able to copy them in some way and apply them to you all.'

'You could replicate the wards?' Azraelle asked, her interest dragging her attention back to the centre of the room but still never looking Xadrion's way.

'I believe so. To create the wards around the castle took multiple sources of magic. I've never been able to replicate it since Hera left. I can use my magic to maintain the wards but not reinforce or create new ones. Now, I believe with Ilyon's help, I could do it,' Emera explained.

'Could you use all of our powers to help?' Azraelle asked.

'It's possible, but I'm not sure,' Emera said. 'Ilyon's would definitely work, but the rest of you might not be as compatible as I need to the origin of the spell. The wards are a means of protection, and it would take a pure form of that to create the unbreakable bonds that form the wards.'

'You can't just use our power as a raw energy form?' Xadrion asked, confused.

'No,' Emera answered, looking disappointed to be giving the news. 'I don't know much of how yours or Tolemus' magic represents, but Azraelle's... I think it would do more harm than good to use her magic.'

'Why?' Xadrion asked.

'Because my magic doesn't come from a source of healing like Ilyon's and Emera's does,' Azraelle said, finally meeting his eyes. She looked at him long enough for him to see the rage behind her eyes before she dropped them from his once more. 'My magic is the partner to Death, and Death is not about protection.'

'I'm afraid so,' Emera answered. 'Your power, Xadrion, doesn't seem to be protection-based either, even if you are descended from Hera. Tolemus is the only one of you three who might be able to help as his link to water could work in favour of being cleansing. We could definitely try.'

'Could you link it to everyone in the room right now?' Azraelle asked.

'I think so,' Emera nodded.

'Do it now,' Azraelle said. 'We need to move on this as quickly as we can. If Zeus finds us before I find Naxos, I fear he'll get away with whatever it is he has been building toward.'

'I will need a few hours with Ilyon to prepare and show him the process. Tolemus, you come as well. I can test if your power is going to be compatible,' Emera explained.

'Very well,' Azraelle said, pouting at the prospect of having to wait. Before anyone else had even thought to move, Azraelle had already made it halfway to the door. Xadrion wanted to stop her, wanted to keep her there in that room with him for as long as he could, but he couldn't think of a single thing that would get her to stay. Instead, he let her leave the room, leaving the remainder of them in somewhat stunned silence.

The door closed behind Azraelle before anyone else had even moved.

'She'll come around,' Tolemus said, looking cautiously to Xadrion.

'I doubt that,' Xadrion responded.

'One thing you have to consider, Xadrion, is your new lifespan. Azraelle is pissed now, and honestly with the intensity of her feelings I wouldn't be surprised if she remained pissed for a couple hundred years, but she will eventually come around,' Tolemus said.

'And yet I can't help but think she will continue to find reasons to be angry with me for as long as we both live,' Xadrion said. Emera and Ilyon had stood and were waiting for Tolemus by the door. Rather than joining them, Tolemus moved towards Xadrion.

'I'm going to say one thing to you now, and I hope sincerely that you listen to it and think about it and make every decision in your future based off it,' Tolemus said. 'Azraelle will never be an easy woman to love. She will never accept it easily or offer it easily in return. If that is what you are after, I suggest you find literally anyone else and leave her be.'

'I know that,' Xadrion snapped.

'No, you don't,' Tolemus said. 'She has been the hand of Death for thousands of years. You told me what images she showed you when she threw her power at you, the ones that had you heaving your guts up. Where do you think she got those? She has seen things and done things since the moment she accepted Death's responsibility, things you couldn't even fathom. And if all of that wasn't enough, she spent fifteen years tortured at the hands of Zeus. The fact she even gave you the time of day after she learned he is your true father is proof enough that you mean something to her.'

'Why are you saying this to me?' Xadrion asked, his anger causing his hands to tremor as the feeling of a strong, electric current swept through him.

'Because she gave me a hope back that I thought I'd never see again,' Tolemus answered sincerely. 'If anyone deserves to be loved, genuinely loved, for who they are and everything they have already given for this world, it is her. I sincerely hope it is you that can give it to her, but I do not want you to be the one if you aren't even willing to attempt to break through her well-deserved walls.'

Emera and Ilyon were outside the door by that point, giving Tolemus and Xadrion space to talk privately, but they were waiting for Tolemus to join them. Xadrion couldn't think clearly, couldn't even process the depth of what Tolemus was saying to him in that moment. The situation felt hopeless, and while Tolemus seemed to be trying to offer him hope, nothing about it was doing anything to make him feel better.

Despite that, Tolemus was totally and completely right.

'Leave me be.' He walked back to his desk and took the seat he had been in before his room had been overtaken. Xadrion sat and turned back to the papers he'd been looking at, signalling clearly he was done talking. Tolemus sighed but left the room, closing the door silently behind him.

Xadrion left his room shortly after, needing to stretch his legs after he'd been in his room for the last day. He headed to the barracks first, taking the opportunity to train with his soldiers once more. Since they'd started training in the old stables he hadn't been back to the barracks, hadn't run drills with the soldiers, had barely even seen to his assigned duties around the castle. Since everything had changed, Xadrion couldn't even think to keep up the façade of his royal duties. It belonged to Ilyon, it always should have, and Xadrion couldn't think to keep his brother's birthright from him any longer.

Even committing a few hours to hard physical training made Xadrion feel no better. When the last session of the day had finished, Xadrion decided to call it a day as well. He headed back into the castle. Restlessness had overtaken him, he wanted to get moving, to help Azraelle in her finding Naxos. Surely the others would be nearly ready to craft their wards.

Xadrion passed the throne room on his way back, the double doors spread open. In a rare moment, Rhoas stood inside the throne room by himself, with the regular guards stationed outside the doors being the only other people around.

'Son?' Rhoas said as Xadrion entered the room and approached the throne. Rhoas had a large book open on the table beside the throne, a pen clutched loosely in his hand. Xadrion couldn't acknowledge the familial term, couldn't think of any pleasantries to fill the silence between them.

'I still don't understand why you didn't tell me Hera was alive,' Xadrion said. He'd come to a stop standing in front of the throne, hands clasped behind his back, ever the trained prince.

'What would you have done if you had known?' Rhoas asked, sitting back in the throne, casually despite the heavy layer of tension that settled in the air between them.

'I would have found some way to bring her back. If everything everyone is saying is true about Zeus, if everything Hera told me about Zeus is true, I would have gotten her and brought her back,' Xadrion answered truthfully.

'And in the process, you would have revealed yourself to Zeus. The only thing Hera ever asked of me was to keep you from his discovery.' Rhoas' brow was furrowed, an expression of sadness visible that he had rarely let Xadrion see before. It was one of the reasons they didn't often speak of Hera, as Rhoas had always retreated to solace when she was discussed at length.

'So, you've left her there all these years, lying to Ilyon and me, for that?' Xadrion asked. Rhoas remained silent. 'I'm leaving with Azraelle soon, today, or tomorrow maybe. I will be helping her find what she needs to go home.'

'He will find you as soon as you leave the castle,' Rhoas said, concern evident in his tone. He made to stand, to approach, but Xadrion took a single step back and he paused. Understanding the message, Rhoas leant back once more, still looking concerned but seeming to accept Xadrion's intentions.

'Maybe, maybe not,' Xadrion said. 'All the same, I will be going. And once I have done that, I will be going to find Hera to make sure she is alive and well. If she is not, I will do whatever it takes to remove her from harm.'

'And what of your duties to Thesadel?' Rhoas asked, a forlorn expression crossing his face.

'I am no rightful heir to you,' Xadrion said. 'That title belongs to Ilyon and should be given to him. I will no longer be accepting the role of crowned prince, heir to your throne. It's time you give that honour to the real son of yours.'

'You are my son, Xadrion, whether you believe it or not. You will always be my son,' Rhoas said. His disappointment was evident but Xadrion did not waiver. It had been everything he was thinking over the last day. After everything he had learned, all he had come to hear, Xadrion could not stay there. He could not fulfil his responsibilities as a prince, not when it was not rightfully his.

'Give it to Ilyon,' Xadrion demanded.

'If that is what you wish,' Rhoas said, quietly.

Xadrion nodded and turned on his heel, leaving the room without another word. He walked through the halls, having one more destination to go before he could leave with Azraelle. Xadrion headed to the chambers that had been allocated to the party from Gaeweth and gave a knock to the door he knew housed the princess. A lady maid answered the door, Romina seated at a table and chairs by the window in the late afternoon sun.

'Prince Xadrion,' the lady at the door said, stepping to the side to allow him access. Romina looked up at him, her face expressionless as he approached.

'May I join you?' Xadrion asked, indicating the empty chair across from her. Romina nodded gracefully.

'To what do I owe the pleasure of this visit, Prince?' Romina asked. Gone was the anger from their encounter in the hallway, instead Romina was the essence of grace and civility.

'I would like to extend a formal apology to you, hopefully doing a better job of it than I did last time,' Xadrion said.

'I don't know if there is much more to be said.'

'You don't have to accept it if you don't wish. You have every right to hold this against me for as long as you like as you have been wronged more than I admitted before. Our kingdoms had an agreement, and I falsely assumed that I would not have to follow through on that simply because I did not want to,' Xadrion said. 'You have always been committed to Gaeweth; more than I can ever say I have been committed to Thesadel.'

'Would you reconsider the agreement between our two kingdoms?'

'I will not,' Xadrion said. At Romina's angered expression, Xadrion went on, 'I will not because it would be doing you a disservice. News has come to light recently, news that changes my standing in this court and in this kingdom. Ilyon will be installed as the crowned prince and I will no longer hold that title.'

'What news could possibly change the order of the inheritance?' Romina asked, her eyes widening in genuine surprise.

'It does not matter. But what does matter is that you do not deserve to marry any less than a king, and I would not hold you to that agreement,' Xadrion said. 'I meant what I said the other day. I believe you should be given the chance to marry for love. Your kingdom respects you and already holds enough power. You do not need to sacrifice for Gaeweth in that way.'

'Will you be marrying for love?' Romina asked.

'I don't know what my future holds, whether love or marriage exists in it at all, but I do hope to leave us both free to find that out,' Xadrion said. Romina was silent for some time, watching Xadrion pensively as she rested her clasped hands on the decorated table between them.

'Very well,' Romina said eventually. 'I will return to Gaeweth with no grudge against you or Thesadel. My father will be disappointed to hear the news, I'm sure, but I suppose he will have no choice but to renegotiate with your father.'

'Thank you for hearing me out, Princess,' Xadrion said. He stood, bowed deeply and left her to her own once more. Night had taken over the castle as Xadrion walked back to his rooms. Maybe the others would already be waiting for him once they had found his rooms empty. Emera had said a few hours but Xadrion had been out and about now for much longer than that. Still, he felt mildly better at the decisions he had implemented.

When Xadrion arrived back to his rooms there was no one there. A note was nailed to his door, signed by Ilyon, that detailed what had happened while Xadrion had been completing his own tasks.

Tolemus was a match. We figured it out but need
rest. Will reconvene first thing in the morning. Ilyon.

Heading deeper into his rooms, Xadrion threw the note to his desk, walked to his bedroom and collapsed onto the bed. One more night of sleep before it began. Something told Xadrion that tomorrow was going to bring with it a complete overhaul on life as he knew it.

Twenty-Seven

AZRAELLE

Azraelle slept poorly after Ilyon had delivered the news of their attempts the night before. They'd figured out how to make the wards and had crafted one around Ilyon and Emera in their practice doing so. Tolemus' power was a match to what Emera needed, which had given them enough to create two wards, but after finishing the wards around Ilyon and Emera, all three of them had needed to recover. When Ilyon visited her on his way back to his own rooms he'd looked as if he hadn't slept in days.

It frustrated Azraelle to have to wait another night, but a small part of her felt relief knowing that at least Ilyon and Emera were protected by wards already. Xadrion and Azraelle would get theirs first thing the next morning and when Emera and Ilyon had recovered enough from that, they would cast their own wards over Tolemus. In the meantime, Azraelle and Xadrion would hopefully be well on their way to finding Naxos.

Azraelle resented having to travel with Xadrion, resented Tolemus slightly for forcing her hand. He had insisted on being the last one warded so that his threat of leaving the castle wards carried enough weight to keep Azraelle there until the moment was right. She would be faster by herself, less detectable, but maybe Tolemus was right and having Xadrion around if something went badly would be a good thing. It didn't mean she had to pretend everything was okay.

Seeing Xadrion in his room after he'd locked himself in it for a day didn't make Azraelle feel any better. He looked like crap, as if he hadn't slept at all, and for the entire time Azraelle stood in that room she could feel his eyes on her. She'd spent half the time paying attention to what Emera had been saying and the other half triple checking the boundaries of her mind to make sure there was no possible point for him to access.

She wanted to be as far from him as she could get, as quickly as she could make it happen. That didn't mean, however, that Azraelle could have left knowing the others weren't protected. Emera's wards made her feel a lot better about the idea of leaving them all. And maybe if she could get back to the Underworld with the right proof, she could request help with implementing consequences on Zeus' actions.

It still didn't make sense to her why he was killing the mortals with magic and Azraelle knew that would have to be the next thing to investigate if she had any hope of putting an end to Zeus' control.

Azraelle was the first one to arrive at Emera's rooms the next morning, but Emera thankfully was already awake. Az resisted the urge to pace the room and tried instead to look calm and collected as she sat on the edge of the desk, her legs swinging and shaking beneath her in her failed attempt at looking calm. Emera poured her a cup of tea and leant against the desk beside Az.

'Are you feeling rested?' Az asked, sipping the tea. As anxious as she was to get started, the tea helped to calm her nerves somewhat.

'I am. The night of sleep helped greatly. If Tolemus and Ilyon are feeling as rested, we should have more than enough for you and Xadrion,' Emera said.

'And we'll be as undetectable as we are within the castle?'

'I think so, but there's really no guarantee. It's a slightly different kind of magic, one that had to be adaptable to move with you rather than covering only a specific area. But yes, I think it should be as comprehensive as the castle wards,' Emera answered.

Emera placed a hand down on Azraelle's knee and let out a gentle laugh. Azraelle's bouncing leg stopped its movement and she felt herself give her own half smile.

'I just want to be moving,' Azraelle explained. Emera nodded but didn't remove her hand from her knee. Az leant to the side, resting her head against Emera's shoulder, and tried to imagine her chest moving at the same pace that she could feel Emera's moving beneath her ear.

'I know. I imagine you're restless to return to your home after all these months,' Emera said.

'Years really. I haven't seen my family since Zeus took me,' Azraelle said. 'I am restless to see them. I'm sad it means I have to leave here for a time but I am eager to see them once more.'

'What will you do if you can't get pardoned?' Emera asked.

'Figure out what's going on,' Azraelle answered. 'I need answers as to how I was even found guilty in the first place. I would find the Moirai and get answers from her. And I would do what I could to look into what Zeus is up to and do my best to stop him from getting whatever it is he's after.'

Azraelle didn't want to think too far ahead, not if her plan didn't work out. She didn't want to let herself start to think about how she could go about regaining her wings, or re-joining the Ravens, if she couldn't even succeed in obtaining her freedom once more.

There was a single knock on the door before it pushed open to reveal Ilyon leading the other two men into the room. Xadrion's eyes went straight to her, straight to where she had her head rested against Emera's shoulder, and Az could see the anger behind his eyes. She sat up properly, not too quickly as to portray that Xadrion noticing had any effect on her but remained seated on the desk.

'Xadrion first,' Tolemus said. Azraelle narrowed her eyes at him. He still didn't trust that she wouldn't leave the moment she was warded. Maybe he was right; she was itching to transform into her shadows and be on her way. Tolemus held her gaze, a slight raise of one brow daring her to say something. Instead, Azraelle dropped her eyes and made to pick at something under her nails as if she were bored with the situation.

The entire process didn't look like much. Tolemus, Ilyon and Emera all circled around Xadrion, placed their hands somewhere on his upper body, and closed their eyes. Nobody spoke a word but Azraelle could feel the moment they began creating the ward. Magic flared throughout the room and Az found herself breathing deeply through her nose, scenting the mix of power in the air. She smelled an ocean breeze from Tolemus, while Emera's gave the impression of a field full of plants, green, luscious and flowering.

Ilyon's scent hit her last and in his power Az was reminded of a similar scent, one she hadn't encountered for many years. Hera's, which she had never once felt in her years on Mount Olympus, was still familiar to her. Az had spent time with her a very long time ago when Hera had come to visit the Underworld for a year. Hera had trained with some of the Ravens, learned their ways, even come so close that Az had nearly considered her a friend.

Az hadn't noticed the scent on Ilyon before, even when they'd been practising over the last few days, but that didn't really surprise her. Magic didn't carry with it a permanent scent and Azraelle had not really allowed herself the time to focus on what her senses told her since she'd been at Fennhall, but in that room, in that moment, when it was being used so strongly, it filled all of her senses.

Silence filled the room for the entire duration of Xadrion's ward being made and the end was only signalled when that beautiful scent of their combined powers died down. Xadrion was looking at the three who surrounded him, his eyes wide. Of course, he must have been smelling what Azraelle had smelt. It was probably the first time he'd really experienced it, or at least knew how to identify what it truly was he was smelling.

Xadrion didn't move and Azraelle did not want to let herself get closer to him. Instead, she stayed seated on the edge of the desk and watched as Ilyon, Emera and Tolemus moved to her.

'Ready?' Emera asked. Azraelle nodded, not trusting her voice to speak. The anxiety to be moving had almost doubled since they'd begun working on Xadrion.

Azraelle felt hands take hold of her, some across her shoulders, some on her back, one even pressed firmly over her chest. The weight of their grasps helped settle Az back into the moment, helped her stay still long enough to let them do what they needed. She closed her eyes as they worked, content to take in their scents and did her best not to let tears fill her eyes at the feeling that accompanied their powers. As it funnelled through her, Azraelle felt their peace, felt herself calm down and be able to breathe clearly for what felt like the first time in centuries.

When she opened her eyes as the magic started to leave her and return to its owners, Az found her eyes locking directly to Xadrion's. He was watching her so intently, as if he could see every thought that had crossed her mind. She knew he couldn't, knew it was just that way he had of unnerving her, but still she dropped her eyes.

Azraelle could feel the wards power around her.

'Check it out,' Ilyon said into the silent room, pulling his shirt up to show a black symbol beneath the base of his ribs on his left side. It looked like a three-pointed star with the middles of the points overlapping at the centre. Between each of the arms there was a small, black dot. 'It showed up after I got warded last night. Emera has one as well.'

Azraelle looked down at herself and pulled her shirt up to expose her own ribcage. She ignored the still twisted skin of Xadrion's lightning strike. It looked much better but still served as an unpleasant reminder of the last few days. Xadrion sucked in a breath from where he sat. Az hiked her shirt up higher and there, in the exact place where Ilyon's mark was, was an exact replica on her own ribcage. Azraelle traced her fingers over it, entranced by the smooth lines now marking her skin. A smile spread across her lips, a feeling of comfort spreading through her at the ink-like colour of the mark.

Azraelle had markings once, several over her body. She'd had a tattoo around her left thigh that depicted a beautiful Raven pattern. She'd had one on the back of her right hand, an ancient symbol from a culture she'd admired that was long since dead that depicted Death, and on the back of her left hand she'd had Hades' brand – a symbol depicting her ability to travel to and from the Underworld freely. She'd had one running from the base of her hair to the tip of her wings that depicted what she imagined her mist form looked like twisting amongst the wind. It hadn't shocked her when she'd awoken in the mortal realm and found them missing, not when they had been gone for several years before her fall.

They'd been taken by a manipulation of the healing powers Emera had used on her several times since she'd arrived. In the cells on Mount Olympus, being tortured over and over, there were methods that could be used to push people beyond their limits. To allow Azraelle to be tortured day in and day out, to allow her to even survive that, they had granted her healing at the end of each day. Wherever she had been struck or branded was healed anew, taking with it any trace of previous markings or imperfections. The only marks Azraelle had left were scars, those of her wings being destroyed as she fell and the evidence from that final day of torture on Mount Olympus. Those they hadn't healed, leaving her body covered with scars that now looked like nothing more than faint white lines scattering her skin.

Azraelle dropped her shirt, not wanting to be reminded of the number of things that had been taken from her. Xadrion had lifted his own shirt to look at his mark, an exact replica of Az's and Ilyon's.

Azraelle turned her attention to Tolemus, who was watching her already. She gave him a pointed look.

'Now will you let me go?' Azraelle asked.

'Yes, restless one, now you may go. We won't be able to speak to you once you're gone, but I expect you to check in with us,' Tolemus answered. Right, demi-gods. She could speak to them; they couldn't speak back to her. It would be harder with distance and with their minds not receptive to the communications of the gods, but she nodded all the same.

'If I hear so much as one word from Xadrion that you have run off on your own, don't doubt for a second that I will refuse Emera's ward and walk outside this castle's protection,' Tolemus threatened.

Azraelle couldn't help the grin that spread across her features, the permission finally being given for her to fly free being enough to set her senses buzzing. She hadn't been made to stay in one place for so long, and now she was finally doing something about the mess she had been dumped in. She turned to Xadrion, not caring in that moment that she was offering him a smile, not even feeling the anger that had overcome her for him. Azraelle donned the weapons she had brought with her to Emera's rooms in preparation for that very moment.

'Try to keep up, boy,' Azraelle said and transformed into her mist of shadows. She didn't pause as she rushed to Emera's window and pushed through it as if she were the wind. It gave out easily and Azraelle rushed into the still early morning sun. As Xadrion responded behind her, the sun began to cloud over and very quickly the sky had changed from its clear blue to cloudy grey.

Her senses in the mist form were different, more expansive than they ever could be in her physical form, so she felt more than heard the thunder as it echoed through the sky. Around her, Xadrion's energy crackled, the lightning carrying him from place to place. Where Azraelle was placed into a different, less physical form when she became her shadows, it seemed as if Xadrion simply disappeared and reappeared in the next place his lightning hit.

His speed was incomparable, Azraelle realised, as she felt the storm moving behind her. Maybe he would be faster than her when he figured out how he could truly use it. He didn't know how to tap into all his power yet, so Azraelle took advantage of her years of experience over him and maintained the lead.

They travelled that way for hours. It was fast, more so than any other means, covering what would have taken them a day in an hour. At some point, after several hours, Azraelle felt the storm behind her begin to die out. He was fading and fast. To be fair, Xadrion had made it further than Azraelle thought he would have in one go.

Azraelle turned herself back, heading to the area she'd sensed Xadrion's power sputter out. He stood at the edge of some woods, the vast plains of Gaeweth extended back in the direction they had come from. The woods, Azraelle quickly realised, signalled the border between Gaeweth and Luzia. They'd covered over half the distance. Azraelle joined Xadrion in the trees, relieved they'd ended up at some cover.

'I didn't think you'd actually stop,' Xadrion commented as she strode toward him.

'Don't push it,' Azraelle remarked. 'I can still keep going if I change my mind.' Xadrion didn't respond, simply turned to survey their surrounding areas.

'Did we make it all the way to Sannigan Forest?' Xadrion asked after some time.

'Mm.'

'I don't think I will ever get over this,' Xadrion said as he stared at the trees around them in wonder. Azraelle walked into the woods, passing him completely, and began to search for a place to rest. Xadrion, to his credit, took the hint and followed behind her. It took a little while, but eventually she found a decent enough patch with trees positioned in an easily defendable design. The ground was covered with the leaves from the shedding trees, the forest all around filled with deep browns and oranges.

'Get some rest, we're moving on as soon as you've got enough power to go again,' Azraelle ordered.

'What about you?'

'Like I said, I can keep going. I don't need the rest,' Azraelle said. 'I'll keep watch.' She wasn't lying either; she felt *strong*. Her power had taken some time to come back, but the night she'd spent with Xadrion had refuelled her in a way she hadn't experienced before. Her power seemed to be singing at any opportunity to be used.

Azraelle leant against one of the thick trees, pulling her knees up and resting her chin on them as she watched the area around. Xadrion looked as if he wanted to speak further but wisely decided against it. He found his own tree, sat down against it and closed his eyes. Azraelle could tell he didn't fall asleep straight away. He shuffled against the tree for the better part of half an hour before he calmed down enough for sleep to overcome him.

Azraelle settled down, less anxious than she had been that morning to keep moving and resolved to give Xadrion a few hours to recover.

TWENTY-EIGHT

XADRION

When Xadrion woke, he could not see Azraelle anywhere in the immediate vicinity. He pushed himself from the tree he'd been resting against and tried to hear if she were still somewhere in the area. There was nothing, no noise, no sight of her. She was gone. Just as she said she could be.

He'd been foolish to think she wouldn't leave him at a moment's notice. If he'd been sleeping for too long and she'd gotten restless she would have left. But it didn't seem as though too much of the day had passed. They'd stopped a few hours after midday and the sun was still shining, although it was beginning to dip out of sight below the tree lines.

Xadrion cast his mind out, searching for any trace of her presence. Surprisingly, he felt her not too far off and perhaps even more shockingly, she opened a space in her mind and let him in.

Stay still, don't make a noise, Azraelle said to him. Xadrion immediately went on his guard, scouting the area around him to see what it was that had caused her warning.

What's going on? Azraelle didn't reply to his question, but he could feel her listening intently to her own surroundings, focusing on something. *Azraelle, show me what's happening.*

Xadrion sensed her frustration but she opened their connection further, allowing him to see more of what surrounded her. She was still in the woods, her eyes slowly scanning the environment in front of her. Xadrion could see no immediate reason she was on edge. But then the sound she had been listening for registered, and Xadrion heard it with her through her senses. Two voices, noticeably quiet, echoing off to Az's left. She turned her eyes towards them but could see nothing.

Her senses changed as she moved forward, so quietly that he wondered how she was not even making a sound. The sound of her thoughts shifted, the senses somehow sharpened, and Xadrion realised he was no longer listening to Az's thoughts in her physical form but rather in her shadow self. He'd never felt anything like the expansiveness of her mind as she held the shadow form.

Her thoughts reorganised and the senses returned to normal a short moment later, revealing now in Az's line of sight two figures walking a decent distance apart from each other. They moved parallel to each other, and spoke quietly, but seemed to have no trouble hearing the other. They had wings, huge and white, that looked so different to the image that Az had shown him once of her own black as night wings.

Who are they? Xadrion asked.

Part of Zeus' legion of scouts, Azraelle answered.

What happens if they find us?

If they see us, they're too fast to catch before they get back to Zeus. If I can get the drop on them, I could kill them, but I fear that will be as big of a signal to our location as being seen would be, Azraelle answered.

So, we hide?

We hide, Azraelle said and shut him out of her mind but not before he sensed her shift back into her shadow form. Within a breath, she was reappearing in front of him. She was so silent in her movement it left Xadrion slightly unnerved.

Azraelle didn't say a word as she surveyed the area, evaluating their options. Xadrion could hear the two others now, coming closer to their location. Azraelle looked up, cocking her head to the side as she evaluated something above them. She looked back to Xadrion and lifted a single finger, pointing up.

Before Xadrion could piece together what she was saying, Azraelle took hold of the tree nearest to Xadrion. It was tall, the lower half of it had barely any branches and looked too smooth to climb almost. It wasn't until much higher up, a good distance off the ground, that the branches started to appear. If they could get to that level the foliage would cover them, thick as it was.

Azraelle found handholds as if they were obvious to her, scurrying up the tree so quickly it left Xadrion shocked. He followed her, grabbing hold of the tree, and did his best to copy her hand and foot placements. Xadrion did not do so well at it. He had never been as good with the agile, lithe movements compared to the brute strength movements. Ilyon would have been much better suited to it.

From not too far off came the murmuring of the scouts. The fact that they were talking was a comfort; at least they weren't aware of their presence so far. Still, if Xadrion couldn't get up the tree faster they would surely be caught.

Xadrion was looking at his feet when he saw the thick tendrils that Azraelle's power materialised as. A few tendrils wrapped around his ankles and Xadrion panicked at the sight of them there. His last memory of Azraelle's shadows touching his body was not a pleasant one. Sharp lancing pain usually followed wherever those tendrils went.

When the tendrils wrapped around his ankles as he climbed the tree, no pain followed. He looked up to Azraelle, catching the tendrils that were moving for his wrists as well. What was she doing? Azraelle was already at the branches, perched effortlessly and looking down at him. She was watching him, focusing on whatever it was she was trying to accomplish.

Xadrion reached his hand up, aiming for the next handhold, and felt as if his hand directed itself towards the small burrow that allowed him to hoist himself up quickly. His feet did the same, finding their next footholds easily, much more easily than he had previously been doing it. Faint pressure remained around his wrists and ankles but his body felt lighter as if Azraelle were somehow supporting him. With her help, he made it to the branches she had come to a rest on fairly quickly.

We need to go a little further to stay out of sight from the ground. Let them lead you, Azraelle said, connecting their minds once more.

Xadrion nodded and followed her the final few branches, letting Azraelle's tendrils take him through the easiest route. When they came to a stop next, they were both perched on a fairly thick branch, both looking down to the ground that now felt like an exceptionally long way off. Beneath them came the scout's voices, as if they were directly where Xadrion had just been resting.

Around them, the tendrils left his wrist and ankles and instead moved into the air. Azraelle's brows were furrowed in concentration as the air around them shifted and contorted, as if the shadows themselves were weaving around them. She was blending them into the trees, Xadrion realised suddenly. Making them as invisible as they could be.

Why are they out here? Xadrion asked.

It's not unusual, Azraelle answered. *Zeus would have scouts in the mortal realm all over, feeding him back information. He's probably increased their numbers since you revealed yourself, but if we aren't spotted it shouldn't be anything to worry about.*

And if we are spotted?

Then we run like hell, as far away as we can get. They're easy to kill so likely won't engage with us, but they are exceptionally hard to catch, Azraelle answered.

Xadrion could not pull his gaze from her as she watched the ground. At once, the proximity of their bodies came to Xadrion's attention and despite the danger of their situation, he felt his body react to her very presence. It was the closest she had allowed him to be since that single night, since the morning she'd laid her legs across his lap and allowed him to touch her face in the way he wished for most. Granted, there wasn't a whole lot of room to move on the branch, but Xadrion could not shake the feeling of electricity pulsing beneath his skin at how close their arms came, at how detailed he could see her expression.

Your mind is open, don't forget, Azraelle warned. She didn't look at him as her cheeks coloured faintly.

Sorry, Xadrion said doing his best to push those thoughts of her from his mind. *I wish you would talk to me.*

Azraelle didn't respond for some time, keeping her attention to the ground far beneath them. The scouts had begun to move away, but Xadrion could still hear their faint voices and knew that Azraelle would make them stay up in that tree until she'd deemed it safe for them to come back down, even once their voices had completely faded.

Tolemus and Ilyon think you didn't have the tools to make the right decision, Azraelle said eventually. *They think you made a mistake that should be forgiven.*

What do you think?

Maybe they're right, Azraelle answered. Hope bloomed in Xadrion's chest. His own anger over Azraelle lying to him about Hera was still present but being separate from her for even the last few days had been unbearable. *They probably are. But I keep thinking about how you said you'd do it again, how you'd do it again for me. And how you called that monster your family. I was never particularly good at forgiving, especially when it comes to Zeus.*

You would ask of me what you wouldn't even ask of your mother? Xadrion asked. Azraelle finally looked at him, tilting her head slightly in her confusion.

What do you mean?

You told me that I should have let innocents die, should have done literally anything else except for signal to Zeus that I was alive. You would have preferred me to hurt thousands in exchange for that remaining secret, Xadrion said. *And yet, you hold no malice towards Nyx for not coming to the mortal realm, for not allowing the mortals to die from her presence. You don't feel any anger at all towards your own mother not coming to rescue you and leaving you to be discovered once more?*

That's different, Azraelle said, and even in their minds her voice sounded like fire given vocal form.

It isn't, Xadrion retorted.

I don't need her to rescue me, Azraelle said. *I can fix this problem myself. I needed you to not send up a Chaosdamned signal calling Zeus' attention to the very place I was.*

And because I did, because I was not willing to risk innocent lives, how long would you have me punished for?

I'm not punishing you.

You are, Xadrion said. *And that's okay. I'll take it. I'll take whatever you throw at me, Az. If you don't talk to me for a century, I'll take it. If you deny me the pleasure of seeing you for a thousand years, I'll take it. I will take any of it for even a crumb of a chance that I will one day get to hold you again, get to kiss you again.*

And if I never allow you that chance? Azraelle asked, her gaze holding Xadrion's. It was the longest she'd looked directly at him since their fight.

Then I'll lament the thought of you for a thousand lifetimes, Xadrion answered. His immortality was still a new concept for Xadrion. He didn't know how he felt about the idea of such endless time, about all the changes that would bring with it. But he was speaking more honestly in that moment than he perhaps ever had before. Tolemus had been right. Azraelle would not be easy to love, would not be easy to convince her to love him, but she was worth it. Xadrion knew he would accept anything she offered him, gratefully, even if it was a glimpse of her every thousand years.

You get given immortal life, and the one thing you commit to doing with it is to chase some uncertain idea of love, why? Why would you choose that path when there is an endless well of opportunities for you to chase instead? Azraelle asked. She sounded like she was trying to stay angry with him, yet from within their shared space her mind circled the questions she was asking. Xadrion had always thought it was her refusal to see love as anything other than weakness that kept her from feeling it, but what if Rhoas had been right? What if Azraelle couldn't feel it? What if she truly couldn't comprehend ever feeling that way for someone?

Because when I think of everything I could fill all those years with, everything that might bring me joy or happiness to spend my time doing, none of it compares to what I imagine it would feel like doing those things with you, Xadrion answered honestly. Az's scoff echoed through their connection.

They've taken to the skies, Azraelle said, tactfully avoiding having to acknowledge what Xadrion had offered her.

What does that mean?

It means we can leave shortly, Azraelle answered. *They'll leave the area much quicker flying, and by the sounds of it they're moving away from where we are headed.* She cocked her head as if to really listen to the direction the scouts had gone, to gain certainty over the safety to move.

Where would they be going?

To the next area, or back to Mount Olympus maybe. Either way, we need to wait for them to leave the area completely before we can move. Your form of travelling comes with a certain level of detectability given the storm that follows you, Azraelle said. It felt like she was making light fun of him and where Xadrion may have previously responded with a jab of his own, he was so grateful for the conversation she'd granted him that he let it pass without his own retort.

Xadrion realised something with Az's most recent words. His form of travelling came with storms, meanwhile her shadow form was only visible from a close distance and only if someone knew what to look for. When she detected the scout's presence, Az could have left and not been discovered. The only thing that kept her from leaving had been Xadrion and the fact that he couldn't travel without gaining attention. She'd waited, allowed those scouts to walk directly beneath that tree with her in it, so that he would not be discovered.

It made Xadrion feel better, both realising that and voicing everything he had. Even if she didn't specifically offer him any hope in return, he'd still spoken more honestly with her than he thought she'd give him the chance to ever do again. Maybe Tolemus had been right, and she would come around... in a century or so anyway.

Don't get your hopes up, Azraelle jabbed and then she proceeded to stand on the branch they had been occupying and drop to the ground. Xadrion's mouth opened in shock at how confidently she stepped from the branch despite the crippling height of it. Azraelle landed smoothly, slipping into a low crouch to absorb the landing, but stood uninjured after her jump.

Xadrion knew there were other aspects that came with being immortal. He knew Azraelle was stronger than him, faster than him, but he never imagined how immortality could have brought resistance to such a movement.

'Jump,' Azraelle said, speaking aloud for the first time in hours.

'You're crazy if you think I'm going to do that,' Xadrion called down to her. He was crouching hesitantly on the branch, looking between Azraelle beneath him and the trunk of the tree he would have to climb back down.

'Don't be a baby, just jump,' Azraelle goaded. Xadrion didn't see how he could walk away from a jump like that, but he trusted Azraelle. Despite everything, she wouldn't have asked him to do something that would actually hurt him, would she?

Xadrion jumped, or more accurately, slid from the branch he had been on and gave in to the trust he had for Azraelle. The air rushed past him and he was tempted to call his power to him to carry him safely down. Anything to stop the dread for the quickly approaching ground.

Xadrion resisted the urge to abandon his jump and followed through all the way to the ground. When his feet hit, Xadrion tried to mimic what he had seen Azraelle do and dropped into a low crouch.

It didn't work. Jarring pain shot from his ankles to his hips and through his spine. Xadrion crumpled to the ground, a pained cry escaping him.

Nothing had broken, Xadrion quickly diagnosed, but his joints and body were rocked with pain. He looked to where Azraelle was standing above him and saw the slight smirk she'd allowed to her expression.

'Is it physical pain you wish to see me in?' Xadrion asked as he began to painfully push to his feet once more. 'Would that be an appropriate punishment for me to have you forgive me?'

'I honestly thought you'd handle it fine,' Azraelle responded, the smirk evident at the corners of her lips, and gave a slight shrug. 'Guess I was wrong.'

Azraelle made to turn from him.

Xadrion stood and reached his hand out quickly, only managing to clasp her fingers as she turned. He tugged gently, spinning her back to face him and took a step towards her. Last time he'd touched her, it hadn't ended well. She'd thrown her magic at him, lashing him in her anger. Az typically responded physically when she was shocked, she had done so several times, sending her power at him with devastating effect. He knew he should probably avoid surprising her with his touch, but he couldn't resist.

In that moment, he just wanted to prolong the moment they'd shared in the trees.

'Like I said, Azraelle, I'll take it. Whatever you throw at me, I'll take it for a thousand lifetimes. I'll take it until you can look at me and tell me that you feel nothing and mean it,' Xadrion whispered, their bodies so close to each other. Azraelle's eyes were glassy as they looked at him, her lips parted slightly. Yes, she was angry with him and would be for a long time, but that look right there told Xadrion everything he needed to know about what other feelings she had for him within her. If she told him, without a doubt, that they had no future, that she did not want a future with him, he would respect that. But Xadrion had not heard those words from her, not yet at least. Their fight had felt like an end, but hope had begun to return that it might not be so.

'Help me escape this cage of mine and we shall see what time brings,' Azraelle whispered. Xadrion grinned, getting all he could have wanted in that moment. She would not give him anything, not yet, but that door was not closed to him forever. Xadrion pulled her fingers up, keeping his hand locked with hers, until the back of her hand was close enough to brush his lips against. He kissed her hand lightly, gently, and Azraelle's eyes fluttered closed.

'Lead the way, Azraelle,' Xadrion whispered against her hand.

TWENTY-NINE

AZRAELLE

Azraelle was grateful for the distance when both her and Xadrion began to move once more. When she looked at him, when she thought about him, she still felt such anger. He'd risked everything, and Azraelle knew if something happened to any of them before she could resolve it, she would find it hard not to blame that on Xadrion. But when he touched her, when he whispered those things into her mind, she could barely think straight. Being so close to him and hearing the words he dared to whisper to her had the depths of Azraelle's gut tightening in pleasure.

Azraelle didn't want to acknowledge what Xadrion had been saying. The idea that he wanted some sort of future with her, that he had those kinds of feelings for her, was too much for her to take on board. He was attracted to her, the tension they'd shared for months and the one night they'd shared in her room was evidence enough of that. But what he had been talking about in that moment was more than physical attraction. He wanted something *with* her.

It was too much to think about, too much for Azraelle to ask herself if she was capable of. There were key events in her mind that needed to happen before she felt she could let herself start to even think of letting anyone in like that. Let alone if she even could, if her past experiences were anything to go by. Would accepting Xadrion bring with it that familiar pain in her mind, that forever reminder of the shield within her own memories?

She needed answers to so many questions. Why had the Moirai deemed her guilty? And what had it meant when she'd said it had to be that way, then asked Azraelle for forgiveness? How was she going to find out why Zeus was hunting in the mortal realms? Why was Deimos doing the killing for Zeus? How was Azraelle going to make sure that Ilyon, Emera and Tolemus were protected when she left? What would happen with Xadrion now that Zeus knew he was alive? There was too much unanswered, far too much troubling her, to even think about opening up to Xadrion.

Plus, she was still pissed. His snide remark about her mater hadn't helped matters. Who was he, who didn't know anything about Az's relationship with Nyx, to comment on why Azraelle should or shouldn't forgive her?

Xadrion had recovered quickly in the few hours Azraelle had allowed him to rest for. When they moved once more, he kept pace with her easily. Within only a few hours it had become night, but they didn't stop. Xadrion did not ask to rest, not even when they'd crossed the final distance and reached Balmoral.

The land was immersed in darkness, the sun still hours from rising, when Azraelle shifted back on the outskirts of the city. Faint sounds could be heard further in, in the occasional house and closer to the market district Azraelle could see from their location. The bakers and other market owners would be awake at that hour, preparing their works for the day ahead, but no one else would be around to witness them.

'How do we find Naxos?' Xadrion asked, leaning against the building Az had stopped by. Azraelle knew he'd pushed himself in those last few hours, not wanting to let her down with his speed. His eyes had dark circles beneath them and he looked exhausted.

'I must find him myself. I'll need somewhere protected in which I can focus. Possibly for as long as a few hours,' Azraelle answered.

'We could rent a room?'

'No,' Azraelle said, and then shifted into her shadow form once more, opening her mind to Xadrion to show him what she was looking for. She moved through the city, getting an idea of where things were and how the city generally was spaced, while searching for a space that served her purposes. Azraelle found the building that would be their hideout, nearly exactly in the centre of the city. She headed back to Xadrion.

'Come on,' Azraelle said and began to walk in the direction of the centre. It wasn't far and bringing a storm into the centre of the city seemed like a bad idea, so she walked, Xadrion keeping pace beside her.

When they arrived at the destination, Azraelle looked up at the building in front of her. It was a bell tower but much larger than the one that they'd visited in the clearing. This tower was designed to ring its bell loudly across the entire city of Balmoral. Still, Azraelle didn't think she appreciated this new theme of bell towers that had taken residence in her life. She'd be happy to never look at one again for all the memories she'd made at one – memories she couldn't even begin to reflect on.

Azraelle unlocked the door at its base with her tendrils and led the way inside. At some point she was sure someone would visit the building to signal the morning, but they wouldn't be found. The ropes to pull the bell hung to the bottom of the tower, but atop a rickety ladder on the top level was a small makeshift room. There, they could hide. Az would be able to keep any mortal from seeing them with her shadows easily enough.

Xadrion ran his hands over the surface of the bell as Azraelle took a seat on the cracked wooden floor.

'I need to search for him. Take this opportunity to rest – you might need your power before the day is out,' Azraelle explained. Xadrion took a seat beside her, close considering how much empty space there was in the room. When he did things like that, Azraelle wasn't sure if it made her feel better or worse. The small sensations of him brushing against her were as powerful within her as the night their bodies had spent entwined together.

Azraelle tried not to think too long on it. It had been a long time since Az had tried to use her powers in the way she now needed to. Part of being the primus of the Ravens was the responsibility of enacting the will of Death. The Ravens were an army for the carrying of all to their next location, but it had been, or maybe still was, Azraelle's task to read the threads of Destiny and ensure their passengers were on the right paths and to find where they needed to go.

Being with Zeus and having her powers suppressed as they had been meant that the last time she performed such a task was the day she revived the young boy, Naxos. Azraelle could only hope that him being the last person she'd done it for would give her some stronger connection to him. Otherwise, the idea of searching through the threads she had encountered, scouring through them to find his individual one, felt much the same as finding the smallest grain of sand on a realm built of sand.

Azraelle closed her eyes and looked to the well within her, the well that had begun to look more and more full as she'd recovered these last few months. She felt more like herself, as powerful as she had once been, than she had since she'd first been captured by Zeus. Drawing on the power and on the memory of what she needed to do, Azraelle imagined casting her mind out to the city around her. She imagined the golden threads that she'd read thousands – millions – of times before appearing in the night sky above the city, showing her the souls of all those around.

It hit her all at once, the threads of the city inhabitants overwhelming in their flooding Azraelle's mind. She could barely distinguish each individual person, but still a giddiness overtook her at the success of her first attempt.

Az realised all at once she'd been genuinely afraid to try this since recovering her power. The idea of not having it, of not having that skill that linked her so closely to the Ravens and her family had left her nearly paralysed from fear in the past when she'd even thought to try it. Now, like an old friend, the threads came back as if they had been waiting for her all along. Had this been what her premonitions had been trying to convince her to do all along?

Azraelle sifted through the threads playing out over the city, their golden lines a text that she was more familiar with than any other. If she took the time to look more closely at the threads, she would see all she could ever come to know about each individual person. Their text would tell her the story of their birth, their death and all that they would ever accomplish in their lives. It was a language, but one she knew only a handful of people would ever be blessed enough to understand.

The process of moving through the threads was one Az knew she'd never be less awed by. Even over her many years, each time Azraelle peered into someone's life threads it always left her with a sense of wonderment. While her physical body remained in that bell tower with Xadrion, she let herself go, travelling corporeally through the city, jumping from golden thread to golden thread. As she moved, Azraelle peered throughout the city, looking for a sign of anything familiar.

There were many thousands of inhabitants in the city and searching them all would take hours, potentially days. Az needed to use more of her power to find Naxos. She cast her mind back to the day she'd saved him, the memories not coming easily to her. The years spent with Zeus hadn't done any favours when it came to accessing those memories. Still, there had to be some trace of recognition for Naxos' thread somewhere in her memory.

Azraelle continued to move through the city as she searched for anything that felt familiar. It started faint at first, the feeling of something tugging her, as if the wind were suggesting her to move to one of the quarters of the city. Trusting that instinct, she let the feeling carry her and, as she did, the tugging became stronger and more insistent. Before long, Azraelle was looking at a blacksmith's shop, a single golden thread drifting into the sky to indicate its sole inhabitant.

Azraelle was not bound to walking in that in between corporeal form, so she reached forward and touched the thread above the building effortlessly. The moment her fingers linked to the soul of the blacksmith, Azraelle knew it was who she had come to find. Just as she'd seen that first time she'd read his destiny, Naxos had centuries ahead of him. Yet it was the information in the past that assured Azraelle it was the same boy, because there, nearly two decades ago, Azraelle felt the presence of herself twined with the boy.

Azraelle opened her eyes and found Xadrion looking straight at her.

'Did you even take the time to rest?' Azraelle demanded, finding it impossible to squash the concern that overtook her at the sight of his worried expression.

'I slept and woke while you were out. I even fetched some food from the city square. It's past midday, Az,' Xadrion answered.

It didn't surprise Azraelle that she'd lost so much time searching for Naxos.

In that place in between the mortal realm and Death, time passed differently. Though it had felt like moments to Az, the glaring sun high in the sky outside told her that half the day had indeed passed. Azraelle looked to the food sitting in front of Xadrion and immediately her stomach rumbled. Had she even eaten for the last day?

Xadrion chuckled at the noise and offered her half the loaf of bread and some hard cheese. She'd been so determined to make this whole trip as torturous against Xadrion as she could before they'd left, but now with all the noise that had surrounded them at Fennhall finally just silenced, she couldn't bring herself to be so icy with him. Instead, Azraelle took his offering and ate it eagerly, the exhaustion of the last day hitting her. Somehow, as angry as Az ever became with him, as soon as she found herself truly alone with him it all just disappeared. Most of it anyway.

She hadn't slept, hadn't eaten, but Azraelle did not want to waste more time and she definitely couldn't let herself think too long on Xadrion and what feelings besides anger he was stirring with her. She'd found Naxos, and now she needed to get to him.

'I found him,' Azraelle said. 'We leave as soon as we finish eating.'

'As you wish,' Xadrion said, rocking back so he was sitting on his heels. He watched her the entire time she ate, his piercing grey eyes almost tracking each mouthful she lifted to her lips. There had been longer times of fatigue in Azraelle's past, even beyond the recent experiences of the last couple of months. A day of high magic use and low rest would not be enough to leave her defenceless, but it still didn't fill her with confidence. Not when Xadrion was so new to his powers and she did not have the Ravens as her usual backup.

When Azraelle had finished eating, or at least eaten until she saw the approval that crossed Xadrion's features, they descended to the lower level of the bell tower. Xadrion took hold of her elbow gently and tugged her to a stop.

'Balmoral is very different to Fennhall,' Xadrion said. He took hold of the hood of her cloak and pulled it over her head, doing the same to his own before they stepped onto the now busy street. 'For different reasons, we would both draw a lot of attention to ourselves so we should do our best to move discreetly.'

'How is it different?' Azraelle asked. She'd been in Balmoral before, of course, but never for longer than it took to pick up a soul and carry them to their next destination. Az had not observed many of the customs of the individual kingdoms of this land.

'Magic is not as accepted here,' Xadrion said. 'It's celebrated in Thesadel, and tolerated in Gaeweth, but here it is persecuted. You may have been fine if you didn't perform magic, but your hair is somewhat of an omen.'

'My hair?' How was such a meaningless thing an omen?

'The white colour. It's not a normal colour anywhere on this land. Anything too far out of the natural order of things is linked to magic, at least in Luzia,' Xadrion answered. Xadrion led the way from the bell tower and through the streets, and Azraelle kept her head down and her hood up as Xadrion suggested. She didn't want to kill her way out of any trouble today, not when she was already so tired.

'And why would you catch attention?'

'Tell me, how many people with skin as dark as mine do you see walking around these streets?' Xadrion asked. Azraelle peeked up to observe their surroundings, to observe the people that they were passing on the street. There was a lot of fine clothing, a sea of blond and brown and black hair all filled with glimmering jewels, but Xadrion's point was not to do with any of that. Azraelle looked to the skin of those surrounding them and saw nothing but various shades of pale and tan. No black, no brown, not anything close to the shade of Xadrion's skin.

'They would persecute you for your skin colour?'

'Without a second thought,' Xadrion said. Azraelle didn't know what to make of it. She'd never known that was something that happened in the mortal realm. For the realm of the immortal's, skin was seen as a point of pride to display where you originated from. Despite the similarities that could occur between gods with familial links, it didn't always work that way. The Ravens had been a beautiful mix of all, despite the entrance to Eviria being through the Underworld, which itself held mostly those with similar colouring to Az. Even the colour of her hair marked her family links, so close was it to the colour of her mater's and Thanatos'.

Poseidon's Pantheon in Atlantis held some of the most beautifully bronzed skin, and those who hailed from Mount Olympus had skin much like Xadrion's or darker. Of course, there was a lot of travel between realms before the years of war between Zeus and Nyx and despite it being a symbol of origin it never demanded being kept to one realm.

'That is appalling,' Azraelle breathed. Xadrion looked sideways at her and she noticed his slight smile visible beneath the cowl of his hood. The glint of his smile against his shadowed face had Azraelle's stomach tightening. She looked away, desperate to keep her head clear from images of him.

'This land holds a lot of beauty, but also a lot of hate. Rhoas has worked exceptionally hard to make Thesadel what it is today, but the rest of the kingdoms that share this land do not share the same belief,' Xadrion said.

'What of Rhoas? Do they respect him in these lands?' Azraelle asked.

'Gaeweth does. They aren't outwardly hateful and they're trying to overcome their biases. The marriage discussions between myself and Romina was a big step for them, but Rhoas has spent many years building that relationship. Luzia do not,' Xadrion answered. 'It still presents as a source of conflict between our two kingdoms.'

'What would they do if they discovered the crowned prince of Thesadel strolling the streets of their capital?' Azraelle asked, her chest tightening at the answer she expected.

'Don't let them find me,' Xadrion warned. Azraelle knew what he meant.

The idea that he'd willingly come with her, willingly stepped into the streets of a city that would hurt him the first chance it got, just to help her find Naxos made Azraelle feel guilty. Yes, she was still angry at the events Xadrion had spearheaded, but she also couldn't keep herself from being thankful for his presence.

Azraelle reached her hand out, slipping it inside Xadrion's cloak and linked her fingers with his. His breathing caught for a moment, and then his fingers tightened around her own, squeezing gently.

'I would never allow them to find you,' Azraelle promised, looking straight ahead.

Az couldn't bring herself to release his hand until they'd arrived at the blacksmithing store she'd seen, and even then, she did so reluctantly. From inside came the sounds of a smithing workshop. Metal on metal rung through the windows and echoed into the streets while crackling from the furnaces kept any silence from occurring.

When they walked through the entry door, Azraelle felt the heat of the workshop and instantly a sense of comfort washed over her. It reminded her so clearly of what it felt like to walk through the main mountain of Eviria, surrounded by the market and trades of the Ravens. They could have gotten their weapons elsewhere but the weapons produced by the Ravens were of such better quality that Azraelle had funnelled as many resources as she could to them to meet the demand of arming the entire Raven army.

Azraelle saw Naxos before he saw them and being in the same room as him solidified every certainty that this was the boy she'd saved all those years before. He was working on a sword, a thick glove covering the hand that held the simmering metal while his other arm moved to bring the smithing tool down onto the hot metal repeatedly.

Sweat glistened across his face, his arms and his chest, which was notably bare beneath the leather apron that covered his front, save for the patterns of ink that covered all she could see of his chest and shoulders. His hair had thick tight braids weaving back into a ponytail of dreadlocks, while Azraelle noted glimmering gold piercings lining the entirety of one ear.

Azraelle thought to the warning Xadrion had given her only a few minutes prior on what it meant to be in Balmoral with anything other than a white complexion and wondered at how Naxos, with his complexion darker than even Xadrion's, had found himself to settle there.

Azraelle pushed her hood back from her head and the movement caught

Naxos' attention as he finally looked up, his arm raised above his head in preparation for another hit on the smouldering metal. Naxos froze, eyes locked directly on Azraelle.

'It's you,' Naxos breathed.

THIRTY

AZRAELLE

'You know me?' Azraelle said, cautiously angling herself closer to the doorway in case they needed to leave quickly.

'I've dreamt of you.' Naxos lowered the hammer from his hand and sat it on the bench in front of him. He pulled the thick glove from his other hand and moved toward Azraelle, his expression one of shock. Azraelle didn't say anything – she didn't know what to say. Instead, as Naxos moved towards her, she watched him for any sign that they were in danger. Naxos looked at her in something more akin to awe, his eyes never leaving her even to notice Xadrion's presence. It didn't feel like a trap, but how would she even know?

Naxos recognised her, which should have been impossible given how long ago it had been for him that Azraelle brought him back to life. Even in that interaction Naxos wouldn't have gotten a glimpse of her. How had he dreamt of her? Or was someone, Zeus maybe, keeping track of him just in case Azraelle ever attempted to do what she was doing in that moment? By all accounts, Zeus thought she was dead – it can't have been him.

Naxos came to a stop within arm's reach of Az, and Xadrion stood stiff at her side as if he were ready to spring into action at any moment.

'You saved me, Azraelle,' Naxos said hoarsely.

'How would you know that?' Azraelle demanded, shocked at hearing her own name come from Naxos' lips.

'The other woman in my dreams told me,' Naxos answered.

'What other woman?'

'I don't know, she never let me see her,' Naxos answered. 'But she showed me you and what you did for me.'

Azraelle's mind was reeling. He had seen her, had seen what she'd done for him. Someone had stepped into his dreams and given him those images. Who would have done that, and how could they have known? There were so few who could have shown him what she'd done. Of those few, Az could think of no one who would have shown Naxos in order to help her. It felt like there was missing information, but Azraelle could not even see where in the story it was missing from. Nothing pieced together.

'What else did the woman say?' Azraelle asked.

'That one day you'd find me, and when you did, I needed to help you,' Naxos answered.

'Help?' Azraelle repeated. 'Help me with what?'

Naxos shrugged. 'Whatever you need help with, I don't know,' Naxos said. He frowned at her then, as if he suddenly had become confused by something he was seeing. 'Where are your wings?'

'My wings?' Azraelle repeated his words, mostly out of shock.

'In my dream, the image of you that the woman showed me, you had wings,' Naxos replied. Azraelle could feel Xadrion watching her, knew the expression that was on his face without even having to look.

'They were stripped from me,' Azraelle answered. Naxos shuddered, as if he had any idea what that truly meant to have had her wings taken from her. Azraelle refused to let herself think on it. She couldn't relive that pain, and she certainly couldn't ponder what it meant for her now to not have them.

'Is this your shop?' Xadrion asked, interrupting the solemn silence that had taken hold of the room.

'Yes,' Naxos replied, looking as if he had just seen Xadrion for the first time. His eyes flickered from Az to Xadrion and back, seemingly unsure now who he wanted to watch more.

'Do you have a room upstairs?' Xadrion asked. 'We've been travelling for some time and Azraelle has not rested.'

Azraelle glared at Xadrion, annoyed at his request. They needed to keep moving; there was no time for them to stop. She needed to get Naxos' memories, to get what she needed and return Xadrion to Fennhall. From there she could summon Thanatos or Nakir and have them take her to the Underworld with the evidence she had.

Az didn't need to sleep, except… maybe she did. While the food earlier that day had been helpful, she could feel the exhaustion approaching quickly. She knew she needed to work smarter not harder, needed to prepare to be at war for the many years to come, but after months of not moving, years of being trapped, it was intoxicating to finally be moving forward again.

She knew how to avoid burning herself out, and the Azraelle from before Zeus capturing her would have been methodical and logical in her approach to this. The Azraelle she was now, this version of her who had so many emotions running through her at any given moment, who could swear her hatred for someone and then allow him to *touch* her merely days later, that version was too unpredictable. It would be that version that would get her killed if she weren't careful.

'Of course,' Naxos answered. He turned and led the way from the simmering workshop and up some rickety steps. Xadrion tactfully ignored any glares Azraelle was trying to send his way and with no choice but to follow, Azraelle found herself staring at the broad width of Xadrion's back as they climbed the stairs. Her anger overcame any pleasure she may have previously gained from the sight. He was right, she knew he was, but she certainly didn't want him to think she thought that.

At the top of the stairs was a single room that held a small kitchen area, a curtained bathroom and a single bed. Azraelle couldn't help but think that the bed would have been much too small for Naxos and his giant frame.

'Why have you come?' Naxos asked quietly, as he watched Azraelle and Xadrion eye the room. He moved to sit on a stool in the small kitchen area, the distance only a handful of steps away.

'What did the woman in your dream tell you about what happened that day I saved you?' Azraelle asked.

Naxos frowned as he seemed to be collecting his memories. 'That I was a pawn in a game much bigger than me – *the pawn that started the match*,' Naxos answered. He furrowed his brow and squinted as he said the last words, as if he were trying to remember them.

'What match?' Azraelle demanded.

'The match that prophesised a queen overthrowing a king,' Naxos answered, as if he were repeating word for word what had been told to him.

Azraelle knew the mortal realm was littered with kings and queens, but when it came to the gods there were much fewer. Persephone, Queen of the Underworld, was the only queen Azraelle knew to still be living. There were many of her kind who had power equal to a queen, if not more than, but none went by that title. Nyx was often called Queen of Night, or Queen of Chaos. But, Nyx had never stepped forward before, had never involved herself in any significant matter save for Hypnos' stupidity. Azraelle couldn't see a world where Nyx was involved in any sort of overthrowing.

As for the king mentioned, there were three of her kind who took that title: Zeus, King of Olympus and God of the Sky; Hades, King of the Underworld; and Poseidon, King of the Sea. The three brothers who had taken rule of each of the immortal realms. Azraelle knew of nothing in existence with enough power to overthrow any of the three kings. Certainly not Persephone; perhaps it was Nyx after all the prophecy was referring to.

'Well, she may be right about that,' Azraelle said. 'When I saved you that day, I was wrongfully imprisoned. A king of my kind twisted the truth and declared that I had meddled with destiny by bringing you back.'

'I was supposed to die that day?'

'No,' Azraelle answered, 'you weren't. But it was said that you were. I read your destiny that day and you had a long life ahead of you. I now need to read it again, to use it as evidence to prove that I was not challenging Destiny by bringing you back.'

'So what do you need from me?'

'Your memories,' Azraelle answered.

'That doesn't sound too bad,' Naxos said.

Azraelle grimaced. She was downplaying the request, but she didn't know how much she could say without sending Naxos running for the hills. Viewing his memories was one thing... taking them was another. To replay them for Hades, Azraelle knew she needed to take them.

'It's not that simple, is it?' Naxos asked, watching Azraelle carefully.

'No, it's not,' Azraelle said. 'For me to use your memories in a way that I can show who I need to show, I need to take them from you. It means you lose them completely. It's also... painful.'

'I don't suppose they would just trust your recollection of viewing them?' Naxos asked, fidgeting his fingers in front of himself.

'No,' Azraelle answered. 'I'm sorry, Naxos. I'd be accused of tampering with them for my own benefit.'

'That means I would never have any memory of you?' Naxos clarified.

Azraelle tilted her head as she eyed him curiously. He seemed... genuinely concerned at the idea he had posed. As if the idea of not having his memories of Azraelle was the biggest loss he faced in all of this.

'That's enough for right now,' Xadrion interrupted abruptly. 'Azraelle, you haven't slept in nearly two days, and you must be feeling it by this point. If you even want to have enough strength to do this you need to rest, let alone if you want to make it back home by tonight.'

'I'm fine,' Azraelle rejected.

'I don't care. You need to sleep. I'll help Naxos get his work done and we can form a plan for when you wake,' Xadrion said.

Azraelle crossed her arms and glared at him. He wasn't wrong but she hated him so much for being right. She hadn't slept when she'd let Xadrion rest in the forest, and she hadn't slept overnight when she'd been chasing Naxos' threads. She'd been expending her power for over a full day, and she was exhausted. Taking Naxos' memories would not be a small effort.

'Glare all you want, it's not happening,' Xadrion said. He gestured to Naxos to leave back down the stairs and turned to follow him down. Azraelle was stuck in place as Xadrion closed the door behind the two retreating men and she found herself left alone in the unfamiliar apartment.

Az felt impatient. She wanted so badly to get what she needed and drop Xadrion back to Fennhall so she could call Thanatos once more. She was still resolved to leaving them, to leaving all the friends she had made in her time in the mortal realm. Az needed to get back to the Underworld, to Nyx and Thanatos, and hopefully eventually to the Ravens. She had a job to do, and it did not involve spending any more time playing with mortals.

But then again… they weren't mortal. As resolved as Azraelle was, she couldn't shake the feeling that leaving them would be her abandoning her own kind, leaving them to figure out their own powers and make their own way without her. It didn't sit right, not when she knew she could help them – Tolemus and Ilyon at least. She knew Emera didn't need her help, but Azraelle knew she would miss them all when she returned home. Az had spent so long of her upbringing hidden from most of her kind, her only company as she came to maturity was Thanatos and Zagreus. When Nyx finally had allowed her to enter the Underworld, Azraelle hadn't found people very receptive to her presence. The friends she'd come to make on the mortal realm had provided her with a feeling Az wasn't sure she'd even felt within the Ravens.

Helping Xadrion was another question entirely. Az knew she would need time before she stopped being so angry with him. She needed to see that nothing bad came of the risks he had taken. Az hoped they had enough time for her to take the space she needed, without him falling into the hands of Zeus, before she could come back to him.

Azraelle looked around the room, noting the cramped space and the lack of anything to rest upon save for Naxos' own bed. She felt wrong to sleep there, so instead Az settled onto the cool wooden floors of the apartment and closed her eyes. She'd slept in worse places.

Az fell asleep quickly but fitfully. She was exhausted. Thankfully, sleep did not play hard to get; however, it did bring with it a premonition, the first she'd had for weeks.

It started too far away from the subject for Az to discover anything immediately. She was looking from a distance upon a travelling group, their figures so small she couldn't make out any details. It was a relatively small group, consisting only of a couple carriages with guards patrolling alongside. Guards… whoever it was had guards, which meant it was someone with either power or gold. Azraelle pushed, trying to get closer, but around her the premonition rippled and faded away.

No, no! Az cried out in her dream state. *Show me who it is!*

Darkness surrounded her, and not the kind that came with sleep. She was still in that space of the premonition but no images could be seen. Azraelle felt a gentle prod at the outskirts of her mental barrier, the feeling of something making itself known and politely trying to request access. The presence was familiar but unfamiliar at the same time. It was one, and many. Az knew exactly who was requesting access.

How dare you come to speak with me after what you did, Azraelle said into the small room she crafted inside her mind for the visitor. How they'd even managed to find her with Emera's wards preventing her being tracked was something Azraelle had no answers for.

Sister, please, came the voices in return. Three of them echoed in the small chamber, each seeming to fill the gaps between the other and combining so easily together that Az felt it would have been less natural to hear them separated. The Fates could have easily spoken directly into Azraelle's mind, one of few who had the power to bypass any mind shields, but instead had chosen to request access.

Show yourself, Az demanded. Around her the blackness shifted and three figures took form. All distinctly feminine, Az knew the Moirai was all that and more. She could be whatever she wished to represent herself as, but she'd chosen to come in her most natural form. Three women, one with hair dark as night, one with hair as white as Az's own and one with hair so red it would have made even Emera's seem brown. The three figures stood pale and covered only partially by the swirling shadows around them.

I need you to listen to me, the Moirai said, the three mouths moving at the same time.

You demand nothing from me. This is entirely your fault, Az retorted.

I know. And I am willing for you to perceive me as your villain for as long as it takes. But, Sister, there is a greater purpose I must ask of you, the Moirai said.

So you deem me guilty, have me thrown from Mount Olympus, have my wings burned from my back as I fall, and now you come to ask of me a favour, Azraelle said. She was so angry, but in that place in Az's mind there was no means for her to physically harm the Moirai, only to speak. No words could have been harsh enough to confront her sister with.

I do. Because it is the reason I deemed you guilty in the first place, the Moirai answered.

Her response stumped Azraelle entirely, so she found herself stammering in response, *What are you saying? What do you mean?*

I'm saying that your capture and your fall to the mortal realm was written into your destiny already. It was my task to ensure it was carried out, the Moirai said.

My destiny has always been and always will be to deliver others. I am only a conduit for Death's will. For what reason would anything further be asked of me?

Azraelle didn't even give her sister time to respond before her mind was running away with the possibilities.

I think, Azraelle continued, *that Destiny has fucking nothing to do with it.*

I think when I was caught by Zeus I became a puppet – for him, for Nyx, I don't know. I was supposed to die when I fell, either to cover up your treachery and involvement with Zeus or because Nyx saw an opportunity to call the war even. But I didn't die, and now you're trying to cover your screw up. There is no larger destiny at play here. To be tortured for fifteen years, to be thrown to the mortal realm in the most excruciatingly painful way, there is no purpose! I was simply expendable – I have always been so. And now you're trying to make yourself feel better by saying there was some grand plan. I don't believe it.

It was the only way you would find them. It was the only way you could find who was required to bring down Zeus. You're right, Sister. The fall should have killed you, but I granted you some of my own power to keep the fall from doing so. I needed Zeus to trust me enough to distract him from finding you, long enough for you to find the pawns, the Moirai said.

What pawns? To what end, Sister? He cannot be killed; he will never accept being overthrown. This will only lead to our deaths, Azraelle all but shouted.

Maybe, but if we do not try Zeus will wipe out half our kind, and most of the mortals, in his quest. The balance of Destiny cannot allow this to happen, the Moirai said. *I needed you to find the ones you have found. Xadrion is the son Zeus thought he lost, the one he memorialised as Ares. One way or another, he will take over Zeus' reign, but Destiny asks you to keep it from being in partnership with Zeus. Naxos, the boy you brought back. His mortal mother was nobody, but his father was Apollo himself. And Naxos is prophesised to have powers far beyond what we yet understand.*

What kind of powers? Azraelle demanded, her interest temporarily piquing over her anger.

I do not know. It is yet unclear how they will come to present. But if they were to fall into the wrong hands, Destiny would stop serving a purpose and would come to mean nothing in the new world.

What is Zeus' plan? Is he the one killing those in my premonitions?

Yes, the Moirai answered. *He found a prophecy, one that foreshadowed his downfall. He is targeting any and all who have descended from our kind and is making plans to clear our own ranks. He will kill thousands, if not more, in the way to keeping himself on that throne.*

I already had my task! Azraelle said, her rage renewing. She had already given so much over her life, had already spent centuries secluded from her own kind before Nyx granted her leave to join the Ravens, had already spent eons delivering souls to their next stops, had never allowed herself a moment of rest when there was work to be done. Her responsibility had been eternal, what more was to be expected of her? *I had Death and everything that came with it. I was doing my duty. Why is it thrust on me to find those who could go against him? I did not ask for this!*

And yet, the Moirai said, *Destiny asks it of you anyway.*

What do I owe Destiny when Destiny seems determined to take everything from me? Azraelle asked, the words escaping her before she could pull them back in. One did not go around challenging Destiny, certainly not to the Moirai.

You owe it everything, the Moirai answered, her voice hardening for the first time. *Keep Naxos with you, do not take his memories. He is going to need them one day.*

How am I supposed to get my proof if I cannot take his memories?

You're smart, Sister. Perhaps the smartest of us all. I'm sure you can find a way.

With the last words, the three women in front of her dissolved into blackness and Azraelle found herself alone once more. Her mind was spinning, and she could not make sense of anything. The Moirai had betrayed her; that was a feeling that was burned so deep into her memory Az wasn't sure she'd ever shake it. And yet, Destiny had asked her to.

Destiny had taken everything from Azraelle, all in its purpose. It was the responsibility of her kind to obey Destiny, and to ensure its protection. But in that moment, in her anger, Az thought Destiny could go fuck itself. All she wanted was to go home, back to Eviria and walk amongst the Ravens. To feel the strength of her wings behind her and to return to her regular tasks. It had been exhausting, and never ending, but it had been simple. It was a task Destiny and Death had asked of her, and she had willingly done it. But now they asked more of her, and Az didn't know if she could bring herself to follow the orders. She was so tired.

When Azraelle opened her eyes, settling back into Naxos' tiny apartment, she found herself no longer on the cold wooden floor but tucked into the single bed. Xadrion sat on a stool beside the bed, his long legs sprawled out away from him, his arms folded across his chest and his chin tucked down, soft snores coming from him.

Naxos was moving in his kitchen, his frame comically large for the size of the small cabinets he moved amongst. The windows showed the sky filled with hues of red and orange, purple and pink. The whole day had nearly passed. They'd wasted too much time and would have to move through the night if they intended to reach Fennhall once more before Tolemus and the party from Gaeweth departed. Az hadn't intended for it to be the schedule she stuck to, but something seemed wrong about letting Tolemus leave without a final goodbye.

Azraelle slid from the bed quietly, determined not to wake Xadrion yet, and moved to join Naxos. She stood on the opposite side of the counter and offered him as polite of a smile as she could manage. Naxos smiled easily back at her, his demeanour inviting and friendly.

'Why would you be so willing to help me when you have no idea what is being asked of you?' Azraelle asked. Naxos shrugged but didn't stop preparing the food he was making.

'All this time I have had, all the time that I ever will have, was because you decided to bring me back. I suppose being brought back from death... it made me wonder as to why me. I always suspected I was brought back for a reason, and that it was my responsibility to see it through in payment for the years I've been granted,' Naxos answered.

'But the years weren't granted to you. They were always yours to begin with, and someone took them from you early,' Azraelle argued.

'Yes, and you gave them back. If you hadn't, I'd be dead, and the years wouldn't have been mine. I am in debt and would like to repay you for that,' Naxos said.

'There's another way for you to help me, one that doesn't involve me taking your memories. But it requires you to leave the life you have here,' Azraelle said.

'For how long?'

'I do not know if I could give you a truthful answer to that question,' Azraelle answered.

'Very well,' Naxos said with an impassive shrug, as if the thought of leaving his life here meant nothing. Azraelle looked at him, closely, curious as to why he could agree so easily. Why was he so willing to throw away his business and his life just to help Azraelle? Is that what she was supposed to be doing when Destiny asked something of her?

'What of your life here?' Azraelle said.

'It is not my life,' Naxos answered. 'I have always felt that I was to be part of something greater than this. I know you don't know me, and you might not understand me, but I know you, Azraelle. I was not always living this life of comfort. I was quickly descending down a much different path, one that would have led to me dead in a gutter, but when that woman started visiting my dreams and telling me your legends, it changed me. I vowed to wait for you, all to help you.'

'You owe me nothing, Naxos.'

'I owe you everything, Azraelle. It is not your decision to reject that.'

Azraelle pondered for a moment, thinking on everything Naxos had said. If the Moirai wanted Azraelle to leave Naxos with his memories, she could do that. It involved a change in her plans, but it was possible.

'Very well,' Azraelle said. 'You have an hour to wrap up any business you have here. Then we leave.'

THIRTY-ONE

XADRION

'What do you mean he's coming with us?' Xadrion demanded.

Azraelle was sitting on the bench of Naxos' small kitchen, and Naxos himself was leaning against the cabinets with his arms folded and a smirk on his features. Xadrion noted with frustration how Naxos' eyes stayed trained on Azraelle constantly.

'I need him to present his memories. There are too many ways I can be accused of tampering with them if I take them,' Azraelle said.

'So he's coming back with us?'

'Exactly.'

'And how are we going to do that? It took you and I over half a day to travel here. With him we'll be back to it taking weeks, if not a month,' Xadrion argued.

'You can carry him,' Azraelle said, as if it were the simplest concept. Xadrion could feel himself staring at her, his jaw dropped. He had no idea what she was saying, no idea what she expected from him.

'You're going to have to explain it a bit more to me, Az,' Xadrion said.

Azraelle clasped her ankles together, swinging her legs gently off the edge of the bench.

'My shadow form involves me transforming into a different substance. Who I am physically ceases to exist in the moments of movement, but you don't. You would remain connected to Naxos, and he would come in and out of the jumps with you,' Azraelle explained.

'Why didn't you say this back at Fennhall? Ilyon could have come, could have offered more protection,' Xadrion said, angry all over again at Azraelle.

'I didn't even want you to come with me, what makes you think I'd suggest a means for someone else to come?'

Xadrion clenched his palms into fists and paced the section of floor he was occupying. He wondered if Azraelle would ever truly stop keeping things from him.

'You're unbelievable,' Xadrion said. It was all he could think to say in his frustration.

Naxos stood from where he had been leaning and shifted his gaze to Xadrion. It gave Xadrion the impression of a giant guard dog standing just beside its owner, begging to be let off the leash. Azraelle looked impassive at what was happening around her. What had happened while he'd slept in that chair? Naxos had been perfectly civilised as Xadrion had worked with him that day and suddenly now that Azraelle was awake, it was as if Xadrion were the threat in the room.

'Fine,' Xadrion eventually said, exhaling heavily in exasperation. 'I'll try. When do we leave?'

'Right now,' Azraelle answered. 'We either go through the windows or we get to the edge of town and leave from there.'

'Might I suggest the windows,' Naxos said. 'At this time of the afternoon, as the sun is going down, it's not entirely a good idea for the likes of Xadrion or I to be caught outside. You either, I suppose.' Both Xadrion and Naxos looked to the white that marked Az's hair. Xadrion was not as familiar with Balmoral as Naxos obviously would be, but he knew enough to know they needed to stay out of sight. How Naxos had lived here for so long without any harm coming to him was something that Xadrion would be curious to understand.

'Mortals have the strangest intolerances,' Azraelle remarked as she pushed from the bench and stood. Naxos followed where she walked in the apartment. She strode to the window and unlatched it, pushing it open wide. It was a small window, only Azraelle of the group would have been able to pull herself through it. But they didn't have to physically move through it, they just had to use it as an exit to the sky.

'So I just hold onto him?' Xadrion asked, eyeing Naxos up and down. He was of equal size to Xadrion, if not broader and slightly taller. Carrying him would be an effort.

'Keeping your arms linked should be enough to do it. But whatever happens, do not let go of him,' Azraelle warned.

Xadrion followed her command, moving to stand beside the window and linking his arm with Naxos'. Azraelle shifted into her mist form and Xadrion noted the look of awe in Naxos' eyes as he observed the transformation.

'Hold on,' Xadrion instructed, and then followed her. It was much harder travelling with Naxos attached. It somehow felt like there was a lag on his power, as if it took a second longer to take the next leap. As they moved, the thunder rumbled in quickly behind them and lightning crackled around them as they appeared and disappeared. Azraelle was almost invisible even to him as they moved, so different were her shadows to his storming presence.

They'd left at sundown and travelled without pause until the sun had been out of sight for hours. They'd cleared the Sannigan Forest once more, Xadrion's storm still following their path, when Xadrion felt the probing at his mind from Azraelle.

Whatever you do, don't stop, she said when Xadrion lowered his shield for her. Xadrion looked to where she had been beside him and found nothing. He threw his mind towards her, trying to locate where she was, when he detected her a fair distance behind and further to the side.

What are you doing?

We're being followed. I need you to keep going or they'll sense that we've detected them, Azraelle answered.

What about you? Are they scouts?

Yes, Azraelle answered. *Two. I need to take them out before they get away, so I need to be fast.*

Dread filled Xadrion's gut, amplified by the fear he felt from Azraelle through their shared connection. If scouts were able to scare even Azraelle, Xadrion knew he should be worried.

Xadrion didn't feel comfortable carrying on as if nothing were wrong. He wanted to turn around and help Azraelle face the danger. She was strong, but could she handle two scouts on her own? He wanted to help, but she'd made it exceptionally clear that if he indicated that anything was wrong, the scouts would turn tail and take the knowledge of their location with them, faster than Azraelle would be able to stop them. Through Azraelle's senses, he could hear the beating of two sets of wings, fast approaching where Azraelle had drifted away to, hiding in wait.

Xadrion could see the grip she held on to her sword, waiting for them to get close enough to her. He was thankful that Naxos had seemed willing to travel in silence so far, so immersed in what he was seeing around them as they moved, and would not have any idea that something was amiss. Naxos, at least, would continue on as an unknowing bystander.

Azraelle kept the link between their minds open, keeping Xadrion informed on what was happening as best she could. The wing sounds came closer and Azraelle reacted. She changed to her mist form, her thoughts and senses at once enhancing and shifting, and she shot towards where the scouts were, approaching them from behind.

Azraelle positioned herself above them before transforming back to her physical form. At once, her shadows lashed toward the scout on her left, wrapping themselves around its wings and arms, locking it into a stationary position. At the same moment, Azraelle landed atop the shoulders of the second scout, burying her sword straight through the back of his neck and, with the force of her drop, so far into his body that Xadrion could only see the hilt grasped in Azraelle's hands through their shared vision. The armour that coated both scouts head to toe had done nothing to shield them from Az's strength and accuracy driving her sword down.

The scout she was on began to plummet quickly to the ground and Azraelle leapt, pulling her sword with her, to the second scout, who was already ripping at the shadows in an attempt to free themselves. They had gotten their wings free and seemed to be about to make their escape when Azraelle latched onto them. As quick as the interaction had been, the second scout had already managed to get some distance between themselves and Az, which meant the only thing she could grab hold of were their wings. Her hands gripped the top of their wings, Az's skin only a few shades darker than the white of the wings in her hands.

'I'm sorry for this,' Azraelle whispered to the scout before she began to tear.

Azraelle's strength shocked Xadrion; the wings immediately beginning to rip from the scout's back. Blood sprayed from the gashes at the top of the scout's wings and their screams echoed through every sense Xadrion had, both his own and Azraelle's. The scout stopped trying to escape and instead became incapacitated with the pain. As soon as they had stopped moving enough for Azraelle to get a better grasp on them, she drove her sword straight through their neck. A few more seconds passed and finally the second scout stopped their movement, their screams already having died out to gurgling cries.

Xadrion turned around, heading straight to where he knew Azraelle would be, on the ground with the fallen bodies of the scouts. As soon as they settled, Naxos flew into action and headed straight to where Azraelle stood. Naxos would have had no idea what transpired but took no time in evaluating the situation before deciding he needed to get to Azraelle and pull her from the dead bodies at her feet. He was a quick thinker at the very least.

'Are you unharmed?' Naxos demanded, pulling her body this way and that so he could get a better look at her condition. Xadrion felt paralysed in place as he looked at her. He'd always known Azraelle was the goddess of Death, always knew she'd had a thousand lifetimes of that world, but she'd never looked so like it than in that moment. Blood coated her, the dark mahogany colour soaked through her clothes and covered her skin. Az's hair, once white and gleaming, looked like it had the first day Xadrion had ever laid eyes on her, dripping with the blood of wings. The colour of the blood was such a contrast to the luminescent streaks of ice white still struggling to shine through. Her hands and forearms were drenched and blood coated her face, dripping from her bared mouth and covering her teeth within.

Azraelle *was* Death.

Xadrion nearly heaved at the thought of so much blood coming from one body, from two gashes Azraelle had made at the scout's wings. Azraelle spat, sending what blood had landed in her mouth to the ground, and let Naxos lead her from the two fallen bodies.

Once clear of them, Azraelle turned to look back once more. Her eyes did not seem able to leave the one whose wings she had torn.

Perhaps truly for the first time, Xadrion thought of what pain it must have meant for Azraelle to lose her wings. Seeing them tear from the scout's body as he had, hearing the screams that had resulted, he could only imagine the pain that had followed. And she had apologised before she'd done it. No matter how badly she needed to guarantee their safety, despite the scouts working for the man who had tortured her and taken her own wings, Azraelle had known what she would be doing by taking those wings in her hands and tearing.

'They had our trail,' Azraelle said, her voice calm and cold.

'Of course. You did the right thing,' Naxos said.

'I know.'

Silence followed the moment, and Xadrion resolved to let Azraelle dictate their next move. Outwardly, minus her appearance, she seemed fine. She'd thrown him from her mind the moment she'd plunged the sword through the scout's throat, so Xadrion had no idea what she was actually thinking. He didn't delude himself into thinking she'd not killed before. In all her years, and with all her responsibilities, it would have been a common occurrence for her, Xadrion was sure. But she seemed so calm in that moment that Xadrion wondered if he was seeing someone who was so accustomed to killing or someone who was very good at putting on an act.

'Let's go,' Azraelle said. 'We'll stop at the first body of water we find so as not to scare the others when we return.' She gave a brief look down at herself, at the blood that covered her hands, and that Xadrion could still see dripping from the ends of her hair and slicking through her brows down her face. Before anyone could say anything more, Azraelle had shifted and was continuing on their path back to Fennhall.

They travelled for another few hours, passing nothing more than a small stream here and there. Eventually, they came to one of the larger lakes of Gaeweth, Lake Gravatos, which told Xadrion they were only a couple more hours from the border of Thesadel, and shortly after that Fennhall. When they arrived at the lake, Xadrion kept a lookout while Azraelle walked straight into the water, fully clothed. Naxos was pacing around, stretching his arms out to the sides as if he were trying to work out a kink, but his gaze never left Azraelle.

Xadrion struggled to pay attention to their surroundings as Azraelle submerged herself into the water. At first, Xadrion found himself amazed at how quickly the colour of the water surrounding her changed. Blood washed from her skin and hair and turned the water a deep red. When Azraelle was fully in and had dunked her head several times, she began to peel the layers of her clothes off. First her cloak, which she scrubbed harshly before leaving the water and hanging it on a branch. Naxos made a small fire beneath the branch to help it dry. Azraelle re-entered the water, leaving her shoes by the fire, and pulled her shirt and pants from her body before she scrubbed those also.

Naxos, to his credit, looked away when Azraelle begun to reveal her naked skin. Xadrion did not want to, did not ever want to look away from her, but did so anyway. It felt wrong to watch her methodical cleaning in that moment. When the remainder of her clothes were hanging on the branches above the fire, Azraelle stayed in the water for a while longer. When she emerged, she'd scrubbed her hair clean and there was no evidence remaining to suggest she had ever been so soaked in blood.

Xadrion kicked himself when it was Naxos who got his cloak around Azraelle's body before he did. She nestled in it and sat beside the fire with her arms folded around herself. They only had two or three more hours to go, and the sun was longer from rising. They had made good time.

'Let's rest for a while,' Xadrion suggested.

'No, I'm fine to keep going,' Azraelle said, staring into the fire.

'You may be, but I'm not,' Xadrion lied. Really, he was fine to cover the last few hours, but he knew Azraelle would never take the moment to herself, would travel the remainder of the way home in dripping clothes. 'Carrying Naxos is taxing me more than I thought it would.'

'Fine,' Azraelle said, pulling Naxos' cloak tighter around her as she stared into the flames.

'Who were they?' Naxos asked, after a long while of silence.

'Scouts for Zeus,' Azraelle answered.

'I've heard his name in the legends the woman in my dreams told me of. Who is he?' Naxos asked.

'Zeus is the ruler of Mount Olympus, one of the realms of my kind. I believe he is the king who the woman mentioned to you,' Azraelle replied.

'Why does he have scouts on these lands?'

'To keep an eye on everything. Lately, I imagine, he is looking for Xadrion,' Azraelle said. Naxos turned to Xadrion with a puzzled expression. So, Azraelle was not withholding anything, throwing Xadrion to the wolves in what she chose not to keep secret.

'He's my father,' Xadrion grunted, the words feeling foreign to say out loud. He still had not wrapped his head around everything.

'Ah,' Naxos said, though his face showed anything but understanding.

'Zeus didn't know Xadrion existed, allowing Xadrion to live a life of peace, until Xadrion thought it would be fun to go knocking on his door to declare his presence,' Azraelle said. She was still angry then. The moment in the trees had not erased that, apparently.

'Az,' Xadrion warned. But he'd meant what he said in their journey to Balmoral – he would take whatever she threw at him. And maybe… maybe Az was not so fine after taking out those scouts as she was trying to lead them to believe.

'I'm going to keep watch,' Naxos said awkwardly, pushing himself to a standing position. 'You guys try to rest for a while. I'll wake you up in an hour.' He walked a slight distance away, out of earshot, and Xadrion was thankful. As suddenly defensive as Naxos had been over Azraelle, he'd at least allowed for them to have a moment together.

'I'm going to sleep,' Azraelle said. She shuffled until she was laying on the ground, her head supported by the hard fallen trunk she'd been leaning against.

'Whatever you throw at me, Az, I'll take it,' Xadrion reminded. 'Just tell me you're okay after earlier.'

She rolled to face him, and Xadrion, noting the expression on her face, immediately moved to lay beside her. Azraelle eagerly adjusted to allow for Xadrion to place his arms around her and settled her head in the crook of his shoulder. The feeling of her in his arms felt right, as if it were the most natural thing in the world. Xadrion pulled Naxos' coat closer around her body when he felt the iciness of her skin.

'You had to kill them, Az. They had our trail,' Xadrion said.

'I know. It just… it doesn't get easier. Battlefields are one thing; on those there is so much chaos that all the faces blur together. On the grounds there is one goal: to take as many enemies out as you can, however you can. I've led the charge to push the front line forward enough times I should be familiar with this.'

'But you're not,' Xadrion said.

'No, I'm not.'

'If it's any comfort, I don't believe killing another should be an easy thing to do,' Xadrion said.

'Maybe, but it's something I'm undoubtedly going to have to do more of, and soon,' Azraelle said.

'Do you truly believe this will end in war?' Xadrion asked.

'I know you have an image of who Zeus is in your mind, and I truly hate to be the one who breaks it for you, but he will ensure it ends in war,' Azraelle said.

Xadrion's fingertips found the scars that lined Azraelle's back and immediately remembered the sounds of the scouts screams as their own wings were being torn from them.

'You said once to Ilyon that you didn't remember the day you fell, the day you lost your wings. That's not true, is it?' Xadrion asked.

'No, it's not true,' Azraelle said.

'Did you feel all of it?'

'Yes.'

Xadrion pulled her tighter, resting his hand in her hair and brushing his fingers through it gently. The noise that came from Azraelle at his brushing of her hair reminded Xadrion of a purring cat. He couldn't help but smile at the sound, continuing to stroke her hair until he felt her relax and eventually slip into a light sleep.

Xadrion did not sleep – he couldn't. The sound of the scout's screams echoed through his memories, and he could not stop himself from imagining it was Azraelle who screamed that way, falling from the sky much the same as she had made both the scouts fall. She had remembered every moment of the wings being torn from her.

He stayed alert until Naxos approached an hour later to wake them.

THIRTY-TWO

AZRAELLE

The sun had just started to rise when Xadrion, Azraelle and Naxos covered the final distance of their journey and arrived at Azraelle's rooms through her window. Az's clothes were still damp from the lake, but the fire had stopped the dripping wetness.

'Well, this is much nicer than my little shop,' Naxos commented, already looking around the room and all its finery. Azraelle hadn't adorned the room with much while she'd been at Fennhall apart from some piles of books and draping of clothes. The room, in Azraelle's absence for the two days, was tidier than it had been when she'd left. She supposed she had Darlene to thank for the cleanliness of her possessions.

'What do we do now?' Xadrion asked as all three stood seemingly lost for thought.

'Now, I go find Tolemus and say my goodbyes before they leave this morning. Naxos, you can stay here and get some rest,' Azraelle commanded. 'Bedroom is that way.' She pointed in the direction of her room, noting Xadrion's grimace at her direction.

'I'll come with you,' Xadrion said.

'No,' Az interrupted. 'You need to go to Rhoas and let him know we've returned. Emera and Ilyon need to know also.'

Azraelle hadn't accounted for them actually succeeding in finding Naxos. Now that they had, it meant she could follow through on everything she'd been telling herself she would for months now. She would be leaving Fennhall, taking Naxos with her, and that meant leaving Xadrion behind. There may have been a part of her that wished she could bring herself to ask more from the people she'd come to know here. She wished she could ask Xadrion particularly to come with her but she couldn't bring herself to do it.

285

So much needed to be figured out, and Az didn't like all the uncertainty already looming over her future. Adding Xadrion into the mix and all that it could mean felt like too much for Az to process at once. As much as a part of her wanted to move forward with him, there was a huge part of her that still couldn't move past his connection to Zeus.

Xadrion caught her as she rushed from her room.

'Az, wait,' he said, catching her arm and turning her to face him. 'Can we talk later?'

'Sure. I'll find you,' she said. Xadrion kept hold of her hand, and Azraelle zeroed in on the gentle strokes he was doing to the back of her hand, the warmth of his touch doing more than he probably realised when it came to thawing her resolve. She needed to get the ice mask on, and fast, or she'd be saying far too many things she didn't want to say.

'I can find Naxos some rooms of his own in the meantime,' Xadrion said.

'Xadrion.' Azraelle pulled her hand away gently.

'What? There's no reason for him to stay with you when we have spare rooms,' Xadrion argued.

'Xadrion… Naxos won't be here long enough to need his own rooms.' It was silent as Xadrion took in what she had said, his eyes never leaving hers.

'You're leaving?'

'Xay,' Azraelle breathed, her voice barely louder than a whisper. 'This was always the plan.'

'Az, please,' Xadrion said, his voice cracking slightly.

'Look,' Az interrupted, 'I'll find you later. For now, I have to go say goodbye to my friend. Go find your father.'

Az shifted to her shadows and left as quickly as she could. Right now, she needed to focus on one thing at a time. The thought of returning to the Underworld had her reeling, and that wasn't even accounting for how shaken she'd felt since ripping those wings. Azraelle had killed before, so many she'd lost count. She'd killed in desperate times; she'd killed viciously and mercilessly. But there had always been a line with wings. Knowing what it was like to have them had Azraelle grimacing even at the thought of causing harm to another's. The sheer number of nerves in the wings would have had that scout feeling searing pain, worse than anything they'd ever felt before. The scouts were fast, though, and Az had done what she'd needed to do to keep them from getting away. It didn't stop her feeling sick thinking about it.

She didn't stay in the shadows the whole time, just long enough to guarantee she was far enough away from Xadrion that he couldn't follow her. It took all of one knock on Tolemus' door before it opened and revealed his quickly smiling expression. A moment later Az was crushed inside his bear grip.

'You made it back in time,' Tolemus said, still not releasing his hold.

'Of course I did,' Az answered. 'Are you warded?'

'They did it that afternoon,' Tolemus answered, finally letting Az pull away. He pulled her inside and led the way to take a seat in one of the lounges. 'How did it go?'

'We found him, and brought him back with us,' Az replied.

'That's great news.'

'It is,' Az said. 'But what of you? Are you all ready to return to Gaeweth?'

'Packed and ready to go. The horses and carriages are being organised now. We'll likely leave within the hour,' Tolemus answered.

'And you're sure you want to go back rather than come with me, or even stay here?'

'I'll be back, Az. I'm merely going to settle my affairs. Gaeweth and its army has done a lot for me, and I wish to settle the mortal part of my life in the right way. Once that is done, I will seek you out once more,' Tolemus said.

'I look forward to that day,' Azraelle said. 'It's somewhat bittersweet, don't you think? You're leaving back to Gaeweth. Now that I have Naxos, I will be returning to the Underworld. Xadrion, Ilyon and Emera will return to their normal lives, although I doubt the princes will settle back into things easily now that their powers have awakened.'

'You're truly going to leave them here?'

'It isn't what I wish to do,' Az answered, playing with her fingers in her lap. 'But it is what must be done. Ilyon is not immortal and bringing him or Emera in will likely end in their deaths. Xadrion is too big of an unknown and far too powerful to fall into Zeus' hands. He must remain hidden here. Besides, there is nothing to say that I'll even be pardoned.'

'But if you are?'

'If I am, it is likely that my kind will be heading to war once more. Zeus must be stopped,' Azraelle said. She relayed everything to Tolemus that the Moirai had said to her when she was sleeping in Naxos' apartment.

'He's the one behind the killings?' Tolemus confirmed.

'Yes. And one way or another I have been tasked to bring that to light, to hopefully stop him,' Az replied.

'Not just you, though,' Tolemus argued. 'You said your sister even told you that you needed Xadrion and Naxos to do it. Why do you insist on leaving Xadrion here?'

'There are a thousand reasons to leave him here,' Az said. 'What if he decides he wishes to side with Zeus instead? He is already pining after his newly discovered father. I could not ever wish to expose him to war amongst our kind, as brutal and scarring as it is. Whether he is fighting on Zeus' side, or on mine, both will bring him agony. Especially if he has to fight against his own father.

I would be all but throwing him into the deepest layer of the Underworld if I were to involve him in this.'

'Azraelle, he is already involved in this,' Tolemus argued.

'I refuse to believe that.'

Their conversation was interrupted by a knock at the door. Tolemus got up to open it to reveal Romina standing on the other side, guards stationed either side of her.

'It is time,' Romina said, then caught Az's eye over Tolemus' shoulder. Her expression hardened instantly.

'Give me just one more moment to say goodbye,' Tolemus said, then turned and strode back to Azraelle. He pulled her in and kissed the top of her head. 'I will find you once more, and you will help me fill these long years. I wish I could come with you to where you are going, but please, if you find Nico tell him I love him and think of him every day.'

. They'd spoken once before about the Underworld, that day Azraelle had told Emera, Ilyon and Tolemus everything. She'd told them they were not able to come with her, even then. Few travelled freely in and out of the Underworld. Az and the Ravens had always been able to, given the nature of their work. Theoretically, most of the gods could traverse between their realms, but Hades kept a strict control over things, monitoring who came and went. He did not believe the Pantheon of the Underworld served any purpose travelling to the mortal realm, so at least the gods who fell under his jurisdiction remained there nearly always.

Mortals who ended up there never left again. Unless they were granted rebirth, in which case they underwent an entire transformation to do so. Demi-gods were much the same, if they died and ended up in the Underworld that usually was where they remained. To take Tolemus in, even in hopes of seeing Nico, would all but guarantee his life remained there.

Perhaps it was something he would want... Azraelle knew it was not her place to withhold the information from him but still, she couldn't bring herself to tell him. Next time they met, under whatever circumstances they were, she would tell him.

'I will find you once more, Tolemus. And we will have lifetimes to live in this friendship of ours. For now, I will carry your message,' Azraelle said. She felt the tears burning behind her eyes and her throat thickening, but she swallowed harshly and fought the urge to let the tears fall. She *would* see him again.

'Stay here and let this be our goodbye. I don't want an uncomfortable walk to the carriages to be our last moments. I will miss you, Az. Please reconsider your choice to shut Xadrion out. You deserve more,' Tolemus said. He pressed another kiss to her head and then he swept away, heading to walk beside Romina once more.

Romina did not leave immediately; instead, she kept her gaze pinned to Azraelle.

'I will pray for your good health,' Romina said as her way of saying goodbye.

When they left, the guards closed the door behind them and Azraelle was left alone in the room. Tolemus she would miss, but Romina she would not. Az had grown weary very quickly of the holier-than-thou attitude and constant disapproval. The kingdom of Gaeweth was highly religious, worshipping even some of her own brothers and sisters. If only Romina knew who it was she was getting on the nerves of, Az was sure she would adjust her behaviour rather quickly.

Az took several moments to collect herself before she left the room and headed back through the castle. Rhoas was next on her list, then Ilyon and Emera. After that, she would bathe and get the sleep she so desperately needed. Then it was time to go home.

She found Rhoas in his study accompanied by Xadrion. Hearing Xadrion's voice through the door had her nearly turning around to come back another time. Fighting every urge she had, she pushed through the doors after the guards nodded their permission and knew immediately she had interrupted a tense scene between Xadrion and Rhoas.

'Azraelle! It is good to see you again,' Rhoas said, his expression immediately shifting to a smile. 'Xadrion was just reporting on your success.'

'Yes,' Az said, feeling unsure and awkward for the first time that she could remember. Awkwardness had never been a feeling of hers. She had been a primus, and she had filled that role in every sense. She was commanding, and controlling, and powerful. She was not awkward.

'I… I just wanted to say that I am so grateful for your hospitality these last months,' Az began.

'Surely you are not leaving so soon?' Rhoas interrupted.

'I intend to leave as soon as I am strong enough and have contacted my family. But again, you have allowed me a place of safety and comfort while I healed from my experiences, and I will forever be indebted to you and yours,' Azraelle said.

'You could repay that debt by staying until we can throw some sort of gathering for you, tomorrow night at the latest? I would like to formally show my appreciation for what you have done for my sons,' Rhoas said.

'I'm afraid I cannot stay that long,' Az said. She forced herself to keep watching Rhoas, to keep herself standing by the closed door. She would not look at Xadrion, not at what she knew she would see on his face. She could feel the prodding of his presence against her mind's barrier, begging to be let in. She ignored it.

'I can offer you a promise instead,' Az continued. 'If I see Hera amongst everything I must do next, I will relay your kindness to her, and I will do everything in my power to free her from the hold Zeus has over her so she can hopefully return to you.'

'That is an incredible promise,' Rhoas said, tears brimming at his eyes. 'Of course, if you could merely convey my thoughts of her, that would be enough. I know the power of Zeus' hold, and I hold no expectations of you to break it.'

'All the same, I will do my best,' Az responded.

'Very well. I will not ask you to stay again, as much as I so wish you could,' Rhoas said. 'Take care of yourself, Azraelle.'

Az dipped into a shallow bow and retreated from the room. Before she had the time to dart away, Xadrion's hand slid into hers, as if the physical contact would keep her from running from him, and he walked side by side with her.

'Please, just let me walk with you,' Xadrion said, eyeing Azraelle as she looked to make her escape.

'You cannot change my mind.'

'I know,' Xadrion responded quietly. 'I wish I could, but I do know you well enough to know you are stubbornly on this path. I will stick to my word, Az. This is not the last time you will see me and I will never stop fighting for you. You can leave me now, you can insist on me remaining in this mortal life of mine, but you cannot dictate what happens a year from now, ten years from now, even a hundred years from now. This isn't the end of our story. So please just let me walk with you.'

'It's better this way,' Azraelle said, allowing him to keep hold of her hand as they walked. 'A hundred years from now you are going to be wishing you had the opportunity to live this mortal life for just a little longer. My world – our world, I suppose – is about to start looking very different. Of course, it is your choice when and how you join us, but I hope you listen to me when I say that you need to steer clear of it while this war happens.'

'Why are you so certain there must be war?'

'Because I know Zeus. Because I know me. If he does not start one, it is my duty to do so.'

'You will go to war for this? What must you even fight over?' Xadrion asked, looking at her with disapproval. He had not looked at her that way since she had refused to save the girl's life at the bell tower, even when she had been coated in that scout's blood. It saddened Az to feel that, despite so much having happened between the two of them, they still could not meet what the other needed. If only he knew what it meant to have her destiny, to be goddess of Death. He would be endlessly disappointed in her.

'I fight for your mortals,' Azraelle spat, her sadness quickly turning to anger. It was the easier emotion to feel. She needed distance; she needed him to let her go. 'The mortals you so carefully considered when you went and signalled your presence. You did so to save thousands of lives. I would go to war to save thousands more. Zeus will not stop until he has what he is after.'

'Going to war will kill thousands,' Xadrion argued.

'Maybe. But Destiny asks it of me anyway.'

'What the fuck does Destiny have to do with this?' Xadrion all but shouted.

'It does not matter. You only need to know that there is no other option for me,' Azraelle answered.

'Can I not just meet with Zeus and get him to lay off this entire thing?'

'Don't be naïve, Xadrion. Do not allow yourself to be so foolish as to think you are the only reason Zeus is doing all of this for,' Azraelle said.

'I know you have him painted as this evil who will stop at nothing, but has he not respected my wishes so far as to being left alone while I think things over? We haven't seen him or Athena at all,' Xadrion said.

'That is not because they are respecting your wishes. They will have been using this time to gather information, to search for you. It is luck and Emera's wards that have kept you from being found thus far. Do not think for one moment that they are respecting your wishes,' Az argued.

They arrived at Azraelle's door and she was feeling so tired from the last couple of days and all the conversations she'd had that day, including the one Xadrion was insisting on having, that she decided she'd find Ilyon and Emera later. For now, she needed to sleep.

'Just… please. Let me handle this, and just stay here. You're right, maybe one day there is something else for us. Right now, I need you to not make things harder,' Az said.

'Why do you perceive everything to do with me as difficult?'

'Because it is! Love, as you so keep wanting to force me to acknowledge, is the hardest thing to account for that there is. I do not open myself to those feelings, and I do that for so many reasons. What vision of us do you want me to entertain when I cannot feel that? We will never live a life of easy love,' Az said.

'You can feel it, you just refuse to,' Xadrion argued.

'What difference does it make? I still do not feel it. Let me do what I need to do. Let me go,' Azraelle said. She pushed her way inside the door and slammed it shut behind her. On the other side, lounging across the chaise with a pile of bread and cheese in front of him, was Naxos. He was looking at her with an expression that showed his attempt to look casual while clearly listening in on what had been happening on the other side of the door.

'Don't say a word. I'm taking a bath and sleeping. We leave tonight,' Az barked and strode into the bathing room. The lake had cleaned the blood from her, but Azraelle could still feel it everywhere. She scrubbed herself until the water had changed from scalding hot to nearly freezing before she finally stood and dressed herself in fresh clothes.

As Azraelle lay in bed, she got caught in her thoughts. Destiny wanted her to work with Naxos and Xadrion, and while Azraelle had spent millennia obeying Destiny's commands and enforcing them, she could not follow this one. Had she not had enough taken from her? Had too much not already been asked of her? Even Naxos, who she had only known for a day, she didn't want to risk. She would take him with her, take him to reveal her innocence, but as soon as she was pardoned, she would ensure he returned to safety. The fight to come, well… that was between her and Zeus and no one else.

Xadrion would never forgive her for killing his father, but there would be no future for them anyway. Anything she had ever said to him otherwise was for his sake and not her own. She would not entertain the idea of loving him. She could not. If she didn't kill Zeus, it only meant her own death. And if she miraculously survived everything that was to come, she still had a long way to go before she ever returned to who she had been prior. How could she open herself to Xadrion when she was not even whole? Her wings were as much a part of her as her immortality was. Not having them for these last months, having them bound for fifteen years before that, had left a searing hole deep inside her.

Sleep came eventually, but no peace arrived with it. Instead, Azraelle found herself back in that premonition, the one she had begun to see in Balmoral. Only now… now she saw exactly who it was that was the target.

THIRTY-THREE

XADRION

Banging, loud and hard, crashed against his bedroom door. Xadrion felt as if he'd just gotten to sleep when it started. When he pulled himself back from the softness of his bed and opened the bedroom door, he was greeted to the sight of Azraelle with her fist raised to bang once more. Her eyes were wide and frantic, and her hair dishevelled, but she was dressed as if she were ready for battle.

She was wearing a set of black leather armour that Xadrion had not seen her in before. Sheaths wrapped around her thighs, weapons buried in each of them, and the leather adorning her top half was thick with metal coatings built in at key places. Xadrion could see the emerald pendant's chain leading beneath the chest piece of her armour.

'What's happening?' Xadrion asked, moving already to start pulling on his own armour. Whatever it was, he'd never seen Azraelle so urgent before.

'It's Tolemus. I had a premonition, and it's Tolemus. We have to get to him,' Azraelle said. Her voice sounded thick, as if she was pushing back threatening tears.

'Fuck.' Xadrion pulled his equipment on faster. 'Go get Ilyon, I can carry him with me. I'll meet you at his rooms. Go!'

Azraelle turned and ran, slipping into her shadows as if by second nature before she'd even taken three steps. Xadrion hurried to pull the rest of his armour on and strapped his own swords to his side. Tolemus... could it already be too late? He didn't know how long he'd been asleep for, but a quick glance outside his window showed the sun much lower in the sky than it had been. Late afternoon, at least, which meant it had been at least half a day since the Gaewethian party had left.

By the time Xadrion reached Ilyon's rooms, Azraelle was already anxiously pacing and Ilyon was dressed and waiting. He met Az's eyes long enough to see how much it was paining her to not already be moving. She had come for him, had waited long enough and asked for help. Finally, something he had wanted her to do so many times before, she had finally done. Xadrion took hold of Ilyon as Az shifted into her shadows and fled out the window.

'Hold on tight, Ilyon,' Xadrion warned, and then they were following Az. It was an effort to keep up with her, given he was carrying Ilyon, and given that Az seemed to be letting nothing hold her back. She was moving faster over the distance than he'd ever seen her do before.

Azraelle stopped suddenly after a while, and Xadrion reappeared beside her. Ilyon was breathing heavily, and Xadrion knew adrenalin was pumping through his brother just as it was him. Ilyon hadn't had to put his training to use before, had never had a fight where his opponent would genuinely try to harm him. Xadrion cursed at not knowing what was waiting for them.

'What is it?' Xadrion asked.

'They're just over that hill,' Az said, pointing in the direction she was referring to. Xadrion could tell every instinct in her was directing her to rush in, but for some reason she had stopped.

'Let's go then,' Xadrion said.Azraelle fidgeted with her fingers, eyeing both him and Ilyon cautiously. She looked worried.

'I can feel the power over there. When we go over, I need you both to keep moving and keep fighting. Do not stop. You haven't prepared for this and if there is more than just Deimos there, we are in for a lot of trouble,' Azraelle said.

'Don't worry about us,' Ilyon said, grabbing her hand and giving it a squeeze. Azraelle's eyes swam with emotion before they hardened. Before him stood a commander, ready for battle.

'I will anyway. Stay alive,' Az warned. 'Oh, and I must stress this, you cannot let even a single person get away. If even one of them gets away and calls for reinforcements, we are certainly dead.'

Then, she was moving again. She soared over the hill, Xadrion close on her trail, and by the time Xadrion had dropped in once more, Azraelle was already moving. Xadrion took a single breath's length to take stock of the situation. There were bodies already littering the ground, all Gaewethian guards Xadrion had seen. Deimos was stalking towards one of the carriages, which had a single figure standing in front of it, their weapon drawn.

Tolemus.

Xadrion knew Romina was inside the carriage that Tolemus guarded. Deimos and Tolemus were already engaged in combat with Deimos' flames enhancing every stroke that they made. Yet, Tolemus was holding his own, somehow. The flames never quite reached him and instead, from what Xadrion could see from his distance, it looked as if he was landing the occasional strike against Deimos with his sword.

The rest of the field had at least ten other soldiers, half with wings and half without. They were the ones chasing down the remaining Gaewethian guards, but as soon as Azraelle had cleared the hill they all diverted their attention to her. He saw fear and recognition on many of their faces but without hesitation, they each redirected and streamed straight for Az.

'Keep them from her!' Xadrion shouted to Ilyon as he ran forward. As he turned, he could have sworn he saw a ripple across Ilyon's skin, like an invisible barrier had spread itself around him. In front of Xadrion was chaos as the Olympian soldiers cut down the remaining mortals in their path to get to Azraelle, screams echoing around the valley.

Azraelle pushed forward, as if she might run straight through the soldiers who descended on her very spot. Her shadows began dancing between her fingers, and as Azraelle moved, Xadrion noticed the size of the black swirling tendrils grow and swirl around her form. Within the blink of an eye, the tendrils had grown and shaped themselves into a shape Xadrion couldn't believe he was seeing.

Spread on either side of Azraelle, her tendrils formed the shape of her wings, the exact wings Xadrion had only seen before in her memories. The wings were writhing as the tendrils moved as one. Azraelle didn't draw her weapons, didn't even pull a dagger. Instead, whips from her shadow wings shot forward, striking at the Olympians who came upon her.

One of the Olympians, seeing the destruction in front of them, diverted their direction. This was exactly what Azraelle had warned them against. If that one got away, all the might of Olympus would surely be on them within moments. Xadrion darted forward, becoming lightning as he shot into the battle, aiming for the rogue Olympian. He appeared in front of the fleeing soldier, who looked at him in shock. The shock turned to pain quickly as Xadrion plunged his sword forward, stopping the soldier in his tracks.

In the distance, on the opposite side of the field, Ilyon had somehow pulled three into battle with him. He'd always admired his brother's fighting. Where Xadrion had always fought with strength and brute force, Ilyon was lithe and fast. He dodged and weaved the incoming strikes with ease. Xadrion couldn't make out from that distance how he was fairing, but amongst the scene were ripples of energy stemming from Ilyon's outstretched fingers. Where the ripple occurred, one of the three he'd engaged nearby would stumble, or trip, and Ilyon would take the opportunity to dart forward with his spear.

Xadrion hadn't had long to train his powers with Azraelle, but now that he was on a field where he could unleash it, he did. The remaining six who had advanced on Azraelle had been flung from her by her tendrils, two lay crumpled on the ground and didn't seem to be moving. The last four continued in their pursuit of her, running headlong into the whips in their attempt to keep her from reaching Deimos. Azraelle showed no sign of stopping.

Xadrion zapped forward, focusing on the one closest to him and appeared close enough to divert the soldier's attention from Azraelle. Xadrion pulled at the energy he could feel in the air around him, the very storm he had caused aiding him in drawing on more power. He could feel his heart thrumming in time with each lightning strike that hit the ground. *This* was what it meant to feel strong and immortal.

Xadrion parried briefly with the one in front of him, his strength quickly overpowering the winged scout, forcing him to the ground with the final sword thrust through the heart. As he looked back up, one of the advancing Olympians had circled behind Azraelle who was still endlessly pushing forward in her desperation to get to Tolemus.

Xadrion pulled the energy from the air and flung the bolt forward as if it were a spear. It soared, burying itself deep in the chest of the Olympian approaching behind Azraelle. A quick glance showed Ilyon still engaged with three, so far successfully darting and avoiding, and the final two near Azraelle.

'Deimos!' Azraelle screamed. 'Don't. Touch. Him!'

Azraelle was a force Xadrion could barely look away from, even in the midst of combat. While one of the two finally noticed Xadrion, Azraelle plunged the tip of one of her shadow wings straight through the second to clear her path to Deimos.

Behind Deimos, Tolemus was breathing heavily as he deflected the blows rained down upon him. Xadrion could see the grin that adorned Deimos' face.

'Xay,' Ilyon cried, dragging his attention to the opposite side of the field. Ilyon was lagging and at the very moment Xadrion looked, he saw the first sign of blood appear on Ilyon's armour. Ilyon clutched at his side as he dodged again, avoiding the blows of the next two.

Xadrion threw himself forward, absently sending another lightning spear in the direction of the final Olympian who had turned to him. He didn't look to see it land; he knew without a doubt it had.

Xadrion jumped forward, deflecting an incoming blow aimed straight for Ilyon's exposed side. His sword clashed against the steel of the opposing blow. While the two swords remained connected, he sent a blast of electric energy over his sword, straight through to the other. Its owner yelped at the shock and dropped the weapon, giving Ilyon time to thrust the spear forward. The Olympian crumpled to the ground in death.

Ilyon and Xadrion took one each of the final two, and without the element of surprise to help bring about their deaths quickly, they both took longer to deal the killing blows of their respective match. Xadrion was breathing heavily and for the first time since running in, took a moment to pause. Ilyon was bleeding from the wound in his side, but a quick inspection showed it wasn't deep enough to do any real damage.

Both the brothers turned to Azraelle at the same time. Deimos had jumped to stand atop the carriage behind Tolemus, a ball of flame dancing across his outstretched palm. Xadrion quickly took hold of Ilyon and jumped them forward to flank Azraelle. Tolemus whirled to face Deimos now behind him, and kept his sword raised as the fighting all at once came to a halt.

'It's nice to see you again, dear Az,' Deimos said, smirking.

'Deimos,' Az said. 'You will not be completing your mission today.'

'I cannot return without doing so,' Deimos said. Xadrion had come to stand beside Az by that point, but he waited, willing to wait for her command. Why she was entertaining a conversation with Deimos, he couldn't guess, but this was her family and by all accounts Xadrion knew she had the right to decide the way forward.

'I am not as powerless as I was that day in the woods. You cannot win. Zeus does not get this one,' Az warned, gritting and baring her teeth in a threateningly animalistic way. Xadrion had never heard her sound so possessive in her speech before, yet as she demanded Tolemus be left alone, Xadrion got the distinct impression that she was claiming him as her own.

'You realise that by interfering today I now am forced to report your existence to Zeus. You had the chance to live your life away from his eyes, and yet you have forced my hand,' Deimos said.

'Out of respect for your parents, I will offer you the chance to go, unharmed. Do not make me tell my dearest brother that I had to kill you,' Az said.

'My favour, Az, I'm calling it in,' Deimos said, their grin mocking. 'I need you to let me kill him.'

Azraelle tensed, her shadows drooping from their winged form until they had returned to mere tendrils playing around her fingers.

'Deimos, please. I can't do that,' she said through gritted teeth, as if the very act of denying the favour was causing her physical pain.

'Zeus has Phobos,' Deimos said, their cocky grin faltering. Azraelle's own expression conveyed pain at the statement from Deimos.

Xadrion felt a probing on the edges of his mind, a presence he quickly recognised as Azraelle. He lowered his guard enough to let her in, eager for her presence despite the danger they were facing.

Deimos will not stop and I am unable to act against them. Zeus is holding their sibling Phobos so Deimos must fulfil their task. My deal from that day in the clearing binds me and I must allow Deimos to act. You and Ilyon are Tolemus' only chance to survive this.

'Please don't do this,' Az said out loud.

'You,' Deimos said, shifting his attention to Ilyon, refusing to acknowledge Azraelle's pleas. 'That slash you landed on me last time took days to heal.'

'As did the burn you landed on my face,' Ilyon retorted.

'Hm,' Deimos said, their eyes glinting as if like fire. 'Very well, I shall call us even. You were... impressive.'

'I'd say the same to you, but I had not even a fraction of my power then and I still managed to land a hit,' Ilyon said. Deimos smirked at him; their eyes focused solely on Ilyon. They appeared to be entertained by Ilyon, their tone almost... flirtatious.

'Maybe I couldn't bear to end such a divine creature,' Deimos said.

'Deimos,' Az interrupted, her anger audible. 'Will you spare him or not?'

Tolemus was standing, his sword still raised, and from behind him through the carriage window, Romina's face peeked through the curtains.

'I cannot,' Deimos answered but made no move to act.

'Why are you stalling?' Az asked, eyeing the area cautiously. Through their connection in their mind, Xadrion felt her hesitation. Something wasn't right. Why was Deimos taunting them and not trying to kill Tolemus?

'Zeus didn't have to find out you were alive,' Deimos said. 'He only wanted that one.' Deimos pointed to Xadrion. 'Oh, Azraelle, you should have seen the sight of Athena telling Zeus that his dear son was still alive. Olympus itself shook with his rage.'

'I can imagine,' Az responded, cautiously.

'And Hera. Poor, dear Hera. Wife or no, Zeus spared no expense finding out how she had kept him hidden from Zeus. She broke, this morning. Withstood days of torture, although nothing compared to the tales of what you were subjected to in your years of captivity,' Deimos said.

'Hera broke?'

'She did. Zeus knows all about the wards she crafted to keep the boy hidden,' Deimos said.

Emera, Azraelle said into Xadrion's mind. *He knows about Emera.*

'He does indeed want this one dead,' Deimos said, flicking their head to indicate Tolemus standing on the ground beneath them. 'But it is not his only goal of today.'

'He knows where the castle is?' Azraelle asked.

'Yes, I do believe Hera broke on that detail also,' Deimos said.

'Let us leave right now,' Xadrion said, speaking up for the first time. 'Leave Tolemus be, take me back to Zeus right now and I will see all of this come to an end.'

'Xadrion, no!' Azraelle said.

'It is in everyone's best interests for you to come with me, as you have offered. But Tolemus does not get to leave today,' Deimos said. Deimos jumped then and as they did, morphed through a series of shapes. Deimos reappeared back on the ground, so close to Tolemus with a clawed hand raised above ready to strike, while Azraelle remained rooted to the spot.

Go! Go! Az cried, while simultaneously letting loose a guttural cry. 'Deimos!'

Deimos did not divert from Tolemus. Ilyon and Xadrion began running as one, lightning shooting from Xadrion at the same moment that Ilyon sent out a gust of air towards Tolemus. Deimos' clawed hand sent a bolt of fire towards Tolemus, but miraculously it didn't reach him. The fire hit an invisible wall and dissolved against it, and the clawed nails of Deimos' outstretched hand sparked as it was deflected against an invisible barrier, as if there were a shield surrounding Tolemus.

Ilyon raged forward, running so gracefully that his long legs led him ahead of Xadrion easily. His spear lanced forward just as Deimos whirled to face him, deflecting the incoming blow.

'Yours, I take it?' Deimos said, gesturing to the invisible shield that had smoke now swirling against it.

'Only way to take it down is to take me down,' Ilyon said, a wild grin on his face. Xadrion had no idea Ilyon had that ability. He hadn't really paid much attention to the training he'd received from Emera.

Before Xadrion could make it the final distance to Deimos, a burning pain swept through him. It started from the point on his ribs where he knew the ward tattoo to be, but quickly seared through his entire body. Xadrion buckled, dropping to the ground. Ahead of him, Ilyon let out a cry and dropped as well. Behind him, another cry came from Azraelle.

'No!' Az screamed, guttural and distraught. Xadrion turned through the pain, seeing Az frantically try to pull her way through her leather armour to see the skin of her ribs. When she finally made it through and lifted her shirt, Xadrion could see nothing but bare skin, no tattoo in sight. The pain didn't subside and Xadrion could not get the strength to lift himself from the ground. Tolemus' cry was the last to join the chorus of screams, and he too dropped to his knees from their seemingly shared pain.

'That would be the second task of the day completed,' Deimos said.

'He killed her?' Azraelle cried, lunging to her feet and towards Deimos. Xadrion did not know how she did it; he could not fight the pain enough to even sit up. Deimos looked worried as Azraelle broke through the pain and hurtled in their direction. Deal or not, Az was going for them. Deimos turned once to look at Tolemus and the shield that the smoke still swirled against. Despite Ilyon being down, his shield held strong.

'Tell my mother I'm sorry. Phobos will pay for this one,' Deimos said, then lunged forward to Xadrion. 'You want to go see Zeus?'

Xadrion looked to Azraelle, still fighting the pain to reach them. She was watching him, eyes wide with fear.

Don't go, please, she begged.

I'm sorry, Az. It was always going to go this way. Her eyes showed the betrayal she felt as Xadrion managed to nod and reached his hand towards Deimos. Deimos took it and before Xadrion could look back to Azraelle one last time, they were gone. When he blinked next, instead of the open fields and the dead bodies, Xadrion found himself now in a room made completely of marble.

A room was an understatement as it was closer in size to the throne room at Fennhall. Bigger, even. At the top of the marbled hall, furthest away, was a dais with a large male figure seated in the middle. His skin was dark, much the same as Xadrion's, but his hair was white, so white it rivalled even Azraelle's. To his left sat a woman who Xadrion did not recognise and to his right, kneeling on the ground with bruises lining her arms, was Hera.

Hera. His mother, who Xadrion had once thought he would never see again. She was looking at him with tears streaming over her cheeks.

As soon as they'd appeared in this new place, the pain that had wracked Xadrion's body disappeared.

'Brother,' a voice said beside him. A hand extended towards him. Athena stood above him, palm outstretched. Xadrion took it and slowly stood. The absence of the pain left him feeling shaky on his feet.

'My dear son,' the man said from the top of the room. The words echoed across the marbled room, each word feeling like a gentle, electric thrum in the air as Zeus stood and descended the steps of the dais, his smile genuine as it reached his eyes. Laughter lines were embedded deep in his skin. 'I never thought I'd see this day.' In a second, Xadrion's face was pressed between the sizable hands of Zeus, who was looking at him as if he were the greatest marvel to exist.

Xadrion couldn't focus, couldn't think through what was happening. *He killed her.* Azraelle had said those words as the pain had wracked their bodies.

'Emera?' Xadrion said, the truth hitting him all at once. 'You killed Emera?' Xadrion couldn't stand but before he dropped to the ground, Zeus moved to support his weight. What had he done? Why had he come here? Zeus had killed Emera, all to find him. He had people inside Fennhall, people strong enough to get through and kill Emera. Who else had been a casualty of that invasion?

'Athena, take your brother to rest. He has had a trying time, it seems,' Zeus said. Something probed into his mind, tearing straight through any wall he had erected and blackness swirled in his vision. Before a moment had passed, Xadrion was unconscious.

THIRTY-FOUR

AZRAELLE

Emera was dead. They weren't warded. Fennhall wasn't warded. Xadrion had gone to Mount Olympus with Deimos. Fuck.

Azraelle stumbled forward, her momentum carrying her to Tolemus. She pulled him into her arms, checking to make sure he was unharmed. Az couldn't collect her thoughts, couldn't think through what she needed to do next. Naxos. Naxos was at Fennhall. If Zeus had others in Fennhall, enough to take out Emera, they could find Naxos or kill him. It would be luck on their part; they didn't know about him, didn't know he was there. Or at least they wouldn't until they got through Xadrion's mental defences. Az didn't trust Xadrion being able to withstand Zeus' probing for very long. She needed to get to Naxos or all of this would be for nothing. If Naxos was gone, she would be unable to do anything to save everyone she had come to love.

Brother, Azraelle said, practically shouting her signal as loud as she could to Thanatos. She could go back to the castle, but Tolemus and Ilyon would not get back in time. They had nowhere safe to go now. Zeus was hunting demi-gods, and without Emera's wards they would be easy targets.

Azraelle? Thanatos responded. Azraelle nearly wept.

I need you and Nakir to come, or someone else you trust. Come to my current location. When you arrive, I won't be here, but there will be two who I need you to take. You need to get Ilyon and Tolemus to the Underworld. I need you to protect them above all else.

Where will you be? Thanatos asked.

I must go retrieve Naxos and hope to Chaos that he's still alive, Azraelle answered.

Nakir and Zagreus are on their way. They will ferry your two, and then meet you where Nakir previously met you. Be safe, Az. Come whether you find Naxos or not.

Zagreus was coming. That was good, he could be trusted. Azraelle did not give much thought to Thanatos' last words. Without Naxos, she would not be welcome in the Underworld. She would never gain her freedom once more. She needed Naxos, and if she couldn't get to him, she would not find a safe place again.

Azraelle moved to Ilyon, checking him over in the same way she'd checked Tolemus over. When she deemed them both safe, Az allowed herself a brief moment to collect her thoughts. From behind Tolemus, the carriage door creaked open and Romina stepped out cautiously, eyeing the destruction of the plains around them.

'They killed Emera?' Ilyon whispered, pulling his shirt up to see his own scarless rib.

'They did. I'm heading back to Fennhall to save what I can. I cannot carry anyone back with me,' Azraelle said.

'What are we going to do?' Ilyon's panic was starting to rise.

'I'm going to go. But you and Tolemus are going to wait here. Two of my kind are going to be arriving shortly. They can be trusted. Let them take you with them – they will take you to safety. I will join you shortly,' Azraelle said.

'Where will they take us?' Tolemus asked, stepping away from Romina and moving towards Az. With the immediate threat gone, the few surviving members of Romina's kingdom were approaching, flocking back to their princess once more. Their numbers had been decimated if the corpses surrounding them were anything to go by. Still, there were enough to get Romina the rest of her way home.

'To my mater, to the Underworld. You'll be safe there,' Azraelle answered. 'Trust only the two who come for you, and Thanatos. I will join you when I can.' Azraelle stepped away, preparing to shift into the shadows and go as fast as she could to Fennhall. She didn't give herself time to look at Tolemus' reaction to the knowledge that he was about to embark to the Underworld.

'Azraelle?' a meek voice said from behind Tolemus. Romina.

'I don't quite have the time for your disapproval right now, *Princess*,' Azraelle spat.

'I am not giving it to you. I only wish to say… thank you,' Romina said. 'You saved me, and a lot of my people today. Gaeweth will not soon forget this.' Romina dropped to her knees, kneeling for her in a way Az was sure Romina had never knelt for anyone. There were too many mortals who put stock in the gods, as if they would deign to help them. Romina had seemed to be one of them, talking often of sin and praying. Now, face to face with what she worshipped, Az could see all of Romina's regret.

'I don't have time for this. Fill her in or don't, but you aren't going back to Gaeweth,' Az said to Tolemus. She never should have agreed to let him out of her sight. Az shifted then, whipping into her shadow form and spearing towards Fennhall as fast as she was able.

The sight that Az faced upon arriving was unnerving. The city around the castle appeared completely untouched. Az could see families through their windows, and occasionally saw people strolling the quickly darkening streets. Nothing seemed out of the ordinary until she got closer to the castle.

Az slipped over the castle walls and through the familiar courtyard she'd walked through countless times on the way to training, or to take her rides in the woods, or even just to stroll through the grounds. It was deserted, save for a single person.

No... not person. A body, pinned to the large, grated doors that marked the entrance to the castle.

A shock of red hair covered the face and tangled around the metal and arms that were tied, but Azraelle knew exactly who she was looking at. That red hair was recognisable to her anywhere. Emera marked the gate; symbolic of the protection she had once offered the castle. Now, as a sign of her wards dropped, she hung from the entrance of the very castle she had tried to protect.

With no one else around, Azraelle slashed at the binds that held Emera with her shadow whips and gently eased her body to the ground. She brushed the hair from Emera's face and took note of what she was seeing. One injury, a single gash across the base of her neck. It wasn't drawn out at least, and Emera likely wouldn't have seen them approach. Azraelle kept the tears back as she brushed her fingers through Emera's hair gently.

They'd taken care to present Emera to be found. Not by Azraelle at least, they hadn't known of her existence. But Xadrion perhaps, if he hadn't first been taken by Deimos, or anyone else who would have thought to help Emera keep Xadrion hidden. Azraelle supposed it didn't matter anymore that the wards couldn't keep her hidden. Xadrion's mind would not hold up to Zeus' probing. It was likely Zeus already knew of Azraelle's surviving.

Emera had never stood a chance. The moment Hera entrusted her with the wards to keep Xadrion hidden, she'd signed her death warrant. Azraelle had just been too slow to realise it. Az hadn't even made time to see Emera one final time, had not found the time to ease the worry she knew Emera would have felt at Azraelle being away from Fennhall.

Azraelle kissed Emera's forehead, choked down all the threatening tears and resolved to move on. Now was not the time to feel that loss, or to think of everything that had changed. Now, she was in battle. It was one move and then the other. For the moment she had the element of surprise, and she could not waste that opportunity.

Moving further into the castle, Azraelle found many more bodies. They lined the hallways, slumped against the stone walls, all the way along. Guards in their armour, mostly. Faintly, Azraelle could hear crying within some of the rooms. They weren't killing all on sight, at least. But most of Fennhall's castle staff would be slain that day, hundreds of innocents.

Azraelle headed to her rooms first, seeing no one on the pathway there. Behind many of the doors along the way, she heard the quiet whimpers of the occupants. The dead in the halls decreased the closer she got, and Azraelle gave herself the faintest glimmer of hope that no one had come this far along, and if they had that her room had been left untouched.

Before the final turn, Azraelle heard voices in the hallway.

'It was definitely this room?' one voice whispered.

'Definitely,' the other replied.

'What if she's there?' the first one whispered.

'She won't be. The memories were unlocked as soon as he'd arrived at Olympus and were conveyed straight to us. She wouldn't have had time to get back here yet,' the second one comforted.

Her. They were talking about her. It was true. To their knowledge, it would have taken Azraelle longer to get back from where they'd intercepted Deimos. Without her wings, it was reasonable for anyone to think her travel would be slower. Only Az's immediate family, and even then not all of them, knew of her ability to shift as she did. Zagreus and Aphrodite were the only two outside of her family who knew of the ability. No one could have expected her to be able to return to the castle so fast.

Azraelle waited until they had pushed the door to her rooms open and went inside before revealing herself. She'd followed them in, silently closing the door behind her so no one walking past might see. The room in front of her was empty, save for the two men who she had overheard in the hallway. They had no wings, which was both a good and a bad thing. Good because they weren't scouts and would be easier to keep hold of. Bad because it probably meant they ranked higher than scouts, high enough that they didn't need wings to give them power. If they had been entrusted with this task, they would have been high in Zeus' army.

From the corner of her eye, the glimmer of steel shone from behind her bedroom door. Naxos stood through the crack of the door, a sword clasped in his hand. If she'd seen him, there was no way the two men hadn't seen him. Azraelle pulled her sword from her side and thrust it forward, straight through the throat of one of the men. Surprise always helped. The second had been in the process of drawing his own weapon to head to Naxos when his companion dropped to the ground, a gurgling sound echoing as he choked on his own blood.

The second man whirled to face her, dropping into a defensive position. Seeing Azraelle in front of him, his eyes widened. Azraelle would have kept moving, swinging straight at the second man, if he hadn't been instantly familiar. His eyes were a piercing blue, so memorable that Azraelle had seen them nearly every night as she'd tried to sleep since she'd escaped Olympus.

'Well,' Azraelle purred, trying to keep the memories at bay. She would not show him what effect he had on her. 'It would seem you've been granted a promotion.'

The man didn't respond but kept his sword raised to use at a moment's notice.

'Come on, still not going to let me hear that voice of yours?' Azraelle coaxed. She hadn't heard him speak a single day during her confinement, during the torture she suffered at his hands. He'd been one of many torturers that Zeus rotated through, but Azraelle remembered him more than the others. He had enjoyed what he'd done to Azraelle's body, over and over. She didn't need to be in his mind to see the pleasure he had gained from trying to break her.

'You don't deserve my words,' the man said, practically spitting at her. The way he looked at her was exactly how he'd looked at her in that cell – as if she was one of the most rotten creatures to have existed, as if she were a pest that needed to be ridden of.

'Careful now,' Azraelle said, pulling the icy façade over every one of her features. She would be Death. She was Death. 'I'm not all trussed up like I was. Now you're standing across from Death's Hand at her finest.'

'Finest?' the man goaded. 'I seem to remember those black wings of yours. How are you at your finest when they're nowhere to be seen?'

'My wings are not my link to Death. They were merely my link to the Ravens. That link may be severed, but the powers imbued within me by Death itself are no less because of the absence of some wings,' Azraelle said, imbuing as much strength into her words as she could, despite the ever-present pain of her wings being gone. Behind the man, she could see Naxos pushing through the door, a sword raised in front of him. He looked like he'd never swung a sword before in his life. He might have been exceptional at making them – for he was very good as Azraelle had noted when she'd been in his smithing shop – but he had clearly never trained with them.

'Death seems to like the sound of her own voice a whole lot,' the man snarked.

Azraelle hissed through her teeth, baring them to show her anger. 'In such a hurry to meet your maker?' Azraelle asked before lunging forward. She whipped past him, blending into shadows as his sword struck where her corporeal form would have been, and resolidified as she passed behind him. Azraelle struck with her own sword, aiming only for his sword hand. It sliced through the exposed fleshy underside of his forearm and the man yelled as his sword clattered to the ground, his grip unable to hold on any longer. Azraelle kicked his weapon away.

The man turned, slashing his arms through the air with only his nails as weapons. Azraelle dodged easily, pulling a dagger from the sheath at her thigh and burying it deep into the side of his leg. He went to the ground screaming.

'You made your move up by torturing a bound body. Do not be so delusional as to think you have any real talent,' Azraelle said, standing above his body. She'd thought of countless ways to kill this man, to drag his own torture out for years and millennia. Now, with him pinned and weak beneath her, Azraelle could not let herself indulge in the time to do those things. Naxos was looking at her, eyes wide in his panic, as she stood above the man who was writhing on the ground.

There were others in the castle, others who would find them eventually. She needed to get Naxos away. Azraelle pushed her sword to the man's chest and held it there.

'Our time must be cut short, I'm afraid. I look forward to seeing you again, perhaps in the deepest layer of the Underworld?' Azraelle said, and only when the man's eyes truly began to reflect the fear she wanted him to feel at that prospect did Az push her sword in, inch by inch, until he lay lifeless beneath her. Yes, she would see him again. He'd been mortal once, and had been granted the afterlife on Mount Olympus, the location most souls she ferried preferred. But oh, now that he had died from his non-mortal life, he would be heading straight to the Underworld for his next sorting. If she made it back there, she would see to it that they got their time.

'Come on,' Azraelle barked, pulling Naxos towards the door. She did not have the time to savour any of these moments. Not until the day was done, and she had escaped... or not.

'Where are we going? What the fuck is going on, Azraelle?' Naxos whispered as they hurried through the halls.

'Zeus found out Xadrion was being kept here and is taking it down,' Az replied.

'But Xadrion isn't here,' Naxos said.

'He got taken to Mount Olympus anyway. For now, you and I need to get out of here. We have a bit of a journey ahead but once we're clear of the castle, we should be okay. What happened here?' Azraelle asked.

'I didn't hear much. I'd slept most of the day away after you told me you had to go find Xadrion. When I woke next, I heard a few screams down the halls and then silence. I found one of your swords but I didn't know what I should do. Then those men came through the door. The whole thing happened so quickly,' Naxos replied.

'I need to check on one more person before we go,' Azraelle said and began leading the way from the room. It was risky to not leave straight away, but Az didn't think she could live with herself if she didn't first check on Rhoas. If she managed to make it out of this and couldn't give Ilyon an answer as to how his father was, she would feel terrible. Although, if Zeus had gained the information of Fennhall from Hera's memories, Az didn't think he would let Rhoas live long enough to see its downfall. Still, Rhoas had welcomed Azraelle into his home, had treated her with such kindness even when he had no reason to. She could not abandon him in this hour of need.

It didn't take long to reach the hallway to the throne room. No soldiers lined the hallways but Azraelle could hear the voices inside. Two clear speakers, a man and a woman, and many mumbles of spectators came from the room. Azraelle recognised the two main voices; she'd heard them thousands of times before throughout her lifetime. They'd been the ones who had led her from that cell to Zeus' platform, the day she received her judgement. Apollo and Artemis. Zeus really had sent in his best – his very own twins.

'Wait here, please,' Azraelle said, ushering Naxos into a nearby empty room. She cast some of her shadows over Naxos to help keep him hidden, and then transformed herself into shadows to enter the throne room. It was risky, but she needed confirmation. If Rhoas was in there, suffering at the hands of Apollo and Artemis, she needed to know.

Slipping through the cracks of the doors, her stomach turned and her heart pounded heavily inside her chest at the sight before her. Several of Zeus' foot soldiers and scouts lined the walls of the throne room. The middle of the room was empty of furniture, still set up from the ball from days ago. Atop the throne at the head of the room sat Artemis, Rhoas' crown perched atop her thick black hair. She leant casually to the side, her cheek resting on the palm of her hand as if she were bored. Azraelle knew she probably was – it was Apollo who had a taste for the extravagant, while his twin Artemis usually kept herself removed from elaborate affairs. The most alive Azraelle ever saw Artemis was on the few occasions she'd gone hunting with her, on one of the rare occasions Artemis had visited the Underworld with Hera.

In the centre of the room was Apollo, using his own power to cast a crown of fire atop his head. At his feet, Rhoas knelt with his arms bound behind his back and his feet tied together. Not that he needed to be restrained; he was a mortal in a room full of gods and their army. He didn't stand a chance. She could end his suffering, but could she do it without drawing too much attention to herself? A well-timed shadow blade would be all that was needed, slicing right through his chest in a way that no one could see the wound. But no, Apollo or Artemis would see the shadow. They'd known her well enough to recognise her powers and Azraelle would never make it out of the room.

Azraelle didn't know what to do. Rhoas wasn't screaming, wasn't even crying, as Apollo pulled his own blade against Rhoas' skin, leaving sizzling flesh wherever he traced. It reminded Azraelle so harshly of the smell of her own skin burning in that cell. Rhoas had been so welcoming, so accepting of her presence, that she knew she couldn't just leave him. She had to help him.

Azraelle had been focusing so intently on Apollo and Rhoas, debating her options, that she didn't see the other twin moving until it was too late. Artemis had pulled her bow to her lap, knocked an arrow and shot it before Azraelle realised what was happening. She didn't have time to swerve away when the arrow shot straight through the centre of her shadow form where she lurked against the wall of the room.

THIRTY-FIVE

AZRAELLE

Paralysis swept over her and Azraelle felt her physical body return. She slumped to the ground, unable to make herself stand and run. Artemis, goddess of the Hunt, had seen her. Of course she had. Her eyes were attuned to spotting enemies. The shock of Artemis' paralysis arrow rippled over Azraelle as she watched Artemis stand and casually stroll towards where she now lay. Around her the soldiers that lined the wall cleared an area near her.

Apollo remained near Rhoas, but his eyes quickly trained on Azraelle's recently appeared form. He held his dagger permanently to Rhoas' throat, who now watched Azraelle with fear lacing every ounce of his expression.

'That was a foolish move, Az,' Artemis drawled as she came closer. Slow, measured steps. She didn't need to go faster; she knew how long the paralysis lasted. Artemis stopped a few feet from Azraelle and cocked her head as if she were listening for something. Artemis showed no expression, she rarely did. Yet, behind Az, the throne room door creaked open and Naxos grunted as he was dragged into the room by a thick, thorny vine.

'Father is going to be so happy to see you once more, Azraelle,' Apollo taunted. 'And to put an end to this foolish plan of yours with your new pet.'

They really had gleaned everything from Xadrion's mind, it would seem. Azraelle couldn't even let herself be mad at Xadrion, despite telling him that was exactly what would happen if he was in Zeus' presence before he built his shields fully. She could only think of the danger he now faced that he was on Mount Olympus. Yet another person she had failed.

'You don't need to hurt Rhoas or Naxos if you have me,' Azraelle said.

'Rhoas was dead the moment he laid a hand on Hera,' Apollo said, yanking on the grasp he had on Rhoas' hair.

'And Naxos has valuable memories surrounding this mystery woman who told him of you,' Artemis said.

Azraelle pushed against the paralysis, weaving her own magic in amongst the bonds and trying to dislodge the hold it had over her. Slowly, she could feel the ability to move her fingers and toes. It wasn't fast enough.

Naxos was thrown to the ground beside her, Artemis' thick vine holding around him tightly. He didn't look scared, but Azraelle could smell his fear easily enough.

'I'm sorry, Naxos,' Azraelle whispered, dropping her head in defeat. She would not go back to Zeus. She had promised herself that every day since she'd woken up in Fennhall. She could not subject herself to that torture again. She could not see what it would mean to watch Zeus slowly increase his hold and capture her family. She could not see what it meant for her sister, the Moirai, to be discovered in her treachery. She could not bear to see Xadrion in the hands of Zeus. She had brought Naxos here, had put him directly in the hands of her enemy, and Azraelle already couldn't live with herself at the thought of what was to come.

It was all her fault. She would die before going back to Zeus but she didn't deserve to die peacefully. There was one more thing she could do, if she could only move enough to do it. If she could, she would save Naxos, and maybe even Rhoas if she got there fast enough.

'Rest your power, Azraelle,' Artemis said, feeling the increase of Azraelle's power pushing against the boundaries of her paralysis. 'It will be easier if you just come with us.'

'I can't do that, Art,' Azraelle replied. 'Zeus cannot win today.'

Azraelle pushed on the paralysis again, and again. She felt it slowly recede, so slowly. Artemis was watching her, her brows pulled together in a mixture of confusion and... maybe awe? Az had never seen that expression on her face before but if Artemis pieced it together before she could move, the element of surprise would be lost. For Artemis could put it together – Azraelle's plan – if she thought to.

The emerald pendant burned against Azraelle's skin, signalling all she needed to be able to reach to see it through. She pushed, and pushed, and pushed. Artemis watched her, as if she were genuinely curious as to what she was witnessing. She'd always liked Artemis more than Apollo. Az had enjoyed her pensiveness and thoughtfulness, had wondered to hear Artemis talk about many topics, especially the art of hunting. Artemis was a peaceful presence, and now served as a centre of focus while Azraelle pushed and managed to free her arm.

Artemis raised the bow, another paralysis arrow knocked and prepared to shoot.

'Stop, Az,' Artemis warned.

Azraelle ripped the necklace from around her neck at the same time that Artemis finally displayed a measure of shock. Behind her, Apollo lurched toward Azraelle, pulling Rhoas by the hair with him. They knew – they knew exactly what the necklace was.

Salvation, and damnation.

She was no longer a Raven, but the emerald pendant was the last surviving gift she had of her time as one. It was bound to her, bound to her body until she deemed it was time to let it go. Every Raven had their own uniquely coded pendant. Azraelle's didn't serve as many functions as the others, but it didn't need to – not when she hadn't obtained her wings in the same way. All the same, she'd been granted a pendant as a symbol of her Raven presence regardless.

The other Ravens used it to keep corruption at bay, to keep the wings they fought for from consuming their souls. A Raven's wings were hard earned, and dangerous to keep, but if a Raven kept the pendant secured it protected them. It kept Chaos unbridled at bay. If a Raven smashed their pendant, usually only done in the most desperate of times, they would be a conduit of that power for a short period of time. Then, usually, they would die.

'Don't you dare,' Apollo shouted, as Artemis loosed her arrow. Not fast enough. Azraelle brought the pendant down, the only person capable in all the worlds of removing that particular necklace from her neck, and cracked the emerald hard against the stone. It fractured as the arrow landed in Azraelle's shoulder. She didn't feel it. Couldn't feel it. Not as power rushed from the cracks in the gem and gushed through her fingertips, deep into that well within her body.

Azraelle had never felt anything like it. She was so closely descended to Chaos, and yet she had never been blessed with hearing its call. Unfiltered Chaos was pure ecstasy. An old sigh swept through her, as if her very bones were sinking at the release, and around her the very material of light flickered and disappeared. Void surrounded her, surrounded Naxos, and was creeping toward Artemis.

Daughter, a voice whispered. It was both in her mind and in the room simultaneously. It felt old, more ancient than even Azraelle could comprehend. It also sounded tired, as if it had just woken.

Father?

Yes and no, the voice replied. *My son, Erebus, wishes me to help you.*

Erebus' parent… that meant, no. No, she couldn't be hearing Chaos itself speaking to her. That voice had never granted her its presence before.

Help them, Azraelle begged. A warmth brushed over her, moving from her toes all the way through to her shoulders, as if she were being scoured. She tasted blood in her mouth and felt a stream dribbling from her nose. Was she crying?

Yes, you are a suitable conduit. I can give you what you want, the voice said.

In front of her, no movement was happening in the throne room. Artemis remained frozen in shock; a single foot raised forward as if taking a step. Apollo had an expression of rage, Rhoas pained as he was pulled along. Everything was frozen.

Yes, please. I'll do anything, Azraelle begged.

Very well. I will do this for you. In return, I will be seeing you soon, Chaos replied.

Yes, it would be seeing her soon. This was bound to kill her. After that, she would go to her first death. She'd never experienced it before. Maybe it would be peaceful after she got there. Maybe Erebus would be there, and they could spend the centuries together before they each returned. Would she return? If Destiny had run its course with her, it could very well be a true death.

Yes, Azraelle agreed. Az released the hold she had on the well inside her, offering every fibre of her being to the ancient presence circling her, probing at her mind. She would not be able to save Xadrion, not in this lifetime. Maybe, maybe one day, they could meet once more. She would do everything so differently.

Blackness swam over her vision, the metallic taste of blood increased in her mouth and her shadows left her, commanded by another. The last thing Azraelle saw before the blackness completely overcame her was Apollo, the fire crown atop his head, shifting and transforming into a spear that shot straight for Rhoas. Time was moving again. Apollo was moving.

The fire spear shot straight through Rhoas' chest, a deathly scream filling the throne room. It ended abruptly, and another began, Azraelle's own scream shaking the very walls of the room. Her vision disappeared, her senses shut down, and Azraelle's last scream sent her to her death.

Soon, Daughter, Chaos' voice echoed into her mind. Soon there would be peace.

EPILOGUE

AZRAELLE

The place where Death lived was not supposed to feel so painful, Azraelle thought. Blackness remained. Sharpness pierced every second of Azraelle's breath. Azraelle supposed it was okay; she did not deserve the peace anyway. She had brought this on herself.

'Don't even think about it, *Primus*,' a harsh voice spat. Nakir? Azraelle could manage nothing but a groan in response. Hard arms circled beneath her legs and shoulders, and suddenly Azraelle felt the cold presence that had been beneath her disappear. Nakir couldn't be here. Azraelle was dead; no one else could be here.

'Azraelle,' a man's voice whispered to her ear. So familiar, so familiar. Why could Azraelle not place anyone around her? It had been… years since she'd heard that voice, she was sure. 'Do not give your brother any more reason to not like me. If you die before Nakir can save you, I swear to Chaos itself I will follow you down and drag you back.'

The name circled her memory faintly, teasing her. Azraelle pushed as hard as she could against her senses, aiming for sight above all else. Slowly, Azraelle found the strings to her eyes and pried them open as best she could. A crooked grin was in her immediate line of sight, a shock of dark hair. Pale skin, a hard jaw line. Zagreus. It was Zagreus.

'There we are,' Zagreus said, his icy blue eyes meeting Azraelle's. 'We're going home. Don't die before we can get there.' His eyes served as a tether, holding her own sight open long enough to gaze at the destruction around her. The bodies… there were so many. All those who had lined the walls of the throne room were piled atop each other, horrible expressions of fear masking what remained of their faces.

Nakir stood a little further away, pulling Naxos to his feet. Apollo and

Artemis were gone; they weren't amongst the bodies. But there… in the middle of the room. Rhoas. Dead.

Azraelle felt the tears break through and couldn't hold back the shuddering sobs as they wracked her body. She closed her eyes, not wanting to see anymore, not wanting to feel anymore. She couldn't breathe, didn't want to. It was time to go to Chaos.

'Nakir,' Zagreus called, panic lacing the word. 'It's time to go!'

The last thing Azraelle felt was the tightening of arms around her, the rigid muscles of Zagreus' torso, and the splintering pain of everything inside her. Finally, after darkness once more encircled her, the pain drifted away, and Azraelle felt herself face to face with the peace she had expected. At last.

About the Author

Jade Andrews has a Bachelor of Creative Arts and a Master of Arts, majoring in creative and professional writing. Her area of study focused on the societal and cultural influence on genre classification, specifically within the distinction of young adult, adult, fantasy and romance.

Fascination with Greek mythology prompted Jade's interest in writing The Pantheon Collection but the desire to explore family and relationship dynamics in the theoretical world of magic and immortality was the more significant factor that shaped Jade's debut fantasy novel.

Her passion for and inclusion in the LGBTQI+ community and her support of intersectional feminism drives her to create stories with characters who reflect all corners of our community, while acknowledging that her own voice comes from a position of previous and existing privilege.

Shawline Publishing Group Pty Ltd

www.shawlinepublishing.com.au

SHAWLINE
PUBLISHING
GROUP